DEAD

A SAM RIVERS MYSTERY

CATCH

CARY J. GRIFFITH

Cover design: Travis Bryant
Cover photo: siraphat/Shutterstock
Text design: Annie Long
Author photo: Anna McCourt
Editors: Mary Logue, Emily Beaumont, Jenna Barron, and Holly Cross

Library of Congress Cataloging-in-Publication Data
Names: Griffith, Cary J., author.
Title: Dead catch : a novel / Cary J. Griffith.
Description: First edition. | Cambridge, Minnesota : Adventure Publications, 2024.
Identifiers: LCCN 2023050170 (print) | LCCN 2023050171 (ebook) |
    ISBN 9781647554019 (paperback) | ISBN 9781647554026 (ebook)
Subjects: LCGFT: Detective and mystery fiction. | Novels.
Classification: LCC PS3607.R54857 D43 2024 (print) | LCC PS3607.R54857 (ebook) |
    DDC 813/.6--dc23/eng/20231108
LC record available at https://lccn.loc.gov/2023050170
LC ebook record available at https://lccn.loc.gov/2023050171

10 9 8 7 6 5 4 3 2 1
Copyright © 2024 by Cary J. Griffith
Dead Catch: A Sam Rivers Mystery (book 4)

Adventure

Published by Adventure Publications
An imprint of AdventureKEEN
310 Garfield St. S.
Cambridge, MN 55008
800-768-7006
adventurepublications.net

DEAD

A SAM RIVERS MYSTERY

CATCH

Also by the author

Gunflint Burning: Fire in the Boundary Waters
Gunflint Falling: Blowdown in the Boundary Waters
Opening Goliath
Lost in the Wild

Wolf Kill
Cougar Claw
Killing Monarchs

PRAISE FOR *DEAD CATCH*

"The terrain is rough—the characters rougher—in this suspenseful mystery set in the wilds of Northern Minnesota. U.S. Fish and Wildlife Special Agent Sam Rivers must wade through turbulent waters to determine if a childhood friend is guilty of walleye poaching and murder or if, as the ex-convict insists, he was set up to take the fall. The author weaves together the rugged landscape and his knowledge of those who inhabit it to spin a tale of corruption and deceit sure to please readers who enjoy a gripping outdoors mystery."
　—Lois Winston, author of the best-selling and critically
　　acclaimed Anastasia Pollack Crafting Mysteries

"*Dead Catch* captures your attention from the opening sentence, and then, like Griffith's first victim in the poacher's net, you're caught in a trap that'll keep you flipping pages until the final twist. You'd best call in sick tomorrow, as this book will keep you up all night."
　—Jeffrey B. Burton, award-winning author of *The Dead Years*
　　and the Mace Reid K-9 Mysteries

"A fascinating and thoroughly satisfying investigation into the shadowy world of illegal fishing"
　—Pamela Beason, author of the Sam Westin Wilderness
　　Mysteries

"Cary Griffith never disappoints. The suspense is taut as Special Agent Sam Rivers spins out a line to land a murderer in the wilds of Northern Minnesota. He pulls in one whopper of a story. This smart and gripping mystery is highly recommended."
　—Mary Logue, author of *The Big Sugar*

"The first chapter of *Dead Catch* by Cary J. Griffith has everything I love in a mystery: a remote setting, wildlife facts, a life in peril, and a twisted murder. Hook, line, and sinker, I was caught.
 —Sara Johnson, author of the Alexa Glock Forensics Mysteries
  set in New Zealand

"Cary Griffith's beautifully crafted *Dead Catch,* like the three preceding novels in his Sam Rivers series, is not a simple whodunit. No, it's about the complexity of life: the importance of love in our lives and what love motivates us to do; the power of compassion and mercy; the need to make amends and begin life anew; and the renewal of a friendship lost in childhood. *Dead Catch* is about all these things and much more. It is a compelling read."
 —Brian Duren, award-winning author of *Ivory Black,*
  The Gravity of Love, and *Whiteout*

"Author Cary J. Griffith's fourth Sam Rivers novel, *Dead Catch,* is an intimate journey into the Northern Minnesota lake country and the inner sanctum of fish-and-game law enforcement.
 —Rob Jung, author of four mysteries, including *Judgment Day,*
  and the host of Minnesota Mystery Night

"*Dead Catch* kept me turning pages as Griffith revealed the high stakes in the walleye poaching industry. This fantastic mystery shows the depths of love, friendship, and the power of being given a second chance. A must-read series for all mystery and wildlife lovers!"
 —Kathleen Donnelly, award-winning author of the
  National Forest K-9 series

For the Canfield Bay Boys:
Jim Gray, Eli Nemer, Mike Reeve, Steve Sauerbry,
and Drew Skogman
Buddies for more than five decades,
we have lots of stories we cannot share.

CHAPTER 1

Holden Riggins lay in the bottom of his boat, still as a stone-cold corpse. The day had dawned clear but sharp. There was a light breeze out of the northwest, causing Lake Vermilion's surface to riffle. The breeze kept the fishing boat's anchor rope taut.

Holden wore a faded black down coat with oil stains blotting its front. He liked to fry whitefish in Crisco, and he worked part-time as a small motor mechanic, so the stains could have been Crisco or engine oil or both. The coat had been patched in two places, obvious because the patching tape was a shade too dark. His Carhartt work pants were worn to a faded taupe, with their bottoms frayed over a pair of scuffed leather work boots.

Holden's feet were splayed out, and his arms flung from his sides like a pair of catawampus windmill blades. The palm of his right hand was face down, with a crudely fashioned S-I-N-K tattooed on the top knuckle bone of each finger. The palm of his left hand faced the sun. You could not see it, but atop his left-hand fingers—cleaner, more stylized, and recent—tattoos spelled F-I-S-H. His face was round and puffy, and beneath a pair of black plastic-rimmed glasses, his eyes were shut tight as a toad. Most people would have thought the tattoo off the corner of his left eye was a mole. It could have been a teardrop. Holden had done prison time, and in convict parlance, a teardrop meant either a long sentence or testament to having killed someone. But it also had the shape of a crudely fashioned, 2-ounce split shot sinker.

Regardless, lying in the bottom of his boat, his body had the kind of terminal flaccidness of someone who had been pole-axed in the middle of the night and left for dead.

Holden was in his late 30s but had the wizened appearance of someone much older. In his early 20s, he had learned to appreciate the day's first beer buzz. By his mid-20s, he followed the beer with harder chasers. By the end of his 20s, he had become intimately familiar with most controlled substances. Growing up in Northern Minnesota, he had always been an outdoors guy, and the sun, combined with hard living, had turned his skin leathery with occasional age spots appearing on his face and across the backs of his hands.

Less than 3 feet from his prone body, an empty bottle of Old Crow rested against the boat's live well compartment. Near the bow lay a half-filled fifth of Jack Daniels.

If not for the above-freezing embrace of Vermilion's red waters and the sun, which an hour earlier had crested the boat's gunwales, the man would have been covered in a patina of hoarfrost, already dead from a heart attack triggered by hypothermia. But Vermilion had kept Holden Riggins alive, though it was uncertain it could keep him alive much longer.

In the distance, the faint sound of an outboard motor cut through the midmorning like a chainsaw felling trees. Holden, of course, could not hear it. The sound did not reach over the boat's gunwales. Besides, his body temperature was nearly 95 degrees. If he had been conscious, he would have been shaking like a man with delirium tremens.

On the leeward side of the boat, 20 yards into the lake, a pair of empty white jugs anchored each end of a 40-foot whitefish gill net. Minnesota DNR regulations were very specific and strict about fishing with nets. Except for a few weeks in late fall, netting was forbidden. Holden knew all about the regulations, in part because he had been fishing his entire life. Also, more than once, he had been arrested and convicted for poaching. The most severe penalty had been eight years earlier, when he was caught selling illegally netted walleye to local restaurants. Technically, it was a violation of the Lacey Act, and because he was selling the fish commercially, he was convicted of a felony.

There had been other violations, although none recently. For the last seven years, Holden had been clean, or at least he had not been caught committing an illegal act. There were a few people who believed Holden was a changed man. He had turned over a new leaf, so some said. There were many others, less sanguine, who believed he had finally figured out how to avoid getting caught. These people opined the Holden Rigginses of the world don't change; they just get smart, or lucky.

Regardless, today, October 14th, there was nothing untoward about Holden's gill net. It was strung 3 feet deep across familiar shallows. The net was perfectly situated to catch whitefish, which in late fall swam up out of Vermilion's depths to spawn. There was nothing illegal about Holden's net because last Thursday had been the whitefish netting season opener, and Holden had a license.

The motorboat was growing closer.

Beyond Holden's whitefish net, the lake bottom dropped to a rugged, well-known 25-foot-deep rocky bottom. Locals knew it as prime walleye habitat and a great place to fish. But again, walleye could never be taken with nets. Minnesota's walleye had to be caught the old-fashioned way, with hook, line, sinker, and live bait or lures or both. Or any one of a huge number of variations involving fishing poles, reels, and tackle.

Walleye fishing in Minnesota was big business. New boats similar to Holden's Lund 1600 Renegade easily sold for tens of thousands of dollars and were outfitted with fish finders, GPS, live wells, rod storage compartments, swivel pedestal seats, steering wheels, gauge-filled dashes, and more. And providing you only used some variation of hook, line, sinker, and bait, whatever boat and fishing technology you could leverage was legal.

But Holden's boat was old. Years earlier, he had purchased it used, and now its hull was scraped and dented. He had none of the newfangled electronics typical of boats purchased today. In many ways, Holden's boat was a counterpoint to the Minnesota DNR runabout, whose gleaming hull rested 30 yards shoreward, tethered to an overhanging cedar branch. Affixed to the boat's aft was a shiny black 150-horsepower Mercury outboard motor, now drifting up and down in the chop, its propeller occasionally scraping against the lake's boulder-strewn bottom.

Twenty yards farther out into Vermilion, beyond Holden's legal nets, bobbed a pair of faux pine branch floats. If you boated by, you would think they were tree debris, to be avoided if you did not want your motor to get caught up. The faux branches anchored each side of a 15-foot-long, 25-foot-deep gill net, set in a way designed to produce a maximum walleye harvest. Pound for pound, a single catch of walleye in that net would fetch enough money to keep a grown man stocked with Old Crow for a year. Maybe Jack Daniels too.

Annually, Minnesota restaurants sold $25 million of the prized fish, none of it commercially harvested in the state. Most restaurants and grocery stores purchased their walleye from Canadian fisheries or the Red Lake band of Chippewa, the only Minnesotans who could legally harvest and sell the fish.

Because of the cold and time of year, there was almost no one on Lake Vermilion. The lake contained more than 40,000 acres of water, dotted with 365 islands. It was strung across Northeastern Minnesota in a series of channels and bays that were so ragged and jagged that it had 341 miles of shoreline, the most of any Minnesota lake. There were a lot of places to lose oneself on Vermilion, which is why the distant sound of the motorboat, growing closer, was surprising.

The index finger on Holden's left hand, the one tattooed with an elaborate "F," twitched.

If Holden had not been nearly comatose, he would have recognized the sound of the approaching outboard. Like the patrol boat tethered to the nearby shoreline, the distant drone was definitely a 150-horsepower four-stroke Mercury, standard issue for the Minnesota DNR. From the approaching noise, he might have suspected the authorities were on their way. If he remembered or had been aware of any of the things that happened the previous night, he might have worried. But he was just beginning to regain consciousness; besides, he would have never guessed that the reason for the patrol's approach was because, five hours earlier, a call was made to Minnesota's Turn-in-Poachers (TIP) line.

"TIP line," Dispatch answered, before dawn. "Can I help you?"

"Uhhh," the caller began, not unusual for TIP line calls. "Think I got somethin' to report."

"A violation?"

"Well, don't know exactly." The voice sounded old, but with that inflection that identified a Northern Minnesotan. A man.

"What did you see?"

"On Lake Vermilion. Out across Big Bay. Near that big island. Two boats, one of them DNR, pretty sure. But nobody in sight. Leastways, that I could see."

"And you think there was some kind of violation happening?"

"Looked fishy, know what I mean? Where the hell was they? And there were net floats. Could a been whitefishin', but looked like there were two nets. That ain't legal. Is it?"

"No, sir. Unless there were two people with licenses. Are you sure one of the boats was DNR?"

"Two empty boats. One of them DNR. I was a ways out, headed to my car. But when I seen the boats I come up close and hit them with my high beam. When no one popped up, I yelled. But . . . nothin'."

"Can you tell me a little bit more about where exactly you saw them?"

The voice paused and then said, "North of the casino water tower. Clear 'cross Big Bay. Just 'bout a straight line, I'd guess. Up close to that long island."

Dispatch repeated the location. She had been to the Lucky Loon Casino and was familiar with that part of Lake Vermilion. She didn't know the island he referenced, but there were a lot of islands on that big body of water, and she thought she remembered seeing a map that showed a long island, due north of the water tower.

"What made you think the boat was ours?"

"It was . . . new like. With a big black Merc on the back. Pushed up to shore, just sittin' there empty. But I seen that DNR sign on its bow. That yellow-and-blue map?"

"Map of Minnesota with M-N-D-N-R in big letters?" Dispatch said.

"That's it."

Lake Vermilion was in District 5, which was Conservation Officer Charlie Jiles's territory. Dispatch had the rosters for all the COs, since they were typically the first to respond to TIP calls. But Charlie had the weekend off, and COs were forbidden to use their official boats for anything personal. She knew Charlie Jiles. He had a reputation. He was a good officer, but he didn't always follow the rules.

"Can you describe the other boat? Was it against the shore too?"

"Nope. Bout 30 yards out, I'd say. A Lund. An old Lund. Just anchored there."

"We'll check it out," she finally said. "Would you like to leave a phone number in case we have any other questions?" Dispatch had already captured the number from caller ID. But something about the caller sounded a little off. She wanted a name and was leading up to asking for it, thinking the phone number would be a good first step.

Then the line went dead.

Most people were reluctant ratters. DNR regulations could be ambiguous, and most were willing to give fellow outdoors people the benefit of the doubt. Others who might recognize a larcenous act refused to get involved because they were acquainted with or related to the perpetrator. And then there were a minority who thought if someone could get away with a little larceny, especially when it involved Minnesota's abundant natural resources, more power to 'em. This caller's voice sounded like it belonged to one of those guys—*a Northern Minnesota good ole boy*, she thought. And if the caller was coming across the lake before dawn, to get his car, he most likely lived in a cabin you could only reach by boat. And if he lived on the lake, surely he knew the name of that big island.

Something was a little off, but one thing was certain: they needed to check it out.

TIP calls were dispatched out of Brainerd, and it had taken nearly four hours to marshal two neighboring COs—Jennie Flag out of Grand Rapids and Bernie Olathe from Two Harbors—and get them over to Vermilion to follow up. Flag had trailered her boat. The pair then put in at the Lucky Loon Casino docks, feeling anything but lucky. The late morning was sunny but cold. Not ideal for being on water that in another three weeks would be solid ice.

They both knew fellow Officer Charlie Jiles. He lived alone in Eveleth, and Dispatch had told them he had the weekend off. Dispatch had called his cell as soon as they'd received the tip, but it rolled over to his voicemail. Must have had it off. Each of the COs tried him on their way over, and then Flag had tried him again from the dock. But again, no answer, which was regrettable because the day was bracing. Flying full throttle across Vermilion's red surface in 26-degree cold was going to be, well, frosty.

Once they motored out of Hemingway Bay, they cut due north, starting across the big open water. Flag pushed the throttle all the way down, and the runabout surged forward. The riffle on the lake's surface was mild enough, so the boat almost immediately planed level, flying like a hockey puck flung across a mile-long expanse of smooth ice. Both officers wore tight wool stocking caps pulled down over their ears, heavy down coats, and wool gloves. All of it DNR khaki green. To avoid the windchill and keep their hats from blowing off, they kept their heads hunkered behind the boat's windshield. Once into Big Bay, Officer Olathe raised a pair of high-powered binoculars, scanning far out over the huge expanse of water, searching along the distant shoreline.

This part of Vermilion is more than a mile across, so it wasn't until they neared the middle that Olathe thought he saw two boats, one of them silver, tucked up close to the opposite shore. He pointed in that direction, and Flag corrected their course.

There was movement, back in the bottom of Holden Riggins's boat. Following the finger twitch, his hand had seemingly come alive. It trembled in the cold. Holden slowly awakened. Almost immediately he felt cold. In direct proportion to his rising consciousness, his body began to shake. And apart from the bone-rattling nature of the shakes, it was a good thing. Intense shivering is the body's way of creating movement and heat. The ambient temperature didn't help, but the overhead sun did.

Now he could hear a boat approaching. He had a vague notion of hope, thankfulness, maybe even luck. But what he felt most was awful. In fact, he was pretty certain he was going to be sick, if he didn't freeze first. He was disoriented and nauseous and trying to regain consciousness and body heat all at the same time, and it was taking a toll.

When he was finally able to sit up, with a touch of vertigo that made the world unstable, he thought he recognized the motor's sound, a 150-horsepower Merc. DNR, if he had to guess. He hoped whoever it was had a bottle of aspirin and blankets or some kind of heater and something to drink. His mouth felt like someone had stuffed it with a dirty sock and wired his lips shut. Sitting up, he could barely peer over his boat's gunwale. He looked out into Big Bay and saw a boat, definitely approaching, maybe a quarter mile out.

Then he had to lay back down, bracing himself with his hands for support. His hands felt like a pair of ice chunks. He knew he had to move. He had to get up and move.

He rolled to one side, coiling into a fetal position. He stayed there for a moment until he was able to push himself up.

He was shaking, but not like a leaf. More like the start of an epileptic seizure. Only Holden's shaking didn't stop, and he swore his teeth were rattling as rapid as a woodpecker's thrum.

He was certain he was going to be sick, and just about the time the approaching boat drew close enough to see him, he managed to place his knees on the boat's side bench, hang his head over the gunwale, and heave.

It was a mix of solids and liquids, something that had no business seeing the light of day. He had a vague memory of last night's dinner at the casino restaurant, a recollection that triggered a gag reflex. He paused long enough to catch his breath, and then . . . this time he choked up bile, accompanied by a low-throated growl. He wavered a little, afraid he was going to pass out, still coming awake. The two COs were within 20 yards.

"You okay?" a man yelled.

Holden barely looked up. No, he was not okay. He was sick. But he was alive. He was at least regaining consciousness enough to both hear what the man said and understand it. He wasn't yet thinking clearly, because otherwise he would have realized it was a stupid question. Neither could he speak yet, so for now he just shook his head once: No.

The other officer was at the helm, and Holden squinted to see her throttle down, edging the boat forward so that in another minute—Holden's head still precarious over the gunwale—the runabout's bow kissed the edge of Holden's Renegade.

Holden couldn't move anything but his head. He bent it and squinted at them sideways, recognizing khaki green DNR uniforms, one man and one woman, but not much else.

"Water," he said, dry and squeaky, like a frog. Making an effort to talk threatened to precipitate another expulsion. This time he managed a dry swallow.

Officer Flag reached down into her pack and brought out a water bottle. She handed it to Olathe, who was gripping the side of Holden's boat. He took the bottle and stepped into the Renegade and sat down next to Holden, noticing the empty Old Crow and half-filled Jack Daniels resting on the boat's floor. No wonder the man was sick.

"You been out here all night?" Olathe said, unscrewing the water bottle cap.

Holden didn't look at the officer. He stared at the water, still shivering, and said, "drink," whispered and raspy.

Olathe started to hand the bottle over but quickly realized there was no way Holden's shaky hands could grip it. He was still leaning over the gunwale, partially prone. Olathe managed to bring the bottle to Holden's lips and tilt it and Holden sipped, some of it dribbling down his chin.

The three-day beard growth on Holden's face was coarse enough to sand the chrome off a trailer hitch. His hair was salt and pepper, short and greasy. Given the F-I-S-H and S-I-N-K tattoos, his raggedy attire, the booze bottles, and disheveled demeanor, Olathe thought the man looked more Skid Row than Lake Vermilion. He looked like a drunk on an all-night bender, just coming around, lucky to be alive.

While Olathe was giving Holden water, Officer Flag stepped back to a rear compartment. She pulled out a DNR-issued wool blanket and handed it to Olathe, who spent the next couple of minutes unfurling and wrapping it around the shivering drunk.

After another couple of minutes and small sips, Officer Olathe said, "What's your name?"

Holden finally looked up at him, as if starting to wake from a bad dream. "Holden," he said. "Riggins," the name squeezing out of him.

By now Olathe and Flag had scanned the area and absorbed the scene. They needed to get over to the DNR boat, tethered against the shore. They could see a standard-size whitefish gill net, strung 100 feet along the shallows, near Holden's boat. Out beyond the whitefish net, Flag recognized the faux pine branch floats. She had seen them at an outfitter's supply store over in Ely. They were supposed to be natural looking floats used to anchor duck and geese decoys, and while those seasons were open, there were no decoys in sight. She wasn't sure how they were being used here, but judging from the fact they hadn't drifted an inch in this light breeze, she wanted to see what kept them anchored.

The COs had also registered a violation of the open container law, given the bottles in the bottom of Holden's boat. Probably drunk while boating. Possibly illegal netting if he didn't have a license. Hopefully, nothing more. But it didn't look good.

And where was Charlie Jiles?

The whole scene was a clusterfuck, as Officer Flag liked to say. She was one of a handful of women COs in the state, so she felt like her language needed to be a little salty. She also grew up the middle child, a girl, in a family of four boys, so she learned their rough-and-tumble ways and how, when necessary, to land a blow. But both officers remained silent because, if Holden was a perp, they didn't want to piss him off. They wanted him to cooperate.

By the time Holden's hands finally settled enough to grip the water bottle on his own, Officer Olathe took another turn looking around. His eyes followed the same objects and jumped to the same conclusions as Officer Flag. They needed to get over to the runabout. They'd checked the numbers and verified it was Jiles's boat. Now they needed to make sure Officer Jiles wasn't lying in its bottom.

When Olathe finally turned to consider the shoreline, he said, "Any idea why there's one of our boats tied up to the shore?"

With some effort Holden swiveled his head and glanced at the nearby shoreline. Then he peered back into the lake and said, "First I seen it."

Olathe caught Flag's eye, and they exchanged a wordless comment, part irritation, part concern, mostly disbelief.

"We gotta have a look at that boat," Olathe said. "Stay put."

Holden nodded, clearly in no shape to do more than drink water and shiver more heat into his hands and limbs.

After Olathe was back in the runabout, Flag pulled away from the Lund, steering toward the shoreline. She nudged the gunwale up close to Charlie's DNR boat, and Olathe grabbed hold of its edge. A red fire extinguisher was out of its side bracket, laying on the boat's bottom. There was no sign of fire. A DNR officer's hat lay near the extinguisher. Beside the captain's chair they saw a Styrofoam cup stuck in a cup holder, frozen coffee dregs in its bottom. It was Charlie's boat, but where was he?

They took another moment to radio Dispatch and tell them what they had found. Other than Holden Riggins, who needed medical care and who they still needed to question, and an empty DNR runabout, nothing.

Dispatch told them they had been unable to reach Officer Jiles by phone. They should secure his boat, search the area, and if they were unable to find him, one of them should drive the boat in.

It was all very strange. They would need to search this part of the island. It was Temple Island, they had seen, finally consulting a map. From Charlie's boat, the shoreline rose rocky, steep, and poplar-covered to a granite overlook. There was a towering white pine way up on top. From there they figured they could get a better view of the entire area, but neither of them was looking forward to the climb.

They still needed to check on the faux pine bough floats, which they both suspected were probably attached to an illegal net. They had decided to check on the floats first, when Holden called over to them.

"Hey," he said, the word still scratchy in his throat, but sounding stronger. "Somethin'," he managed, "in my net," pointing to the net's middle.

Flag pushed away from Charlie's boat, put her motor in gear, and puttered to where Holden had pointed between the two white buoys. But it wasn't until they were right on top of it that they recognized, through Vermilion's red water, a body caught up and submerged in Holden's net. When they squinted through the lake's choppy surface, they noticed the body was dressed in khaki greens.

CHAPTER 2

S am Rivers awakened in the Twin Cities suburb. He had been following the media's coverage of the frost line as it crossed the Canadian border, traveling south, and took another two days to hit the Cities.

"A cold front," the meteorologists called it. "We knew it was coming, and it's finally here."

Sometimes, Sam thought, weather people predicted the inevitability of a Minnesota winter the way ministers predicted sin, with a rueful smile and the certainty that something bad was about to happen. Minnesotans could count on it.

Sam knew the cold snap wouldn't last. They were predicting four to five more days of low temperatures, and then some kind of warming trend. They didn't use the phrase "return to summer" because the idea the first hard frost would be followed by a few days of the year's most beautiful light, color, and heat would put a positive spin on their dour prognostications. It was the time of year for the meteorological glass to be half-empty. Regardless, Sam, who usually considered himself a glass-half-full type, refused to let the predictions of continued cold affect him.

He pulled on a pair of smart wool socks, faded blue jeans, a blue and gun metal gray Pendleton shirt, and a black lightweight down coat. He found a pair of black fleece gloves in his coat's pockets, from when he had stuffed them there at the end of spring. He decided it was another example of how fortuitous circumstances happened all the time, if you were open to considering them in that kind of light.

He also found a black headband, reminding himself the cold was only bothersome if you failed to prepare for it. Finally, he pulled on his hiking shoes, which brought his lean 190 pounds to just over 6 foot, 2 inches.

Hiking shoes weren't exactly U.S. Fish & Wildlife standard issue, but since it was Sunday, he wasn't exactly following protocol. Not that Sam Rivers, a special agent for the USFW, cared about standards or protocol. He cared most about teasing the right result out of the morass of details that threatened to swamp our daily lives. When working on a case, some people called it finding justice. Sam, who believed justice could be ambiguous, would never use such a charged word to describe his work or life's choices. He appreciated ambiguity and believed what he did was more akin to choosing the right path, in life as well as work. The clear choice almost always presented itself, though it wasn't always the easiest one to make.

He was thinking along these lines partially because it was Sunday. In many cultures Sunday was a sacred day. Sam, who considered himself more spiritual than religious, appreciated the day because it was the only morning he woke up with his phone turned off. And he would keep it off, at least until he and Carmel had a chance to spend time together, preferably in a way that honored the spiritual focus of the day.

The weather, day of the week, and the phone notwithstanding, Sam was preoccupied. He was thinking about choices. Big choices. Hard choices. When it came to Carmel, the woman he had been seeing and living with, off and on, for several months, he knew there was a discussion they needed to have. About their future. Together.

Were they marching toward matrimony? Despite several months of profound intimacy, he couldn't tell for certain how Carmel felt. Or how he felt. Not about love. Sam loved her. Intensely. And she loved him. But how did they imagine their paths continuing?

Was she expecting him to kneel on bended knee? The idea of proffering a ring seemed so . . . old-fashioned, traditional. Nothing wrong with it, Sam knew. But neither of them considered themselves traditional.

When he imagined their conversation, he was damned if he could feel the right words surface, the ones that would accompany the right next step. He wanted to feel centered about what to say, and when. And he wanted to have a sense of what Carmel wanted, and how she might respond.

He felt as good and right about Carmel Rodriquez as he had about anything in his 37 years, a bone sense and soul certainty.

And yet doubt awakened him in the middle of the night, like an owl pestered by a murder of crows.

The more he thought about it, the more he realized the simplest course of action was to put it out of his mind.

The status quo was practically perfect, so why rock the boat? Why interject the complexity his question was certain to create? There was Carmel's 12-year-old daughter, Jennifer. She was a great kid, who had a devoted father and mother, and Jennifer and Sam got along well. But how would she feel about a change in her mother's circumstances, even if it were only on paper?

His assignment from the USFW's Denver office to Minnesota was temporary, which meant it could change at any moment, sending him back out West. Carmel's life was firmly entrenched in Minnesota. Sam was familiar with long-distance relationships. From his experience, the success of distant relationships was directly proportional to the miles between them. Anything longer than a two-hour drive was doomed to fail.

And then there was Carmel.

Sam was certain she liked the idea of continuing to live together, providing the stars were in alignment. But glimpses into anything beyond the next week or two, let alone a lifetime, were about as clear as two ships stuck in a Lake Superior fog.

Compounding Sam's doubt was the baggage they both shouldered.

Carmel had been married to Carlos for 10 years. Then Carlos fell in love with another woman. When he asked her for a divorce and told her why, it hit Carmel like a runaway freight train. It had taken a year of struggle, but finally she'd realized she and Jennifer could survive the wreckage, even though it would take some time for her heart to catch up to her head. That was four years ago.

The demise of Sam's marriage had been more like a morphine drip for a terminal patient. Sam and his ex-wife, Maggie, both knew their marriage was over long before either of them had the courage to say it. It had finally been Maggie who summoned the nerve. Sam felt relieved. And then he spent several months feeling profound sorrow and anger and a sense of inadequacy—he had known the truth, but he lacked the courage to speak it. For a long time after Maggie, he felt like he had wandered into Minnesota's trackless Big Bog and was hopelessly lost.

What their pasts told them was that the best intentions could, over time, go awry. Seriously awry. There were no road maps for journeys of the heart. The idea of spending your life with another person was like binding one of your legs to your partner's and running a three-legged race through a Byzantine maze. A maze that ran to the end of days, if you were fortunate enough to have that kind of run.

And while he and Carmel often professed love for each other, there was no guarantee that if Sam asked her to marry him, Carmel would say, "yes." She would be well within the bounds of reason to say, "no," or "let's wait," or even, "really?"

At some point, Sam knew, he trusted his instincts and his fallible heart would tell him the right time, the right words to say, and the right path to take.

In almost all things Sam Rivers believed he knew the right choice, the right next step. He just had trouble taking it.

Earlier, Carmel had rolled off her side of the bed and began getting dressed. She pulled on black hiking pants and wool socks. She donned a gray fleece pullover that hugged every contour of her strong upper body. Her hair fell thick over her shoulders. If Sam was being objective, he would have said she was 5 feet, 6 inches tall, with a medium build. True enough, but for him there was nothing medium about her. She didn't worry about her weight because she ate well and either spent time in the gym, or outdoors, or was busy caring for the myriad animals that entered her veterinary practice. Most evenings she fell into bed literally dog-tired, since many of her patients were canines, some requiring a strong hand and firm mind. She liked sex, on her schedule, but usually in the morning, or in the afternoon on the weekends, or occasionally at the end of a late night after plenty of wine, in the dark. She had a pair of opalescent eyes that missed almost nothing, especially when they settled their high beams on Sam. And she liked to laugh, with Sam and at him, and especially at the antics of their canine family. Occasionally, something could ignite her wrath—bad drivers, animal abusers, stupid politics—turning her normal equanimity into something fierce and fiery. But she was quick to recover her temper and never stayed angry long.

Perhaps most importantly, she shared Sam's reverence for animals and the natural world.

Once she had finished getting dressed, she pulled on a light down purple jacket, thin black wool gloves, and hiking shoes.

While the two adults finished dressing for the outdoors, their three dogs—Frank, Liberty, and Gray—each reacted in familiar ways. Frank and Liberty were Carmel's dogs. Liberty was a 45-pound black-and-white springer spaniel mix—the one who always woke them in the morning with a smile and the need to pee. Liberty was shifting her intent eyes from Sam to Carmel and back again, looking for the certain sign. Carmel finally obliged and made a playful step in Liberty's direction and the springer jumped like a horse doing giddyap, racing toward the door. Then racing back. Then repeating the back and forth, unable to contain herself.

Frank was a 60-pound energetic chocolate lab mix with the agitated intensity of an adolescent on Adderall. *Or maybe a buzz saw*, Sam thought. When Liberty did her giddyap, Frank followed in hot pursuit, ricocheting down the stairs toward the back door.

"You love to rile them up," Sam said.

"One of my favorite things," Carmel said, grinning. "After riling you up."

Sam's wolf-dog hybrid Gray had now matured into a 2½-year-old who stood 36 inches at the shoulder and weighed 97 pounds. He was regal and intelligent and, Carmel had once said, "one of the finest specimens of canine-lupine crossbreeding I have ever seen." Though she was always quick to add that she opposed wolf dogs, all things considered. They could be problematic, even dangerous pets. "But sometimes you get lucky."

Gray was a rescue animal. Breeding wolf dogs was legal in Minnesota. But more than a year earlier, Sam had busted a breeder for cruelty to animals. One of the few wolf dogs that survived was the 6-month-old Gray, who bonded to Sam as instantly as superglue. And Sam, still rattled after his divorce, had welcomed his companion the way a brother welcomed another into the pack.

Gray peered at his two agitated cousins and cocked his head, as if to say, "It is hard to imagine I am genetically connected to you two." Gray knew a walk in the woods was about to ensue. And while he was excited, too, his temperament was more reserved, providing no crimes were being committed or no pack members were being threatened.

Carmel's house backed up to a 47-acre wood. While Frank and Liberty vied to be first through the door, Gray hung back, wanting no part of their frenetic, meaningless competition. Gray knew he would get out the door in good time. He also knew he was a born alpha, head of the pack the three dogs made while hunting through the woods.

Finally, Carmel managed to open the door, and all of them headed for the back steps. Frank and Liberty leaped, while Gray joined Sam and Carmel, following them onto a frozen, leaf-littered woodland path, heading into the frost-covered trees.

They moved 50 yards up the path. The dogs were out in front. Every footfall left an imprint. At the top of the path, they turned right and hiked along a trail that cut through a new stand of poplars, their leaves rustling golden in the morning light. Many of the leaves had already fallen, and now the five of them walked over the golden path through the trees.

For the next half hour Sam, Carmel, Gray, Frank, and Liberty hiked through the woods. The dogs remained off leash. They hunted left and right through the trees. The humans talked about their day and planned their afternoon. Jennifer was coming over after dinner, the start of her week with her mom.

"I can help you move your stuff into the study," Carmel said. "Maybe set up the Murphy bed and give you a massage."

It was a euphemism, they knew.

There were two promontories in the woods and the pack summited both, taking their time at the top to consider the view.

Finally, feeling energized by their immersion in forest and field, they returned to Carmel's house.

Once inside, their pack considered them expectantly, knowing breakfast was about to appear.

After preparing their bowls, Sam finally retrieved his phone, turned it on, and checked his messages. Overnight he had received two calls, both from an old friend, Vermilion County Sheriff Dean Goddard. The sheriff had called again this morning and left a message.

"Hi, Sam. Dean Goddard again," the sheriff said. "Can you give me a call when you get a chance? This morning, if at all possible?" And then the recording ended.

Other than occasional, infrequent texts, it had been almost two years since Sam had spoken with the sheriff. But he knew him well enough to recognize the man's brevity. Something was afoot, especially because he was calling on a Sunday morning. And judging from the sheriff's tone, rather than the more familiar gibing with which both men were familiar, whatever he wanted must be important.

Sam hit "call back" and after two rings the sheriff picked up. "Special Agent Rivers."

The sheriff was the same height as Sam, but thicker through the shoulders, chest, belly, and legs. A big man, providing he hadn't changed. The minute Sam heard the voice he imagined him sitting, his booted heels resting on the corner of his messy desk.

"It's been too long, Sheriff," Sam said. "At least a couple of years. And you're still sheriff?"

"They keep electing me. I keep at it."

Two years earlier, before an election, the sheriff's extramarital affair became public. After the dust settled, the good citizens of

Vermilion County recognized the complicated situation for what it was. They put politics and cultural considerations aside and kept Dean Goddard in the job for which he was born. The sheriff had subsequently gotten divorced and then married Susan Wallace, one of the area's most prominent doctors.

"And how's Dr. Wallace?"

"She went and got herself pregnant."

"Ha!" Sam said. "She should know better."

"She claims it was planned, but I don't remember that part."

"When's she due?"

"Due date was last Friday, but she thinks it's going to be early this week. It better happen soon because every spare moment of mine is spent in some kind of complicated nesting ritual. Later today I'm supposed to paint the kid's bedroom robin's-egg blue."

The image was incongruous, but people change, Sam thought. "You having a boy?"

"Yup."

"You're in for a wild ride, sheriff."

The sheriff chuckled and said, "I believe I'm ready for that kind of ride."

Sam and the sheriff were around the same age. Sam told him he could understand the sheriff's perspective.

The sheriff asked about Sam and his latest exploits. They discussed the drug busts Sam had made the previous spring. Sam's work had made another splash in the Twin Cities press, and the sheriff had followed it with interest and chagrin. Sam never tried to shine a light on himself or his work. But the nature of the crimes on which he worked made it difficult to keep a low profile. Especially when his wolf-dog partner Gray was involved.

The sheriff remembered Gray and asked about him. Then there was the sheriff's curiosity about Sam's personal life, and Sam told him about Carmel.

"You sound serious."

Sam paused. "Maybe."

"Fish or cut bait, Rivers."

Sam smiled. "For a man who likes to come right to the point, I still have no idea why you called."

"Well," he finally said. "I've got a situation up here."

"And you think I can help."

"I don't know. That depends. Do you know a guy by the name of Holden Riggins?"

CHAPTER 3

It had been a long time since Sam had heard the name, but it only took a second to recall him. They had been best friends their 12th summer, living on the edge of Defiance. Sam remembered a short, stout boy wearing a dingy, nondescript T-shirt and dirty jeans. He had round, wire-rimmed glasses with lenses so thick they magnified his eyes. His belly pushed out over the lip of his beltless pants, holding them tight. His stringy brown hair was unruly. Sam remembered how Holden's mother, a sweet woman like Sam's own, cut Holden's hair with shearing scissors, to keep it out of his eyes and off his collar.

"I know him," Sam said. "Or knew him. When we were kids. But it was a long time ago."

"Hard to imagine you were friends with Holden Riggins."

"It was just a summer. I think we were, what, 12?"

"I guess your good sense and respect for the law didn't wear off on him."

The sheriff's remark reminded Sam of the fatal accident that resulted in their parting of ways. Holden had been pestering his dad all summer to take them fishing in the Boundary Waters. The weekend before school was set to resume, the three of them entered the woods. On their first day they set out in a canoe to fish the middle of Pine Lake. As they neared the lake's center, Holden's dad, who was drunk, failed to recognize a storm building on the horizon. It hit them like a juggernaut, and howling wind and rain capsized their canoe. Holden's father, who had used his life vest for a cushion, drowned.

After Holden's dad died, Holden's mom moved them across Minnesota's Iron Range to the city of Virginia. Sam recalled feeling sad about Holden's departure. Holden had been his first good friend, and when he left there was an unexpected emptiness in Sam's life, at least for a while.

After their move, Sam hadn't seen Holden until the 9th grade. Growing up and attending different Iron Range schools, Sam and Holden's paths occasionally crossed at inter–high school events. But when they did, Sam barely recognized Holden, acknowledging him with a slight nod. When Holden did the same, Sam assumed it was because Holden would just as soon forget anything that reminded him of their fishing trip into the wilderness.

From what Sam had heard, Holden's high school years had been troubled. Run-ins with the law. Alcohol. Drugs. Nothing like the boy Sam remembered.

"His dad died in a canoe accident," Sam said. "Too young. I think it was hard on Holden, afterwards."

"Fathers can be tough," the sheriff said. He knew about Sam's father, who the sheriff at one time tried to arrest for murder. Before the sheriff managed the arrest, Sam's father escaped into a subzero Northern Minnesota night, where he was attacked and killed by a feral pack of wolf dogs.

"My old man was different," Sam said. "He was mean from the start and lived long enough to inflict plenty of pain. When my old man caught me stepping out, there was hell to pay. Holden's dad was just a quiet guy who drank too much and died when we were kids. I don't think he ever laid a hand on Holden. But he never paid much attention to him, either. When my old man died, I felt relieved. Holden was devastated."

"Did you know Holden racked up quite a record? At least in his younger years."

"I heard something about that. But I haven't spoken to him in years. After his mom moved them to Virginia, we pretty much lost touch. I'd heard he started hanging out with the wrong people and did some stuff. Mostly drugs, as I recall."

"Definitely drugs. Busted for selling marijuana. Then dealing meth. He was arrested for B&E, but plea bargained to a lesser charge to avoid jail time. DWI three times in his 20s. There are a few drunk and disorderly, one involving assault. But the thing that got him a year and a half in lockup was poaching and selling walleye. There are some other game violations, but you know how those went."

Sam did. Hunters and fishermen could pile up a stack of game violations but only receive misdemeanors. They'd get fined, which stung them. Sometimes they had their firearms, fishing poles, or nets confiscated. They almost always lost their hunting and fishing privileges, at least for a while. But they always avoided jail time. That is, unless they were caught poaching and selling their catch commercially. In 1900, Congress passed the Lacey Act, which, among other violations, made the sale of illegally acquired fish a felony. Violators of the Lacey Act could be fined *and* imprisoned.

"Holden was selling the walleye commercially?" Sam said.

"Until he got caught. He was netting walleye out of season, cleaning them, and then passing off the frozen filets to local restaurants as Canadian. Did pretty well, so I've heard."

"Until he got caught."

"Yup. Did 18 months for the felony. And appears to have been pretty much clean ever since. That was," there was some shuffling paper in the background, "seven years ago, when he turned 30."

Sam and Holden were both 37.

"Nothing after that," the sheriff said. "Until now."

"Poaching again?"

"We think so. And murder."

"Murder?"

"Looks like it. For now, we're holding him on lesser charges. But I suspect he'll be charged with murder in the next day or two. A couple of conservation officers answering a TIP line call found him midmorning yesterday. It appears he was illegally netting walleye, though he denies it. He had a legal whitefish net, and a license for the whitefish. The local CO was tangled up in his whitefish net. Dead."

"Oh God," Sam said. "Who was it?"

"Guy by the name of Charlie Jiles. Do you know him?"

Sam didn't.

"I've met him a few times," the sheriff said. "Kind of a glad-hander. Single. No kids, thank God."

"How old?"

"51."

"What's Holden say about it?"

"Not much. Knows nothing about the walleye net, even though it was his and it was set 20 yards in front of his whitefish net. And of course, he doesn't know anything about the conservation officer. Other than he knows him. Or knew him."

"Did it look like murder?"

"Definitely. CO Jiles was experienced on Vermilion. He never struck me as a guy who took great care of himself. He was a little heavy and out of shape, the kind of guy who visited the bars and cradled a few too many longnecks. If he fell overboard in that cold water, it wouldn't have taken long for him to become hypothermic and drown. But he had a nasty blow on his head. Either it was the blow that killed him, or he was knocked out and fell in the lake and drowned. That's what we think, anyway."

"Any sign of a weapon?"

"A fire extinguisher. In his boat."

"A fire extinguisher?"

"Yeah. One of those emergency extinguishers. It was bagged on site and tested back here. It has the victim's blood and some of his hair on it. And Holden's prints."

"So, you've got him," Sam said, with a pang of sorrow for his old friend.

"Pretty much. Except he denies ever touching the thing. Or knowing anything about it."

"What's he say about his prints?"

"At first he said they couldn't be his. When we assured him they were, he stopped talking."

"That doesn't sound good."

"No," the sheriff agreed. "When the COs got there, Holden was out cold in the bottom of his boat. Hypothermic. He's lucky he didn't freeze to death. When he started coming around and he was talking, he claims the last thing he remembers is having dinner at the casino, night before."

"So, maybe he did it in a drunken rage and passed out."

"He was definitely on a binge. We found an empty fifth in the bottom of his boat, beside a half-filled bottle of Jack Daniels. But he claimed the bottles weren't his and he didn't drink them."

"Did the COs test him?"

"On site. Blew a .06."

"I guess he drank something."

"Looks to me like he drank a bottle and a half of whiskey."

"And doesn't remember anything."

"When they found him, he was shivering like a dog. Couldn't even hold a water bottle."

"Did you check the bottles for prints?"

"His all over them."

"What's he say about that?"

"That's when he stopped talking."

"Maybe he was starting to remember it," Sam said.

"When I told him about his prints on the bottle, he just looked at me. But in a weird way, like he was boring holes into my head."

"You mean, threatening?"

"No. Not that. Like he was reading me. Trying to figure something out."

During the summer of their childhood friendship, Sam remembered Holden as a smart kid, but a risk taker. One of their favorite activities, living in Defiance, was to dare each other.

"Bet you can't stick a grasshopper down your pants."

"You can't swallow a live minnow."

"Can't jump off the river bridge."

"I'll give you a quarter if you run through Defiance . . . naked."

It was kid stuff. Nothing dangerous. Meant to test them and have a laugh and keep the boredom of a Defiance summer at bay. But Holden always had the last word on dares. He always took them the farthest.

None of the crimes the sheriff now related sounded like his old friend. Still, people change, especially when fired in the crucibles of puberty, high school, and early adulthood. And if he was still drinking and doing drugs or both, there was no accounting for the actions of an addict.

"Did he give you blood and urine?" Sam said.

"Yeah. Didn't really have a choice. We're having it tested. But it takes a while. They're saying at least a couple of days because they're backed up. We'll see."

Sam thought about motive and all the incriminating evidence. "If Holden got caught netting walleye and then selling it to local restaurants commercially, he'd go back to prison. This time longer."

"Yup."

"The CO catches him. Holden boards the CO's boat. They fight and Holden hits him with the extinguisher. The CO falls in and drowns. Holden, raging drunk, gets in his boat, but passes out before he can take off."

"That's what we think. Something like that."

"When are you getting the medical examination (ME) report?"

"Probably late tomorrow. Could be Tuesday. That should tell us for certain when the victim died," the sheriff said. "Holden works Monday, Wednesday, and Friday at a marina on Vermilion. All day Friday, he was working until late in the day. Then he boated to the casino for dinner. He's got solid alibis, at least until dark."

"Guess you'll just have to wait and see what the medical examiner says," Sam said.

"When they searched Holden's boat, they also found an unregistered .45 pistol taped under one of the floorboards. But it hadn't been fired and there was no gunpowder residue on his hands."

Sam remembered a .45 from when they were kids. During that summer they had spent hours trying to get into a locked cupboard above Mr. Riggins's workbench. Holden had finally picked the lock with one of his mom's hairpins. The cupboard held half-filled liquor bottles, three *Playboys*, and a .45 pistol with several boxes of ammunition. Sam had been raised on guns, but the military .45 was a novelty. The *Playboys* too.

"Unregistered?" Sam said.

"Yup. And like I said, he's a felon."

Felons were not allowed to own or carry firearms. And no one is supposed to have an unregistered weapon.

"Another violation," the sheriff said. "Like the open bottle. Since we didn't catch him operating his boat, we can't get him for

DWI. But we're running ballistics on the weapon, just to see if anything turns up."

"Not that you need anything else."

"No," the sheriff said. "It does not look good for Holden Riggins. Other than Holden's bizarre behavior, denials, and refusal to talk, which would be any attorney's advice, the evidence is stacked against him. At least enough to deny him bail, given his record."

"Who was your investigator?"

"Smith Barnes."

"Deputy Barnes hasn't retired yet?"

Smith Barnes was long and lean and had been getting ready to retire, last Sam heard. He was also incredibly thorough, intelligent, and quiet as a cat.

"After that stuff with your dad's gun club, he took some time off," the sheriff said. "He was thinking about retiring. Said he was going to use some of his vacation time to consider it. He was out two weeks before he came back to the office. Said if that was retirement, he wasn't interested."

Sam smiled. Sounded like Deputy Barnes.

"Barnes got some help from two of our newbies. Deputies Joe Haman and Sandy Harju."

"So why are you telling me all this?"

"Well, this isn't Holden Riggins's first rodeo. He's been here before. This is the first I've dealt with him because my term started 5 years ago. But before I started, Sheriff Diggs, who had been sheriff for almost 20 years, told me about certain people in the area you needed to keep an eye on."

"He gave you a list?"

"Nah," the sheriff said. "That wouldn't be right. Might even be illegal. We were just talking. Holden's name came up, but I almost forgot about him because it's been seven years and nothing," the sheriff paused. "But Holden has had enough practice with the whole arrest and lockup routine to know he's entitled to a phone call and a lawyer. Probably more to the point, he knows the first advice he'd get from an attorney would be to shut up. So I told him he could make his one call, thinking he'd call a lawyer." The sheriff paused again. "Personally, I believe the best predictor of future behavior is past behavior. And I think Holden Riggins was headed in this direction, at least 7 years ago. Maybe he just figured out how to beat the system. The guy looks like a cross between a Northern Minnesota backwoodsman and a gangbanger. This time he did a really bad, bad thing and got caught."

Both men fell silent, thinking about the death of a conservation officer, an extremely rare tragedy.

"I still don't see how I can help," Sam said.

"Holden knows you're a USFW special agent. If anything, a guy like you is gonna be investigating his crimes and making some kind of recommendation to our prosecutor's office. But still, since his arrest, other than the handful of comments he's already made, which wasn't much, he's basically said three words: 'Call Sam Rivers.'"

CHAPTER 4

The sheriff was correct about Sam Rivers. Working for the USFW, poaching was one of the crimes he frequently investigated and prosecuted. Fish and game laws were in place for solid reasons, mostly to do with the species they were protecting. When people poached, to Sam's way of thinking, they violated the species. That kind of violation required the maximum penalty.

"Any idea what he wants to talk about?" Sam said.

"He won't say," the sheriff said.

"Do *you* want me to speak with him?"

The sheriff paused. "Well, we're not getting anything out of him. I'm not sure what the USFW could do, but it's worth a try."

"Okay. Set up a call."

"Holden's insisting he'll talk to you in person. Privately."

"Given the circumstances, I don't think Holden's in a position to insist on anything."

"He is not. But it sounds like he has something to say, and speaking in private, one-on-one, is the only way he'll do it."

"He's got one call," Sam said. "If he wants to call me, so be it."

Sam was willing to listen to his old friend, but he was also thinking ahead. It was Sunday. Tomorrow was the start of Sam's work week. He had been planning to head into his St. Paul office. Apart from catching up on overdue reports—something he had been putting off until his boss, Kay Magdalen, threatened him with a transfer back to Denver—Sam had nothing else on his schedule. Except, possibly, Carmel, and his conundrum about how to address the next level of their relationship. But a trip north had never figured into his plans. Especially in the service of an ex-con in Holden Riggins's predicament, who had apparently been poaching again. And worse.

"Uhhh," the sheriff started. "I understand, Sam. But there are extenuating circumstances. I assumed you'd want to speak with him, and I knew you were in the Cities, so I let him have his one call, which he made. To a lawyer."

"So," Sam said. "Give him a second call. It's been done before." Then, "It's a bad time to be out of the office."

"Sam, I wouldn't normally push it. But like I said, something happened out there. I'm interested in what Holden Riggins remembers about it. Especially since I know the victim and he's a law enforcement officer. Frankly, the guy was well-known up here. He had a lot of friends. Holden's not talking, but I'm pretty sure he knows something. We can throw the book at him and probably convict, given the evidence. But we haven't seen the ME report or the results from Holden's blood and urine. The two COs who found him said he had to be out cold all night. And we know he was last seen at the casino the night before, after dark. Depending on the CO's time of death, it could throw a wrench into our murder charges. At least it could give a good public defender a possible alibi on which to build a case."

Barring the ME report and time of death, which would never change the other corroborating evidence—murder weapon, prints, proximity of victim, illegal net, etc.—it felt to Sam like the sheriff was pushing his participation unnecessarily hard. Then he thought of something.

"Any other extenuating circumstances I should know about?"

A pause. "We could use some outside help," the sheriff said.

"Help?"

"Smith Barnes has no problem running with the investigation. He and Holden have some history that precedes me, and if given a chance, especially given the evidence, he'd just as soon take Holden into the woods and hang him from a white pine."

Sam thought about it. "Smith needs to recuse himself."

"I have two deputy investigators, but neither one of them are ready to lead an investigation. And I can't, 'cause at any minute Dean Junior's gonna show up."

"You're asking me to lead the investigation?"

"No," the sheriff said. "Not at all. I'm asking you to hear what Holden has to say. And if he doesn't confess, to follow up informally. I can give you Sandy Harju to help. She's smart as a whip. In a year she'll be running the place."

"Wait a minute," Sam said. "The dead man has . . . had a lot of friends. The evidence is overwhelming. The perpetrator is a known felon. But if by some bizarre chance a good defense lawyer can raise enough doubt in a jury to get Holden off . . ."

Another pause. "You see my problem."

"You need someone from the outside, in case there's some

heat," Sam said. "From the public. From the dead man's colleagues and friends."

"I won't deny it," the sheriff said. "That's part of it. But it's not just the politics. If Holden doesn't confess, I need to make sure he gets a fair shake. If some of my deputies were found to be biased, it could jeopardize our case."

"I used to be his friend," Sam said. "Don't you think that could jeopardize your investigation?"

"Maybe if it was someone else," the sheriff said. "But it's you, and your policing of wild places and the critters that inhabit them is well documented."

Sam knew it was true. He also knew he would follow the facts wherever they led, regardless of his past friendship with Holden Riggins, as tenuous as it may be.

"Maybe if you'd been friends your entire life," the sheriff added, "instead of one summer when you were 12. As it is, nobody's going to have problems with you helping out."

"And I'm an outside federal employee. And when I'm done, I'm gone."

More silence. But both of them knew Sam's status as an outsider, a federal employee, and an official who would return to the Cities when he was finished were all helpful to Sheriff Dean Goddard.

Under the circumstances, Sam understood. And he was willing to help out an old friend . . . two old friends . . . even if he felt a little used. But if he told his boss he was headed up to Vermilion County to assist with a county law enforcement matter, her face would shade apoplectic. The request would need to be handled with care.

"Do you remember my boss?"

"How could I forget Kay Magdalen?"

Over the phone, Sam's boss conveyed a sentiment that was a lot like a bull in a China shop, but with righteous intelligence instead of brute force. She was one of those people who could project power over airwaves.

"You need to call her and request my services. Tell her it's an emergency. Tell her it's a Lacey Act violation and involves the murder of a conservation officer."

There was a long pause. Then, "Send me her phone number," the sheriff said.

Sam said he would.

"I know it's Sunday, Sam, and this came out of the blue. If you can get up here by this evening, I'll make sure there's a room for you at the Vermilion Falls Motel. Holden's not going anywhere. Then tomorrow we can meet for breakfast and talk about this, before you have a chance to hear Holden out."

"Is Barnes done with the arrest report?"

"Should be by this afternoon."

"Have him send it when he's done."

"Sure. And Sam," the sheriff paused. "Thanks for this."

Sam reminded the sheriff he hadn't done anything yet and hung up.

Definitely surreal, Sam thought. The best friend from Sam's 12th summer was reaching out over all those years to ask for Sam's help? Or to confess? Or, what?

On the other side of the ledger, the county law enforcement officer Sam respected and considered a friend was asking for help in the same matter.

Sam's current friendships were all with people he had met through work. People like Sheriff Dean Goddard, Kay Magdalen (who was more friend than boss), Carmel, and others. But when he thought about Holden Riggins, it was a friendship born out of an entirely different dimension.

They had bonded over difficult fathers, during a time when their only concern was how to spend a summer's day in the woods and waters around Defiance. Before their fateful trip into the wilderness, Sam recalled a moment when they stated, in definitive terms, their intentions to lead good lives, when they made their first cross-your-heart and hope-to-die pacts.

"Let's never drink," Sam recalled.

"And never smoke again."

"Be good to our moms."

"Study at school."

"Do hard things."

Sam recalled the statements because of how they'd sealed their pledge. Holden had seen a Western movie in which two Native Americans professed their friendship by cutting their arms with long knives and mixing their blood. Blood brothers. Neither Holden nor Sam was interested in inflicting so deep a wound, but even as boys they recognized the need for some kind of ritual to honor what they both considered sacred. So, they held the sharp end of a safety pin over a match flare, purifying its tip. Then they pricked their thumbs, pressing small beads of blood onto a sheet of paper, under which they signed their names.

"Blood brothers forever."

They bonded with one another in childhood, long before knowing who either of them would become. Long before it mattered.

That they'd been too young to know how the other would turn out, or the tenor of each other's character, wasn't entirely true. Most psychologists believe that by the age of 12, your character has been established. Not that it's been set in concrete. More like a clay pot before it's fired. Until it's been tempered by flame, there's ample opportunity for change. As Sam thought about his old friend, he tried to reconcile the kid he knew with the man he had become.

After Holden moved away, he had clearly changed. They'd been kids, and they'd done stupid kid things, but they'd done nothing that presaged the kind of record Sheriff Goddard had shared with Sam. Especially not the wildlife violations, which were, Sam had always felt, sins against the natural world. From Sam's perspective, anyone who violated the natural universe was, in no small part, violating themselves. Violating everyone.

Sam remembered the boy as smart, funny, and gutsy. He'd been curious about the world, especially the natural world, much in the way Sam had been as a boy. Those were the traits to which Sam had been drawn. They liked doing many of the same things, particularly exploring the woods, fields, and waterways around town. But their trip into the Boundary Waters had changed everything, especially for Holden.

CHAPTER 5

After the sheriff finished his phone call with Sam, he phoned Deputy Joe Haman, who was out on patrol. The sheriff needed someone to visit the victim's house.

"I'm going to text you Jiles's address," the sheriff said. "Technically, Jiles's house could be considered part of our investigation. I don't want you to break in. But if he was like the rest of us the place is probably unlocked, or there's a spare key hidden somewhere, maybe on the porch or under a back stair? We need to make sure nobody's taken advantage of his passing. And look for his cell phone, would ya?"

No one knew it, but Deputy Joe Haman and CO Charlie Jiles had been friends. More like accomplices. When Charlie Jiles was alive, Deputy Haman had watched him reach up above the back-door lintel, take down his spare key and use it, and then replace it, before both of them entered Jiles's house.

But all Deputy Haman said to the sheriff was, "Sure. I can check."

More than three years ago, not long after Joe began working in the sheriff's office, he ran into Charlie at an assisted living facility.

44

At that time, Charlie's mom was in a bad way. Joe's mom had just become a resident. Charlie and Joe commiserated about the final stages of their mothers' lives. Joe's mom was still in reasonable physical shape, but she was beginning to have memory issues, which was the reason Joe had been forced to leave the military and return home. Charlie's mom was well beyond memory issues.

The two shared their angst over parental plights and the high cost of the care facility. And since both were in law enforcement, they had plenty in common. Joe had worked in Iraq and Afghanistan as an MP, so he had stories. Charlie had been a CO for more than two decades; he could match Joe, story for story. Apart from the considerably different venues, the pair of officers had similar perspectives about some of what they'd experienced, especially when the crimes they investigated involved ill-gotten gains. They enjoyed swapping details about perpetrators and schemes they'd busted and decried the criminals they were certain got away.

In fact, they had witnessed so much over the years, it was hard not to feel disillusioned, and maybe they envied those they were certain reaped benefits from their misdeeds and then slipped away.

The two could not be more mismatched physically. Joe Haman spent a lot of time in the gym. The Army had instilled in him a rigorous routine of morning calisthenics. Over the years, he'd augmented that routine with weights and running. The man was as fit as the comic-book hero GI Joe. In fact, with his short-cropped crew cut, square jaw, and sparkly incisors, it was surprising the nickname GI Joe Haman had never taken root. Perhaps because, unlike the comic hero, Deputy Joe Haman had a temper. Three times during his tour of duty, that temper resulted in blemishes to his MP career.

He was cited for using "excessive force" once in Iraq, two times in Afghanistan. The second incident in Afghanistan involved drunk and disorderly conduct. After the drunk called MP Haman a *pussy*, Joe dislocated the man's arm and broke his jaw.

Similar to Joe Haman, Charlie Jiles sometimes went too far. But it involved women he encountered in the field. If they were younger than 50 and passably attractive, Charlie sometimes stood too close. With women, at least, Charlie Jiles was known as a close talker and a toucher. Over the years there had been a few complaints, but nothing that resulted in a formal report on his HR record. Charlie's boss, Ben Connors, had to speak with him. But it was a conversation between a couple of guys, and in addition to the verbal reprimand, the two bemoaned the new state of male/female relationships, particularly in light of the #MeToo movement.

The fact that both Charlie and Joe sometimes crossed lines was another trait they shared. Men like Charlie could be discreet, but part of the joy of sexual conquest was being able to brag about the encounters with friends. Men friends, of the right temperament. Similarly, when Deputy Joe Haman talked about his work in the military, overseas, he could not help but mention the times he'd "taught that asshole a lesson he'd never forget."

Charlie had concurred.

Joe also shared his experiences visiting foreign brothels. Asian women ran them and recruited exotic women to work in them: Russian, Tajik, Chinese, Filipino, and Tamil girls—young women from poor countries. Relating these stories, Joe was more circumspect than Charlie, in large part because Joe preferred the young men working the brothels. Joe was smart enough to know

Charlie wouldn't understand that preference, so Joe conveyed his experiences by replacing his memory of the young men with descriptions of the young women.

The two men bonded over their waning mothers, the high cost of assisted living care, indiscreet liaisons, their disillusionment with law enforcement, and the persistent problem of never having enough.

It was the problem of scarce financial resources that finally prompted Charlie to say, "I'm working on a little something. A way to generate some quick funds. Interested?"

"Does a fish have lips?" Joe said.

Charlie smiled.

"What's cookin'?" Joe said.

"Well, it isn't exactly on the up and up."

Joe thought about it. But only for a moment. "Well, there's pulling over a babe for a traffic violation, just to have a look. That's not on the up and up. And then there's murder. Where does this fall?"

Charlie laughed. His friend was interested. So he explained about an operation that leveraged Minnesota's considerable natural resources in a way that could throw off serious income. But no one would ever be hurt, and if they played their cards judiciously, no one would ever find out. And frankly, the less Joe knew about it, the better. All Joe needed to do was provide periodic intel about the location of county law enforcement personnel.

"You mean our patrolling routes? Stuff like that?"

"Let's say for some reason county law enforcement was going to fire up one of their Lake Vermilion boats, or trailer one of their boats to some other nearby lake, or maybe drive a cruiser along a remote wilderness lake, just to have a look around. All I'd need to know is where and when. Intel."

"And it never involves anything like B&E?"

"Nahhh," Charlie said. "This is really under the radar."

Joe thought about it. He knew where to find the departmental rosters, and every Monday they had their deputy briefing, when the sheriff shared the week's upcoming activities, stakeouts on nearby highways, patrols in the area, and so forth. Providing intel would not be a problem.

"Well, I guess the question is . . . how much is this kind of intel worth?"

"That's something to ponder. Not that I've given it much thought, but I'd say a few hundred bucks a month would be about right."

Now they were dickering. Both men enjoyed this part of their transaction. Negotiating prolonged their conversation over something nefarious. It was strangely entertaining. In a way, they both thought the whole process was enabling them to get back some of what they were owed.

Joe alluded to hearing about the cost of intel overseas. It was definitely north of $1,200 per month.

Charlie said leveraging Minnesota's prodigious natural resources had to be done carefully, and there was only so much cash such an operation could generate.

In the end, after a couple of beers and an hour of conversation, they agreed.

For more than two years, Charlie had been paying Joe $1,000 per month, cash. Over time, Joe was pretty certain he'd figured out the source of the illicit cash; someone was poaching fish from area lakes. And given that, in two years, there'd been no mention of it in the local press, or on any of their law enforcement networks, people were being careful.

And that made Deputy Joe Haman smile. At least until the unexpected demise of his friend.

Joe knew there were others involved. The kind of operation that threw off enough cash to pay off two law enforcement officers had to be big enough to involve others. But he hadn't known any details, and he definitely didn't know any names. And he didn't want to. More importantly, Charlie assured him he was a silent partner. If the loose-mouthed Charlie Jiles could be believed, no one knew who provided the county law enforcement intel.

When Joe heard that the person responsible for Charlie's murder was Holden Riggins, he wasn't surprised, given the man's appearance and record. Joe knew criminals could be idiots. But this guy—using his own clearly identified equipment to illegally net walleye just yards from his legal whitefish net—was brainless. Joe had no idea why the perp killed Charlie. Probably a disagreement over money. Knowing Charlie, there could have been a good reason. But getting drunk, committing murder, and then passing out was a new level of stupidity.

Regardless, given Joe's relationship with Charlie, he couldn't help but manhandle Holden Riggins, when escorting the suspected murderer from the casino to county jail. It was expected, considering Charlie was a fellow law enforcement officer. Also, Deputy Smith Barnes let his sentiments be known. There should be *no special treatment* for Riggins, even though technically he had not yet been charged with murder.

Deputy Barnes was disappointed Minnesota wasn't a capital punishment state.

But in transit, Holden Riggins had been so hung over or sick or preoccupied, he barely noticed Joe's rigid, too-tight handcuffs, or the way he shoved him into the back seat of the cruiser. Riggins never even looked in Joe's direction. The one positive outcome from their brief interactions was Joe's certainty the errant outdoorsman knew nothing about Joe's work as an insider. If he had, he would have used it.

Joe thought it was a good sign. Maybe Charlie *had* kept his mouth shut.

Still, Joe worried Charlie could have left tracks to find. A trail that led to Joe.

A man who could blather like Charlie, rarely engaging the prudent filter that kept important facts to himself, was dangerous. Especially to anyone else with whom he was associated. Joe worried his old partner could have left something sitting around, some kind of incriminating evidence.

The sheriff had also told him about the investigative support they were going to get from USFW Special Agent Sam Rivers, who was coming into town later that day. When Deputy Haman wondered about it, the sheriff was vague. Rather than ask too many questions, Deputy Haman knew he'd be doing some investigative work of his own, trying to figure out if Sam Rivers was a threat. And if so, what he should do about it.

Any good investigator, including Deputy Sandy Harju, would subpoena Charlie's phone records. Joe couldn't care less about Charlie's cell phone. If they found it and got a warrant to look at Charlie's cell log, they'd find a handful of calls to the deputy's personal cell. Easily explained, given their shared connection to the assisted living facility their mothers called home.

Whenever they discussed their other business, Joe had insisted on Charlie's use of a burner. Nevertheless, Joe knew the man was sloppy. Now he was going to search for anything untoward Charlie might have left behind.

As Joe turned into Charlie's driveway, he reminded himself to be thorough. Given the amount of cash their venture threw off, Charlie probably had a stash. If Joe could find it, he'd take it. Because dead men don't need cash.

Joe also needed to keep an eye out for anything incriminating, or that might lead back to him. Eveleth homes were well spaced. While Charlie's house was small, it sat on more than an acre of ground and had a detached garage with a parking space in the rear. Joe parked behind the garage and used the key above the lintel to let himself in.

The first thing he noticed was a putrid stench. When he glanced around the kitchen, he saw a box of takeout pizza sitting on the counter. Beside it, Joe recognized the takeout cartons from a local Chinese restaurant. The counter surface hadn't been cleaned . . . at least recently. The kitchen table was similarly crumb-covered and jam-smeared. A saucer held a half-eaten stick of butter. Dishes were piled to the top of the sink, with more over-flowing on the counter.

Joe followed the stench to an undercounter cupboard, where he found an overflowing trash bucket. At least it was lined with a plastic bag. He pulled it out. A rotten smell overwhelmed the kitchen air. Joe held his breath, yanking the bag out of the recepta-cle, tying it off, and placing it on the back step.

Joe Haman was a neatnik.

Charlie Jiles kept his house like a frat boy on a binge.

The rest of the house was in similar disarray. Clothes hung over chairs. A master bathroom was covered, sink to wall, with various soiled items. Obviously, Charlie hadn't been expecting any visitors. But then again, neither was he expecting to die.

Joe began a thorough perusal of the dead man's house. He peered into the obvious places: under Charlie's bed, under his mattress, in the freezer, through his closet shelves, in each of his multiple pairs of shoes. The man had a collection of tennis shoes that rivaled a player with the NBA. The upper closet shelf con-tained stacked shoe boxes, some empty, some containing brand-new shoes, some containing shoes that were worn to nothing. The man, Joe guessed, had some kind of fetish.

Joe searched through every box and every pair of shoes but found nothing.

Charlie had a bedside nightstand with a drawer above a book-shelf. It was the only place where he had books. A half dozen books were stacked beside a dog-eared dictionary. Joe pulled them out far enough to peer behind them. Then he checked the nightstand's drawer. But again, nothing out of the ordinary—only a couple of pairs of eyeglass cheaters, a blank mini-spiral notebook, two pencils and a pen, and some paperclips.

He pulled out the man's dresser drawers, rifled through their contents, lifted them to examine their bottoms, and examined the empty dresser drawer slots.

He pulled down an attic ladder and ascended to its dusty confines, where he found a patina of dust so thick it was obvious no one had set foot or hand in the space for years.

By late morning, Joe sat down in Charlie's overstuffed easy chair to think. "Now where in the hell is your stash?" he said aloud.

He tried to imagine. Suddenly he thought, *the chair*. He stood up from the chair's stuffed comfort. And then he examined every part of it, tipping it on its side, looking underneath, feeling through the stuffing for an anomalous bump or object.

But again, nothing.

He left the house and walked back to the garage. He turned on the overhead light.

He spent almost 30 minutes perusing the garage's contents. Like the house, it was a mess.

Earlier, the department had found Charlie's red truck in the Lucky Loon Casino lot, with his boat trailer affixed to the hitch. Joe and Deputy Sandy Harju had already searched it, but in the end, like the garage and house, they found several fast-food wrappers on the passenger side floor but nothing else.

Because Joe was experienced, and because he was a good investigator, he guessed that Charlie hid his illicit cash elsewhere. Or more likely spent it on slot machines and whores.

Finally, before noon, Deputy Joe Haman locked the back door. He returned the key to the overhead lintel. His report to the sheriff would be brief. Nothing found, particularly no cell phone.

But as Joe backed out of Charlie's drive, he could not shake the niggling notion that, despite his thorough efforts, there might still be damaging evidence the dead man left behind.

CHAPTER 6

S am had come into Carmel's study to take the call from Sheriff Goddard. The room was furnished with a wooden desk against the back wall, in front of a window overlooking the forest. Bookshelves were built into the walls on either side of the window. They were filled with an assortment of veterinary medical, contemporary fiction, and nonfiction titles. For the most part, the books were Carmel's. But in the five months Sam had been staying with her, he'd added some volumes of his own.

A Murphy bed was built into the opposite wall. When it was 12-year-old Jennifer's week with Carmel, Sam pulled down the bed and slept alone in the study. Carmel was raising her child as a good, smart kid. She had told Sam she wanted to avoid questions of sleeping arrangements, since her daughter was on the verge of becoming a woman and questions of sex, marriage, fidelity, and all the rest were sure to follow. Also, Carmel had a good relationship with Carlos, her ex-husband and Jennifer's father. Carlos, who had a little of the old patriarchy in him, appreciated their discretion.

Sam respected Carmel's sense of propriety, especially since it did not preclude bedtime visits in the dark, after Jennifer fell asleep.

Sam sat in front of the desk, staring out at the trees and thinking.

Carmel walked into the room.

"Are you done with your call?" Carmel said.

"Sort of. The sheriff wants me to come to Vermilion Falls. Tonight."

"Tonight?"

"I know. Bad timing. Do you remember me telling you about an old childhood friend of mine named Holden Riggins? Or at least that canoe accident in which his dad died?"

Carmel remembered. Now Sam conveyed more details, especially about Holden and him as a kid in Defiance on Minnesota's Iron Range, their Boundary Waters trip, Holden's subsequent life, and now his latest alleged violations.

"That's awful," Carmel said.

"You mean what he did?"

"I mean all of it. Especially what happened with his dad. That must have been traumatic for you too."

"It was," Sam said. "Nothing like that had ever happened to me. I'll never forget Holden's broken face, holding onto that capsized canoe. When he realized his dad was gone. Hard to recover from something like that. It was one of the first times I experienced trauma, though I had no idea it was happening. What happened to Holden was worse than terrible. But for me it was useful, given the truckload of crazy my old man dished out."

Carmel had heard about Sam's father, a prominent Iron Range attorney who used the law for his own nefarious purposes. Sam's father had been as different from her father as two men could be.

Her father came from an Old-World sense of patriarchy. He was a gentle and doting father who lived to support and provide for his family. He loved them without reserve or conditions, similar to the way he loved the animals for whom he cared. He was a veterinarian, and despite his perspective about the differing roles of men and women, it had been his guidance and example that had enticed Carmel into the same profession.

Not long after getting to know Sam, Carmel realized he reminded her of her dad, except Sam had a more modern sense of gender roles. It was one of the traits that drew her toward him. Among others.

"Doesn't sound like you have a choice," Carmel said, about heading north.

"I have a choice," Sam said. "We always have a choice. But my gut tells me it's a journey I need to make. That I want to make, truth be told."

There was a pause during which neither of them said anything.

Carmel finally broke the silence. "Will you take Gray?"

"Sure. He'll prove useful, somehow. He always does. Besides, Gray loves Northern Minnesota. It's where he was born."

"I'd think he would hate it, given his first six months in Angus Moon's hell kennel."

"I'm sure there's trauma, but I've never seen it. He just seems to have accepted what he was born into as the way it was. I think it's the wolf in him; he lives in the moment, unburdened by the pain of his past or hope for his future. He just is. And I think he especially feels it up north, in wolf country. Besides, where I go, Gray goes."

Some partners might have been jealous about Sam's relationship with Gray, and that Gray was a constant companion when sometimes Carmel was not. But for Carmel, it was another one of those traits she loved.

"Of course," she said.

Both of them paused, considering the different ways their week was beginning to unfold.

Then Carmel said, "You know, I'm speaking to a group of conservation officers about the latest research on Lyme disease on Tuesday. Some kind of annual CO conference. In Duluth."

Sam remembered. "You were going up for the day."

"That was the plan. But I could come up and stay. The conference is actually Tuesday through Wednesday."

"What about Jennifer? And your practice?"

"I could trade a night with Carlos. Jennifer would understand. And Dad loves covering for me now that he's retired."

"I need to interview some COs. I wonder if they'd be at that conference."

"I think all the COs will be attending, except a skeleton crew in the field," Carmel said.

Sam thought about it. "That might work. Problem is, I'm not sure what I'm walking into. Can I call you tomorrow, later in the day? I should know by then."

"Sure," Carmel said. Then Carmel reached over Sam's shoulder and lowered the window blinds. She twisted the slats shut and the room darkened. She turned to the Murphy bed and pulled it down.

"Before you go . . .," Carmel said. She pulled off her gray fleece top and stood staring at him. He was reminded again that, along with everything else, there was that discussion they needed to have.

But he didn't think now was the right time for it.

CHAPTER 7

Cray Halverson sat at his small kitchen table, bug hunting. The table was covered with a plastic, red-and-white checkered picnic cloth. Atop the table sat an antique minnow bucket lamp. The old bucket formed the base of the lamp. A rusted iron stem rose out of the bucket's center. Affixed to its top was a yellowed lampshade. The shade was covered with numerous fly-size red-and-brown stains, the remnants of Cray's previous safaris.

Cray's live-in girlfriend, Rowena, had seen a similar lamp in a Hibbing antiques store. She liked it, but at $125, she knew it was priced for fat cats out of the Cities. She came home and scrounged through Cray's boathouse and garage until she found enough spare parts to cobble together something of her own making. It was *similar* to the antiques store piece, though slightly less polished. Still, Rowena felt proud of her lamp, considering it an example of both her craft prowess and common sense about dollars, of which she had few. And since the lamp attracted the omnipresent bugs, Cray liked it too.

Cray sat quiet as a statue, waiting. Beside his left hand rested a tumbler of Jack Daniels, three fingerfuls of amber liquid cooling over ice. Normally he avoided Jack in the middle of the day.

But there was nothing normal about the shitstorm of the past few days. Besides, he hoped the drink would help settle him, maybe give him some bright ideas about what in the hell he should do next, all things considered.

Cray's lake home was perched at the end of Tamarack Lane, a quarter mile out a long peninsula that until five decades earlier had been pockmarked by black spruce bogs. Then in the 1970s, a developer out of the Cities used drainage tiles to filter off the excess swamp water. Prior to development, the place had been home to mosquitoes, black flies, mayfly hatches, army worms, and just about every other form of Northern Minnesota affliction. The only permanent resident had been Cray and his father, Boggy Halverson. There had been a handful of temporary residents, the occasional women Boggy brought home. If the women stayed more than a month, Boggy told Cray he could call them mom. But none of them lasted more than a year, and Cray grew up thinking mom was another name for girlfriend.

Growing up, Cray's luck in romance was only slightly better than his old man's. Before Rowena, he lived alone. Part of his lackluster lady luck was due to appearance. He had a sharp nose that tapered to a point over a pair of thin lips. The nose punctuated deep-set gray eyes. Since Cray made his living outdoors, his 43-year-old skin was weathered. His nose usually carried a slightly higher red tint, especially after whiskey. At 5 foot 6 and 190 pounds, he was short, wide, and strong. He had the kind of power that was well suited to making a living as a logger, fisherman, hunter, and guide. And though he had not matriculated beyond the 12th grade, he had northern backwoods smarts, wilderness savvy, and bush country instincts that kept his cabin cozy, his cupboards well provisioned, and his cabinet filled with bottles of amber liquid, mostly Jack Daniels.

Four years earlier, after the midnight close of Daisy's Supper Club, Rowena agreed to come home with Cray. Mostly because Cray *had* a home—the small, rustic cabin at the end of Tamarack Lane that Boggy had willed to him. Prior to Rowena, Cray's stockiness and disheveled clothing choices were keep-away signs for most women. But Rowena had a special appreciation for Mackinaw Wool, red-checkered being Cray's favorite. Wearing a gray wool Mackinaw hat atop his head, the outfit set off Cray's pointy face in a way Rowena thought, eventually, she could come to love. But love wasn't in Cray's vocabulary, which was fine by the robust Rowena, who had been settling most of her life and was okay settling for Cray.

Cray sat still, his eyes narrow and intent, like a reptile awaiting prey. Four or five blue bottleflies buzzed around the lamp like electrons around an errant nucleus. One finally settled on the yellowed shade. Cray's right index finger and thumb tightened over the fly swatter's wired handle. The blue bottle skittered, licked at a lampshade stain, and skittered again. The unsuspecting prey paused, long enough for Cray's arm to trigger forward faster than a chameleon's tongue. The swatter flattened the bug, smashing it into another glistening red stain.

Cray felt a familiar jolt of satisfaction. He took a long swallow of Jack Daniels, draining half the tumbler. The whiskey burned his throat but settled his nerves. Unfortunately, killing flies and sipping whiskey was, for the moment, all the rough woodsman could think to do. His absence of inspiration was problematic given the challenges ahead.

At any moment, Char Peigan, the head chef and regal owner of Field & Sea down in the Cities, would drive up Tamarack Lane, looking for her bimonthly shipment: 20 (50-pound) boxes of walleye filets, all carefully cleaned and frozen, each waiting for a $27-dollar dinner plate. Or to be sliced into digit-size walleye fingers and served in a basket with three handmade sauces. The basket fetched almost as much as Char's renowned fish dinners.

Cray's garage was a mini fish-processing center. Along one wall were two rubber aprons, one for Cray, the other Rowena's. Besides occasional sex, woodchopping, and craft assembly, one of Rowena's most appreciated skills was cleaning fish. If she and Cray put their backs into it, using electric carving knives, they could clean nearly a half ton of walleye a day. Once the filets were ribbed and washed, they were flash frozen and packaged in plastic bags, tied off at the top, and placed in white boxes. Exactly as though they'd been caught, cleaned, and packaged north of the border.

If they had been caught and shipped from Canada, the wholesale cost would have been $10 per pound. For a few customers, Cray had touted his special contact in the Canadian fisheries, which enabled him to sell the precious cargo for $8 a pound. One thousand pounds every two months, for $8,000. And Char Peigan, whose latest creative interpretations of walleye were just one of the reasons she was angling for a James Beard award, saved $2,000 every two months on the wholesale price of walleyed pike.

In the Cities, the restaurant business was cutthroat, so Char kept the secret of her inexpensive walleye supplier to herself. Besides, Char was suspicious about Cray's Canadian contacts, though she never questioned them. Golden goose, as she saw it. As long as the filets kept coming, Char was satisfied with the arrangement. Besides, if shit ever hit the fan, she had taken the woodsman at his word; he had an inside contact from Canada.

Cray heard Rowena stir in the narrow bed. In a few more hours, she would get ready for another day of work. After tonight, she would have a couple of days to herself, when she would not need to worry about covering her bruises with jeans and a long-sleeved shirt. The weather was starting to turn, but Rowena ran hot, and when home she liked to dress in shorts and a T-shirt regardless of the cold.

Although "romantic love" wasn't the kind of phrase that had ever graced Cray's lips, he recognized Rowena's value, never more so than in the last few days. He cared about her. And it wasn't only because she could wield a woodcutting axe or a power saw as well as any professional logger Cray had ever known.

As the clock neared 2 p.m., Cray sipped his whiskey and kept hunting bugs.

The last three days had discombobulated the normally even-keeled woodsman. He had a lot to think about, and he had never excelled at considering all the angles and planning out his moves. He had always relied on instinctual scheming, which until now had served him well. But last Thursday, circumstances took an unexpected turn and one gut reaction had been followed by another until he found himself wondering if the choices he'd made were the right ones.

To Cray's way of thinking, it was as though he had started out on a clear path through the woods, following the trail's familiar twists and turns, and then a windstorm felled all the trees, not only making the trail impassable but also impossible to find. Now he felt like a wanderer trying to pick his way through a wilderness he had never seen.

From down Tamarack Lane, he caught a vehicle glint through the pines. He stood up from the checkered tablecloth and peered through the kitchen windows, waiting for Char Peigan.

Cray walked into the garage, grabbed the door's handle, and lifted. The door shuttled up, making a racket. Recent events notwithstanding, Rowena knew Sunday afternoons, once every two months, were set aside for Char. It was the time Cray wheeled out 20 white boxes of prime walleye filets.

Normally, Rowena helped them move the shipment from the garage to Char's Mercedes Sprinter. But today her ache and soreness felt bone-deep, and she was in no mood to assist.

The Sprinter emerged out of the woods and turned at the bottom of his driveway, backing up so the Sprinter's rear was 3 feet from the garage entrance. Then a tall, thin Char Peigan cut the engine and put one well-heeled foot down, stepping out of the van.

"Cray," Char nodded. "How's it going?" Char's breath clouded in the cold air.

"Been better," Cray said, an unusual response.

"Oh?" Char said, noticing Rowena's absence. "Is Rowena okay?"

"A little under the weather, but she'll be okay."

Char stood 6 feet tall in her Frye brown leather boots. She wore a powder-blue down vest over a designer Western shirt with mother-of-pearl buttons. Her blue jeans had elaborate designs stitched into their back pockets, front waist, and zipper fly. Her brown hair was long, and Cray could never tell if the streaks of gray running through it were colored or natural. She had a striking, Nordic face that was set off by a pair of intense blue eyes.

"Got a little problem with my contacts north of the border," Cray lied. Cray had always suspected Char knew where his fish came from; it was simplest to maintain their charade.

"How big a problem?" Char said.

"Big enough to dent my supply for a while."

Char frowned. "I need a little more notice than this," she said. "We're coming into the holidays. My big season. I was hoping I could pick up the next shipment a week early?"

Cray thought about it. He hated to disappoint. Especially Char, whose teeth were as straight and white as bleached ivory. Char Peigan was as unlike Cray Halverson as a beauty queen to a troll. He appreciated seeing her once every two months. He loved the feel of her hand when she passed him a fat envelope of cash. It was the nearest he would ever get to royalty.

Cray knew the smart move. Stop their netting and take a break, at least for the rest of the year, until the law cooled down with the weather. But the Jack Daniels was working in him, along with the chef's presence.

"One more shipment. Then we gotta back off for a while," Cray said.

Char nodded. "That should work," she said.

They finished loading the boxes in silence. After they were done, Char handed Cray his envelope, the chef's hand grazing the woodsman's chafed knuckles.

"You always deliver," she said.

Then she returned to her Sprinter and backed out of Cray's driveway.

He knew where he could secure the quantity of fish Char needed fast, though he didn't want to go there. But given the circumstances, he didn't feel like he had a choice. They had to move while law enforcement was caught up in their own underwear. And no other way around it; he would need Rowena's help. For the break-in, and setting the net, but especially to haul in and process their catch.

He pulled down the garage door and re-entered his cabin.

He needed another drink. Maybe it would help him figure out how to tell Rowena she needed to return to Smugglers Creek.

CHAPTER 8

After Sam made the decision to head north, he and Carmel made the most of the remains of their day. After a torrid encounter, they were reluctant to leave their island of bliss. They reached for their latest books and leaned back on comfortable pillows, legs sprawled over each other, reading and reveling in an unspoken, skin-on-skin closeness.

Sam opened *Factfulness*, a nonfiction book chronicling several of the reasons that, contrary to most peoples' opinions, social media, and daily press coverage, the world was becoming a better place. Sam appreciated the positive spin in the book, but especially the way that spin was explained and supported using solid evidence, science, and facts.

Carmel was reading *The Signature of All Things*. They were both reading for more than an hour, occasionally sharing interesting anecdotes and passages. And then Carmel read a section from her novel in which one of the chief protagonists, a young woman, enjoyed (and was troubled by) her sexual awakening. It was funny, poignant, and erotic. It took Carmel about five minutes to get through it. By the end they were laughing in the way two profoundly intimate companions do, with open hearts and unfettered humor. Not unexpectedly the passage triggered longing in both of them. They put down their books and turned toward each other.

Finally, reluctantly, Sam rolled out of bed. He checked his watch and saw it was nearly 4 p.m.

"We've got to get going," Sam said.

Carmel understood.

Gray quickly realized they were departing. He accepted it the way he accepted everything; it was fine, as long as he was accompanying Sam.

There was a long kiss goodbye and the promise of a call tomorrow, at first light. Then Sam and Gray headed north.

It was a little over two hours to Cloquet, the halfway point to Vermilion Falls. Sam stopped at Gordy's High Hat for a quick dinner. Then he continued north, where the forest gradually shifted from mostly deciduous trees to mostly coniferous.

Until the change in terrain, Sam had thought about Carmel, his plans, and the call he knew he'd be getting from Kay Magdalen. But as the forest thickened and grew denser, and then they crossed Hellwig Creek, continuing north—water and bogs on both sides of the road—it was as though Sam was driving back in time, to his 12th summer with Holden Riggins.

It had been a season of firsts. Sam grew more than an inch that summer and was the first to reach 5 feet. His features sharpened, acne sprouted across his forehead, and his biceps began to show definition. Down as soft as a young rabbit appeared under his arms, and around and below his navel. His head hair turned shiny and lank, finally taming the boy's cowlick that until that summer had stuck out like the splinters from a broken green branch.

That summer they left no log unrolled and no stone unturned. It was a time of garter snakes, grubs, field mice, earthworms, and roly-polies (those small bugs that looked like armadillos and burrowed under things).

"Dare you to put one in your pocket," Sam said.

"Pfft," said Holden, picking up not one but six of the small bugs, cradling the mini armadillos in his palm. "Double down dare," he said, dropping all six into his right front pocket, while his buddy looked on, grinning, certain this would end in entertainment.

It wasn't long until the bugs opened up in their warm cloth confines. They started nosing around, perilously close to where it mattered most. Holden's shoulders twitched, trying to shrug it off, pretending it was nothing. But after a minute his eyes panicked, and he dropped his pants so fast they knotted around his ankles and toppled him.

"They bit me!" he said, bending and checking for marks.

Sam, laughing, said, "You're the roly-poly king!"

That summer was the first time they stole a cigarette (from Holden's dad's Marlboro Reds). The first time they smoked, trying to be older than they were, physically sickened by the effort. The first time they ate olives, exotic fruit of Italy. And the first time they used a stick to flip the carcass of a dead racoon, discovering its seething, maggot-ridden underside. They leaped back, horrified. And then stepped forward, morbidly curious.

It was the first time they ducked behind Mr. Armstrong's grape vines and sated themselves on forbidden fruit. At least until they saw his door burst open. And then it was the first time they ran so long and so hard—beyond any speed and distance either of them thought possible, straight into the Defiance woods—they felt certain their hearts were going to explode. They fell into a sumac thicket, breathing hard. After five minutes of quiet they knew they were in the clear. And then the terror they had felt moments earlier was eclipsed by laughter they could not quell.

Sam recalled that, by late July, they were regular campers in Holden's backyard. Sometimes, in the middle of darkness, they shared things they would have never shared in daylight.

"My dad never talks to me," Holden once said. "All he does is come home, eat, and head out to the garage. Doesn't talk to Mom, neither."

"At least he lives with you," Sam said.

"Might as well not."

"My mom won't let me go out to my old man's place," Sam said. "Afraid of what might happen."

"Like what?"

Sam shrugged in the dark. "I don't know. He just . . . gets mad sometimes. Especially after drinking."

"That why your mom moved you guys into town?"

Another pause. "When he gets mad, he . . . he hits her. More than a couple of times."

Holden wasn't sure what to say. "When was the last time you were out there?"

"Before the end of school, when we moved out."

"You seen him much?"

"Sometimes. Keeps sayin' I should move back. Just me and him. Sometimes I think about it. But I don't really want to. And so far, my mom keeps tellin' him, let us settle first."

Holden thought about it, wondering what it would be like living with just his dad. "Only thing my dad does is work in the garage and drink beer," he said. "I don't think he'd ever hit anyone. He mostly just doesn't talk."

Sam said, "I bet he loves you."

If it was true, Holden didn't feel it. "Then why don't he say so?"

"Some guys don't," Sam said. "It's stupid, but they don't."

They paused in the dark, thinking about it.

"Mom says drinking makes you stupid," Holden finally said.

"Drinking turns my old man mean."

CHAPTER 9

Rowena Melnyk shifted on the narrow bed in their spare room. Since the rape, she had holed up in there, unable to return to their bed. She could hear Cray move through the rest of their cabin. She sensed his worry and struggle over knowing what to do. It was wrong to shun him. He had done nothing but help her.

But he was one of them. One of that sex with whom she'd contended her entire life. So, for now, she could not look at him.

She wore an old pair of cotton pajamas that had been washed so many times the fabric was threadbare. Faded blossoms spread across a dingy white background. She appreciated its pattern and soft embrace. Especially now, when she was trying to put so much behind her.

Whichever way she turned, she ached. There was a fist-size bruise on her backside, ugly as a storm cloud. She hadn't been struck there, exactly. Three days earlier, she had gone over backward and toppled onto a bow seat. Then she blacked out. Other aches were the result of what happened after she was down. She did not want to think about it. She tried to forget, to put it behind her. But her pain's persistence refused to give her respite.

Both wrists felt as though they'd been twisted. Given the pang in her shoulders, her arms must have been yanked back behind her. She had a slightly swollen ankle from a wrench that happened when she fell. Her knees were chafed and red.

But the deepest pain was inside her. Where she had bled.

At 5 foot 4 and 165 pounds, Rowena Melnyk was a physically powerful woman. She had a shapely large chest, two stout arms, and a pair of legs thick as a 20-year-old oak. Nearly two decades earlier, she had been a slugger on her high school's fastpitch team. Her senior year batting average climbed to a respectable .326. There was talk of a full ride at the University of Minnesota, but her grades and test scores barely made her eligible to play in high school. Other colleges with more relaxed academic standards didn't offer her enough to make it worth her while.

But no doubt about it; she had a natural affinity for swinging a bat, her left foot stepping into it and her full, ample figure leaning into the follow-through.

Out of high school, she worked odd jobs until she turned 21. Then she was hired as a barmaid/waitress at the Sportsmen's in Vermilion Falls.

Most men didn't pay a lot of attention to Rowena. Until Cray, her boyfriend—partner, she liked to think—she'd had a hard time with men, especially the guys who frequented the Sportsmen's. Those guys usually took advantage of her easy nature. She was born with a trustworthiness such that she *believed* some men, when after a few drinks, they told her she was "stunning," or "amazing," or "one of the most beautiful women they'd ever seen."

As a Sportsmen's barmaid she had learned about food . . . and sex.

First, she could eat and drink anything she wanted and not gain weight. She was already stocky, so it was a blessing to live on a steady diet of pizza and beer with no appreciable increase in size.

Second, she discovered that she enjoyed sex. Quite a bit. And though she desired a steady beau, eventually knowing she wanted to settle down, she decided her early and then mid and then late 20s were fine to devote to playing the field. She could sow her oats. Experiment. There'd be time enough to settle down.

She became known as a girl who could not only party, but wanted to, developing a reputation. And then as she neared 30, she grew bored with it all, recognizing the need to throttle it back. She also grew tired of the way some men used her. They were rough and selfish in sex, which was part of the reason she eventually backed away completely.

Unfortunately, it took a while for some of her previous partners to get the message. One oversize lumberjack forced her to perform in the woods behind the Sportsmen's. After it was over, she slapped him, hard, rattling his teeth.

Startled, he stuck a finger into his mouth; when it came out bloody, he returned her blow. After a fierce brawl they finally became untangled, exhausted. Rowena told him she was going to file rape charges.

The lumberjack, wheezing, waited until he caught his breath. "With your fucking reputation?"

In the Sportsmen's shadows, recognition that the lumberjack might have a point hurt worse than the physical abuse. It was a turning point. That night she quit the backwoods bar and never went back.

Less than a month after her brawl in the woods, she walked into Daisy's, a supper club nestled into a cove on Vermilion's east end. She sat down at the bar and ordered a large slice of meat lover's pizza and a 16-ounce Budweiser. Waiting for her meal, she noticed Cray Halverson. She had seen him around. Cray was quiet. He had no reputation. He wasn't particularly good-looking. He liked to occasionally go out just to hear bar chatter. And he had a house on the lake. So, she thought she might give the reticent woodsman a try. And once she got him into bed, it was enough.

Rowena wasn't the kind to share details about how she spent her 20s. Cray had been around long enough to know what was what. While he didn't know any particulars about her numerous partners, he knew enough. When it came to women, Cray thought his dad, Boggy, left him with good advice. Often enough, Boggy had brought home women whose characters some might question. When an acquaintance passed judgment on one of Boggy's girlfriends, he was quick to defend them, paraphrasing Jesus's admonition, "Let whoever is pure as the wind-driven snow throw the first punch."

For the last four years, Rowena and Cray had been partnered up, through good times and bad, through lawful pursuits and others that might be considered flying beneath the legal radar. From Rowena's perspective, their latest business was not meant to harm. Yes, technically, it was illegal. Technically, if they got caught, they'd be in trouble. But it was only something she vaguely sensed, leaving the details to Cray. She did what Cray asked of her, and over the last couple of years, they had made a great team and better money. Definitely better than what Cray could scrape together from logging jobs, or her tips waiting tables four nights at the casino, though they still needed both to appear legitimate.

Cray was a smart woodsman. Cray had figured out how to make sure they would never get caught. Cray had been careful about almost everything.

Except Charlie Jiles.

There was a soft knock on the spare bedroom door.

Rowena rolled over and winced. "Yeah," she said, her voice gravelly.

The door opened and Cray stood in its threshold, not daring to enter.

Rowena lifted herself up on one elbow and finally looked at him, movement and attention that until now had been difficult.

Cray thought her willingness to make eye contact was a good sign.

"Need your help," he said. "Need to get another net. And set it. One last catch before freeze up."

"I got work."

On Sunday nights, the casino restaurant and bar stayed open until 10 p.m. Then it took Rowena and a couple of her colleagues another hour to clean up and get the place ready for the following day.

"Tomorrow," Cray said. "We get the net. Set it Tuesday. Harvest the next."

There was a pause. Then, "Let me get through work," she said. "We'll see."

Those were the most words she'd spoken in three days. Again, a favorable sign.

"Okay," Cray said. A long pause, during which Cray wondered if he'd pushed it too far.

Rowena knew what Cray wanted. In the back of her mind, she remembered their earlier taking and setting of nets, the violation so recent she alternated from rage to weeping, trying to forget what she knew she never would.

Then, laying in bed, she felt something different, like the calm on the horizon while the big lake raged.

"It's gonna be colder than a gravedigger's ass," she finally said, a familiar comment that until this moment she had been unable to make.

"Not if gravediggers dress for it," Cray said, also familiar.

The words broke some kind of ice.

"How much you need now?" she said.

"Twenty boxes for the holidays. Char's last shipment . . . for a while."

Rowena always left the details to Cray, but she knew enough about their business to do the math in her head. Twenty boxes meant $8,000. Hard to turn down.

Rowena dropped her elbow, rolled onto her back, and stared at the ceiling. Flipping onto her back made her hurt again, reminding her the bigger ache was still too close for words, even with Cray. She closed her eyes.

Then she expelled a big sigh and said, "Where?" Pretty certain she knew the answer.

Cray wished it could be somewhere else. But it was the only place he knew, this time of year, with fish enough to fill Char's order.

"Smugglers Creek," he finally said.

The words hit her. But even Rowena knew, all things considered, it was the best place, and one she could not ignore forever. So, she nodded. Just once. Enough.

Then Cray backed out of the threshold and closed the door.

CHAPTER 10

By the time Sam and Gray arrived at the Vermilion Falls Motel, it was well after dark. The rear of the motel was bordered by a stand of woods. After checking in, Sam parked in the back, so Gray could stretch his legs. Afterward, he retrieved Gray's oversize dog bed from the Jeep, got him settled, and fixed him a dinner of raw venison with kibble.

The morning, the unexpected peculiar news, and the ride up to the Iron Range had taken their toll on both man and dog. They turned in early, looking forward to getting some shut-eye.

After Sam recollected his 12th summer, it was hard getting Holden Riggins out of his head. Especially the way it ended, with their fishing trip into wilderness.

Holden's dad knew how to get into Pine Lake, east of Trout, north of Lake Vermilion. The boys did all the work. They slogged gear up to the Trout Lake portage, then paddled against a headwind up the east side of Trout, finding a small river that took them into Pine. It was laborious and the bugs ate them alive. But they loved the journey into wilderness and setting up camp on an island in front of a clear expanse of blue water.

The next morning broke gray and cool. Holden's dad had breakfasted on whiskey. By the time they all climbed into their canoe, the wind kicked up like an omen. As they readied to paddle out, the breeze out of the west stiffened. The overcast sky was opaque as vellum. But Mr. Riggins either did not notice the weather or, if he did, was unfazed by it. The boys took the father's lead, too young to have anything but confidence in a grown-up's judgment, even if, Sam wondered, it may have been impaired.

Before they got into the canoe to push off, Holden's father made them fasten their life vests. Then he wrapped his own around the canoe's middle strut, making a comfortable backrest.

Holden stepped out of the shallow water into the front of the canoe, fishing pole nearby, paddle at the ready. Sam's pole was already leaning beside his paddle. He pushed off the bank, stepped into their craft, and seated himself. Once steadied, the boys dug in, fore and aft.

More than 100 yards out, the waves started to build.

"Smells like rain," Sam said.

For the first time, Mr. Riggins raised his head to consider the darkening sky. "Little rain never hurt anyone. Besides, that chop on the water is good for fishing."

The waves were blowing west to east, their peaks rising, the troughs growing wider and deeper. More than a football field ahead, Sam glimpsed worrisome whitecaps. But it was, after all, his first canoe trip into wilderness and, as Mr. Riggins said, a little rain never hurt anyone. Besides, while the air temperature had dropped, the lake water felt warm. And when he glanced toward Holden in the bow, he watched his friend continue digging into the dark water, pulling their canoe forward, steady on toward adventure.

The boys kept paddling. The swells continued to rise. The canoe lifted with each wave and slid sideways into the trough. Their course was perpendicular to the wind, and though Sam wasn't a seasoned paddler, he suspected it would be better, safer, if they were paddling *with* the waves rather than sideways to them.

Out front, Holden could see the waves building. "I think," he stammered, the wind ripping the words from his mouth, "we should turn. Go with the waves!"

Mr. Riggins finally glanced forward, sensing his son's alarm, for the first time rising from his comfortable recline. He squinted more intensely into the west, considering the blow. On the distant shoreline the trees swayed, their canopies appearing to fracture in a sudden, intense gust of wind, as though some invisible colossus was rattling the old growth by its roots. Near the edge of the lake, they watched a curtain of rain fall onto the water's surface in one thick torrent, heading toward them. The surface turned a mottled gray, agitated by the downpour.

Suddenly they were battered by a cold gust of wind.

"Turn, Holden!" Sam said. "With the waves! Make for shore!"

The waves washed over their gunnels. The air turned colder. And then the deluge hit like a pounding juggernaut, obliterating the shoreline. All they could see was the foaming water, the rain falling wild across its surface.

"Paddle!" Holden said.

The boys tried mightily to turn the craft toward the eastern shore, to paddle with the blow rather than against it. Mr. Riggins finally flailed his cupped hand over the side, digging his palm into the water in a useless effort to help turn the craft. His awkward lean into the lake began to tip the wave-swept canoe.

"Dad!" Holden said.

Sam dug in as earnestly as his 12-year-old shoulders could manage.

And then, as if in slow motion, they could feel the moment the canoe's tilt reached maximum shift. In a futile attempt to stabilize them, Holden plunged his paddle deep. The center tilted toward the waves. Sam watched Mr. Riggins's hand disappear into the lake. Then his entire arm. The canoe's aluminum edge dipped to the water's surface. Mr. Riggins struggled, as though something beneath the surface was pulling him down.

"Dad!" Holden yelled again.

And then they all tumbled into the water. Sam held onto his paddle. Both boys' life vests bobbed them to the surface. Holden grabbed the gunwale with both hands. Sam managed to catch its edge with his one free hand. They coughed, trying to hold on.

Holden's dad finally appeared on the wave side of the canoe, sputtering, flinging one arm over the canoe's bottom, white knuckles gripping its keel. Their gear had disappeared into the gray-green depths. The wind and rain grew more intense. Mr. Riggins glanced fore and aft, his eyes unfocused, wild. To the west, with the mounting weather, they watched a swell rise toward them. From the bottom of its trough, the wave's peak climbed and then broke over them. For a moment their entire world was water.

When the boys bobbed to the surface again, the weather worsened, pounding the middle and back of their canoe, making it impossible to see more than a foot into the storm.

Sam coughed out water, keeping his head upright. He spit, breathed, coughed, and spit, breathed, and coughed again. He gripped his paddle, his other hand clinging to the canoe's stern.

Eventually—seconds or minutes, he could not say—the storm began to ease. The rain slackened. The lake's surface grew slightly less furious. Sam could see down the canoe's length to where Holden gripped its bow, his pole and paddle gone.

Holden's dad had disappeared.

"Dad!" Holden called, in a higher, more urgent pitch.

The rain blanketed the canoe, the boys, the lake, for the moment obscuring everything except the two of them in the center of the tragic universe.

"Dad!" he repeated, a child's plea.

Sam looked down the length of their canoe, praying Mr. Riggins sought shelter beneath it. Carefully, still holding onto his paddle and the metal edge, he worked along the canoe's length, kicking beneath it, hoping his feet would find purchase on the grown man's leg. But his feet flailed against empty darkness.

He reached for the center keel, holding its edge. Then he took one deep breath, went underwater, and popped up beneath the canoe's overturned hollow. The weather still pounded overhead, making a metallic roar. Sam felt the man's life vest still fastened to the canoe's strut. But Holden's dad was gone.

After ducking and resurfacing into the storm, Sam managed to turn toward his friend. The storm and plunge had ripped Holden's glasses from his face, following Mr. Riggins into the depths. The boys peered at each other through the deluge. The life jackets kept their heads bobbing above the waves. Holden's eyes, now open, frantic, naked, and searching, held something Sam had never seen and would never forget. His friend's face held terror, etched so deep and inscrutable Sam wondered if it would ever fade.

And then Holden Riggins began to wail.

CHAPTER 11

Monday, October 16

In the predawn, Sam awakened in the Vermilion Falls Motel. He kicked off the covers and sat on the edge of the bed. His last thought before falling asleep was about Holden Riggins. It was hard to put a memory like that behind you. But everything he had heard about the man Holden had become made him realize they were friends no longer. Sam had a hard time figuring why a man like Holden Riggins had asked to see him. Maybe to confess, he hoped.

He stood and ambled to the bathroom, feeling creaky. Sam bent over, splashed water on his face, and toweled off. Then he put on a pot of coffee.

After Gray rose and stretched, carefully, he wandered over to greet his partner. Once Sam said "morning," Gray wagged his tail once, twice, and then returned to his oversize dog bed, awaiting breakfast and his morning walk. Gray knew the routine.

Sam fired up his laptop, poured himself a cup of coffee, and waited for his screen to come on.

He spent an idle moment remembering his previous day with Carmel. A much more pleasant business than anything else he had thought of this morning. Hard not to smile about it.

Finally, he logged onto the motel's Wi-Fi. Near the top of his email list, he saw Sheriff Goddard's message, sent late last night.

"Here's the Arrest Report on Holden Riggins" was entered in the subject line. Sam opened it and read:

> It took Deputy Barnes longer than expected to finish his report (attached).
>
> As I mentioned on the phone, it doesn't look good for Holden Riggins.
>
> All I'm really looking for, Sam, is to find out what he knows. I'm not sure what he thinks you can do, but if he's willing to share info with you, we'll take it. Better yet, if you can get him to sign a confession, that'd be a slam dunk.
>
> We can discuss next steps over breakfast, providing Dean Junior hasn't decided to make an appearance. If so, Barnes can fill you in. Hopefully, I'll see you around 8:30 at Rafferty's.
>
> —Dean

Sam checked his watch: 6:30. Plenty of time. Rafferty's, Sam recalled, was a local café on Main Street.

He opened the report and began reading.

The first page contained the usual cover information: date, time, location, names. Most of it Sam already knew. Near the top right corner was Holden's ID photo. Sam barely recognized his old friend. He wore thick, black plastic-rimmed glasses and his head was covered by short mottled-gray stubble. It had been two decades since he'd seen Holden, but this man's face appeared older and more weathered. Obviously, he had spent a lot of time outdoors. Sam had seen similar wear and tear on chronic drug users, alcoholics, and smokers. The photo must have been taken soon after Holden arrived in the sheriff's office because it looked like Holden was on the verge of losing his stomach contents.

There was a one-page image of a map included on the last page of the report—probably printed from GoogleMaps—depicting the approximate location where the boats, nets, and men (the conservation officer dead) were found, near Temple Island on Lake Vermilion. Sam knew nothing about netting whitefish or walleye, only that there was a short fall season for the first, and that netting walleye was illegal. Period. He had been on Lake Vermilion a few times when he was young. He remembered it as picturesque, huge, and troublesome to navigate. What struck him about the map was the location of the illegal net.

The report mentioned Holden's license for whitefish netting, so with regard to the whitefish net the location appeared fine, as far as Sam knew. But with regard to the illegal net, if it was Holden's, it was set in an odd place. First, Temple Island appeared to have quite a few cabins on it. Cabins showed up as dots on the map, and though there were no interior cabins on the island, there were many dots spaced intermittently along much of the 6-mile-long island's shoreline. It was a big island, to be sure, so there was plenty of space and many gaps where there were no cabins at all.

The area where the boats and body were found was in the middle of a cabinless half-mile stretch of shoreline. But there were enough cabins in the surrounding country and on the lake to make Sam think the area was probably well-trafficked. Even though few would be on the lake during this time of year, the few who were would likely be traveling within eyeshot of where the boats, nets, and men were found. And directly across Big Bay was Lucky Loon Casino, a sizable, popular destination. Maybe the location was particularly rich with whitefish and walleye, Sam wondered. It must be in order for someone to risk placing an illegal net in that location. On the other hand, if it was Holden's net, maybe he thought the best place to set it was right under the authority's noses, especially with the cover of his nearby legal whitefish net.

The arrest report was specific with regard to the nets and their placement. The illegal walleye net was smaller than the 100-foot-long whitefish net. Also, the floats for the whitefish net bobbed on the lake's surface. The whitefish net itself extended 3 feet down. The walleye net had been submerged in the bottom 10 feet of a 25-foot depth of water, presumably to avoid detection. That meant there was much less on-the-surface length to the illegal net, so significantly less net was exposed. Of course, Holden still needed to mark the submerged walleye net with fake pine bough floats, so he could find and retrieve it. Also, the location made him think that, if it was murder, it wasn't premeditated. A crime of passion, probably; Sam's best guess was that CO Jiles happened upon Holden, and Holden, rather than spend any more time in prison, killed him.

As Sam read the arrest report, he noticed Deputy Smith Barnes did his best to convey only facts. But it was easy to sense, between the lines, the seasoned lawman's perspective. The deputy believed Holden was guilty of both illegal netting *and* murder. The deputy's tenure as an investigator pre-dated Sheriff Dean Goddard's election. The sheriff mentioned Barnes knew Holden, at least during the years he'd been breaking the law and getting caught.

Sam held a similar perspective to the one espoused earlier by the sheriff. The best predictor of future behavior was past behavior, which didn't bode well for Holden, unless you gave the man credit for staying out of trouble the last seven years.

But people could, and did, change, Sam knew.

The report also described how the victim was placed into Holden's whitefish net.

> *"The victim was found in the center of the net, 2 to 3 feet below the surface, directly above the net's heavy center weight. The body was pushed against the net and rested sideways near its bottom, face toward the webbing. The victim's right hand and right foot were tangled in the lower net section and accounted for why the body was held below the surface. CO Jiles was in uniform, including his badge. Judging from the placement and depth of the victim, as well as the way the hand and foot were tangled, the body appeared to have been placed into the net, rather than pushed into it by wind or currents and becoming entangled."*

The idea CO Jiles had been placed in the net was peculiar, unless by placing him there the purpose was to hasten his drowning. But if it was Holden who had struck the CO on the head, why would he place him in his legal whitefish net? It would make more sense to get rid of the body, particularly when there was so much wilderness in which to ditch it.

When Sam first read the report, he'd again noted the reference to the half-filled bottle of Jack Daniels and emptied Old Crow. If Holden had emptied them, even if he was an alcoholic, it was hard to imagine that much whiskey wouldn't put him down . . . at least for a while.

Sam was aware, all things considered, that he was bringing his own set of prejudices to this incident. There was part of him, an old, deep, nearly unconscious part of him, that remembered his old friend. He recalled Holden as a kid who took risks. But nothing he remembered presaged a heart capable of murder. Sam had also wondered, off and on over the years following Holden's move to Virginia, that if things had unfolded differently, and if Holden's father had not died tragically, would Holden have remained in Defiance, and would they have remained friends?

Eventually, at the age of 14, Sam's old man convinced him to move back to the farm. It had been a tragic mistake. Sam knew it was wrong, but it took him three years to realize the severity of his mistake. Then Sam, beaten senseless by the old man, nearly murdered his father. Would have, if the old man hadn't broken three of Sam's ribs before Sam threatened him with a .22 rifle. Fortunately, the beating had been so severe that Sam had forgotten to load the rifle.

After the awful row, his father, a prominent attorney, threatened Sam with attempted murder, a charge Sam knew his old man could, and probably would, pursue. At 17, he had been too young and weak to face down his old man. So, he fled. But the experience taught him the legal system didn't always reach just conclusions. It also taught him people could be driven into corners that made them capable of just about anything, including murder. Were getting caught with an illegal walleye net and the fear of returning to prison big enough motivators to make Holden Riggins a murderer?

Now it made Sam wonder how both their lives—his and Holden's—might have turned out differently, if Holden had remained in town.

But those were ifs, and their lives had unfolded in entirely different ways. Sam found solace in wild places and entered a profession that enabled him to protect them. Holden saw the natural world as something to exploit for his own ill purposes.

Still, Sam reminded himself the best way to approach crime scenes and criminal acts was with a mind open to all possibilities.

After rereading Smith Barnes's arrest report, Sam turned to Gray. The wolf dog had been lying down, his eyes open and waiting. As soon as he caught Sam's eyes, he rose, tail wagging, and came over to nuzzle Sam's hand.

"You're hungry," Sam said.

Gray's tail wag hastened.

Sam prepared Gray's breakfast. While Gray wolfed down his food, Sam showered and dressed. Then he and Gray walked into the forest behind the motel, long enough for Gray to do his business and Sam to clean it up.

When he came around the Jeep's driver's side, he saw that his right rear tire was flat. "What the . . . "

The tires had less than 20,000 miles on them. Wrangler tires were rugged and built to withstand just about anything. Sam bent over to examine it and, at first, couldn't see anything. He wondered if someone had let the air out of his tire. Then he noticed two screws, one on the ground, misshapen but definitely stout enough to have caused the damage. He found another in his tire. It appeared the hole for the one on the ground was near the other.

It also appeared, if he wanted to attribute it to chance, that he could have run over both screws at the same time, maybe near a construction site?

But Sam didn't think so.

The previous night, he had parked in the rear of the motel, backing his Wrangler into the parking place. Now he examined the ground behind the Jeep. He cradled one of the screws in his palm and held it in front of Gray's nose.

"Smell anything?" Sam said.

Gray was definitely interested in the screw. But it was a small piece of metal. The likelihood he could pick up any kind of scent from it was doubtful. But possible.

Sam spent a couple of minutes working the other screw out of his tire tread. Then he cradled both in his palm, let Gray smell them, and said, "Find."

Gray knew the routine. He turned and started back toward the tree edge, his nose to the ground.

There were bent stalks, but not much else. Something, or someone, had been behind the Jeep in the weeds in front of the trees. The trees were near enough to provide cover. Gray followed a narrow game trail through the woods. Sam followed for about 50 yards, until they reached another road. It was a narrow dirt turnoff tucked back into the edge of woods. Sam could see someone had parked here. But there was no way to know if any of the tire tracks were recent. Also, that game trail could have been made by a deer, or even a bear, on the outskirts of Vermilion Falls.

"Could have just been an accident," Sam said to Gray.

But he didn't really think so.

CHAPTER 12

Rafferty's Café was on Main Street. There was a glass picture window on the front of the long, narrow eatery. Bent gold letters declared Rafferty's, in chipped and fading script.

When the Iron Range boomed with good jobs and pay, it was because of mining. And while mining had never roared back to provide the region with the kinds of salaries and economic largesse it once enjoyed, the area was still doing well enough to support a local cafe. Admittedly, the local economy and rural traffic didn't generate enough money to enable Agnes and Gene Rafferty, the aging proprietors, to install new countertops and appliances or repaint the faded gold letters of their name. But the old couple, who Sam vaguely recalled, worked behind the counter most days, logging the kinds of hours only people who loved what they did could endure.

While Rafferty's was clean, its threadbare environs reminded Sam why someone like Holden might be tempted to break a few game laws and make some easy money.

Sam had texted the sheriff and let him know he would be 10 to 15 minutes late, the time it took to change his Jeep's tire. Now he glanced around the room and saw one long, uniformed arm rise into the air from a rear corner booth.

Sheriff Dean Goddard sat alone. Sam appreciated the back-booth location, which was out of earshot of most of the customers. From Sam's experience, rural cafes were excellent sources of local information, in large part because the locals who patronized them possessed keen eyes and ears well practiced in the art of eavesdropping.

As Sam wound around the tables and entered the far aisle, several of those patrons turned to consider him. They recognized a stranger, glanced at him long enough to register it was no one they knew, and returned to their food, coffee, and conversation. Sam knew his visit with the sheriff would generate interest and speculation.

The sheriff stood as Sam approached, extending his hand. "Special Agent Rivers. Great to see you again."

More than two years earlier the officers, working together, had learned more about each other than either of them cared to divulge. Rather than make them wary, the personal details—the sheriff's extramarital affair and partial acquiescence to blackmail, and Sam's childhood trauma and illegal entry into his mom's Defiance home and his old man's ranch house—had brought them closer.

"Sheriff," Sam smiled, shaking his hand. "I guess your son hasn't made his entrance yet?"

Compared to the last time Sam had seen him, the sheriff had added some extra pounds. But he still had close-cropped, sandy hair parted neatly on the side. His face was a little more rounded but still set off by a pair of piercing, hazel eyes. A belly lip protruded over his black leather belt. Sam guessed marriage to his doctor wife was making him content and keeping him home at night. The sheriff's demeanor conveyed the familiar, sincere warmth Sam remembered. As well as conviction and strength.

"He's already following in his father's footsteps," the sheriff said. "He'll make his appearance when he's good and ready."

The sheriff smiled and Sam laughed.

"Sorry I'm late. Had a flat tire this morning."

"Hate it when that happens."

"Looks like a couple of screws," Sam said. "But they're new tires, and it's a Wrangler. Pretty odd."

"You think," the sheriff said, wondering about it. "You think somebody messed with your tire?"

The way he asked, Sam knew, conveyed doubt.

"I'd be surprised," Sam said. "Does anyone even know I'm up here?"

"Smith Barnes. And some of the deputies. But no one else, far as I know."

Sam thought about it. "Gotta be an accident."

The sheriff considered it. "My guess," he said. "When did you get in?"

"Late last night."

"Found the flat this morning?"

Sam nodded.

"Screws do cause a slow leak," the sheriff said.

Sam agreed.

"How was the motel?" the sheriff said.

"The rooms are clean and they accept dogs. That's all Gray and I need."

"How is Gray? Gotta see him."

"Of course," Sam said. "I would have brought him in, but the locals might not appreciate a wolf dog wandering by their table."

"Is he back at the motel?"

"He's in the Jeep. And he's great. Especially up here, with so many of his wild brethren in the surrounding country marking their territories."

They settled into easy conversation, talking about the area's wolves, Sam's drive up, the sheriff's family, and several other topics they hadn't discussed since the last time they'd break-fasted together.

While they talked, Agnes Rafferty came out of the kitchen, nodded to the sheriff, reacquainted herself with Sam, and poured them coffee.

After her cursory hellos, Agnes said, "I heard about Charlie Jiles." Her face turned serious. "He was kind of a regular. We'll miss him."

"I appreciate that, Agnes," the sheriff said.

"Don't know that guy who did it. Heard he was a no-account. I hope you put him away for good, Sheriff."

The sheriff paused. Then, "We'll make sure justice is served."

Agnes seemed to like that answer. She nodded and turned with her coffeepot, refilling cups across the room.

After she left, Sam and the sheriff talked a while longer about law enforcement. The sheriff wanted to know how extensive Sam's contacts were in the Minnesota DNR. Sam was familiar with one or two COs, but none in Northern Minnesota. And he had limited visibility into the organization.

"The DNR doesn't lose a lot of officers," the sheriff said. "You can visit their website and find a list, with a small bio, of every officer they've lost in the last 50 years. So it's a big deal. As you heard," he said, glancing toward Agnes refilling coffee. "I'm glad I have someone in custody. Most people don't know he hasn't yet been charged with murder. If we don't do it soon, I'll be hearing about it."

"Given his record and the circumstances, a judge should let you hold him as long as you need to. At least until you can clear up some details and build a more solid case."

The sheriff paused. "True enough. But a sheriff always needs to consider the politics." His eyes grew wary. "As I think I mentioned, I didn't know Charlie Jiles well, but he had a lot of friends. The longer Holden's in custody without charging him, the more I'm going to hear about it."

"I understand," Sam said. "Seems like you already have enough evidence to book him, given his prints on the murder weapon and the CO in his net."

"Agreed. But I'd like to wait for the ME report. And ideally, I'd like to have his blood and urine test results. And he still needs to speak with his attorney. Right now, if we moved on him without an attorney, the judge wouldn't like it. The real slam dunk would be if you talked to him this morning and he confessed."

After a short wait, plates of eggs, hash browns, sausage, and toast arrived.

"So, the sooner we get at it, the better," Sam said.

"The sooner we get his signed confession, the better." The sheriff was talking between bites. "Comments from the public, like Agnes's, are coming in pretty solid against Holden Riggins. And you can imagine Jiles's DNR friends are waiting for swift justice to be done. Especially those who have seen the man's mug shot and read about his record."

Sam agreed. Holden's rough appearance didn't help his cause.

"And if it's someone who's ever had anything to do with Holden Riggins," the sheriff added, "like Deputy Smith Barnes, they're just about ready to take matters into their own hands. Our suspect has a rep."

Sam knew the sheriff well enough to know his attitude toward the law was immutable. The notion he might railroad an innocent man into a conviction for a crime he did not commit, just to appease his constituents, was absurd. But it didn't change the fact that the most logical candidate was in custody. The public and their fellow law enforcement officers would be pressuring the sheriff to take the next logical step.

"Sometime," the sheriff said, "preferably sooner rather than later, I'd like you to check out Holden's place on Vermilion. He's got a small cabin on the back side of Temple Island. He claims the net they found near his other net was stolen from his shed. Says he's got another one and wants us to check on it."

"You believe him?"

"I have no idea. Seems pretty stupid to use one of your marked nets for illegal walleye netting. But as we know, perps don't always make the smartest decisions. Frankly, I don't want some derelicts hearing about his incarceration and figuring it's an opportune time to rob the place. Or worse, going vigilante over the poaching charge or the murder of a friend and burning his place down."

"Minnesotans love their walleye."

"Resort owners depend on a healthy walleye population to attract customers. And recreational fishermen, particularly the locals, want to catch fish."

In Sam's line of work, policing the wild, he was familiar with all sides of the poaching issue. A decided minority of outdoors people chafed at the idea of game limits. But when your livelihood depended on the availability of wild game, nobody liked a poacher.

Sam told him he'd check on Holden's cabin, though there were a few other things he needed to check on first. "What are you holding him on now?"

"Illegal netting. And he's a felon with an unregistered weapon. And suspicion of murder. That's a triple whammy. Oh, and a violation of our open bottle law."

From Sam's experience, those caught committing crimes often denied any knowledge of the event, even if they were caught in the act. Or, as in Holden's case, they were caught on-site, with the damning proof in their possession. While their knee-jerk reaction was to deny, they sometimes eventually recognized the absurdity of their denial and confessed. He hoped it would be the same with Holden.

"Has Holden completely recovered?" Sam said.

"Seems like it."

"Last I saw Holden Riggins was in high school, and he had no interest in speaking to me."

"Well, he wants to talk to you now," the sheriff said.

"I'll talk to him," Sam said. "But if he's followed any of my work, he should have realized talking to me may not be in his best interests."

"He knows all about your work," the sheriff said. "He knows about the work you did up here. He knows about how you uncovered that fake cougar kill in the Minnesota River Valley, and your work last spring breaking up that Mexican drug cartel."

Sam was surprised.

"I know," the sheriff said. "But maybe he thinks a childhood friendship has loyalty that reaches beyond crime?"

"Friendship would never trump any crime," Sam said, "for me."

Both men looked over their finished plates, thinking about it. Then the sheriff said, "Frankly, what I worry about is going down some kind of rabbit hole that draws this whole thing out."

"I can't see that happening. But if it does, you can blame it on me. Isn't that one of the reasons you followed up on Holden's request and called me?"

The sheriff's eyes turned wary again. "True enough," he said. "I can't deny Holden asking to see you was, well, lucky. Especially with my son on the way."

Sam agreed.

The sheriff paused for a moment, looking at Sam. Then, "If Holden Riggins declares his innocence, the heat could get considerable, given the charges."

Sam shrugged. "The heat's never really bothered me. Especially during a cold snap."

CHAPTER 13

Gray seemed to smile when the sheriff stopped by Sam's Jeep to say hello. He wagged his tail, which was unusual behavior for the regal Gray, who was typically more reticent.

"I think he remembers you," Sam said.

"I should hope so. I was one of the first to welcome him into the world, after springing him from Angus Moon's death trap. When you come in, bring him. I bet Barnes would like to say hello too."

Sam knew Gray's reaction to the sheriff could also be instinct. Occasionally, Gray seemed intuitive about people. Not always, but there were times when Sam would introduce him and his reaction was either friendly or decidedly cool, maybe even wary. On some of those instances, if Sam had a chance to get to know and understand the person, it seemed to him as though his partner's instincts were prescient.

The sheriff's offices housed county dispatch, a warren of deputies' cubicles, and side offices for the sheriff and undersheriff. In addition to 12 deputies, the sheriff managed five people manning county dispatch, plus two clericals. There were two interrogation rooms, but they were used so seldomly one of them had file boxes along the wall.

When the sheriff, Sam, and Gray approached the third-floor door, the sheriff peered through the bulletproof glass and knocked at the nearby attendant to buzz them in.

Deputy Smith Barnes was waiting. Apart from more gray through his short-cropped hair, he was still fit and wiry. When Sam shook his hand, he felt strength and the kind of callouses that come from wielding hand tools.

"Deputy," Sam said, nodding. "Last time I was here you were close to retirement."

Deputy Barnes managed a rare grin and said, "Still am." And then he bent down to greet Gray. Almost as soon as Gray heard Deputy Barnes's voice his tail wagged. Gray had a long memory, if not for faces, for sound and scent.

"We were all a little surprised to hear you knew Holden Riggins," Deputy Barnes said.

"Long time ago."

"Was he a bad kid?"

"Not that I remember. Just kid stuff. Stealing grapes off neighbor's vines. Smoking his dad's cigarettes. Normal stuff. We were 12."

The deputy made a sound as though it figured. Then said, "Some people are just born bad."

Sam had dealt with lots of bad people. Many of them, like Angus Moon or his own father, had been evil, if you wanted to put that kind of distinction on it. But Sam knew his father's childhood had been as bad as his own. Angus Moon had been raised by the swamp. Both men had been parented by abuse, addiction, and neglect. There was a reason they became who they were and did what they did. Not that it changed what they'd done. But *born* evil?

"I don't know about that," Sam said. "If stealing grapes and smoking your dad's cigarettes are signs of bad character, you'd better include me." When Sam thought of his old friend, he thought about watching Holden's dad drown. It's tough for that not to affect you, in one way or another. "I just don't remember Holden that way. Evil."

"I arrested him once. About 10 years ago. Drunk and disorderly," the deputy said, looking off and thinking about it. "He took a swing at me."

Sam was surprised. "What happened?"

"Not much. He was drunk and his swing went wide. But I felt the wind of it. So, I thumped him. Pretty hard. And charged him with assaulting an officer. Did some time in County, as I recall. But I don't think it taught him anything."

"Hasn't been arrested for a while," Sam said.

Deputy Barnes considered Sam with a guarded eye. "Men like Holden Riggins don't change. He just figured out how to avoid the law. Until now."

"It's been seven years," the sheriff said. "Could be he was still doing things but managed to dodge the law. Could be he's stayed clean. At least until now."

"Could be," the deputy said. "But I don't believe it for a second."

The deputy told them Holden had been brought up from the county jail and was waiting in Interrogation Room 2.

"We can watch Gray," the sheriff said.

"I want him with me," Sam said. "I'd like him to meet Holden Riggins."

The sheriff nodded. "Your call."

"Got anything that could be used as a weapon?" the deputy said.

"My Glock's back in my Jeep."

"Got a pen or pencil? Anything sharp like that?"

Sam shook his head.

"The guy did a year in lockup. That's where he got that tear-drop tattoo, I bet. Probably learned a few things too. Like how to make a shiv out of just about anything."

Sam had interrogated many he considered far worse than Holden. At least the Holden he remembered. He felt certain he wouldn't have any issues with someone he had once considered his best friend, regardless of what he had become.

"I'm not worried," Sam said. "Besides, I have a special weapon." He nodded toward Gray.

"I believe you do."

Sam thanked the deputy, then he, Gray, and the sheriff headed across the floor.

CHAPTER 14

Yesterday afternoon, the sheriff sent out a departmental email informing the staff about Sam Rivers's assistance. The email gave no clear reasons for the extra help.

Then at this morning's briefing, Chief Deputy Smith Barnes said he knew Sam Rivers, and that he and Sheriff Goddard had worked with him before. But the chief didn't know anything about why Rivers was on loan from the USFW. When one of the deputies asked for how long, the chief said he didn't know but that the sheriff would share more details about Sam's assistance in the near future.

Deputy Joe Haman remained silent through the briefing. When it was over, he returned to his desk with the rest of the deputies.

Joe was scheduled for a casino patrol run, then a radar setup through the afternoon out on Highway 7. But he told the chief first he needed to finish some paperwork from last week.

Joe prolonged his morning efforts because he was concerned about Sam Rivers. Joe had been Charlie's partner in crime. Joe did not know why Charlie was dead. Clearly, Holden Riggins had murdered him. But Joe did not know the suspect and was only mildly interested in knowing why Riggins killed Charlie. Joe was much more concerned about keeping Charlie's taint off of him, so no one would ever suspect. If he had to go after Sam Rivers to keep him off the scent, so be it.

The chief deputy intimated that Rivers was an investigative expert. Joe disagreed with the chief deputy's perspective, but he wanted to look Sam Rivers in the eye and shake his hand.

Deputy Joe Haman had spent Sunday afternoon researching Sam Rivers, and what he read about his work made him think the man was more Boy Scout than expert.

In one account Sam Rivers was described as the "predator's predator." That made Joe laugh. Joe knew predators. In the service, Joe had dealt with drunks, scofflaws, and a wide assortment of other deadbeats. But the number of genuine predators he had encountered could be counted on one hand, without using all his fingers.

Joe's old man had been a predator. When Joe was growing up, he'd been forced to help his dad slaughter pigs and cows. Heavy cables, chains, and meat hooks hung from the barn's rafters. When there was an animal to slaughter, Joe's father reveled in the ugly business.

The old man had taken deer out of season and run a permanent line of leghold traps across their farm's property. Whenever he found the tracks of a large carnivore (wolf, bobcat, bear, coyote), he'd set out bloodied hares laced with strychnine.

Sometimes, the leghold traps held a chewed-off foot, the remnant of whatever poor beast had been trapped and held. When it happened, his old man smiled.

Growing up, Joe had never been able to keep a dog because of the poisoned baits.

Finally, when Joe was in high school, his old man died. Joe's mom sold the farm. When Joe returned home from his tours of duty, he'd driven out to the place. The house was vacant and, like the barn, in disrepair. Joe walked the property. Meat hooks still hung from the rafters. Rusted traps lined the walls. When he was a boy, he thought the barn, with its accoutrements of death, looked like a torture chamber. After his tours of duty, he understood it had been.

Joe had been raised by a predator, so he felt a special appreciation for them, one that had been bred in the bone.

Joe read about Sam's work in the Florida Everglades, tracking down a hunter who was poaching rare Key Deer. If the hunter was stupid enough to sell Key Deer venison in the local newspaper want ads, he deserved to get caught. Even a rookie like Sandy Harju would have figured it out. After the crime surfaced, there was a sensational photo of Sam Rivers, looking disheveled in front of the developer's bulldozer blade he had, according to the reporter, "single-handedly idled."

Bullshit, Joe thought. The Keystone Cops could have arrived at the same conclusion.

Then there was the dustup involving Sam Rivers's father and the Iron County Gun Club. That's where Sam got to know Sheriff Dean Goddard. But again, the trail of clues that led to the secret cabin in Skinwalker's Bog could have been painted by a pavement lining crew.

And then last year Sam had broken the case involving the alleged cougar predation of a prominent citizen of Savage,

Minnesota. Joe believed that if the local authorities were stupid enough to think a cougar killed someone—an accident rarer than a lightning strike in the same place twice—then they deserved the public shaming they received when Rivers and his mutt followed the obvious trail.

People were idiots. Especially the authorities in Savage County.

The one thing Joe thought had been missing from all three of these sensational cases was pushback. The miscreants involved hadn't sent Rivers the proper signals at the right time. The perp who wounded Sam Rivers's mutt almost made a difference. If that guy would have killed Rivers's dog, Rivers would have become too distraught to continue, or at least to focus. And Joe wouldn't be worried about the mutt and its master now.

On the other hand, if Joe finished off the dog surreptitiously, he was pretty sure that kind of pushback would stymie Rivers's investigation and get the so-called expert off his tracks.

The previous night, after Joe had finished his research, he had cruised by the Vermilion Falls Motel, looking for opportunity. It was late and the motel windows were dark. When Joe drove through the rear parking lot he noticed the Jeep with Colorado plates—had to be Rivers's vehicle.

Joe Haman circled out of the lot, turning onto Main Street. He took a right on Flanders, another right on Bushman Street, and then he pulled into a dirt turnoff that backed up to a wooded lot. At this time, Sunday night in Vermilion Falls, there was little or no traffic.

He carried his tools through the woods until he came out onto the back side of the motel, approaching Rivers's Jeep in the dark. It took less than five minutes to turn the screws that flattened Rivers's Jeep tire. Normally, Joe Haman liked to send a more direct message, one not open to interpretation. But he wasn't above seizing an opportunity to convey a little mayhem when it arose. He hadn't planned on flattening Rivers's tire, but even if the Boy Scout interpreted the diversion as an innocent accident, Joe Haman knew that somewhere in the back of Rivers's mind a worm would turn. If it made Rivers wonder for a second, the worm would start feeding on his thoughts the way maggots chewed through a rancid carcass.

Flattening Sam Rivers's tire had been the opening salvo of a clandestine campaign Joe was going to wage against the special agent and his mutt. By the end of it, Joe figured, Sam would think the gods were against him. He would be so preoccupied picking up the pieces he would no longer give a rat's ass who killed Charlie Jiles.

When, in truth, the person who had thrown him off the case was just a genuine predator.

Monday morning, sitting at his departmental desk and feigning paperwork, Deputy Joe Haman waited for his opportunity to meet Sam Rivers and look him in the eye.

Take the measure of the man, Joe thought. *Especially when he's your quarry.*

CHAPTER 15

The 12x12 room's cement block walls were pale yellow. There was a white cafeteria-style table in the room's center, flanked by two beige plastic chairs. Holden sat on the far side, facing the door. When Sheriff Goddard opened it, the prisoner stood.

"Holden," the sheriff nodded, "Sam Rivers."

Sam paused in the threshold. As a man, Holden was bigger than Sam expected. Not tall, but short and wide. His arms were stout and stuck out of a short-sleeved orange prison jumpsuit. The skin on his hands and face was darkened and weathered. He wore thick-lensed, black plastic-framed glasses and Sam noticed the tattoo off the corner of his left eye, peculiar and maybe anomalous in the kid he remembered at 12. Sam recalled a mop of hair on Holden. Now it was cropped to his skull, dotted with salt and pepper—in the style of a monk, or a skinhead.

Sam had seen the teardrop tattoo, if that's what it was, on other prisoners. If it was a teardrop, the tattoo artist (Sam was being generous) had been an amateur. There were more tattoos on the backs of Holden's hands. But what Sam noticed most, what he caught in those first seconds of greeting, was caution. In the way he stood and held himself. Sam sensed Holden's guardedness, like a dog familiar with ill treatment.

Maybe it was the prison jumpsuit or maybe it was the weathered look and his demeanor, but Sam understood how some might think Holden had the appearance (if not the vibe) of a hardened criminal. In one glance, the memory of Sam's childhood friend was almost erased. The only thing Sam recognized were the eyes, which were wide, brown, and slightly enlarged under thick-lensed glasses. The eyes were open and familiar.

"You okay if my partner joins us?" Sam said, nodding to Gray, who stood attentively beside Sam's side.

Holden glanced from Sam to Gray, his countenance serious.

"I like dogs," Holden finally said. "Can't say I've ever seen a wolf dog. This Gray?"

A surprise. Sam assumed Holden knew Gray's name and lineage from news accounts of their past investigations.

When Gray heard Holden say his name, he looked up, quizzical.

"You've heard of him?" Sam said.

"Read about him, anyway. Seen his picture."

Holden came around the table far enough to greet Gray, keeping his distance. He leaned in and held out the back of his left hand, thick and freckled, with sausage-like fingers. Sam noticed F-I-S-H tattooed on the back of Holden's fingers, up near his knuckles.

Gray nosed forward, taking a couple of steps to close the distance between himself and the prisoner. Then he sniffed, cautious. He didn't wag his tail, but neither did his lip curl. He peered up at Holden, unsure what to make of him. Holden finally stroked his head and Gray allowed it, examining him out of one curious blue eye, and one yellow.

"He's got the wolf eye," Holden said. "And the other, maybe Husky?"

"Malamute," Sam said. "The different-colored eyes are a condition called heterochromia. It's a pigment thing."

"He's got a wolf build. Leastways the wolves around here. Big and rangy, with big paws."

Holden looked up at Sam and reached out a hand. Sam took it and they shook. Then Holden returned to the other side of the table and sat down.

The sheriff told Sam to come get him when they were done and backed out of the room.

After the door was closed, Holden said, "Talked with an attorney yesterday. She couldn't be here but said I didn't have to see you and shouldn't. Shouldn't talk if I did."

"Probably good advice."

"Same advice they always give. Can't say it ever did any good." Holden paused. "I read about your work with the sheriff. About that Gun Club. Your old man's club, I think it was?"

Sam nodded. "Two years ago. I couldn't have done any of it without the sheriff."

The two men paused for a moment, uncertain.

"I guess the sheriff thinks talking to a lawyer makes more sense than Fish & Wildlife, given the shit I'm in." Holden paused. Then he glanced up, straight into Sam's eyes.

Sam recalled the measured pools that held intelligence and mischief. Now they were wary and intense.

Sam shrugged. "I guess," he said.

"I didn't ask for you 'cause we used to be friends."

Sam waited.

"You're an outsider," Holden finally said, letting the words sit there. "Not from around here, since you were a kid. And you're not DNR, exactly, and not one of the sheriff's people."

It sounded like criticism of people and organizations Sam trusted. "Technically, the USFW isn't part of the DNR or local law enforcement. But they're my colleagues. We work as a team."

"I haven't had any issues with the sheriff or the DNR in a long time."

The comment almost made Sam smile, given the evidence against Holden, and the fact he was dressed in a prison jumpsuit and in jail. But he waited. And ignored the urge to smile.

"You're not local, but you know the area. And you work for Fish & Wildlife."

"The USFW isn't keen on illegal netting," Sam said. He was going to add, "or murder," but he didn't want to make Holden edgier than he already seemed.

There was a pause while Holden glanced away. Then he looked back at Sam.

"Somethin's going on here," Holden said. "I got no right to expect you or anyone else to believe me, given I haven't exactly followed the law most of my life. I've done things I wish I could take back. But this that's happening here," he paused, his head turning and his left hand opening, as though to emphasize candor, "I done none of it."

He looked away again. Sam watched his lower jaw shift a little, in the way of someone with more to say, trying to figure out the best way to tell it.

"I didn't know that conservation officer," Holden said. "Jiles. I mean, I knew him. But last time I saw him was more 'n two years ago," he paused again and looked away, thinking. "Gettin' ahead of myself," he said. "I don't know anything about Jiles and how he got into my net. I mean, it was my whitefish net. I set it Thursday. But it was legal. I have a license. I don't know nothin' about that other net, the illegal one set near mine. I know it wasn't there when I set my net on Thursday. Nobody was there. I never saw anybody on the whole damn lake. And I don't know anything about those bottles in my boat. Or the DNR boat near shore. Last thing I remember was having dinner at the casino. I do that, Fridays. Last Friday, after work, I went to the casino. Sat down to dinner. I admit I had a couple of drinks. That's what I do. Fridays. Couple of drinks. But that's it."

He stopped, still staring at Sam.

"What do you think happened?" Sam said.

Holden paused again. "Only thing I can think is somebody drugged me. They slipped me somethin' and knocked me out."

"And then set you up?"

"I don't know," Holden said. Now both his hands were open. "Maybe they killed Jiles and needed somebody to blame? Who better than somebody like me, with a record. I'm guessing whoever it was knew me." He paused again. "Only thing I can think.

Because I've been quiet for seven years. I mean, I've been straight. For seven years. I think whoever did it needed cover and they knew about my past and knew the law wouldn't think twice about whether I'd done it. Throw 'em off the real murderer."

Sam sensed Holden's sincerity. But someone with a record like Holden's—and who had, Sam guessed, been an addict at one time—would be an accomplished liar.

"What about before? Anyone in your past want to get even? Looking for revenge?"

"I admit I've done a lot of shit. Bad shit. But I can't think of anything I ever did that would piss somebody off bad enough to set me up like this. At least that I can remember."

Sam considered it, glancing down at Gray. His partner was sitting quietly, staring at Holden. Sam wondered what those heterochromic eyes were thinking.

"Didn't you have some assault charges?" Sam said. "Maybe somebody you beat up?"

"That stuff was more 'n 10 years ago. And I knew all those guys. We were just drunk and things got out of hand. None of 'em would have done anything like this."

"The evidence isn't good, Holden."

"I know," he said, short and irritated. "I know."

"Your prints are all over those bottles, and on that fire extinguisher. Sure you didn't go on a bender? Finish dinner and head to the nearest liquor store? And then you went out to set that illegal net and CO Jiles caught you?"

Holden peered at Sam, with what Sam thought was a flash of anger. And then his countenance softened.

"Good point," Holden said. "Nearest liquor store is Tower, I think. If I did buy those bottles, somebody sellin' that night would remember. Because if I did, I was so drunk I don't remember driving there, or coming back, or getting in my boat. And I never touched that extinguisher or that other net. I never set foot in that boat because that boat wasn't there. At least when I was."

"Maybe you already had the bottles?"

"I do two drinks a week. At the casino. Fridays. I haven't bought liquor since I stopped drinking regular. Eight years ago. Ask around."

Sam knew he would. Ask around. He reminded himself to check out all the nearby liquor stores . . . couldn't be that many. He'd need a better photo than the mug shot.

"If we follow up on anything, it would be good to have a rea-sonable photo," Sam said.

"Got a phone?"

Sam did. He pulled it out of his pocket and aimed it in Hold-en's direction. In response, Holden looked into the lens, not with a smile, but not like a criminal either. Sam snapped a couple of takes, examined them, was satisfied with the results, and said, "Okay."

Sam wondered if Holden could have purchased bottles from the casino. Casinos weren't licensed to sell off-sale liquor. But if Holden knew someone or had a contact who was willing to deal, Sam guessed it could happen. A casino would have video. Lots of it. Probably of the entire premises, given their business. What-ever happened last Friday night was probably recorded. At least the early part of it.

"I can check," Sam said. "If you didn't touch the bottles or the extinguisher, why were your prints on them?"

"Easy enough to do, if I'm out cold."

Sam knew it was. "So you think someone gave you something?"

"Only thing I can think. But I didn't see anything like that. Maybe the bartender, Amy? But I watched her make those drinks, so unless she put something in it, I don't know. And Amy wouldn't. Got no reason to."

"But if someone gave you something, sounds like it would have been done at the casino?"

"Only thing I can think. But I know them. I can't believe anybody there'd do that. No reason."

"At a casino, it could have been anyone. A customer." Sam considered. "Why didn't you tell any of this to the sheriff?"

Wariness crept back into Holden's eyes. His demeanor too. He looked away, staring at the right-side wall. Then he gazed back at Sam.

"Somethin's going on up here," Holden said. "I mean, somethin' not right. Not just this that happened to me, but on the lakes up here. My place is on Vermilion. I'm on that lake every day. I fish it. Especially walleye. I know lots of people who fish it. Last couple years, walleye stocks are down. On Vermilion." He paused again. "And I've tried some of the other nearby lakes. Crane. Kabetogama. Over on Elbow. Big, good walleye lakes. Stocks are down in every one of 'em. Somethin's going on."

"You mean poaching?"

When Sam learned about Holden's record and the illegal walleye net, the obvious conclusion was Holden's return to poaching.

Maybe he had resurrected his network and was selling the fish commercially. But given the CO in his net and the other circumstances of his arrest, it would have been stupid to get caught the way he did. But again, criminals didn't often demonstrate forethought or good judgment.

"Only thing I can think," Holden said.

"So why not tell the sheriff. Or the DNR?"

"If the walleye count is down on all those lakes, it'd be more than one person doing it. There's gotta be insiders. A group, maybe including the law."

"You think the sheriff's office?"

"Sheriff. DNR. Gotta be others if they're poaching Vermilion, Kabetogama, Crane, Elbow. Those are the only other ones I fished, so they're the only ones I know about."

"The DNR checks the fish population every season. They'd see it. They'd know about it."

"Maybe they know and haven't said anything," Holden said. "Maybe it's down, but only a little. Maybe they're the insiders?"

"The DNR biologists?" Sam was trying to be fair, but he had always been skeptical of conspiracy theories. Especially those involving law enforcement people he knew and the Minnesota DNR, an organization he respected.

Holden shrugged. "Another thing to check on," he said, serious.

"I can do that. But I just don't see it. Especially the sheriff. Or the DNR biologists. Makes no sense."

"I'm not sayin' it's the sheriff. Maybe a deputy? Someone inside who could let people know what's going down? Someone who could look the other way. And I'm not sayin' it's a fish guy, like one of the guys who does counting. But it could be somebody at the DNR. Leastways, I'm pretty sure that conservation officer, Jiles, might have been involved."

"The dead man?" Sam knew if he suggested the idea to law enforcement—especially the sheriff and the DNR, but also any of Charlie Jiles's numerous friends—there would be outrage. It would convince them Holden was guilty and trying to cover up his crimes by maligning the reputation of a dead man, one of their own.

"Two years ago," Holden said. "I ran into Jiles. At the casino. I knew him, but not well. Knew him because of my past. I'd had run-ins with COs. Plenty of them. Had one with Charlie Jiles once, but he cut me some slack. He was like that," Holden paused. "That night at the casino he told me he'd had some luck. Blackjack, he said. Wanted to buy me a drink. I don't make a lot of money. Only thing I really spend money on is dinner at the casino and a couple of drinks. And only Fridays. This was a Friday, and I hadn't yet gone to the bar. So, I said, sure, thanks."

Holden paused and looked away again, trying to recall details. "We went over to the bar and sat down, and I ordered a Manhattan. My drink. Charlie Jiles got a beer, the way I remember it. And then we just talked. Nothin' special. Talked fish. Talked Vermilion. Fifteen, maybe twenty minutes. Maybe longer. When we finished, he wanted to buy me another. I told him it was my turn, but he insisted. Said he'd gotten lucky. I should keep my money. Bought me another Manhattan. And we kept talking. Said he liked to eat at the casino. Liked their take on walleye. They do it different ways. So, we talked about different ways to cook walleye. Like, with

almonds. Deep fried. Cooked in lemon butter. Stuff like that,"
Holden continued. "Then he says, 'But it's so damn expensive.
Here. Over at Daisy's Supper Club. In town. Seems like everybody's going upscale.' Then he talked about the good ole days,
how you could get good fried walleye cheap from just about anywhere. 'But now it's a delicacy,' he said. 'Delicacy' I remember he
called it. This was all a little strange to me, you can guess. Guy like
Charlie Jiles, a DNR conservation officer, buying a known poacher
and felon a drink at a casino."

Sam agreed. It sounded odd, if it happened the way Holden
described. But it also occurred to him that Charlie Jiles might have
been cultivating an informant. Who better than a man with Hold-
en's record?

"Then Charlie Jiles finally got around to it. He said, 'Be easy
for somebody to set up a few people, some fishermen to net walleye and sell 'em. Vermilion's so damn big netters would be hard to
catch. Make a considerable profit, I expect.' I remember looking
at him," Holden said. "Like, I wasn't sure if it was an insult, or he
was fishing for illegal stuff or if I'd heard anything about poachers
or what? But he just looked back and smiled and said, 'I mean,
seriously, guy could put away a fair amount of jack. Especially
given what my friends the DNR fish biologists are finding about
Vermilion's stocks. Stocks in other lakes too. Bouncing back like
fish populations in the 80s.'

"I said, 'Probably could, but it's against the law.' And he
paused, looking at me, like he was trying to size me up, or wondered about how much more to say. I didn't say anything. Then he
said, 'What a fisherman like that'd need would be a little help from

people in the know. Like running interference on a football team. Couple of strong blockers in the backfield to watch for tacklers, know what I mean? Nobody'd ever get caught because they'd know when trouble was coming and where it was coming from.'"

Holden paused again. "I did a year for netting and selling walleye. Caught most of it out of Vermilion. I've been in county jail more than I'd like. Never thought I'd be here again," he said, indicating the pale-yellow walls. "And I figured Jiles knew all about that. But I wasn't going to remind him. So, I just shrugged and said, 'I expect so, but it's against the law.' And then I tried to talk about something else.

"But Jiles looked around, like, over his shoulder to make sure nobody's close enough to hear. And he says, 'Just keep it in mind,' and winks. I just nodded, like okay. And then changed the subject again. I can't remember to what because my head was spinning. I didn't want any part of anything. I wanted to get out of there. But I wasn't about to piss off a CO. So, we talked, not about fish. And I finished my drink and thanked him and shoved off. I left. I walked out and didn't even bother with dinner, 'cause I was spooked."

Sam had heard of inside jobs, some involving law enforcement officers. He had never heard of a dirty conservation officer, especially in Minnesota. Sam guessed there were plenty of instances when DNR officers, who entered the profession out of an interest, knowledge of, and love for the outdoors, recognized they were in a position to get away with technically illegal activities, and maybe did so. Little stuff. But Holden was suggesting Charlie Jiles, who as far as Sam knew was a well-respected or at least likable CO, was trying to put together some kind of concerted fish-poaching ring?

The idea was so far out of bounds, Sam thought it was more likely that Holden had conjured the entire story, or series of stories—considering Holden's excuses for all the other evidence against him—as a way to give his predicament plausible deniability. He was claiming he'd been set up. Framed. Worst case: Holden was finding a scapegoat on whom he could blame everything, someone who couldn't defend himself because Holden had murdered him. Or if there *was* any truth to Holden's interaction with CO Jiles, it was more likely Holden had misconstrued CO Jiles's intentions. Maybe Jiles *was* fishing for illegal activities. Just doing his job.

"What about the .45?" Sam said.

Sam asked the question as a surprise, wondering if Holden would lie about it too.

But he didn't.

"Mine," Holden said.

"Unregistered?"

"Didn't know it was unregistered," he said. "It was Dad's. Before Mom and me moved to Virginia, I took it out of that cupboard. Do you remember that cupboard in our garage?"

Sam did.

"Mom didn't know anything about it, and I never told her. I took the gun and ammunition. Took the bottles, too, and the magazines. Me and my new friends drank the liquor before I was 15, and the magazines disappeared, you can guess. I took Dad's tools too. They're the only things I still have from him. And the .45. But I didn't know the gun wasn't registered. Not that it matters, being a felon."

"Why didn't you turn it in?"

"It was Dad's," Holden said, explanation enough. "So, I kept it." He looked at Sam, but Sam didn't respond. "And when you spend as much time in the woods as I do, especially fishing and stuff, it's good to have a weapon. Every bear I've seen I scared off by yelling. But you never know. And up here, there are wolves and moose to scare away. And people. I know some bad people."

Sam knew it was true. "So, what is it exactly you want me to do?"

Holden paused, glancing away. Then he looked back to Sam and said, "Sheriff Goddard's been square so far. But I don't know about bringing in the DNR on this other stuff. Especially given my conversation with CO Jiles."

"They've got to get involved sometime. No way around it. CO Jiles was one of their own," Sam said.

"I'd appreciate it if you could at least take a look. Maybe start careful? If I am right, and there's somethin' going on. Some kind of poaching. If word gets out, it'll shut down faster 'n stink on shit."

Sam considered it. "I'll do what I can," he said. "Me and the sheriff."

Holden nodded. "Like I said, you got no reason to help," he said. "And I never would have called you. But you know us. You know the territory. You grew up here. But now you're an outsider. And I've read about your work and how you seen things others haven't, or don't. It sounds like you have a nose for stuff like this. So," he said, "I appreciate whatever you can do."

It was sincere, but Sam wanted to make sure Holden understood Sam's perspective about *investigating*.

"Long time ago we made a promise to each other," he said.

Holden was listening.

"One of the things we promised was that we'd *do hard things.*"

Holden nodded. "I remember."

"None of what they've got on you looks good. I gotta say I don't expect it to fall out well for you."

Holden's expression didn't change. But he was attentive.

"So, any way you cut it, this is going to be hard. And if I find anything that implicates you in any way, it's *not* going to be hard to turn it over to a prosecutor and recommend prosecuting. You understand? It won't only be a hard thing. You'll do hard time."

Holden nodded. "I'm not looking for favors. I'm looking for the truth."

CHAPTER 16

After coming out of the interview, Sam saw Deputy Barnes across the room, sitting at his desk in front of the sheriff's office. Since his head was bent over paperwork, Sam approached and said, "Deputy."

When Deputy Barnes looked up, Sam said, "We're done with Holden Riggins, for the time being." By we, Sam meant he and Gray, who had wandered out with Sam.

The deputy nodded and pushed away from his desk. "How'd it go?"

It was a strange interview, but Sam remembered Holden's concerns about local law enforcement. He still didn't know what to make of Holden's comments, but for the time being he figured reticence was at least prudent.

"It was different," Sam said. "Definitely different. Gonna have to think about this one."

"So," the deputy said, still fishing, "no confession?"

"Not exactly," Sam said.

"You mean, he sorta confessed?"

Sam paused, thinking, then said, "Not exactly."

"Who's the pup?" came a voice from behind them.

Sam and Gray both turned and saw two deputies approaching, a man about Sam's age and a younger woman. They both stopped, 6 or 7 feet back, their attention focused on Gray.

"This is Sam Rivers and his partner, Gray," Deputy Barnes said. "Sam, Deputies Joe Haman and Sandy Harju. They're a couple of our newer recruits."

Joe Haman took a cautious step forward and extended his hand. "Sam Rivers," he said. "Heard a lot about you." They shook while Deputy Haman said, "I been with the department three years. I guess compared to Barnes that's *newer*," he smiled.

Sandy Harju also shook Sam's hand. "Been here two years," she said. "Guess that makes me the newbie."

Deputy Haman had short-cropped, military-style hair with eyes so blue Sam wondered if they were chipped out of turquoise. His hair was blonde, and a prominent jaw was set off by a Teddy Roosevelt grin. Sam's immediate impression was Dudley Do-Right, with maybe a little lady-killer thrown in. Clearly, he was no stranger to exercise.

Deputy Harju's hair was fair, not exactly blonde, and twisted into a tight bun behind her head. By appearance she was definitely the youngest deputy on Sheriff Goddard's staff, at least that he could see. Deputy uniforms were not exactly testaments to fashion, but both Haman and Harju filled out their khakis in a way that made them excellent advertisements for law enforcement. Similar to Haman, Harju gave off the physical impression that she could complete an obstacle course with no problem.

Deputy Haman seemed affable. The vibe Sam picked up from Deputy Harju was cooler. Sober and serious.

"You two investigated with Deputy Barnes," Sam said, remembering. "The conservation officer incident?"

Both deputies nodded. "That's right," Joe said. "Barnes was good enough to let us tag along and benefit from his years of experience. Me and Deputy Harju."

"Deputy Haman was an Army MP," Smith Barnes said. "He came to us fully trained."

Joe grinned. "I was in for 10."

"Which included 2 years in Iraq, 2 in Afghanistan," Barnes said.

"Didn't want to stick it out for the pension?" Sam said.

"I liked the military. Would have stayed in longer, but I needed to get home."

"How was your interview?" Deputy Harju said.

Sam wondered if his morning meeting with Holden was common knowledge. But all he said was, "Like I was telling Deputy Barnes, it was interesting. There were a few things I learned I need to check out. We'll see."

"Did he continue to deny everything?" Joe said.

"Not exactly," Sam said.

Deputy Haman looked at Sam, considering. "Well, maybe we're making progress." When Sam didn't respond, Joe said, "If we can be any help checking stuff out, let us know."

"Ditto that," said Deputy Barnes. Then, "Joe. Holden Riggins needs to get back to lockup."

"I'm on it," he said, and turned, starting across the floor to the interrogation room. "After I get the perp squared away, I'll be out on patrol."

Deputy Barnes nodded.

Gray's focus was intent on Deputy Haman crossing the floor.

Then Deputy Harju looked in Gray's direction and said, "Is Gray friendly?"

Sam introduced Gray, and Harju stepped forward carefully, apparently familiar with dogs. She reached her hand down with an open palm and said, "You're one handsome dog."

"He's a wolf dog," Sam said.

"I wondered. And the eyes?"

Sam explained about Gray's benign condition.

"I've seen that in people," Harju said. "But only a couple of times."

"It's rare," Sam said.

"He looks rare," Harju said. After Gray sniffed the palm of her hand his tail wagged, briefly. She leaned forward and reached behind his ear, scratching. Gray turned his head to the side, pushing into her scratch, his eyes squinting.

"He's shameless," Sam said.

Gray had a nascent way of charming people, in particular women. But he had more or less charmed Holden, too, Sam recalled, remembering how he had warmed to Gray. And vice versa.

Once Gray's scratching session was done, Deputy Harju stood. "Well, if I can help in any way, just let me know."

"Thanks," Sam said.

The deputy turned and started across the room.

Both men watched her leave. Then Smith Barnes said, out of Harju's earshot, "You can see that woman's good-looking. What you can't see is she's whip-smart."

"She looks too young to be investigating a murder scene," Sam said, thinking about Lake Vermilion.

"She is," Barnes said. "And don't think it didn't ruffle a few feathers. The sheriff took some heat for it. But she's got a lot more going on upstairs than the rest of the deputies combined. Minus Joe Haman, of course. And me."

"Haman looks competent."

"The sheriff has a couple of ringers in those two. I'd say give them a few years and they'll be as good as me."

Sam smiled.

But Barnes shrugged and said, "Well, maybe."

That made Sam laugh. Finally, Barnes grinned.

"Deputy Haman came home to family?" Sam said.

"His mom got sick—that's why he's home. Otherwise, he'd still be in the service."

The sheriff's door was open. When he heard Sam talking, he stood in the entryway to his office and waited for Sam to finish. Then he called Sam over. The sheriff stepped around his desk and sat down, ready for the debriefing.

After Sam and Gray crossed the room's threshold, Sam turned and closed the door.

"That bad, huh?" the sheriff said. His chair creaked as he leaned forward, both hands resting on the edge of his desk, waiting.

"Not at all what I expected," Sam said. "Though I'm not sure what I expected."

"Did he mention his lawyer?"

"Only that he wasn't going to be quiet, regardless of his lawyer's advice."

The sheriff turned and looked at a gray metal vertical file cabinet, nicked and scarred from use and age. Four drawers high, the top two drawers were labeled PENDING. On top of the cabinet rested a photo of the sheriff and Dr. Susan Wallace. It was taken in a boat on a lake. Judging from the light and tree-lined shore, it looked like mid-spring. "Nice shot," Sam said, peering at it.

"That was at a friend's cabin on Vermilion."

"You guys look good."

"You sound surprised."

Sam grinned. "I'd love to introduce you both to Carmel."

"Let's do that," the sheriff said. They both paused for a moment, wondering how and when that could happen. Then, "So, what did Holden Riggins say?"

"Well, he confessed, at least to something," Sam said.

"Now we're gettin' somewhere."

"But not to any recent allegations."

"What did he confess to?"

"A felon owning an unregistered firearm."

"He'd already copped to it," the sheriff said. "He doesn't want to get any of these current crimes off his chest?"

Sam paused. "About that," he said. "There are a few things I need to follow up on."

Sam shared what Holden told him. The sheriff listened with surprising patience, particularly when Sam conveyed Holden's suspicions about possible insiders. Not only in the DNR, but also county law enforcement. Sam explained that at least to begin, he'd like to keep the investigation simple. He could take the lead on most stuff. It might be good to have someone from the sheriff's office, someone the sheriff trusted, who could occasionally assist. Sam referenced his interest in reaching out to all the local liquor stores with Holden's picture, asking about whether or not Holden had made any recent purchases. Any for the last year, for that matter.

"What about Barnes?" Sam said.

"Too busy. He's my acting undersheriff. And at any minute I'm going to be out of the office for a while."

"You should appoint him."

"Tried to. He refused the job. I've asked him to pinch-hit for a while. I'm hoping he gets a feel for it and changes his mind."

"Smart," Sam said.

"I thought so."

"What about Joe Haman?"

Sheriff Goddard looked at Sam, thinking. His eyes didn't blink. He said, "I think Sandy Harju could help you out."

Sam thought the sheriff's reaction was peculiar. But then again, given Haman was a seasoned law enforcement officer, the sheriff probably wanted to make sure he had a good investigator at the ready, if anything else came up.

"That'll work," Sam said. "Can you just let her know she needs to keep this between you, me, and her? And no word to anyone else about how she's helping out, or what she's doing."

"Sure. For starters, Deputy Harju isn't a big talker. So, you don't need to worry. Particularly after I have a word with her. Also, you'll find her more than capable. She's one of those people who dots every i and crosses every t. She's good. And it's my studied opinion she won't be in this position long."

"You going to promote her?"

"I'll get her officially promoted to investigator. That should hold her for a little while. But she's that good, Sam. She's going to master it in a year or two and move on."

"That's what Barnes said. She's smart."

"Definitely smart. But for a law enforcement officer not yet 30, she's also a professional."

They talked for a while longer. The sheriff told Sam he was doubtful anyone in his office or the DNR was involved. It was possible, he said, but improbable.

There was something in the way the sheriff made the comment, Sam thought, that was less emphatic than it could have been. Still, he'd take the sheriff at his word. Improbable.

The sheriff appreciated Sam leading the investigation and keeping it simple. But he reiterated it was more because of scarce county resources and the politics involved than fears of an insider. He gave him Harju's number and told him he'd talk with her this morning.

"Just make sure I'm in the loop," the sheriff said.

"Of course," Sam said.

"For the time being, I'm going to keep Deputy Harju on the roster. I'll tell her when she isn't helping you, she needs to be out on her usual patrols.

Then Sam asked about Charlie Jiles. "Anyone been to his place? Checked his car?"

"Truck," the sheriff said. "He had a practically new Dodge Ram 3500. We checked it, but other than a little mess, didn't find anything unusual."

"Check his place?"

"Deputy Haman went over yesterday. The guy lived in Eveleth. Found a key above his back door. Said it looked like a bachelor pad. Takeout boxes. Kind of a mess. A pretty nice big-screen TV. But otherwise, pretty sparse."

"Bank accounts? Cell phone?"

"We're working on his accounts. That's a little harder. Especially without a will. Can't find his cell. Wasn't in the boat. Wasn't on him when they found him. We checked his whereabouts. Last active cell tower ping was in Tower, on Lake Vermilion. Could have pinged from anywhere in the vicinity. Including just about anywhere at that end of the lake."

"Maybe it fell in the lake?"

"We've got one of those MarCum underwater video cameras. Deputy Harju spent the better part of half a day on the scene. She had the same thought you did. Checked all over around where we found Jiles's boat and where we found him in the net. Checked the bottom around that illegal net too. We've got lights with it. But nothing."

Sam thought about it. First, he would get Sandy Harju checking the liquor stores. While she was working that angle, Sam would visit the casino and see if he could check out the casino's video. He told the sheriff he'd learned, from the arrest report, that the TIP call that originally alerted the DNR to Holden's and Jiles's whereabouts, had been placed from a pay phone at the casino docks. He would also be checking out the dock video, if they had any. If they did, maybe he could get a photo or image of whoever made the call, try to ID him, and follow up. And he wanted to see the video of the bar from Friday night, where Holden had dinner and drinks. He wanted to speak with anyone who had seen Holden that night.

The sheriff gave him a name and number: Amanda Goodacre, head of casino security. He'd call ahead and let her know Sam would be over after lunch. He also told Sam she was ex-military and knew what she was doing.

"I'll let you know what I find out this afternoon. Tomorrow I'd like to go down to Duluth. The DNR's having some kind of convention. I'm hoping to talk with the two COs who found Jiles, and some fish biologists. Maybe Jiles's boss too. See what I can find out about Charlie Jiles, given Holden's accusations."

"You could do it by phone," the sheriff said.

"I know. But I'm not sure who all I need to speak with, and I prefer meeting people one-on-one, face-to-face, where I can see how they react."

There was, too, the fact that Carmel would be in Duluth tomorrow night.

"You believe Holden?" the sheriff said. "And you think Jiles was into something?"

"I have no idea. Right now, I have more questions than anything else. And Holden has a long record, while Jiles was a law enforcement officer," Sam said, thinking out loud. "I hadn't considered it, but maybe Holden and Jiles were working together?"

Both officers thought about it. For now, there were just too many possibilities and too few certainties. At this point, everyone and everything was suspect, especially Holden.

"But Holden's raised enough questions to create some doubt," Sam said. "Especially if Smith Barnes is right about Jiles being dead a while."

"Maybe, like you said, it all happened Thursday afternoon. Holden puts him in his net, thinking it would be too obvious to be believed. And then he went about establishing his Friday alibis?"

"And then on Friday night he gets hammered, boats out to the murder scene, and passes out?" Sam said. "And stashing Jiles in his whitefish net to make it look obvious sounds like a Hardy Boys mystery. It just doesn't make sense. Especially when he could dump the body in the woods and scuttle his boat or leave it drifting in the breeze at the other end of the lake. And if he did it Thursday, and the CO's boat was tethered to that Cedar tree for a day and a half, don't you think somebody would have come along and checked on it? Reported it?"

"Maybe there wasn't any traffic on the lake that day," the sheriff said. "That was the start of our cold snap. People are always more likely to hunker down in a cold snap."

Sam still thought there were more anomalies than puzzle pieces that fit. "When are you getting the ME report?"

"Should be in by this afternoon. Evening, latest."

"What about Holden's blood work?"

"Tomorrow, or the next day."

"Well," Sam said. "The more information we get, the more we'll know, which right now isn't much."

CHAPTER 17

S am and Gray were back in their Jeep, pulling out of the county offices parking lot, when his cell phone rang. A local number.

"Sam Rivers."

"Agent Rivers. Deputy Sandy Harju."

"Deputy," Sam said. "You spoke with the sheriff?"

"I did. He said for the time being I should give you a hand."

"Are you sitting at your desk?"

"No. I'm in the women's restroom. The sheriff told me to be discreet. There aren't many women in the sheriff's office, so it's a good place to go if you want privacy."

Sam smiled. "Did the sheriff tell you why we need to be discreet?"

"He said because the victim was law enforcement, we can expect increased scrutiny of our work. Best to keep it to ourselves. I am to take my direction from you and no one else. And I'm not to share what I'm doing or what I find with anyone but you and the sheriff."

There was, of course, more to it. But Sam appreciated the sheriff's discretion. "That would be good, Deputy Harju. Because Charlie Jiles was an officer, I'm sure you'll get questions about what you're doing and finding. If you do, tell them you're just helping out with some clerical follow-up. If they persist, they can talk to me."

"I can play dumb," Harju said. "But it doesn't come naturally."

Sam chuckled. "The sheriff tells me you have outstanding aptitude and instincts, which I appreciate. I'm sure they'll prove useful as we try and figure out what happened here."

There was a pause. Sam wondered if she was surprised by the sheriff's compliment. But finally, she said, "So how can I be of service?"

The sheriff had also described her as professional.

Sam told her about checking all the liquor stores within a 50-mile radius to see if they remember selling anything to Holden Riggins. Anytime in the last year.

"I'll text you an image of Holden," Sam said. "They may recognize he's wearing a prison jumpsuit and have questions."

"I know," Deputy Harju said. "Play dumb."

She reminded Sam this was Northern Minnesota, so there were a fair number of liquor stores within 50 miles of Vermilion Falls. But she was confident she could get back to him by the end of the day.

"Perfect."

After Sam texted her Holden's photo, he called ahead and spoke with Amanda Goodacre, the head of casino security. They agreed to meet at the casino entrance around 1 p.m. He also reread the arrest report and found the contact information for conservation officers Olathe and Flag, the two who were first on the scene and found Holden Riggins and CO Jiles. He knew he would eventually need to speak with both of them, so he sent out emails and suggested tomorrow afternoon. Maybe in Duluth, providing both were attending the conference?

Amanda Goodacre was tall and angular, and her black hair was cut similar to Deputy Joe Haman's: short-cropped, almost in a crew cut.

"Sam Rivers?" she said, coming forward.

"Ms. Goodacre?" Sam said.

She smiled and stuck out her hand. "Amanda's fine. Any friend of the sheriff is a friend of ours."

Amanda had a politician's smile and way of greeting, as though you were the most important person in the room. The tint of her native skin and a pair of obsidian eyes made her teeth appear preternaturally white. She conveyed confidence and command.

"I appreciate that," Sam said. When Sam shook her hand, he thought it had the feel of someone familiar with chopping wood and carrying water.

Amanda suggested she give Sam a brief tour and they talk while they walked.

"The sheriff didn't spell it out. What are you looking for?"

Sam knew the Director of Casino Security would need to be briefed about some of the details of his investigation. When he thought about Holden's suspicions, he considered, briefly, whether anyone at the casino could be involved. But the likelihood of a casino employee helping with a walleye poaching ring, if one existed, seemed remote. So, Sam shared the details about Holden and what he'd told him.

"We knew CO Jiles, of course," Amanda said. "He wasn't exactly a regular, but he would come in for dinner every so often. We monitor local law enforcement scanners, so the DNR checked in with us when they brought his boat and body back to our docks. And Holden Riggins, in handcuffs. I figured we'd be hearing from someone."

"You know Holden Riggins?"

"Oh sure. He comes into the casino every Friday, for dinner. Never gambles. Always sits at the same place at the bar. Always orders the same thing. He's a creature of habit."

Sam was surprised she tracked Holden enough to know when he came in, where he sat, and what he ordered.

"I don't normally stalk customers. But I gotta say, the first time I saw Holden, I thought he looked dangerous. He has a certain," Amanda paused, "kind of look."

"Like he's an ex-con?" Sam said.

"I'd call it a cross between gangster and Northwoods lumberjack. He always looks like he's just spent the day working outside. Maybe he has? He's not the best dressed casino customer. And not exactly clean shaven, but of course up here he's not alone."

Sam wondered if there was anything else she could tell him about Holden.

"He doesn't talk a lot. But he's polite to the serving staff and once you get to know him, he seems like a nice enough guy. I was surprised to hear he killed CO Jiles."

"You ever see them together? Jiles and Riggins?"

"No. Never saw much of Charlie Jiles. But you can ask the waitstaff. They might be able to tell you more."

When Sam told Amanda what he wanted to see . . . the restaurant tapes from last Friday night, she told him they were already queued up. After she gave him a quick tour she'd take him to Cal in the media room, who could show him whatever he wanted.

"That'd be great. Do you have video of your dock?"

"Docks," she said. "It's a pretty big operation. And yes, we have some. Mostly the boathouse. We don't worry too much about the actual docks. What are you looking for?"

Sam told her about the TIP line call made from the pay phone predawn the previous Saturday.

Her lips pursed and she looked doubtful. "Gotta warn you. If it was dark, we might not see much. But we can look."

"I'll take whatever you've got."

After touring the public casino facility, Amanda pushed through a rear door that opened onto a long, gray hallway. Amanda walked to an unlabeled door near the back end of the building.

"We call this our Eyes-in-the-Sky room," Amanda said, letting herself in. Once on the other side, they were ushered into a nondescript stairwell. Amanda started climbing the steps, with Sam following.

"We're in the process of upgrading our CCTV system cameras to IP security devices. They'll have better resolution and give us options we don't have right now. But our existing system is pretty good."

"You cover everything?"

"Pretty much every inch of the place. We have some issues with lighting, but mostly at night. Some of our corners get a little shadowy. But our entrances, exits, and every machine and table in the place is pretty well lit. We want to be able to see if anyone's gaming the gaming tables," she said.

The video room was intensely lit, with a bank of overhead monitors against the near wall. Each monitor displayed a wide shot of a different casino section, most of the scenes focused on the gaming floor. Inside the video room, four people sat in over-size chairs, their eyes trained on a bank of monitors. Their desk-tops contained keyboards and more monitors, two to a keyboard.

When Amanda walked into the room, the near person turned and nodded and said, "Amanda," in greeting, but he didn't get up. He was boyish looking and big, filling the ample black leather of his chair. The others kept staring at their screens.

"Hey, Cal."

Amanda introduced them, and Cal said, "I've got the video from Friday night, of the bar. But do you have a time?"

Remembering what Holden had told Sam, he said, "Can we start at 5:30?"

It took Cal only a moment to pull it up. A poorly lit restaurant and bar came up on the screen. It was much less well-lit than the overhead screens illuminating the gaming floor. The restaurant and bar customers appeared a little grainy, but clear enough to distinguish. By 5:30, there were several people at the restaurant tables. Sam watched a bartender pouring drinks. *Amy Winter*, Sam remembered Holden saying.

In a moment Sam watched Holden walk into the restaurant and cross through the tables to the end of the bar. "There," Sam said. "There's Holden."

"That's Holden alright," Amanda said.

They watched Holden sit at the bar and fold his hands in front of him. Amy was mixing drinks for one of the waitresses. After she finished, she looked toward Holden and said something. Holden nodded. Then Amy moved to her right and pulled down a bottle of what appeared to be Canadian Club, a whiskey. Beside it was another bottle with a red foil top and yellow label. Beside the yellow label was a smaller bottle—much smaller. Amy used the bottles to mix a drink, mostly whiskey. She finished it off with some maraschino cherry juice and dropped one of the cherries into the drink. Then she carried it with a napkin to the end of the bar and placed it in front of Holden.

They watched him nod and smile and say something.

Amy smiled and laughed, though from the camera's vantage point they could only see the front left side of her face.

And then she returned to hustling more drinks. And Holden took his first sip.

Sam asked Cal to rewind the video to the point where Holden first sat down at the bar, and they watched Holden again, this time waiting until his food had arrived. They watched as Holden focused on his food. At this point his first drink was nearly finished.

"You going to watch for a while?" Amanda said.

"Until I see him leave."

"I'll leave you to it, then. But let's see if we can find your pre-dawn caller first. Down at the dock phone?"

Sam agreed. It took Cal a couple of minutes to call up the appropriate video segment on his second monitor. He started the camera with a lower-right periphery including a clear shot of a pay phone mounted on the side of a building.

"That's the boathouse," Amanda said. "Only place there's still a pay phone on the whole premises."

"Try the whole county," Cal said.

Cal queued the video to 4 a.m. Then he fast-forwarded. At 4:37 a figure sped into view. The fast-forward was happening so quickly the figure sped through the footage and was gone in a matter of seconds.

"Hold it. Go back," Sam said.

Cal rewound the recording to 4:36. Then he slowed it to normal speed and all three of them watched the shadowy figure approach the phone, his back to the camera. He was wearing one of those bombardier hats, but with the furry brim and ear flaps unbuttoned so they stuck out, obscuring his head. When he came into the circumference of light from the overhead bulb, they could see a small piece of the side of his face, blurry in the predawn darkness. They watched him dial and apparently talk for a short time—the TIP line call. And then he hung up and kept walking with his back to the camera, until he was out of view.

"Recognize the guy?" Sam said.

"Can't see his face," Amanda said. "But . . . can you play it back?"

Cal rewound the tape and they watched it a second time.

"That walk looks familiar," Amanda said. "I think I've seen him before."

"Here? At the casino?"

"Only place I'd probably notice it. I'm careful about what I see while I'm at work. Part of the job," she said. "But I'm kind of in that mode all the time, so it could have been somewhere else."

Sam could understand it. "Take another look," he said.

They watched a third time.

"I'll have to think about it," was all she said. Amanda told Sam she had to make her rounds, and to call her when he was finished. Sam reminded her he would like to speak with some of the folks who were there last Friday night, if that was possible. She assured him it was, but that not everyone was working.

"The bartender?" Sam said.

"Amy starts at 3," Amanda said. "If you're still here then you can talk to her."

Sam suspected he would be. "And the waitresses?"

"Look through the video. Cal should be able to confirm who was here. If they're working tonight, you should be able to speak with them. Mondays are usually slow, at least in the bar."

CHAPTER 18

Joe Haman cruised along the casino's back lot. His patrol was legitimate. The sheriff had an agreement with Amanda Goodacre. Periodic appearances of county law enforcement, even if it was just a turn through the casino's parking lot, showed the presence of law enforcement, should anyone consider taking advantage of the casino's largesse.

After meeting Sam and shaking his hand, Joe was left with confirmation of his earlier opinion: *Boy Scout.* Joe could see it in the man's eyes. There was plenty of strength in those eyes, and in Sam's grip. But the cases the man and mutt had worked on so far, at least those getting press recognition, had been amateur hour for boy wonder and his sidekick.

Joe drove slowly along the outer edge of the lot. He knew there were cameras. But he also knew those cameras didn't reach more than 20 feet beyond the building's perimeter. Once a patron walked out to his or her car, they were invisible.

Like Joe Haman's cruiser.

He circled the lot. It took two turns to spot the Jeep, which had been parked near a stand of red pines. When Joe drove by he couldn't see the mutt, but he assumed Sam parked near the back edge of the lot so his animal wouldn't be bothered.

The road to the casino had a two-rut turnoff that backed up into the stand of red pines near the casino parking lot. Sometimes county deputies backed into the turnoff, concealing themselves in the woods with a radar gun. Or when they use the bush edge to take a piss.

The authorities claimed catching speeders was to deter fast drivers. Joe Haman figured it was about raising revenue.

Joe backed into the turnoff and picked up his radar gun. But he didn't switch it on. He waited to make sure the afternoon traffic was sparse. Then he set the gun down, got out of his cruiser, and backtracked through the stand of red pines to the edge of the lot. The largest pine had a 2-foot-diameter trunk surrounded by thick alders, their leaves still thick and green.

Joe took a moment to relieve himself on the red pine trunk. Then he turned his attention to Sam's Jeep, parked in the lot less than 20 feet from the giant red pine.

Still no sign of the mutt. He found a pine cone and, careful to remain concealed, flung the cone toward the Jeep. It fell short of its mark. His next effort hit the Jeep's rear left tire, soundlessly bouncing against the rubber sidewall and falling to the ground. Finally, he picked up a heavy, thick cone, hurled it, and thumped the Jeep's side window. Suddenly the mutt's muzzle peered out.

Even though Joe was concealed, he swore the animal stared straight at him. The window was cracked for air, so maybe he smelled Joe, hidden in the trees? Maybe he smelled Joe's piss? Joe had heard wolves used piss to mark their territories. If that was the case, Joe had, unbeknownst, marked his.

If you know what's good for you, you'll steer clear of Joe Haman's territory, Joe thought. Not that it mattered.

The dog's gaze remained unwavering.

Then Joe thought he heard a low rumble from deep in Gray's chest—a threat, or warning, or both.

Joe didn't move. Neither did Gray.

For a few minutes the two focused . . . on each other. Joe was certain he was hidden. But Gray's eyes remained unwavering, and he growled again.

If Gray had stared down someone else, Joe thought, the animal's fixation might have been unnerving. But Joe was the hunter. The mutt might have been a wolf dog, but Joe was the alpha.

Finally, Joe backed out of the trees, precipitating another growl from inside the Jeep.

What Joe's reconnaissance told him was that Sam's pal needed to be taught a lesson. Maybe it was time the mongrel got the ultimate lesson.

Deputy Haman remembered the affinity between man and beast. The deputy had never understood it. But he understood how that kind of sentimentality could be a powerful weapon, if it was wielded in a way that cut deep enough into the owner's heart to throw him off the scent. Besides, he didn't think the mutt liked him, or showed him the respect he was due.

Every dog has his day, Deputy Haman thought. *And this dog's day is coming.*

CHAPTER 19

Over the course of the next three hours, Sam watched the casino security video carefully and repeatedly. Holden sipped his first Manhattan, then received his food—what appeared to be a steak, baked potato, and green beans—and began eating. He finished his first Manhattan midway through his plate of food. Almost the second he finished his first drink, Amy delivered another. Sam had to rewind to watch her mix it, using the same process and bottles she'd used earlier. He rewound the video a third time and kept his eye on the bottles and cherries. He never saw anyone touch those containers, including the second glass the bartender used to mix Holden's second Manhattan. And he never saw anyone mess with Holden's drink, once it had been delivered. In fact, while Holden ate and drank, no one came within 5 feet of him.

The only peculiar development happened after Amy mixed Holden's second Manhattan. Sam watched her pitch both the red-foil bottle and the smaller bottle, which appeared normal enough, if they were empty. Also, the Friday-night bar was a busy place. But again, Holden sat near the end of the bar and kept to himself. He looked like a bar patron enjoying a leisurely dinner and drinks on a Friday night, after a week of work. Nothing odd, until he took his last bite of food.

And then he looked up, sudden-like. Sam watched it at least five times to be sure. Something startled Holden. Sam couldn't see anything to account for it. He could see most of the restaurant, but there was no plate crashing to the ground, restaurant patron being loud and obnoxious, or anything else that might have caused Holden's reaction. Besides, Holden was the only one who appeared startled. To be sure, Sam couldn't see the entire bar, but the way Holden stiffened and turned his head, quickly, like he was thinking about something, seemed peculiar. And then he signaled for the check, hurriedly.

Amy delivered it. Holden placed two bills on the bar and stepped away, starting into the hallway. He *lurched* into the hallway, and then disappeared.

Sam continued watching, but Holden never returned. He watched Amy take the money, stack his dishes, wipe the bar top, and then carry the dishes back to the kitchen. Nothing unusual.

Sam fast-forwarded, watching the timestamp tick off 15 minutes. But still no Holden.

"Hey, Cal," Sam said.

"Yo." Cal turned.

Sam rewound the video and showed Holden getting out of the chair and entering the hallway.

"Looks like your guy needed to use the bathroom in a hurry. There's a head down near the end, right before an exit door that opens onto the parking lot."

"You have video for the hallway?"

Cal looked at Sam, and said, "The public frowns on being filmed heading into bathrooms. But I've got video of the exit door."

"Can you pull that up? From around 6:37 on?"

Seconds later Cal had pulled up the outdoor video for that exit. Other than the faint glow from nearby overhead parking lights, similar to deep twilight, the exit was dark.

"Bummer," Cal said. "Looks like the overhead exit light burned out."

They watched the exit and when the door opened, they could see what appeared to be a large man. Holden was wide and it was about the right height for him, but the image was dark and grainy. The figure was backlit by the hallway light, but only for a second. It was too brief, and the light change was too much for the camera to refocus and show anything more than a blur. Once the door closed, the video went dark. It took maybe 1 second to refocus, and then the video screen showed a dark exit door. Whoever exited was gone.

"Can you blow up the blurry image of the guy? Or enhance it?"

"Not with our current setup. We'll be able to do it once we get these CCTV cameras replaced. But until then, this is as good as it gets."

Sam had him rewind it. They watched again, but it was impossible to see who or what it was. The timestamp showed 6:47. Presumably Holden had used the men's room, and then stumbled out the exit.

"How often do those bulbs go out?"

"All the time. But they usually get replaced immediately if they're out."

Sam wondered about it.

"Would there be a record of when it was replaced?"

Cal turned toward Sam and smiled. "We take security seriously, but not that seriously. But we can ask maintenance. They'd know."

"Can you do that?"

Cal shrugged. "Sure." He turned to his screen, pulled up a blank email, and took a moment to draft a quick memo to maintenance.

Sam remembered Holden told him he'd boated to the casino marina. After seeing Holden depart, they turned their attention to the boathouse and marina. They didn't have good video of the three long docks that reached out into the bay, but they could see the occasional traffic coming off the lake and heading out. There wasn't much because of the cold snap, the first of the season. People were staying indoors.

Sam watched the boathouse from 6:45 until 10 p.m., but there was no sign of Holden.

It appeared someone—must have been Holden—departed the dark casino parking lot side door, and then disappeared into the rows of parked cars, in a lot that was mostly full on a Friday night at 6:47. But while the casino's video was quite thorough and particular of the entire casino building and its interior, once customers ventured beyond a 20-foot periphery, they disappeared.

By around 4:45 p.m. Sam had exhausted the casino's video footage of Holden, the bar, and the side entrance. He'd watched Holden arrive, come off the docks, head up and through the casino, and into the bar. No one came within 5 feet of him. Sam had also viewed kitchen footage. He watched a cook fix Holden's meal. The cook used salt, pepper, and butter. Lots of butter, but it was taken from a 1-pound block. Similarly, the rest of his food was taken from spice containers and pots that, had they been spiked, would have poisoned others.

Other than Holden's peculiar turn into the hallway and exit, which was definitely odd but understandable if Holden had some kind of GI issue, Sam saw nothing strange or unusual.

It occurred to Sam that Holden could be lying; he was never drugged. From what he'd seen so far, that was the logical conclusion.

While Sam was reviewing all the video he noticed a few people he wanted to question. In addition to Amy, the bartender, there were two waitresses working that night. Sam asked Cal if he recognized them.

"That one walking in the bar is Rowena Melnyk. That blonde is Julie Schuman."

Sam wrote down the names.

From the dock footage Sam asked about the guy working the dock when Holden arrived. Later, after Holden apparently left from the side exit, there didn't appear to be anyone at the boathouse.

Cal gave him the name of the dock worker on the early part of the recording: Dirk Swenson, a high school kid.

"This time of year, the boathouse is only staffed until 6. The casino doesn't get a lot of traffic after that, at least from the lake."

Sam finally thanked Cal and called Amanda Goodacre.

"Meet me in front of the Eyes-in-the-Sky doorway in 5," she said.

As Sam stood to leave, Cal said, "Maintenance got back to me on that exterior light. They said it was changed Saturday morning. Before that they don't recall."

So, the bulb probably just blew out. A coincidence?

CHAPTER 20

After cruising the casino, Deputy Haman drove 6 miles west to a familiar radar gun location outside the small town of Tower. There was a county highway that cut through the woods from Tower to Ely, 30 miles east. It was a favored route of the locals, plus the occasional out-of-towners who might be following their GPS.

Like the rest of the deputies, Joe had a quota. The sheriff never referenced it as such. But Joe understood. Like all the deputies, he was supposed to "monitor traffic, so we can deter the speeders," the sheriff said.

There were three or four places on this winding blacktop where speed limit violators had no idea they were being tracked by radar, until it was too late. If Joe caught someone exceeding the speed limit by more than 10 miles per hour, he went after the driver like a muskie after baitfish.

Joe had come to this hidden spot along the county highway to both work on his quota and think. After seeing Sam Rivers with his mutt, Deputy Haman knew wounding or killing the animal would stymie Sam's investigative enthusiasm. The question was, how far to go, and how to do it?

A call came in on Joe's private cell, startling him.

Joe had been very careful about his phone. It was in his mother's name. There were definite advantages involved with being his mother's guardian and managing her finances. Not that it wasn't a colossal pain in the ass. But since she could barely remember her own name, Joe didn't worry about questions. He'd put the phone in her name and paid for it with her money. It was foolproof because the only thing his mother had asked him over the last 6 months was, "Do I know you?"

The only calls that *ever* came in on his private phone had been from Charlie Jiles. Joe always made Charlie use a burner, so every few calls the number coming onto the screen was different. If Joe didn't recognize the number, he didn't answer. If the call was immediately repeated, he'd pick up.

Now surprised, he fished the rarely used phone out of his backpack. The screen said, "Blocked."

Not a burner then. Someone using *67, to keep their own number anonymous.

Joe waited through five rings. Then it went dead.

Scam call, Joe guessed. Or some kind of marketing hustle that was ignoring the do-not-call list. Probably from overseas.

Whenever Charlie had called, it was always about intel. Charlie kept his calls brief because he called anytime and knew Joe might be with colleagues or others who might overhear the call. Joe would share what he knew about the upcoming patrols and any out-of-the-ordinary activities. Charlie would listen, which was hard for Charlie Jiles. Occasionally there'd be a follow-up question or two, some kind of clarification about a lake or river or park being patrolled, or a particular section of county highway.

Joe's private cell buzzed again. He was so startled the phone nearly jumped out of his hand. He glanced at the screen. "Blocked."

Joe let it ring another five times before it went dead.

In the silence he sorted through the possibilities. His best guess: marketing scam from overseas. Some kind of phishing venture. Especially considering the phone was in Martha Haman's name, age 78.

But it also occurred to him that Charlie Jiles hadn't kept his mouth shut. Despite Charlie's promises to keep Joe's identity secret, Charlie might have shared his private cell number. Joe knew their venture involved others. Charlie had never shared the nature of what they did, or the identities of anyone else involved. But from the intel Charlie wanted, Joe had figured poaching. He guessed Holden Riggins was involved. But Riggins was in lockup, without access to a phone. Moreover, he had no reason to call a number that had previously been used to provide information about law enforcement patrols.

Joe's cell buzzed again.

Goddammit!

If it was phishing, it could be easily addressed. Or if Charlie had shared his private number, what else might he have shared?

Joe picked up, but he didn't answer.

After a long silence, a man said, "You don't know me."

Joe waited.

Another long pause.

Joe thought about hanging up, but the call was *not* marketing. A salesperson would be launching headlong into a pitch about roofing, or tree removal, or the latest cure-all vitamins. This person was quiet. And patient.

"And I don't know you," the man finally said.

If he had to guess, the voice came from around here. Minnesota's Iron Range. He couldn't put his finger on it, but it sounded, from the few words spoken, like the guy was local. Made sense.

The safe play would be to hang up. End the call and never answer again.

But Joe Haman needed to know.

"Where'd you get this number?" Joe finally said.

"Jiles. Insurance," the voice said. "Know what I mean?"

Joe thought he did. But he sure as hell didn't like it. He still didn't say anything.

"I got a need to know. What Jiles shared, when alive."

"I think we're done," Joe said.

"Jiles is dead," the voice said, quick before Joe hung up. "But it doesn't change the money. The money's still good."

Joe waited. Then, "Listenin'."

"I don't know who you are, and I don't know how you know what you know, and I don't care. But I need the information you gave Jiles. One last time before the freeze. Then we stop. For . . . a while."

Joe could give the caller what he needed. What he couldn't figure out was how, since Charlie was dead and this man claimed not to know Joe, he would get his money.

"How do I get paid?" Joe said.

"Dropped at the bottom of a buoy in Vermilion," the voice said. "East end. Send you the GPS numbers."

Joe knew it could work. But he had no idea if the man knew what he had been getting paid. And he didn't care. The situation had changed. Things were more dangerous now. Risky.

"How much?" Joe finally said.

Another long silence. "Twelve hundred," the man said.

Joe thought about it. If the man wanted, he could send the GPS coordinates and then conceal himself, someplace nearby. Scope Joe Haman and see who he was. A trap. There was no way Joe would ever let himself walk into a trap.

"Two thousand," Joe said. "There's a lot more risk this time. And the drop's gotta be somewhere with a lot of water around it. Where I can see nobody's nearby, looking." Vermilion was big enough.

"Big Bay," the voice said. "Reef in the middle."

Whoever it was knew the lake. At least the east end. That was the kind of silent partner you wanted. Someone you didn't know, who didn't know you, but knew their shit.

"Need to know," the voice finally said. "Vermilion. East end. Quiet?"

Joe had sat through this morning's briefing. The east end was clear, except for Deputy Joe Haman. Sam Rivers was nosing around. But given that the sheriff's investigators had already picked over the crime scene (Deputy Harju having scoured the lake bottom for nonexistent clues), the nearest Sam Rivers would get to the water was the casino. At least for the next couple of days.

So, Joe told him. The east end was clear and quiet.

Afterward, the voice at the end of the line, said, "Two thousand, Big Bay reef. I'll call tomorrow and Wednesday to make sure nothin's changed. If we're still good, I'll leave the money on the reef. Wednesday."

Then the line went dead.

CHAPTER 21

B y around 5 p.m., the sun was lying golden across Lake Vermilion. It was cold, but since there was still sunlight, Sam figured he'd start outside first. Amanda walked with him to the boathouse.

Sam told her what he'd seen on the videos, which wasn't much. She was concerned that anyone in her casino might have been drugged, or somehow poisoned. Especially someone she knew.

She told Sam about two previous instances involving customers who had been drugged. Both involved men slipping what turned out to be date-rape drugs into women's drinks, when the two women weren't paying attention. They'd captured the attempts on video. Luckily, the women had only become sick and had left before the men could take advantage. The casino had tracked down both perpetrators, arrested them, and prosecuted them to the full extent of the law.

"It was so obvious, both of them pled guilty."

"I saw nothing obvious today," Sam said. "Nobody came near enough to Holden to stretch out and touch him, let alone dose his drink or food."

"Maybe that makes his story suspect."

"Maybe," Sam said.

"Do you believe in karma?" Amanda asked.

"You mean the idea that if you do bad things or good things, you're likely to reap bad or good things as a result?"

"Yeah, more or less. Seems to me Holden Riggins's karma is catching up with him."

Sam had been around long enough to have generally witnessed the karmic effect. Bad usually begat bad, and vice versa. But he had also seen evil people doing evil deeds and, for all intents and purposes, getting away with it.

"But in this instance Holden claims to be the victim," Sam said.

"Maybe the victim of his own bad karma. Maybe he pissed someone off and now they're getting even?"

"I guess it's possible, given I didn't see anything on the tapes. At least anything obvious."

"From what I've heard, he had a pretty long rap sheet," Amanda said. "From before. Maybe it just took a while to catch up to him?"

"You're saying if someone drugged Holden, as he alleges, it was because of bad deeds in his past?"

Amanda shrugged. "All I'm saying is Holden alleges he was drugged. Then, if I understand how his story goes, he was put into his boat, which was anchored near his whitefish net. Then whoever drugged him set a walleye net near his boat, and then put the deceased officer in his whitefish net? I mean," she said, "it sounds a little far-fetched."

"I know," Sam said. "And Holden claims someone stole the walleye net from his work shed to make it look like he was poaching."

Amanda chuckled and shook her head. "That's a hell of a lot of logistics. If you think about it, it sounds like something out of *Mission Impossible*."

Sam knew she had a point.

There were three large casino docks. Set off to the far side of one were two covered boats that looked like permanent residents. Otherwise, the docks were empty.

High schooler Dirk Swenson was in the boathouse, staring at his iPhone. When Amanda pushed through the door, Dirk set down his phone, as though he'd been caught loafing, which was the case.

Amanda asked about last Friday night. Dirk had staffed the boathouse from 2 to 6 p.m., but it was quiet. He pumped gas for three boats, but that was it.

"This about that Riggins guy?" Dirk asked.

"You heard about it?" Amanda said.

"I worked Saturday, when they brought in that conservation officer's boat. And his body. And the guy who did it."

Sam guessed it had been quite a scene. "Was it busy?" Sam said.

"Nobody but those guys on Saturday," Dirk said. "Not even locals. Too cold."

Next, Sam and Amanda visited the bar/restaurant. The conversation with the bartender and one of the two waitresses working last

Friday night was a little more interesting, though not necessarily in ways that helped Holden's cause.

Like the docks, on Monday night the restaurant was slow. There was one person at the bar and two couples at tables, all easily managed by the bartender from the video, Amy Winter, and the waitress, Julie Schuman, both of whom had plenty of time to answer Sam's questions.

Amy was young, fit, and attractive. There was a glint to her green eyes. Her long black hair was pulled back into a braid; when she spoke, she had an engaging smile Sam figured would be pleasing to most bar patrons, especially men.

Sam asked Amy about Holden Riggins.

"This about what happened on Temple Island?" Amy said.

"You heard about it?" Sam said.

"Oh, yeah. Everyone at the casino has. Holden was a regular, so even though he kept to himself, people knew him. We were surprised he was mixed up in that officer's death."

"Why?"

"He seems like a regular guy," Amy said. "He looks a little rough. But he's kind of quiet. Always comes in at the same time, Fridays, and orders the same thing. Top Sirloin and two Classic Manhattans."

"Does he ever eat with anyone?"

"Every now and then there's a woman. I think she works at the high school. We've razzed him about it, but all Holden says is, 'she's just a friend.' Otherwise, he sits alone at the bar, down near the end over there," she indicated the end of the bar near the hallway. "But he's polite. I've noticed he likes to watch me mix his Manhattans," she said, smiling, a little mischievous, aware of the attention.

"When was the last time he ate with the woman?"

"I don't know. Maybe a month ago?"

"Has he ever said anything to you?" Amanda said. "Come onto you?"

"Holden? Oh, God no. He's got me by maybe 20 years."

Sam didn't think Holden was that much older. Maybe 10 years. But he remembered Holden appeared older than his chronological age. "You never get hit on by older guys?"

"All the time," Amy laughed. "We all do. Get a few drinks in a guy and just about anything is possible, at least in their minds. But not Holden. He never drinks more than two Manhattans. So he never gets drunk enough to be stupid, like some guys." She laughed again.

"Last Friday, when you mixed his drinks, you threw away two of the bottles. Do you remember?"

She didn't. "Must have been empty," she said. "We go through a lot of drinks, especially on the weekend. I toss a lot of bottles."

Sam noticed two fresh bottles of the kind that had been tossed, on the rear shelf behind her. He asked her about them.

"Sweet vermouth and bitters," Amy said. "The good stuff." She turned, walked over, and picked up the bottle with red foil and said, "This is Carpano Antica." When Sam and Amanda didn't respond, she picked up the other, smaller bottle and said, "Angostura Bitters. The good stuff," she said again, with emphasis. "We have regular Manhattans and Classic Manhattans. The Classics are made with this stuff."

"And Holden always drinks Classics?"

"Always. Two of them. They're twice the cost of regulars."

"How much?"

"Ten bucks. The regulars are six."

Sam was surprised Holden Riggins would pay $20 for two Classic Manhattans. But Sam remembered he had told him they were the only drinks he had all week. At the time Sam doubted it. But if it were true, maybe he could afford to splurge? Still, he was a part-time small motor mechanic, if Sam remembered correctly.

"How do you make the regulars?" Sam said.

"With Manhattan mix. It's a lot easier, but some people, like Holden, like the real deal."

"Do most Manhattan drinkers drink Classics?"

"Nah," Amy said. "I make maybe 5, 10 a week."

"So how often do you run out of the premium stuff?"

"I don't know," she shrugged. "Maybe once a month?"

"How easy would it be for someone to come in and switch the bottles?"

"Well," Amy said, thinking about Sam's question. "I guess it's possible." She turned around and looked at the bar, considering. "But it'd be tricky, right? I mean, somebody would have to come in behind the bar with a couple of bottles and replace them? If it was a customer, somebody'd notice. A customer behind the bar."

"What about an employee?" Sam said.

"I guess," she shrugged. "But why would a casino employee swap out the bottles? I just don't see it. For starters, it wouldn't be that easy. Unless it was me. And I didn't do it," she said, again with a laugh.

"No one's suggesting that," Amanda said.

"Not easy," she said.

After tending to the two tables with people, Julie Schuman joined them at the bar. She was also someone the bar patrons would consider nice to watch. Julie reiterated what Amy said. She hadn't really spoken much with Holden Riggins because he always sat at the bar. Amy waited on him. She'd spoken with him on occasion, mostly small talk. But she'd never had any problems with him.

Thinking about what Holden had been accused of, Julie said, "Goes to show, you just never know about people."

Sam and Amanda ignored the comment and asked about the other waitress working last Friday night.

"Rowena?" Julie said.

"Yeah. Is it Rowena Melnyk?"

"Yeah. She works the late shift, Thursdays through Sundays."

"Has she ever talked about any problems with Holden?"

"Nah. She's always here on Fridays, when Holden comes in. But since Holden always sits at the bar, we never wait on him. It's always Amy."

By the time Sam finished at the casino, it was dark and well after 6 p.m., and he knew Gray would need a run. He'd also be looking for dinner, sooner rather than later.

Sam thanked Amanda, who said, "Any time," and "Please keep me posted."

When Sam returned to his Jeep, he found Gray staring out the rear side window toward a stand of red pines.

"You gotta go?" Sam said. "Sorry it took so long."

He opened the door and let Gray down onto the parking lot. But Gray didn't turn straight toward the woods, where Sam had assumed he would relieve himself. He paused, taking a long sniff at some nearby pine cones.

"Hey," Sam said. "I'm going to run you. If you don't need to piss, let's get going."

Gray ignored the comment and walked over to the woods. Sam could see him enter the bush edge. There was a large red pine in the middle of some alders. When Sam approached to keep an eye on Gray, he saw him through the leaves, sniffing the trunk edge.

Another dog, Sam assumed. Or maybe a wolf? Whatever it was, Gray was interested. And then he lifted his leg and left a scent of his own.

Calling cards, Sam knew.

After both of them returned to the Jeep, Sam drove out of the casino and down the two-lane blacktop until he found some open trees off to one side, with a marked public trail. He parked in a small side lot, and he and Gray spent 20 minutes hiking into the chilly woods and back again, long enough for Gray to do his business and get some exercise.

Sam thought about everything he'd seen and heard and done for the day. He had heard a lot of opinions about Holden. Law enforcement opinions were almost unanimous: Holden was guilty. Either of murder, or something nefarious, as Amanda Goodacre thought. Others were more sanguine, though no one declared him innocent. The more Sam thought about it, the more he realized he had found no solid evidence exonerating Holden or supporting his version of events. He had found several peculiar coincidences that suggested something could have happened. But nothing definitive.

Once back in his room, he fixed Gray's dinner. Then he sat back and ate a sandwich, thinking.

Before he finished, his phone rang. This time he recognized the number.

"Rivers," Sam said.

"Agent Rivers, it's Deputy Harju."

"You can call me Sam, Deputy."

"Oh," she paused. "Okay. You can call me Harju."

There was a pause.

"I reached out to every liquor store in a 50-mile radius," Harju said. "I shared Holden Riggins's photo with all of them, and his name. Several wanted to know what he'd done, but I told them I didn't know. None of them had seen him, that they could recall. Some needed to share the photo with other staff, and they'd let me know. But given that none of them remembered him or even knew his name, I'd be surprised if we got a hit."

"Okay. Nice work. Thanks."

"I was done by around 4. I had a little more time to kill, so I reread the arrest report and noticed he works at White Pines Marina, near Cook."

"I remember," Sam said.

"I was thinking another way to cross-reference his whereabouts would be to speak with his employer. The arrest report doesn't list his hours of work, but if it was during the day, we could at least account for his time during work."

"He's part-time," Sam said, remembering Holden's comments about it. "He told me he was at work all day Friday, and then he headed over to the casino for his usual dinner. He didn't work Thursday. He was mending and setting nets. His whitefish net. At least that's what he said."

"Oh," Deputy Harju said.

"But we need to double-check. Tomorrow I've got to drive down to Duluth. I'll be staying in Duluth tomorrow night. Can you drive over to that marina and speak with Holden's boss? Verify when he was working and nose around a little? It would be good to hear his boss's perspective."

"Sure," Harju said. She sounded pleased by the prospect.

Sam guessed it would be a whole lot more interesting than answering a domestic or chasing down speeders and writing tickets. Sam told her to phone him with whatever she found. Then, "Harju, is your gut telling you anything about Holden Riggins?"

"Gut?" she said.

"Sorry. Instinct. Intuition, I guess."

"About Holden Riggins?"

"Yeah. About his guilt or innocence?"

"Well," she paused. Then, "All I've done is see if he made any purchases at any liquor stores in the area. I haven't spoken with him. By the time we got out to the site, he was already in custody, and he wasn't talking. And I only saw him this morning, briefly, when Deputy Haman escorted him back to his cell."

"But you saw his arrest report. And you know about his record."

"Yeah. I read the report. A couple of times. And everyone in the sheriff's office knows about his record."

"And it sounds to me like everyone in the sheriff's office has a pretty strong opinion about Holden Riggins. Do you share their opinion?"

She paused.

"It's not a trick question," Sam said. "I'm just looking for what you think."

"No. I didn't think it was a trick question," she said. "I guess I'd say I don't know enough yet to have an opinion."

It was a good answer, Sam thought. But all he said was, "Okay. Call me after you speak with Holden's boss."

By 8 p.m. he phoned Carmel.

"What are you doing?" Sam said.

"I'm getting ready to go to bed with my pack."

"You mean with your partial pack?"

"Yes," she said, a smile in her voice. "I wish the rest of my pack were here, so we could all sleep together."

"Where's Jennifer?"

"She's in bed. Reading." Then, "I guess what I meant was, I wish my whole pack was here so I could spend some time in the study."

"What would you be studying?"

"Are you getting ready to launch into some sex talk?"

"Of course not." He quickly considered several racy comments.

There was a pause. Then Sam said. "What if the rest of your pack visited you tomorrow night in Duluth?"

"You can come down to Duluth?"

"I've got to interview those two COs and hopefully some other DNR folks. The COs should be at that conference, so ending up in Duluth tomorrow night should work."

"I'll share my room with you, providing you promise to rub my back."

"Is that sex talk?"

She ignored it and said, "So, tell me what you've found out about Holden Riggins."

Sam took the next several minutes explaining about Holden.

"None of that sounds good," she said.

Sam agreed.

"But I gotta say," Carmel said, thinking about it, "it's a little too perfect."

"Like the sheriff said, it doesn't look good for Holden Riggins."

Sam often shared details about his casework with Carmel. Sometimes she saw things he didn't, and it was useful. In this case, she articulated what he had already thought—though he had not uttered it aloud.

Carmel took a few minutes running through the logistics to explain how Holden's version of events could have happened. Hustling an unconscious Holden into his boat, getting his boat to his whitefish net, getting the CO's boat and body out there, and then getting away.

"Sounds like a lot," she said.

Sam agreed.

"But it's possible, especially given the cold snap, when nobody would be on the lake."

Before turning out the light Sam checked his email. He was expecting the ME report. When he didn't have any messages from anyone in the sheriff's office, he texted the sheriff. "Did you get the ME report?"

In less than a minute, the sheriff texted, "Contractions. Close together. Talk to Barnes."

"Good luck!" Sam texted, and then signed off. He was excited for Sheriff Dean Goddard, who he knew would be occupied and offline for at least the next 24 hours. Probably 48.

Sam suspected Deputy Smith Barnes was already home, so he sent him an email. "Did the ME report come in on Conservation Officer Jiles?"

Sam thought for a moment. Throughout the day there were several moments when he thought of more questions for Holden. Tomorrow, Sam was going to be busy. He needed to end up in Duluth, but he wanted to speak with Holden first. Now that the sheriff was indisposed, he added to his email for Smith Barnes.

"I'd like to speak with Holden Riggins again. Can he be in the interrogation room by 8:30 or so?" Then Sam thanked the deputy and signed off.

CHAPTER 22

Near midnight, Cray Halverson throttled down his boat's engine. The temperature was in the mid-20s. The sky was an impenetrable black. Cray wasn't worried about being seen or heard because nobody would be out in darkness like this, especially during the prolonged cold snap.

He was worried about Rowena.

If she missed catching the dock edge, the Crestliner might ram it, leaving a telltale mark on the dock and his boat. Signs that someone had been here. Evidence it had been him.

Rowena's stocking cap had a built-in two-light headlamp. Before he could tell her, the darkness was bathed in red.

A good sign, Cray guessed.

The dock emerged from the edge of red light. The night's black maw kept everything beyond 10 feet in darkness.

Midnight, the darkness, cold, and their shadowy purpose prompted Cray to say, "You okay?"

There was a pause while the boat drifted. "Okay," Rowena finally said.

The angle of Cray's boat was off by several feet. He turned the wheel and in another few moments the right side of his boat's gunwale coasted along the nearest wooden post and Rowena grabbed it.

Cray cut the engine and the still night deepened.

Cray had been unable to deny Char Peigan. He had immediately known where to find the fish the chef needed. It would be one last haul before he and Rowena ceased operations, at least until the business with Holden Riggins played out and blew over. Cray knew a final catch was risky, given recent events. He knew Charlie Jiles's death had set off alarm bells. Even though Riggins was in jail, people were watching.

Cray's nets were unmarked. If anyone discovered them, it would be difficult to trace them back to him. But they needed mending, which is when Cray realized where they could put their hands on a net they could use. A licensed net; one that if found would be traced back to its owner.

They needed to get that net tonight. Tomorrow, they would set it.

Rowena's long black hair stuck out beneath her cap, hanging over the top of a goose-down parka. Rowena was thick, and her coat, and a pair of black woolen pants pulled over jeans, made her appear bigger. But the extra layers didn't diminish her ability to move, and—still holding the wooden post—she halted the boat's forward movement and stepped onto the dock. Bow line in hand, she made two quick dock knots and moved to the rear of the boat. Cray tossed her the stern line and she fastened it to the nearest post. Then Cray stepped onto the dock.

"Ten minutes," he said.

Cray knew the less time spent here, the better. He wasn't worried about being seen. He was worried Rowena might lose her nerve.

Normally, at dusk or dawn when it was reasonably clear, Cray could set a net by himself. But the mouth of Smugglers Creek was tricky, and black clouds had scudded in with the cold, obscuring floats, netting, weights, and underwater buoys. Rigging and setting a net alone in the creek's currents would have been impossible. And it wasn't only the setting of it in difficult circumstances. They needed to be careful about how and where it was laid out and submerged.

Cray knew a gill net, this time of year near the end of Smugglers Creek, where the walleye would be feeding on baitfish, would quickly fill. He would need Rowena's help hauling it in, processing the catch, and getting it ready for Char. The risky part would be dusk, Wednesday, when they would need at least partial light to haul in the catch, fast as possible, and stow it in the Crestliner's secret compartments.

Now that Cray had made contact with Jiles's informant, he would use it tomorrow and Wednesday night, to make sure law enforcement was nowhere near Smugglers Creek.

Once off the end of the dock, Cray flicked on his own red light and walked over flagstone steps, turning where the stones veered toward Holden Riggins's work shed.

Last Friday, late, he had made this same trip. By then Rowena's rage had passed, replaced by a determined calm, ensuring she could finish her shift while Cray took care of things.

He used the stolen ring of keys until he found one that slipped into the lock and opened the door.

The shed had been surprising. It was big as a barn, with skylights overhead letting in a clear night sky. The workspace was clean and neat, with a side bench containing an assortment of tools on pegs, all positioned according to size. He was most startled by the room's center, where a nearly completed birchbark canoe lay overturned on two sawhorses. He had been hurried, but afterward he remembered the fresh birch bark, carefully crafted. A latticework of black seams marked the places where the bark had been sewn with some kind of natural thread, and then daubed over with pine pitch. The seams appeared sticky. But he'd had no time to consider it.

Last Thursday, after finding Rowena bloodied and adrift and nearly catatonic, a plan entered Cray's mind whole cloth. Charlie Jiles had once told Cray he had tried to recruit Holden Riggins before enlisting Cray, but that Riggins had begged off. Charlie assumed it was because Riggins already had some kind of poaching gig in play. The man, Charlie told Cray, was competition, and if they ever got the chance—if they found out where Riggins was setting illegal nets—they should alert the authorities and turn him in. Or set him up.

Given Rowena's rape, Cray wished Charlie Jiles had partnered up with Holden Riggins when he'd had the chance. But now Charlie was gone, and Cray had the chance to use Riggins to throw the authorities off their scent. It was a sudden, perfect plan, and they had followed it.

Seeing the nearly finished birchbark canoe had been a hiccup. Cray admired the unexpected craftsmanship. But like a thief who was already too committed to back out or change his mind, there had been no other way forward than the one he had taken. He and Rowena.

It had been late, and he was alone, so he hadn't worried about intruders or being seen at this end of the lake. He hurried because there had been much to do.

Rummaging through work bins along the wall, he found what he was looking for. There were two nets in the bottom of the bin. He considered taking both, but at the time he only needed one.

That night, so much had happened he'd been forced to return Holden's keys to his pocket. He hadn't wanted to raise suspicions about someone burgling Holden's cabin, or have Holden alert the authorities about his missing keys.

But that meant tonight, he had no keys.

Cray circled the building, his light flashing over the clapboard sides. The flagstone steps ended at the building's door. There were two windows in back and two on each side. Like the door, the windows were closed and locked.

A burglary, then. Someone taking advantage of a vacant cabin and shed. Cray knew eventually someone would discover the break-in, but time was short and options were few.

He kicked, hard, planting his foot to the left of the knob. The thud and crack reverberated through the dark.

Cray waited, but the night remained still.

He kicked again and the jamb splintered. The door eased open.

The canoe still stood in the center of the room. Cray's red light flashed over it, and then turned quickly to the near bin. He walked over to the bin and opened it. Its bottom was covered with the bulky net, buoys, and weights, all neatly folded. He gathered the net in his arms and hoisted it out of the bin.

If someone had broken in, had taken advantage, they would have stolen more than nets. What else, Cray wondered. But when he looked around the room, he knew he didn't want to be weighed down with tools, or a birchbark canoe, for God's sake.

He turned and hurried out the door, careful to close it behind him and re-affix the lock, at least enough to hold it in place and make it appear, from a distance, as though the premises were secure.

Discovering the break-in would take time, Cray hoped. Figuring out what, if anything, was missing, would take longer. By then, his walleye should be safely fileted, boxed, and sitting in garage freezers, waiting for Char to arrive with one last fat envelope of cash.

Cray was looking forward to ice over, when they'd take a page from the area's bears and burrow into a dark hole until the weather changed.

CHAPTER 23

Tuesday, October 17

When Sam awoke, the first thought he had was about Carmel. He remembered her recitation of the logical steps involved with Holden's proposed version of events. She'd left out the first step: Holden being drugged. Sam hadn't found definitive evidence of drugging, but as Carmel noted: "It was possible."

Whenever Sam shared case details with Carmel, she shared insights he sometimes hadn't considered. She had natural instincts about people and animals. *Which doesn't explain why she's involved with me*, Sam thought.

They still needed to have the conversation about their future. But he felt no clearer about the subject and timing of that conversation than he had last Sunday. For Sam, illumination in matters of the heart always took time.

He turned to his emails.

He hadn't heard from the sheriff or Deputy Barnes, but he assumed he would be able to see Holden this morning. He had an email from Conservation Officer Jennie Flag:

This afternoon should work. If you also need to speak with Bernie Olathe, we can meet you at the same time. We're at our annual meeting in Duluth, at the DECC, but we have some free time from 1–4. Text me with a time and we'll figure it out.

The DECC was the Duluth Entertainment Convention Center. Sam had been there once before, down in or around Duluth's canal park. He hadn't heard from Conservation Officer Olathe, but he quickly responded to Jennie Flag and told her he was planning on being in Duluth later today and it would be great to meet and speak with both of them. Could she let CO Olathe know? He'd text her later with more details.

He turned to Gray and said, "Ready for some chow and a morning walk?"

Gray was born ready.

Around 8:30, Sam and Gray walked through courthouse security and greeted Deputy Smith Barnes.

"No word yet," Barnes said.

"From the Medical Examiner?"

Barnes stared for a moment. "No. From the sheriff. About the kid."

"Oh God, yes," Sam said. "Of course. Nothing?"

"Not a goldarn thing. He left a message with dispatch around midnight. They were headed to the hospital. I gotta believe that boy's popped out by now."

"I'm sure we'll hear about it soon," Sam said.

"The whole department's on pins and needles."

Deputy Barnes was wiry and tough, with rugged features that could have graced the advertisements of everything from Harleys to Marlboros. "You don't strike me as a 'pins and needles' kind of guy," Sam said.

Barnes seemed to think about it. "Others in the department," he said.

Sam smiled. "Did you get my note about Holden?"

"Oh, yeah. He's in the room. Same room as yesterday."

"Any word on the ME report?"

"Nope. I sent her a note this morning, after I saw your email. Was supposed to be last night, so I'd be surprised if we didn't have it by end of day."

Sam told Barnes to keep him posted.

"As soon as we get it, I'll send you a copy," Barnes said. "And I've already got an email set for when the kid arrives."

"That's excellent."

"I know you've got Deputy Harju helping you on this, but the minute you need reinforcements, let us know."

"Will do," Sam said.

"That whole being drugged story is fake news."

While Sam was trying to honor Holden's request, about keeping knowledge of his investigation limited, as the lead investigator and acting undersheriff, Deputy Barnes was aware of many of the details surrounding Holden's case. Including, apparently, the suspect's claim he may have been drugged.

"Way I see it," Barnes said, "he started to worry about the evidence he'd left at the scene, boated out to do some cleanup, and when he was done, he had a few. Had a few before he got there, no doubt. When he passed out and got caught, he made up that cockamamie story to cover himself."

Sam couldn't disagree. "Sounds like he was pretty sick when the COs found him."

"One and a half bottles of whiskey will do that to you. A real binge, even for a drinker like Riggins. He can be three sheets to the wind and look more sober than a church mouse."

"He claims he doesn't drink much anymore," Sam said.

Deputy Barnes snorted, a cross between disgust and disbelief. "He's a drunk," Barnes said, definitive. "No doubt he can hold his liquor. Problem is he had two bottles of whiskey in his boat and almost all of it was gone. I don't care how much you can hold, that's going to put you down."

With his prints on the bottle, Sam thought. But all he said to Barnes was, "Definitely."

When Sam and Gray entered the interrogation room, Holden stood up from the other side of the table. The skin under his eyes was dark and puffy, signs of a sleepless night. But he nodded, cordial.

Sam stepped forward to shake his hand. Despite his tired appearance, his grip was firm.

Holden turned to Gray and said, "And morning to you too." Gray was standing at Sam's side. Holden moved his hand forward, palm up.

Gray peered, sniffed, and wagged his tail twice.

Deputy Barnes wasn't warming to the suspect, but Gray was.

"Gotta meet with an attorney later this morning. When she found out we'd talked, she was pissed. Told me to keep my mouth shut until I met with her."

Sam considered it. Holden's face was serious, his brown eyes intent.

"So," Holden shrugged, "what did you want to know?"

Sam thought he saw Holden grin. Regardless, he appreciated Holden's willingness to cooperate. He glanced through his notes from yesterday's interview. "You said the last thing you remember at the casino was dinner?"

"Yeah. I sat down to dinner. I had a drink. I remember gettin' my steak, and a second drink. I finished. That's when I started to feel . . . sick, I guess. It came on pretty fast. Like, I might blow chow. Then I don't remember nothin'."

"Do you remember stepping away from the bar and going into the nearby hallway?"

He thought about it. "I think so. But I don't remember much else."

"Do you remember going to the bathroom?"

"Nope. I know there's a head down there. But I don't remember hitting the head."

"What about going out that side exit?"

"Got nothin'," Holden said. "Don't remember anything until I woke up about froze to death."

Sam made a note.

"You looked at the casino's video?" Holden said.

Sam nodded.

"You didn't see anybody slip me anything?"

"Nothing obvious, that I could see. And I looked through a lot of video. More than once."

"Well, somebody slipped me somethin'. Somehow. Somewhere. I've put my body through a lot a' shit. Lots of stuff. But nothing ever made me black out quick like that and wake up 12 hours later. What about my blood tests?"

"Maybe today. Or tomorrow."

"I gotta believe something strong enough to put me down for 12 hours would still be in my blood."

"Probably," Sam said. He returned to his notes. "They said you sometimes have dinner with a woman?"

Holden looked surprised. "You mean Ruth?"

"Bartender said you normally eat alone, but sometimes there's a woman. From the high school?"

"Yeah," Holden said. "Ruth. Only woman I seen in the last eight years. She lets me buy her dinner. Maybe once a month. But . . . it's nothing serious."

"You weren't with Ruth last week, were you? Or anybody else?"

Holden paused. "It's not that way with Ruth, if you're thinking we spend nights together. I wish. There was a time we hooked up. For a few months. But I fucked up, and that was a while ago."

"What about others? Others who might have seen you since last Wednesday?"

"My boss," Holden said. "Check with him. Jim at White Pines Marina. Jim Aho." Holden thought about it. "I worked Wednesday and Friday, 8–5. Do you know when that CO died? Jiles?"

"Not yet. The ME report is due in today. That should tell us."

"Well, like I said, after work on Friday I boated to the casino."

"But if he died Thursday?" Sam said.

Holden shrugged. "I was mending and setting my whitefish net. Thursday, before dark. I set it where they found me. But just the one net. For whitefish. I got a license. That other net was mine, but I didn't put it there. And it wasn't there when I set for whitefish."

"And you didn't work Thursday?"

"No. On Thursday I was getting my whitefish nets ready. It takes a while to fix all the tears and holes, from mice and stuff. I got three nets and I always start with the worst, to fix it. That takes a while. I fix all of them, just in case."

"Is that out at your place?"

"My work shed. Over at my place on the back side of Temple." That reminded Holden. "What did they do with my nets?"

"I don't know. But I can find out."

"I want the nets back," Holden said. "I set that legal whitefish net. Somebody took that other one from my shed. I told the sheriff to check my place. If whoever did it stole the one, they might have stolen the other."

Holden told Sam where to find the key that worked for his cabin and his shed; hanging on a nail under the front top stair. The whitefish net was in a bin along the back shed wall.

Sam knew the sheriff's department would have confiscated the nets they found in Vermilion. Also, Holden's boat, the .45. Everything.

"Right now, I don't think you should worry about your nets."

"Maybe. But when they figure out I had nothin' to do with this, I need those nets back. I'll go right back out there and set it. It's a good spot."

"For walleye too?" Sam said.

Holden's eyes flashed. Then he shook his head. "In the spring and summer, if you're using a pole and fishing legal. Lot of people fish off those cedars for walleye. Usually pretty deep. But this time of year, lakes turn over. The water changes and fish move shallower to breathe. Another reason setting that poaching net there was stupid. No way in hell I'd ever set one there and expect to catch anything. I mean, if it was legal, which it ain't. Truth is, nobody with any lake sense, or fish sense, at least for walleye, would have set a net there. And hoped to catch anything. I bet when they hauled up that net it was empty."

Sam made a note. He suspected the COs retrieved the nets. He would check on the catch in the illegal walleye net, for what it was worth.

"But it's a good spot for whitefish?" Sam said.

"Whitefish are different. All year they stay at the bottom in deep water. In the fall they go to shallows like the ones close to those cedars. To spawn. You can't be deeper than 6 foot if you're netting whitefish. I was in about 4 foot."

"So do you think your whitefish net was full?"

"Not with a dead man in the middle of it. Would'a scared off most of the whitefish."

Sam made a note to ask the COs about the whitefish net too. Just in case. "Why whitefish?" he said.

"Lots of reasons. For starters, they're the best eating."

"Better than walleye?"

"I think so. Lots of people think they're the best. But they're not easy to catch. That's another reason I like 'em."

"You can't catch them the usual way? With a fishing pole?"

"Nope. You can try. Some people get lucky. But they're finnicky. I been fishin' walleye my whole life," Holden said. "But I never caught a whitefish with a hook, line, or sinker," he said.

"Other than netting," Sam said.

"Yup. Netting is about the only way. And it's the best way. In two or three catches you get enough whitefish for the year. And it ain't easy. There's DNR regs. But you also gotta know when they spawn and where to find 'em." He paused. "When we were kids it was all about catching the biggest and most. Now I let the biggest go. So they can make more fish."

"You're a conservationist," Sam said.

"Whatever," Holden said. "I just been fishin' long enough to know the big ones make a lot more fish. For next year."

A conservationist, Sam thought, but he didn't push it.

"That tattoo near your eye? What is it?"

"Split shot."

"A split shot sinker?" Sam remembered them from when they were kids. They were different sizes of lead spheres with slits for fitting and clamping down on the line. They weighted the fishing line, so your bait sank to where the fish swam. And hunted.

"Yeah," Holden said. He looked away. "Ruth says it's 'crude.' I was gonna try and get it removed, but the ink's too deep."

Sam wondered why anyone would tattoo a split shot sinker next to their eye, like a teardrop.

"Was a time I wanted a reminder," Holden said, anticipating Sam's question. "Keep my eyes straight, or sink."

"Eyes straight?"

"Stay clean. Put it here too," Holden said, holding up his left hand. "I see it in the morning. I see it at night. And I see it when I work."

"And F-I-S-H?" Sam said.

"Did that later. To remember why I stay clean."

"So you can fish?"

"Fishing feeds me. Not just the food part of it, but it's something I always liked. F-I-S-H. Maybe crude, like Ruth says. But people do all kinds of tattoos for all kinds of reasons."

True enough, Sam knew. When Sam was working on the Florida Key deer case, he'd gotten a barbed wire tattoo around his neck and a large alligator up his right arm. Made him look like an Everglades hunter. But they had been henna tattoos. Eventually, they wore off. But for a time, Maggie, his ex-wife, said she kind of liked the look.

Sam and Holden talked for a while about fishing. For a backwoodsman, Holden Riggins had a complicated perspective about the activity. He talked about how he had always loved throwing a line in water, letting the lures or bait sink below the surface, and then seeing what came up out of darkness. The way he talked about it was metaphoric, though he didn't say that. He talked about getting to know the fish and their habitat. He didn't explain it with those words, but his comments, when punctuated by his tattoos, told Sam that, for Holden, fishing was a spiritual practice. Sam had read about Naturalism and Animism. From what he remembered, Holden's perspective seemed like it was grounded in some kind of -ism. But again, Holden never used those terms. Sam suspected, despite the way he talked about fishing, he had never thought of the practice in spiritual terms.

His reasons for netting whitefish were, like his perspective about fishing, complicated.

"Not many people net whitefish," Holden said. "The season is late fall and it's too damn cold for most. And hard. Another reason I like it."

Sam said, "You like the cold?"

"I like the quiet in the fall. I like the way the lake goes flat, like a mirror. And nobody's out on it." Holden looked away, seeming to think about it. "Used to be I liked to party. Never would have put in the work to catch whitefish, before. Too much trouble. Too damn cold. I liked the bar scene," he said. "I liked to fuck around."

"And now you don't?"

"Lost my taste for it."

"What about the casino?"

Holden sighed. "My casino visit is a reminder. Once a week. A steak dinner and a couple of drinks. To remember what it was like, back then. And to see if anything's changed. If there's some part of me that misses it. The partying." He paused. "It's like getting a shot for something that made you sick."

Either Holden was an excellent liar, or he was being sincere. Sam thought about following up on his comment, then decided he needed more time to think about it.

"So how did you get into netting whitefish?"

"It wasn't just one thing," Holden said. "It started with Ruth." This time he looked down and grew quiet.

Sam watched him, but Holden kept his head bowed.

"I guess, I just changed," Holden said.

"You just changed and started netting whitefish?"

Holden looked off again, thinking. "Things happened. Then I stopped drinking, for starters. Netting whitefish is a lot of fuckin' work. No way you could be drinking like I used to, or using other stuff, and netting and cleaning whitefish. Cleaning whitefish in the cold is another reason not a lot of people do it. Sometimes you gotta clean in the snow."

"So, you got sober."

"More or less," Holden said. "That was the start of it."

"Most alcoholics I know never drink again. They worry that if they do, they won't be able to stop."

"I never thought of myself as an alcoholic. I liked to party. Party hard. I quit partying the way I was. Fridays are a reminder. I never worry I won't be able to stop."

"What about last Friday?"

"Last Friday was the same as all the others. I had two drinks. Then I got sick. Drugged, is what I think. Somebody did something, but it wasn't me."

Sam remembered watching Holden order and drink two Classic Manhattans, nothing more. And then he walked away.

"Let's go back to last Thursday," Sam said. "Was there anybody around your boathouse or cabin who might have seen you? Or seen you out there setting your whitefish net?"

"This time of year, not many stay on Temple," Holden said. "Thursday, the weather turned cold. I don't remember anyone on the lake. I was inside my work shed, mending nets, mostly. Late afternoon I set the net. But I didn't see anyone." Holden paused.

Sam looked back to his notes.

"Where can I find Ruth, if I wanted to talk to her?"

Holden looked surprised, but he gave Sam her cell number.

"If you talk to her, tell her not to worry. Tell her you're working on finding out the truth."

Sam paused, looking at Holden.

"My words," he said. "Not yours."

CHAPTER 24

On Sam's drive from Vermilion Falls to Duluth, he stopped in Finland long enough to refuel and check his messages.

He had a text from CO Jennie Flag, confirming their afternoon meeting, and that Bernie Olathe would join them.

"Around 3, if possible. But we're flexible," she said.

There was a forwarded email from Deputy Smith Barnes. "Forgot to include you on this," he said. The baby had been born around 8:30 in the morning, 7 pounds, 8 ounces. John Michael Goddard. "Mother and son are doing fine." Meanwhile, if anyone needed to get in touch with the sheriff, they should reach out to Deputy Barnes.

Sam thought about how the sheriff's life, as well as Dr. Wallace's, was about to change. It was a good thing. He couldn't help but smile. And then he couldn't help but think of Carmel. He was looking forward to dinner. And spending the night.

There was a follow-up email from Barnes with the subject heading "ME Report," but no attachment.

Sheriff asked me to send you a note about the ME report. Still not done, but we did hear from them. They wanted us to get lake water samples from where CO Jiles was found. Since I know you're working with Deputy Harju, we asked her to take care of it. She said she would and will let you know when she's done.

There was nothing else in Deputy Barnes's message, especially no reason given for why the medical examiner would want to see samples of lake water where Jiles was found. Sam assumed they'd want lake water samples to test and compare to the lake water in the victim's lungs. But why? It was Vermilion. Did they think he drowned in a different lake?

He also had a confirmation from the head of Minnesota's northeast region of conservation officers, Ben Connors, who was at the DECC. He had time this afternoon around 1:45. He told Sam there were tables in the back of the main floor and he should look for Grizzly Adams.

Big guy with a beard, Sam thought.

Moreover, he told Sam he'd try and find a couple of fish biologists from the region to join them.

Sam called Carmel, but she didn't pick up. Then, as he and Gray were getting ready to head south, she returned his call.

"If you're busy, we can talk later," Sam said.

"Not busy. Preparing for my seminar about Lyme disease. I didn't want to disrupt my preparations with steamy language."

"Well, I don't want to keep you from Lyme disease."

"Say what you want, Rivers, but it's pretty interesting."

"You can tell me about it over dinner."

Carmel had heard good things about an Italian restaurant, Amore, down by Canal Park, so she'd booked a reservation for 5:30.

When Sam walked into the DECC's rear open meeting area, it was busy. There were probably 25 round tables spread out over a large area, and nearly every table was occupied. He took a moment to scan across the tables.

Ben Connors was easy to find. He sat in the middle of the room, dressed casually in khakis and a red plaid shirt. He had thick brown-and-gray hair, with an accompanying salt-and-pepper beard, and a barrel chest. An older Grizzly Adams, maybe 60. But instead of a bear as a companion, he was accompanied by a younger woman and a man, both sitting at his table.

"Ben?" Sam said.

"Agent Rivers," he said, standing up.

Ben Connors introduced him to Cindy Hill and Andy Nivens, DNR fish biologists from the northeast region. Cindy was small with cropped blonde hair. Andy was bald with a thick, bushy brown mustache, and he appeared to be about the same height and weight as Sam, and probably about the same age. Cindy, Sam guessed, was around 30.

After shaking hands, Ben said, "They got coffee and dough-nuts over there, if you're interested."

"Just ate. Thanks."

"Tragic about Charlie Jiles," Ben said.

"It is," Sam said. "It's always tough to see a law enforcement officer die in the line of duty."

"Glad to hear they've got someone in custody," Ben said.

Sam nodded. It wasn't the time or place to surface questions about Holden's role in Charlie Jiles's death, particularly to Charlie Jiles's boss and colleagues.

"Nail him," Andy Nivens said.

When Sam glanced at Cindy Hill, she appeared quiet and serious. Sam suspected there were few women fish biologists in the DNR.

"Snagged these two before their 2:30 meetings," Ben said. "If you've got questions about Vermilion's fish stocks, these are your guys."

Sam glanced at both of them and said, "I was mostly curious about the walleye in Vermilion. And in Crane Lake."

"What about 'em?" Andy asked.

"Well, I've heard walleye stocks are down on both lakes, and maybe in some others in the area?"

"Who said that?" Andy asked.

It was Holden, but Sam didn't want to mention it. "A local guy who fishes both lakes. It was anecdotal. But he fishes a lot and says he's noticed fewer fish. Sounds like others have too. I mean, fishermen."

Andy considered for a moment. Cindy seemed fine to let her colleague, who Sam guessed was her senior, take the lead.

"Well, Agent Rivers, that's interesting." Andy paused. "We haven't exactly publicized it, but walleye stocks on both lakes are down a little. Why are you interested?"

"When we found CO Jiles, there was an illegal gill net near his boat. In fact, it might have been the reason Jiles was killed. I'm just trying to figure out if the illegal net was a one-time thing. Or maybe CO Jiles was onto something and there was some kind of consistent poaching going on? If there was, I figured it might be reflected in your counts."

That made Cindy turn and look at Andy, waiting for him to respond. But Andy kept staring and thinking.

"You seeing anything like that?" Sam said.

Finally, Andy turned to Cindy and said, "Do you remember those numbers?"

"Down 6% on Crane," Cindy said, with certainty. "And 7% on Vermilion. I'd have to check my records to be sure, but that's what I remember."

No one doubted her numbers.

"Any idea why?" Sam said.

Andy shrugged. "Fish populations fluctuate. Sometimes it's weather. Sometimes changes in habitat. Sometimes increases in predators and predation. Lots of reasons."

Cindy frowned. "Thing is," she said, "the predatory species for walleye fry are northern, muskellunge, bass, and perch. They've remained stable on both those lakes. At least according to our counts."

"That what you remember?" Andy said.

She nodded. "The weather has been pretty constant. I mean, unchanged, year over year. And there hasn't been any change in habitat, that I recall. Those are two of the best walleye lakes in the state, in terms of habitat."

"Definitely," Andy agreed.

"Could it be from poaching?" Sam said.

"First I heard of poaching," Andy said. Then he glanced at Cindy.

After a long pause, Cindy looked at Sam and said, "I'd wondered if there might be some poaching going on." She glanced back at Andy.

"That's true," Andy said. "She mentioned it after this spring's count."

"Did you talk to anyone about it?"

"Charlie Jiles," Cindy said.

"We told the CO to keep his eyes open," Andy said. "Charlie knows a lot of people and has lots of contacts. Or did. He told us he'd keep an eye out, but we never heard anything, so figured the walleye stocks were fluctuating due to natural causes. Fish population changes of less than 10% year-over-year aren't that unusual. If it happens three years in a row without rebounding, we'd be a lot more concerned."

"And suspicious," Cindy said.

They talked more about Vermilion. Sam asked them if they'd encountered any kind of concerted fish poaching on the lake, or any other lakes in the area. Andy, who had been a fish biologist for more than a decade, remembered Holden.

"That guy had quite the deal going. It's the only other time I remember hearing about a big poaching effort like that. I'm sure there have been occasional busts for people catching over their limit. But nothing organized, like what that guy was doing."

"Did it affect the walleye stocks?"

"Oh, yeah," Andy said. "Down about 5% for two years. But again, we didn't have any evidence it was going on, until he got caught. And, like I say, some fluctuations are normal. Hell, the stocks up on Lake of the Woods have shot up almost 10%."

"Seven," Cindy said.

"Seven," Andy shrugged.

"Do you have a business card, Agent Rivers?" Cindy Hill asked. "In case we think of anything else?"

Sam didn't carry business cards. But he did have a pen and used it to jot his email address and phone number on a napkin. He did it for all three of them. Both Cindy Hill and Andy Nivens were better prepared and gave Sam their cards.

"One last question," Sam said. "Are there a lot of whitefish in Vermilion?"

"It's a stable population," Andy Nivens said. "We don't stock it with whitefish because it doesn't get the kind of fishing pressure as other game fish. Basically, a legal netting season in the fall."

Andy explained how few sportsmen actually pursued white-fish netting because it was too damn hard and cold.

"It's a different species than the others on our lakes," Cindy said. "One of the better eating fish, but not nearly as popular as the other game fish."

There was a pause while they all thought about whitefish. Then Andy looked at his watch and said, "We gotta get going." He stood up from the table.

Sam stood, too, shaking their hands and thanking them both.

Then the pair of fish biologists turned and headed toward the DECC's meeting rooms.

Sam spent a few more minutes speaking with Ben Connors. The head of the northeast region's COs was an old friend of Charlie Jiles. He had a lot of respect for the dead man. They'd worked together for a long time, and though Charlie was almost always in the field, anytime they'd met at meetings, back in the office, or when Ben had visited Charlie's home turf, he'd been impressed. Mostly by Charlie Jiles's affinity with the locals. He seemed to have a natural affability with just about everyone.

"He wasn't the most punctual guy," Ben said. "Especially with his reports. And he wasn't always thorough about what he put in those reports. But he was covering some of the busiest areas in the state, fishing- and hunting-wise, I mean. I never heard many complaints about Charlie, at least with regard to his field work." Then Ben paused. "There were a couple of instances, few years back, when he was accused of harassment."

"What kind of harassment?"

"Let's see," Ben said, looking off, considering. "It was a while ago, so I don't remember all the details. But . . . Did you know Charlie was a bachelor?"

"I'd heard that."

"Between you and me, the man liked women. Whenever we got together and met for lunch, say, and there was a nice-looking waitress, Charlie put on the charm."

Sam knew the type—the kind who had a captive audience and would notice a waitress's name tag, if she had one, and then use her first name, telling her his own. And then there'd be banter. Sometimes there might even be innuendos. It was harmless stuff, really. But Sam knew when servers' livelihoods depended on their tips more than their wages, they felt forced to play along.

"So, there was an instance when an admin up in his region filed a complaint. She said, as I recall, that he was coming onto her and that he missed the cues that should have made him stop."

"What happened?"

"She left before there was any kind of follow-up."

"Did she leave because of Jiles? Because he threatened her?"

"No, no. She got a better job, as I recall."

"There was another instance?" Sam asked.

"There were two women fishing on Vermilion," Ben started, again trying to remember the details. "It was warm. Late summer. August, I think. Oh, and they each had an open beer. And I think they'd already had a few, when Charlie stopped them."

"Out on the lake?"

"Yeah. He stopped them and checked to make sure they had their licenses. And, of course, it was a drinking violation. DWI. Open container," Ben said, looking away. "They claimed, later, that Charlie Jiles suggested he would let it all slide, providing they wanted to party."

"Party?"

"I guess he was suggesting one or both of them might be interested in sex. At least that's what they said."

That sounded a little crazy, Sam thought. "Did they file a complaint?"

"Oh, yeah. One of them knew somebody in HR. DNR's human resources," Ben said, with an eye roll. "She never filed a formal complaint. But she insisted something be put in Charlie's record about it."

"Did they get tickets?"

"Charlie wrote them up for the open containers."

"I presume CO Jiles denied it."

"Sure. Said it never happened, and they were trying to smear him because he ticketed them."

"So, nothing came of it?"

"Well, it was a 'he said, she said' situation. And frankly it was a little over the top, even for Charlie. He wasn't that dumb. I mean, Charlie liked women, but I don't think even Charlie would have suggested a twofer in exchange for not ticketing them. That's just stupid. Charlie might have had a reputation, but he wasn't stupid."

Ben grinned a little.

The two talked a little more about COs, and how the workforce was changing. There was a crop of older COs who would be retiring over the next couple of years, making way for a younger crop, some of them women. The ranks were definitely shifting, Ben said. Then he told Sam he was probably going to leave in the next year or so himself, because it was time.

Sam told him it was similar in the USFW. More women were becoming special agents, and rangers. Sam, at 37, was straddling both worlds; the older workforce, comprised of men like Ben Connors, and a younger, more diverse workforce. Personally, Sam thought the evolving diversity of the workforce was a good thing.

While waiting for COs Jennie Flag and Bernie Olathe, Sam bought a hot green tea from the nearby barista and brought it back to the table, sitting and thinking about his conversation with Ben Connors. Until now, the only negative things he'd heard about Charlie Jiles were from Holden, and maybe the sheriff.

But cradling a few too many longnecks and being out of shape wasn't a crime. When he heard about the two old harassment claims, he wondered about them. He'd asked Ben if there were only the two, and Ben assured him those were the only formal complaints, and that they were old. He reiterated that Charlie had a reputation and clearly liked women.

Male/female relationships were evolving, and CO Jiles's age put him in an older crowd—when women had fewer options. So, he might have had an old-fashioned perspective about women, but that wasn't illegal. Other than those minor blemishes, Charlie Jiles seemed to be a good CO, at least according to his boss.

Still, Sam thought he'd picked up some kind of vibe from DNR fish biologist Cindy Hill. She'd asked for his contact info in a way that made him think she wanted to speak with him, possibly later, in confidence. He made a note to call her.

Sam had a few minutes before his meeting with COs Flag and Olathe. He used his phone to check his email. The only item of interest was a note from Deputy Sandy Harju.

> Deputy Barnes forwarded a request to me from the medical examiner. She wanted samples of the lake water from where Conservation Officer Charlie Jiles was found. We took down the coordinates when we were investigating, so getting to the correct location wasn't a problem. But I was curious about the request and wanted to make sure I got them what they wanted, so I called them. I hope that's okay.

Not only okay, Sam thought, but it demonstrated one of the most important traits of an investigator: curiosity. Harju continued.

The medical examiner read the arrest report. She wondered about where CO Jiles was found, about the water quality. The coordinates are in the AR, so she called it up on her map app but didn't see a nearby creek or river. I told her I didn't remember seeing one and all she said was, she wanted to get some samples of the water, in and around where we found the CO. Some up close to shore. When I asked her why, she said for further analysis.

I spent the afternoon getting out to the site and getting the samples. Because I knew it was important, I hand delivered the samples to the medical examiner's office in the city of Virginia. I gave them to her assistant. When I asked about when we might see the final report, the assistant didn't know for sure, but said probably later tonight or tomorrow.

If you want to talk about it, give me a call. But that's pretty much it. Look for the report tomorrow. I assume the mystery of the water samples will be explained in the final report.

I was not able to visit Holden's workplace, White Pines Marina. But I did call his boss, Jim Aho, and interviewed him over the phone. He said a lot of positive things about Holden. He only works part-time, M-W-F, 8–5.

But he's always on time, does excellent work, and in six years he's never taken a sick day. Aho said if he had more like him, his job would be a lot easier.

I'm on regular duty tomorrow, unless you've got something more for me to do. Frankly, this is a lot more interesting than my usual workload, so . . .

The sheriff was probably correct; Deputy Harju wouldn't be with his department more than another year or two. In another year or two, she would make a helluva undersheriff. But Smith Barnes was also a good cop, and it would be politically difficult to promote Sandy Harju, the youngest officer on his force, to undersheriff. So, Sam thought, her days there were numbered. But someday she'd make a good sheriff, maybe in a neighboring county.

He could tell she preferred being in the field to working traffic stops. And what he had already learned about Charlie Jiles made him wonder if they should take a closer look at the CO.

He sent her a text:

This request is just between you and me. I'm hoping you know the local judge, someone who can help us subpoena Charlie Jiles's phone records. I know we haven't found his phone, but we should be able to review his records. Can you look into it?

After working on the subpoena, if you can visit White Pines Marina to see Holden's workspace, truck, etc., and speak in person with his boss, that'd be good.

Also, can you reserve the department's runabout for tomorrow afternoon? The sheriff wanted us to check out Holden's cabin, and I told Holden we'd make sure all was okay.

Let's talk in the morning.

CHAPTER 25

S am watched two uniformed conservation officers move across the meeting room toward his table; they had to be Jennie Flag and Bernie Olathe. When they approached and confirmed Sam's suspicions by introducing themselves, Sam said, "You two look a lot more official than your boss, Ben Connors."

Jennie Flag was blocky with short-cropped brown hair. Bernie Olathe was a little taller than Officer Flag, but also broad through the shoulders and middle. He had a high, prematurely balding forehead that shined under the overhead DECC lighting. They both wore the customary dark-green cargo pants, thick black belt with accoutrements (including weapons), light-green shirt set off by a dark-green tie, and white undershirt. Since they were both a little heavy, their uniforms stretched across their middles as taut as a drumhead.

"That's 'cause our boss told us we had to present at 4," Officer Flag said.

"What's the topic?"

"CO cooperation in the field," Flag said.

"Dos and don'ts," Officer Olathe added. "Jen's covering the dos, I've got the don'ts."

They both chuckled.

"Let's talk about what you saw," Sam said. "Out there, when you found Holden Riggins, the suspect, and CO Jiles."

"A major clusterfuck," Flag said.

"First of all," Olathe said, "that Holden guy was sicker than a dog. Nearly froze to death and barely alive. But alive enough to puke." He reiterated how, as they approached, Holden leaned over his boat's gunwale and heaved.

"Couldn't even hold a water bottle," Flag added. "And there were nets all over the place." She mentioned the whitefish net, clearly marked and nearby. And the illegal net. It was a little less conspicuous, but to trained eyes, an obvious violation.

"Did you guys pull up the nets?"

"Eventually. It took a while to get the area secured. And then the sheriff's folks came out and blocked off the crime scene so they could cover everything. But yeah, we pulled up both nets and threw them into Holden's boat. We towed his boat, with the nets."

"I drove Jiles's boat back," Olathe said.

"What did you find in the nets?"

"Not much," Olathe said.

"Okay. In both nets?"

"A couple of whitefish at the ends of the whitefish net," Flag said. "Jiles's body probably scared away most of the fish."

"Walleye net was empty," Olathe said.

Sam remembered Holden had said the location of the illegal net was not the place you would expect to net walleye, this time of year.

"Are you guys familiar with the lake? With its fishing spots?"

"Not really," Flag said.

"That was Jiles's territory," Olathe added. "We wouldn't know about Vermilion. Jiles didn't share much."

Sam made notes and considered some follow-up questions.

"Were you concerned about Holden when you were out there with him?"

"How do you mean?"

"I mean, for your safety?"

"No," Flag said, definitive. "That guy was so fucked up. First, he was nearly froze to death when we found him. He began to come around a little, but it took a stay in the hospital, I heard, to bring him back to normal."

"They told you we found an empty fifth and another half-full bottle in the bottom of his boat?" Olathe asked.

"It's in the arrest report. Did he seem drunk?"

"He seemed just about dead," Flag said.

"I've seen some benders in my day," Olathe said. "Maybe even had one or two of my own," he smiled. "But never a fifth and a half of whiskey. And never passing out in that kind of cold and nearly freezing to death. That guy was damn lucky. He had one foot in the grave."

"Other than being sick, did anything else strike you about the suspect?"

"It looked to me like it was some kind of fight that got out of hand," Flag said. "I mean, when I saw the CO's boat there, and the illegal net, I figured CO Jiles was out patrolling. He stopped to do a check. And he and Holden Riggins got into it. And maybe

Riggins, who I understand has a record and has poached before, and done time, hit him too hard."

"A crime of passion," Sam said.

"Something like that," Olathe said. "Holden said a few things to us out there. Did they tell you that?"

"No. The sheriff said he sort of clammed up."

"When he started coming around," Flag said, "he said he didn't remember anything after having dinner at the casino, across the bay there."

"He said something about thinking he must have been drugged," Olathe said.

"But when we asked him a few questions, he seemed disoriented," Flag added.

"The way you would be if you nearly killed yourself drinking and then passed out in the cold," Olathe said.

"And then he shut up."

"Did they find anything in his blood?" Olathe said.

"Haven't gotten the tests back yet." Sam said.

"He killed him," Olathe said.

"I have to say, out there he was like a goddamn lamb," Flag said.

"The guy had just committed murder and then drank himself silly and passed out in the middle of a cold Minnesota night," Olathe said, his voice a little higher. "He's lucky to be alive."

Flag shrugged.

After a pause, Olathe added, "What bugs me the most is that he was cut down like that in the line of duty."

"You mean CO Jiles?" Sam said.

"Yeah. Jiles. Could have happened to any of us."

"For sure," Flag said.

"The only silver lining is that we caught Holden Riggins in the act," Olathe said.

They all grew silent for a moment.

"How well did you guys know Charlie Jiles?"

There was a pause. Then Flag said, "I didn't know him that well. I saw him at conferences and meetings like this one. I heard him present a couple of times. He was okay."

"He was funny," Olathe said. "He had a lot of stories from the field and he knew how to tell them."

"He did," Flag said. She paused for a moment. When no one spoke, she added, "From my perspective, Jiles was kind of a dinosaur."

"What do you mean?" Sam said.

"Well, for starters," she turned to Olathe, "how often did you hear from Jiles?"

"I didn't. I'd talk to him at conferences like this one. But other than that, he was one of those guys who sort of practiced one of our don'ts: he kept to himself, at least among colleagues."

"Early on, I actually called him a couple of times, just to touch base," Flag said. "But he never got back to me."

"You mean . . ."

"I was hoping to learn pointers, the dos and don'ts, from somebody who had been in the field for a while."

"But he didn't call you back?" Sam said.

"Uh-uh," Flag said.

Olathe, too, shook his head no.

"The dinosaur comment was because he didn't communicate?" Sam said.

Jennie Flag thought about it.

"When I first started," Flag said, "I was one of two women COs. Our minority status wasn't lost on Jiles. We were down at a meeting just like this one. For all the COs. He was heading up some kind of session. I can't remember the topic. Right at the beginning of it I remember him saying something like, 'What's the world coming to, women becoming COs?' He said it as a joke, for a laugh. And some of the guys got a chuckle out of it. Mind you, this was a while back, before perspectives about that kind of comment changed. But me and Eileen, the other CO, didn't appreciate it. Bad enough being outnumbered. Then somebody needs to single you out."

"I don't remember that," Olathe said.

"You're a guy," Flag said. "You probably laughed."

Olathe didn't say anything. Then he finally shrugged and said, "Probably."

Sam could tell Flag and Olathe were friends. Not romantic. Flag wore a wedding ring. Olathe's hand was ringless.

Sam looked at Flag and said, "Did you ever hear of CO Jiles making inappropriate gestures toward any of the women in the DNR?"

"Gestures?" Flag said. "You mean, did he ever come onto anyone?"

Sam nodded.

"Nah. Never to me," she said, with another grin. "And not Eileen, either. Eileen's a lot like me; straight shooter. If one of our male colleagues came onto either one of us, we'd cut their balls off."

Olathe grinned. "She's serious."

CHAPTER 26

S am made his way back to his Jeep. Gray was glad to see him. Sam drove to their hotel, which was large and spacious and right on the water. After parking in the lot, rather than checking in, he and Gray started out along Duluth's boardwalk. Sam was meeting Carmel at 5:30 at Amore, so they had 15 minutes to air themselves.

Sam was trying to set his meeting with the COs aside. Like most, they assumed Holden's guilt was obvious, and were pleased the alleged perpetrator was in custody. But they didn't know all the details, and the more Sam learned, the less he understood.

That said, he was trying to focus on the big, gray lake. It was beautiful, with the wind whipping off its surface, intensifying the cold, and keeping most people indoors. Sam wore his down jacket, and it was sunny, so he was comfortable enough. He could feel the cold, but it didn't prevent him from enjoying the walk, or Gray from wanting to leap into the water.

Sam reflected on the picture he was getting of the dead CO, Charlie Jiles. The sheriff pretty much said he was out of shape and drank too much. The Raffertys talked about him in a way that made Sam think CO Jiles was one of those friendly officials who would just as soon strike up a conversation with a stranger as keep to himself. But then, COs Flag and Olathe, colleagues, described him as aloof. Maybe he was professionally aloof, but when it came to the public, he turned on the charm. But then there was Ben Connors, Charlie Jiles's boss. Clearly, he liked Jiles, so maybe Jiles was good managing up? Connors also mentioned the instances in which Jiles allegedly committed harassment. The first sounded like an effort to kindle an office romance gone astray. Since the woman didn't stick around, the incident was dropped. The alleged incident on Lake Vermilion involving the two fisherwomen was bolder and more problematic. But again, that could have been revenge perpetrated by violators who were angry about being ticketed.

Sam suspected if Jiles really had harassment problems, Jennie Flag would probably know about it, or at least have heard about it. Flag was forthright. You understood she wasn't the type to pull punches about sharing someone's misdeeds, even if they were a colleague. Further, if anyone had ever approached Flag with untoward intentions, by her own testament, she "would have cut his balls off." Sam didn't doubt she'd do it, at least figuratively. If Charlie Jiles was as gregarious as some said, Sam knew a couple of minutes spent in Jennie Flag's presence would make him realize she would not be receptive to advances of any type.

Sam found Amore, parked, crossed London Road, and started up the sidewalk. Carmel drove by in her Expedition, alone. He watched her turn into the lot in front of him and disappear. After a couple minutes Carmel walked around the corner, 40 yards away. She saw Sam and smiled.

And then he smiled and thought, *How suddenly my life has changed.*

The first time he'd met Carmel was the first time she worked on Gray, more than two years ago. She had cleaned and stitched a bullet graze along Gray's back side. At that time, he'd been impressed by her examination of Gray, a notorious hybrid. She was a focused, serious, superb veterinarian. As soon as she placed her hands on the wounded Gray, he settled, and so did Sam. She had that kind of bearing, that kind of presence.

Back then she'd been separated from Carlos, and Sam had been divorced for about a year, but was in a relationship with Diane Talbott, a reporter. Then six months ago they'd both been single and collided, fast and hard, like two celestial bodies caught up in each other's orbits.

Over the last six months they had shared plenty of details about their marriages. About themselves. Sam had tried to recall falling in love with his first wife, Maggie. But he could not remember anything like this feeling of contentment, this kind of solace and connection.

"Hey, cowboy," she said, coming forward and leaning in for a kiss.

"Hey," Sam said, returning her kiss. Then he opened the restaurant door and Carmel walked in.

"You look preoccupied," she said, in front of him.

"I guess," he said.

"Busy day?"

"Really busy." But it wasn't his day that was distracting.

And yet there was still something inside him, some hesitancy, some unwillingness to put it all out there, to rock the boat, to threaten capsizing their perfect balance.

As he walked behind Carmel, he tried to distract himself by looking around the restaurant.

"How did you find this place?" he asked.

"Mary Fest," Carmel said. "She's a local vet and kind of a foodie. She said it wasn't just a restaurant; it was a dining experience."

"How'd it go?" Sam said.

"The conference?"

"Yeah. What can you tell me about Lyme disease?"

"Laugh all you want, Rivers. My attendees were riveted."

"I'm serious," he said. Though they both knew he wasn't. Not exactly. "Tell me."

Carmel began detailing the parasite. Clearly, she was enthusiastic about her subject. She talked nonstop for 5 minutes before the waitress finally came over, told them the specials, and asked if she could start them with something to drink.

They ordered a bottle of Chianti. Then Carmel ordered the chicken with roasted walnuts, Craisins, and sun-dried tomatoes tossed with fettucine in a light cream sauce. Sam ordered the Squash Ravioli in tomato sauce.

After Sam poured them each a glass of wine, Carmel lifted it in front of her. A toast.

"To wonderful surprises in the middle of the week," Carmel said.

Even before the excellent Chianti crossed Sam's tongue, he had felt a kind of heady inebriation at the notion they'd be spending the night together. It was Carmel. She emanated some kind of irresistible force, and he was caught up in it. When he stared at her, he saw a pair of beautiful, opalescent eyes staring back with sincere and honest affection.

And then she finished sharing her knowledge about Lyme disease. Sam loved the fact she could get passionate about a parasite and bacterium.

Finally, Carmel asked about his day, and Sam shared its more bizarre moments. His early morning meeting with Holden. His interviews with the DNR folks. And beneath it all, or threading through it in a dense, impenetrable weave, his confusion. About what it all meant.

"And you still don't have Holden's blood work?"

"No. Probably tomorrow."

Carmel thought about it. "You're going to remain confused until you get more definitive information. Holden's prints on the weapon and liquor bottles weren't really definitive, since they could have been planted. It's like Lyme disease. The symptoms can lead to a diagnosis, but until you do a blood test, it's only conjecture."

The food came and for a moment they were busy with their plates, sharing bites and exclaiming about its quality. Mary Fest had been spot-on. Carmel was going to see her tomorrow and would let her know. It was the kind of food that was both cooked to perfection and seasoned in a way that summoned Tuscany. Tuscany with butter. It was delicious and transporting.

By the end of it all they had finished the bottle of wine and both shared their plates and their days. And then their thoughts turned toward the next stage of the evening. The anticipation of it seemed to rise inside them like a huge Lake Superior wave. But it wasn't cold and gray. Incongruously, it was golden and warm and suffused with dusk light.

When their waitress asked them if they would like dessert, Carmel said no thanks, in a way that belied her keen interest in moving on. Sam asked for the check, also hurried. Then Sam looked at Carmel, and he was pretty sure she was thinking what he was; their just dessert was at the hotel.

Paused on the threshold to the restaurant, they embraced and kissed, and Sam, feeling inebriated because of the wine or the food or this kiss or all of it, said, "Do you know how to get there?"

"Of course. I booked it. I'll meet you there in a heartbeat." And then she smiled and was gone.

Sam and Gray were in their car less than a minute when Sam got a call. He figured it was Carmel, wanting to talk steamy. But when he hit the answer button, a woman came on the line. Not Carmel.

"Agent Rivers?"

Startled, Sam said, "Yes."

"Cindy Hill. I'm one of the DNR fish biologists you met today, with Ben Connors?"

"Sure," Sam said.

"Sorry to bother you at night. Do you have a minute?"

When Sam had placed the location of their waterfront hotel in his map app it was a 12-minute drive. "Of course."

There was a pause. "And I need this to be confidential."

"Of course," Sam said. Despite his previous effulgence, he was tracking now.

"I mean, I don't want this to get back to my colleagues. Especially not Ben Connors. But frankly, no one at the DNR."

She had his attention. "Okay," Sam said. "I can go along with that. Unless what you tell me involves breaking the law."

"Oh no. No. Nothing like that. I mean, as far as I know, no laws were broken. It's more of an ethics thing. Or maybe one law was broken, but if so, I don't have first-hand knowledge of it. I'm just passing along what a friend told me."

There was another pause. "Okay."

"It's about Charlie Jiles."

"Okay."

"First, I don't like talking bad about someone who just died," she started. "But I need to tell you a couple of things about Charlie Jiles." She said these last words quickly, as though she had rehearsed them and needed to get them out. "Charlie was one of those guys. He came onto a lot of women, I think. And he wasn't great about picking up the cues that he should back off."

"Did he come onto you?" Sam remembered Cindy Hill as young and cute. He could imagine she got her share of attention from her male DNR colleagues.

"This meeting we were in today is an annual event. One in which a lot of DNR people attend, including us fish biologists. But also COs. And others."

Sam waited.

"Some people kind of hook up at these meetings. So I'm told."

Sam was familiar with the phenomena.

"In my book, all's fair among mutually consenting adults. As long as they're single," Cindy added.

"I agree."

"So, two years ago, Charlie Jiles kind of came onto me."

Given the age difference, Sam was a little surprised. "Okay."

"I guess he didn't *kind* of come onto me. He definitely came onto me. And he was a little pushy. I finally got my point across, that I wasn't interested. First, I told him he was old enough to be my dad. When he persisted, I told him one of my best friends was Ethan Meirovitz, one of the higher-ups in the DNR's HR department. Then he backed off. Truthfully, I was completely grossed out."

Sam was always surprised by the sexual predation of some men. "Did you report it?"

"Oh, God no. I don't really know Ethan all that well. And Charlie Jiles was kind of a guy's guy. I mean, among some of the older guys in the organization."

"You mean, the DNR?"

"Yeah. There are a lot of women in the DNR. Just not many women COs or fish biologists. And a lot of those guys are older. They grew up together. I mean, with Charlie Jiles. They've known each other for years. And they stick together."

"I understand," Sam said.

"That's part of the reason I wouldn't want any of this to get back to my colleagues."

"Of course."

"Charlie Jiles not only knew a lot of people in the field. But I think he and Ben Connors are, were, pretty good buddies."

"I kind of picked that up."

Charlie Jiles clearly liked women, Sam thought, and acted on it. Sam wasn't sure what it meant, other than the CO had balls, hoping to get lucky with a young woman like Cindy Hill.

"So, you just wanted me to know?"

"Oh. Yes. But that's just part of it. I have a cousin Rita, who works at the Holiday Inn lounge up in Orr. We get together quite a bit. More like sisters than cousins. After this meeting two years ago, I was telling her about Charlie Jiles coming onto me. When I mentioned his name, she said, 'oh my God.' She knew him. He was sort of a regular at the lounge where she works. She said he'd come by once in a while, usually on a weekend. He'd come in, have dinner, and try and chat up any single ladies in the place. I guess sometimes he'd get lucky. I don't know.

"But one time a woman complained that Charlie had drugged her. She was embarrassed because they'd slept together. Said she didn't remember much about it, but remembered going back to her room. Remembered Charlie at her door, helping her into the room. Next thing she remembers is waking up alone in bed, in the morning, naked. Said it was obvious she'd had intercourse. Or someone had intercourse with her."

"Did anyone confront Charlie Jiles about it?"

"Oh, yeah. The manager talked to him. But he denied it. Not the sex. He said it was consensual, that she just had too much to drink. But even if that was the case, who does that?"

Sam agreed. Maybe the woman did have too much to drink, Sam thought. But still, who has sex with a woman so drunk she can't remember it?

"Then Rita told me, a couple of months later, she was working a shift on a Friday night. In walks Charlie. He checks out the bar, sees a single woman sitting alone, and goes over and sits right next to her. He ordered dinner and had a couple of drinks and ended up talking to this woman. Must have been some kind of traveling saleswoman kind of thing. Then, later in the evening, the woman gets up. I guess to go to the bathroom. My cousin's across the room working her tables, but when she glances up, she notices the woman heading off to the bathroom. By now Rita is kind of curious, you know? Like, she wonders if they're going to go off together. Maybe to the woman's hotel room? While she's glancing over at Charlie, wondering about it, she sees Charlie glance around, and then drop something into the woman's drink."

There was another pause. "Did she say anything?"

"Rita has dated her share of creeps. In fact, she sort of expects the worst until she sees something different. If she sees something like this, some old guy trying to drug a woman, she can't help herself. It's not only calling out a creep. It's also saving a sister. She went right up to Charlie Jiles, got in his face, and called him on it. Told him what she'd seen."

"He denied it," Sam said.

"Yeah. But the manager likes Rita. And given they'd already had a complaint about Charlie, he asked Charlie to leave. At first, he refused. Then Rita suggested they have the drink tested. Then she said Charlie Jiles got really pissed. He started yelling at Rita and the manager. Then he backhanded the drink and it flew across the bar and shattered. Then he took out his wallet, threw down some bills, and left."

"That was convenient."

"Wasn't it?" Cindy agreed. "After Charlie stormed out, the woman returned. When she asked what was going on, Rita told her. She acted surprised, said she kind of *liked* the guy. Can you believe it? I guess to some women he must have been charming. But I never saw it."

"Did you mention any of this to anyone at the DNR?"

"I didn't. Like I said, Charlie Jiles has . . . had a lot of friends. He was well liked by many. So, I decided to let it go. Besides, it happened to Rita, not me. So it would have been secondhand. But when you started asking questions about him, about what he was like, I thought you should know."

CHAPTER 27

Smugglers Creek was hidden behind an island, across the channel. The creek flowed out of the northern wilderness before being turned 90 degrees by a spit of land near Vermilion's shoreline. The land and bend of water made the creek's mouth indistinguishable from the mainland. The only obvious sign there was flowage was the current that came into the lake, cutting along thick bush at the lake's edge. Here, Cray Halverson knew, it was deep water. Here there were always fish, feeding on what the creek brought down from the Boundary Waters. Here he had always been lucky.

But not last Thursday.

It was growing dark. Cray used his Crestliner's GPS to navigate around the island, pulling the boat up near the creek's mouth. He was thankful the sky was covered by a thick bank of clouds, ideal cover for setting their net. More importantly, Rowena would only see outlines in the vague dusk light, nothing to trigger what happened here. He brought the boat near enough to catch the creek's current, but far enough from the shore to be in 25 feet of water. Then he dropped anchor and turned to ready the net.

Rowena still ached, but over the last four days the intensity of the pain had subsided. Her maelstrom had passed. Now there was just . . . the recollection of actions she wanted to forget, knowing she would never be able to.

She was familiar with male abuse. Years earlier, the lumberjack behind the Sportsmen's Lounge had taken liberties, forced himself on her. But she had known him before. They had sexual history. If she was honest, she had returned his initial advances and let his hands wander before telling him to stop. But he didn't.

None of her initial indiscretions legitimized the lumberjack's actions, which is why they ended up brawling.

But what happened to her in the mouth of Smugglers Creek was on a different level altogether.

As she helped Cray with the net, her swollen wrists felt tight. Her right ankle, where it had twisted, was thick in her boot. The bruise on her left hip had grown uglier. Part of the healing process, she knew. Like time. Lots of time would need to pass before she would begin to feel herself again.

For now, she was thankful she felt good enough to bend, hoist, and thread the floats through the net's top. She fastened extra weights near the net's bottom, to keep it submerged. She tried to focus on her immediate tasks. She had helped Cray before and knew what had to be done. Prepare the net. Make sure it was untangled. Feed it over the side as Cray kept the boat steady, floating with the current. Play out the heavy bottom weights. Make sure the top floats remained near the top. Let the narrow twines unfold and open wide so when walleye moved through them, their gills would be caught in the thin cord.

She was thankful for the near darkness. She was thankful to move through this black night, without anything to remind her of calamity, of storm, or pain. As Cray kept the boat steady in the current, Rowena kept feeding out the net.

Then, as the twine unraveled into the black water, the smell of swamp water and leaf rot drifted up out of the cold. A trace. And a trigger.

The scent returned her to that moment. She felt a piercing jolt beneath her sternum. She remembered blacking out. She recalled the moment her eyes fluttered open to find his bulk behind her, struggling. The odor of decay filled her senses like a mist off the River Styx, as awful as his sour breath.

Cray, keeping the boat steady, noticed Rowena had stopped playing out the net, threatening to drag and snag it behind them.

"Rowena!" Cray said, loud enough to startle her.

The yell returned her to the present. Her memory faded. A bad dream. A nightmare. All commingling with their red headlights cutting through the dark.

"You gotta play it out," Cray said. "Don't stop. The net!"

Last Thursday, midnight had been her friend. The cold front had protected them. Her. But the cold could not protect her from the stench of rotting water.

Everything about that day had been different. She had expected none of it. The afternoon had been clear. Sunny. Warm. She had been hellbent on teaching him a lesson. This time there would be no proffered drink to poison her mind and make her forget. This time she was going to pummel him with righteous fists.

But he had surprised her.

Then, darkness.

"Rowena!" Cray said, throttling the boat back to keep it steady in the current.

Finally, she returned to her task. Fumbling, at first, with the playout of the net. But coming back to it quickly, like a fighter against the ropes, startled back to consciousness.

In another 10 minutes the net was set, carefully. This time the weights had been heavy enough to submerge the faux branch floats—at least enough so they would not be obvious on the surface. If anyone came to the mouth of Smugglers Creek, they would need to be directly overhead to spy the floats. And then they would be easily mistaken for waterlogged branches, stirred from the bottom of the creek by its current, suspended in the lake water while they soaked enough to sink.

Satisfied with the setting, Cray revved the Crestliner's engine and turned around the near island. They switched off their red lights. Cray used his GPS to navigate through the dark into the main channel, out into Big Bay and then home.

Rowena sat back in one of the Crestliner's front seats, feeling the icy wind waft over the boat's windshield, blowing any remnant of scent behind her. Still, bent over in the boat's bow, Rowena trembled. Not from the cold. Her back was sweaty with the memory of pain, and she ached.

CHAPTER 28

An Adidas shoebox lay on the passenger side floor of Joe Haman's cruiser, out of sight. He steered through the dark toward the back side of the Vermilion Falls Motel. Inside the shoebox lay a bloodied, dead cottontail.

Earlier, Joe had returned to Charlie's Eveleth home, an hour before sunset. Deputy Smith Barnes was busy, pinch-hitting for the sheriff during his absence as he tended to the new kid. Doubtless catering to the wife and new mother too. Joe knew there were no evening patrols in Charlie Jiles's neighborhood. So, there was no one to stop him from having another look-see at Charlie's home. He still hoped to find Charlie's money, or anything damning Charlie might have left behind.

After using the key to enter the house, he'd expanded his previous search. He'd checked under the bathroom vanity drawers, flashed a light down a basement sump pump drain, opened the water softener lid, and looked in every other nook and corner he could find. Nothing.

When Joe glanced out of Charlie's bedroom window he noticed a cottontail, munching on overgrown weeds in front of a basement window well.

Goddamn vermin taking advantage of a dead man, Joe thought. And then he thought of a way he might be able to take care of Sam Rivers once and for all.

Charlie's gun rack held a 12-gauge shotgun, a 30.06 deer rifle, and a .22 caliber pea shooter. Joe had earlier considered lifting the 12-guage. He wanted to take several items from Charlie's house. But if someone had pictures of the place, or some kind of inventory, or a previous visitor remembered items, or if Joe was seen hauling something out, there could be questions. So, he'd left everything in its place.

Joe guessed Charlie had used the .22 to keep rabbits and squirrels out of his yard and woodpeckers off his siding.

There was a drawer in the bottom of the gun rack, filled with ammunition, including shotgun shells, 30.06 cartridges, and a box of .22 shorts. Joe pulled it out and shone his flashlight into the empty space where the drawer had fit. He lifted the drawer above his head, to examine its bottom, but there was nothing.

Joe took the .22 rifle off the rack. He opened up the box of .22 shorts and loaded one slug into the chamber, all he would need. Then he approached the bedroom window, careful to stay down out of sight. He took his time unlatching the catch and opening the window and screen to a six-inch gap. The bunny paused, glancing left, then right, but not up, which was when Joe Haman put a bullet through its head.

He wasn't sure if he should feel frustrated or relieved by his search of Charlie's house. He had found neither extra cash nor any evidence that he and Charlie had been partners in anything, or that he even had a relationship with the man. But he wasn't sure he had turned over every stone.

Again, if they subpoenaed Charlie's phone records, they would find a handful of calls made to Joe Haman. But those were easily explained, given both their mothers resided in the same assisted living facility.

The more Joe thought about it, the more he thought he was probably in the clear. Even if there was evidence and cash, he felt certain that if he couldn't find it, no one else searching the place would find anything. Especially Sandy Harju and her Boy Scout sidekick Sam Rivers. Besides, you could not find something that did not exist.

But Joe had no illusions. Sam Rivers was still a problem.

After leaving Charlie's place, Joe took a drive in the country. First, he passed by his childhood house and barn, to make sure the place was vacant. The rancher who purchased the property let them know he had no intention of living there. He'd wanted the land, which he'd planted in a steady rotation of crops. This year it appeared the fields beyond the dilapidated house and barn had been planted in already harvested corn. Cornstalk stubble stuck out of the ground like a field of pungi sticks.

Once he was certain the place was vacant, he turned the cruiser around and headed up the weed-covered drive. Joe followed the familiar ruts up and around to the back side of the barn, where he parked out of sight. He took out his utility flashlight and made his way to the barn door.

The door was padlocked. There was a side grain chute to the right of the door that was latched from the inside. The latch had been flimsy when Joe was a boy. Now he moved over to it, steadied himself, and kicked. The chute panel flung open. Joe shone his light into the barn, and then ducked and stepped into the open space.

Inside, Joe's light flickered over chains and hooks still hanging from the rafters. Rusted leghold traps hung against a far wall. The place was still as creepy as Joe remembered.

On the other side was the old man's workbench. Joe walked straight to the far-right drawer and opened it. It was a deep drawer containing a hodgepodge of items: several random tools, an old cigar box containing arrowheads, a spare hammer, lots of random nails, a couple of small jars with nuts and bolts—the old man never threw anything away—and a small container marked *Mac-Millan's Quality Strychnine.* Beneath the lettering was an image of a skull and crossbones.

Back in Joe's cruiser, the dead bunny lay in the shoebox, now stuffed with enough strychnine to kill a pack of wolves.

Joe remembered the approach to the rear of the motel, through the woods behind the parking lot. Now he came through those woods, looking for Rivers's Jeep. There were two cars parked in the back lot, neither of them Rivers's. The Boy Scout was probably out for a late dinner, Joe guessed. Probably with that young deputy, Sandy Harju. Maybe the Boy Scout was hoping to get lucky.

Regardless, Joe knew Sam Rivers would need to air his dog before bed. Definitely first thing in the morning. And he knew the most likely place for it, at least at the Vermilion Falls Motel: the rear stretch of woods.

He backed up 10 paces from the parking lot's rear curb. He found a plausible opening on the ground, large enough to hold the whole rabbit's carcass. And then he carefully emptied it onto the ground.

It was still early, but dark. Joe guessed Rivers would soon be home. With luck, his mongrel dog would enjoy a midnight snack before bed. His last.

CHAPTER 29

Wednesday, October 18

S am woke up with one arm flung over Carmel's side. She was backed up into him, her thick brown hair flung over her pillow. It had a sweet, musky smell. She was breathing slowly—rhythmic and steady—deep sleep. There was not a micron of space between their languid nakedness.

Outside, the early dawn was just beginning to light their hotel curtains. Gray, like Carmel, was taking long, slow breaths.

Sam closed his eyes, remained still, listened. He thought about their evening, when they'd both finally made it into the room. Things had gotten hectic. Sam arrived first. He had enough time to fix Gray's dinner, set his bowl down, wait until he was finished, and then get him out to relieve himself.

Then Carmel let herself in, her luggage in tow.

And the rest Sam tried to put out of his mind because he knew the memory of it would cause a physical response, and he and Carmel were spooning.

But he couldn't help it.

She felt him. The rhythm of her breathing shifted. And then her hand slowly moved, reaching back behind her, groping until she found her way to the impertinence that had awakened her. And then she squeezed.

They spent the next 15 minutes fooling around.

Carmel got out of bed first, padding to the bathroom. By the time she returned, it was Sam's turn. When Sam came back to bed, Gray had risen, stretched, and padded over to receive a head rub and some cooing sounds from Carmel.

"You're charming us both," Sam said.

"You boys make it easy," she said.

"I'm so glad we had our Duluth."

"Won't be the last, sailor," Carmel said. "But now it's back to the real world. There's an 8:00 on heartworms."

"Eight?"

"Fraid so. Mary Fest is bringing us coffee and croissants."

"Tell her we enjoyed our experience."

"I'm not a kiss-and-tell kind of girl."

"I mean the restaurant. Our dining experience. What are you talking about?"

"Rivers," Carmel said.

It took them 45 minutes to shower and get dressed. By the time they were done, they were already thinking about their days. Sam needed to check his emails and return north. He imagined there would be some other investigative chores that arose, but right now the only one he had on his list was checking out Holden Riggins's place on Vermilion. He expected to finally get the ME report, and Holden's toxicology report. They should both be interesting.

Carmel was back to more classes, and then she had to return home by around 3. She needed to re-assume command of her practice, and her daughter, Jennifer.

"When do you think you'll be back?" Carmel said, nearly out the door.

"I have no idea. It depends on how the rest of today and the week unfolds."

"You think you'll be up there this weekend?"

"Might? I don't really know. But I will definitely know more tonight."

"Did you know the forecast is for a really warm weekend? And sunny all over the state?"

"Maybe we should do something."

"If you're going to still be up north, we could do Vermilion. I've heard it's nice. Me, Jennifer, Frank, and Liberty."

"You guys would love it."

"Maybe I can look for a place. A place with a boat."

Sam came over to her. He wrapped his arms around her, and they kissed. "I love how you think."

"And I love how you . . . "

Sam fed and aired Gray and got him back to their room. Then he stopped by the complimentary breakfast for coffee, a hard-boiled egg, and a bagel.

Back in the room, he checked his messages. One of the first he noticed, because it was near the top (so sent this morning), was an email from Deputy Smith Barnes. The subject line read: *Medical Examiner's Report.*

> Sam,
> Got the ME report late last night, attached. The sheriff said I should get it to you asap. I haven't had a chance to review it (too busy here without Dean). Take a look and let us know.
> —SB

Sam downloaded the PDF and saved it to his PC. Then he opened it, perusing its contents.

Sam had read his share of ME reports. He skimmed over the header material, Autopsy by Dr. Melanie Spivak, date and time performed, attending assistant, and so forth. Sam was looking for details he didn't already know.

Under **EXTERNAL EXAMINATION** he found his first. This part of the autopsy explained what the victim was wearing, his age, height, weight, and described in detail the contusion on the back, right side of CO Jiles's head. "According to the arrest report, the blow appears to have been made by a Class ABC fire extinguisher. We found minute particles of red metallic paint in the victim's head contusion. Similarly, the shape and indentation of the blow was consistent with that piece of equipment." Skimming further Sam read: "As noted earlier, the victim had been floating in lake water for approximately 48 hours."

Forty-eight hours? Sam skipped back to the report's beginning, to the *Estimated Time of Death*: "Body temperature, rigor and livor mortis, and stomach contents approximate the time of death between 1:30 and 3:30 p.m. on Thursday, 10/12."

CO Jiles had died a full 24 hours earlier than they had thought. If the CO died where they found him, off Temple Island, and his boat had been tethered to the shoreline for every passerby to see for more than 24 hours . . . it didn't make sense. First, someone would have recognized an empty DNR boat and stopped to investigate. The cold snap started Thursday, so lake traffic was probably down. But it was hard to imagine no boats going by.

And Holden wasn't on the scene until late Friday. He had already told them that on Thursday he'd set his whitefish net at that location. Holden had said he'd set it Thursday afternoon. If that was the case, did Holden kill CO Jiles on Thursday? If so, wouldn't the obvious choice have been to scuttle the CO's runabout up a creek, or ditch it someplace? Or at the very least take the body into the woods? And why would he leave his whitefish net at that location, as well as his illegal net? Again, didn't make sense.

Sam skipped back to the autopsy's EXTERNAL EXAMINA-TION section and continued reading. After the comment about "floating in lake water for approximately 48 hours," Sam read: "The victim's pubic area and underwear contained fresh blood and semen, indicating recent sexual intercourse."

Jiles had sex before he died? And being in water for nearly 48 hours didn't wash it away? If that was the case, Sam guessed, once Jiles hit the water he probably didn't move.

Sam skipped down to the autopsy's LABORATORY DATA and read: "The victim's semen was found in his boxer briefs, commingled with blood, possibly menstrual."

Again, Sam was astonished they could find enough semen and blood in Jiles's clothes to determine CO Jiles had sex with a menstruating woman?

Also, Sam didn't consider himself prudish, especially in matters of human sexuality. But he was guessing sex while menstruating was an uncommon practice.

This part of the report also indicated the victim had a blood alcohol level of .06. So CO Jiles had been drinking, but not much.

Finally, there was a brief note about lung-water analysis. "Particulate found in the victim's lungs was primarily decomposing leaf litter, consistent with flowage from a watercourse."

What?

Sam skipped to the autopsy's INTERNAL EXAMINATION section. He quickly skimmed and found the following: "The victim's lungs were filled with water, consistent with drowning. While the blow to the head likely caused unconsciousness, the body's autonomic functions continued to operate, and the victim continued breathing. Presumably he was knocked into the water and, face down, aspirated water into his lungs, drowning from suffocation."

Sam skipped back to the LABORATORY DATA and read: "We subsequently analyzed the lake water in the area where the victim was found, but it contained no particulate. Given the differences in water analysis, we assume the victim drowned in a different location. Except for the organic particulate, the water quality was consistent with Lake Vermilion water, suggesting the watercourse was elsewhere on the lake, but not in the immediate vicinity in which the victim's body was found."

The medical examiner was saying CO Jiles died elsewhere? Around the mouth of a creek or river? Given that she believed it was most likely a creek or river that fed into Vermilion, that narrowed their possibilities. But it begged credulity. Sometime Thursday afternoon, CO Jiles was struck, fell unconscious into the water, and drowned. Then, more than 24 hours later, Holden moved him to a different location, along with his boat, set up his illegal walleye net beside his legal whitefish net, placed CO Jiles in his legal net, and then got blinding drunk, passed out, and nearly froze to death?

The more he considered the anomalies, the more incongruous they became. And rather than support the idea that Holden was the murderer, it suggested an entirely different scenario. Though admittedly, Sam had no idea what that scenario might entail. Or who it might involve. Or where Jiles was murdered.

Finally, he drafted an email to the sheriff, Deputy Barnes, and cc'd Deputy Harju. In it, he surfaced three new facts about CO Jiles's death.

"Apparently, CO Jiles had sex with a menstruating woman not long before his death by drowning. Identity unknown.

"CO Jiles died Thursday afternoon, 10/12. This was, in part, consistent with Deputy Barnes's perspective that the victim may have been dead longer than first thought.

"Perhaps most surprising, CO Jiles did not drown where they found him. The location of his death was the mouth of a creek or river that flowed into Vermilion."

Sam thought about calling up Google Maps and looking for watercourses that emptied into Vermilion. But then he remembered someone with enough detailed knowledge of the lake to quickly identify the possibilities, including watercourses that might not show up on Google Maps.

He emailed Deputy Smith Barnes.

"I need to speak with Holden again. I'm in Duluth, but I can be at the department by 11 or so. Can you please make sure he's in the interrogation room? Thanks."

Sam checked his map app. If he left now, he'd arrive in Vermilion Falls by 10:41.

"Let's go, buddy," Sam said.

Sam opened the door and Gray accompanied him to the Jeep. As Sam and Gray walked out, Sam thought about their day. If Holden gave him some likely Vermilion places to check, where creeks or rivers flowed into the lake, maybe he and Deputy Harju could have a look, after they checked on Holden's cabin. All things considered, he thought meeting Deputy Harju at the casino docks around 1 p.m. should work.

He phoned Deputy Harju and she picked up.

"You got my email last night?"

"Yes. I've already been in touch with the local judge. We've worked with her before. Because Jiles died under suspicious circumstances, and the investigation is ongoing, she didn't think it would be a problem. Also, turns out his phone was part of a DNR contract for conservation officers. Technically, it's an official phone."

Which Sam knew meant whatever Jiles did on the phone could not be considered privileged and confidential communication. The DNR had the right to look at whatever phone data they could retrieve.

"Good," Sam said. "Then the DNR will know which carrier to contact."

"Yes."

He told her he was heading back now, but that he needed to interview Holden Riggins again. He was pretty certain he and Gray would be able to meet her at the casino docks by 1 p.m., if that worked. She needed to commandeer one of the department's boats.

Harju said she'd already reserved one, and hung up.

Then Sam stowed Gray and his gear and got behind the wheel.

"Another day in paradise," Sam said.

Gray seemed to agree.

CHAPTER 30

Cocoa, the half-miniature dachshund, rose out of his dog bed in the Vermilion Falls Motel. He sat on his rear haunches, staring at Berta's bed, whining.

Berta's breathing was interrupted by occasional snorts. For Cocoa, this was the sign of a new day and his opportunity to sniff canine calling cards and leave one of his own.

"Judas H. Priest," Berta finally said, awakening to Cocoa's whine. She knew what it meant, peeled off her covers, and glanced around the room for her slippers and coat.

The Vermilion Falls Motel had only one area to walk dogs. The rear parking lot was bordered by a 10-foot swath of weeds before it disappeared into dense woods. The start of a few trails wandered off through a mixed pine-and-birch forest. The patch of woods stretched for about an acre before it hit Bushman Street. Beyond Bushman the woods continued into wilderness, which is probably how the mangy coyote managed to conceal itself as it meandered through fields and trees, following the powerful scent of a dead rabbit.

Berta wore a long black winter jacket against the chill, hanging over her pajamas to mid-calf. She'd slipped on her tennis shoes before leading Cocoa behind the motel. There were a few cars in the lot. Turning around a large, red GMC pickup truck, she was just about ready to let Cocoa off leash—a minor violation of Vermilion Falls's leash laws, which Cocoa appreciated—when she noticed movement at the tree edge.

Cocoa noticed the movement too. He strained against Berta's leash, his spine hair bristling.

"Cocoa. Cocoa!" Berta said, catching a glimpse of a ragged coyote. Half the animal's fur was in clumps. A bad case of mange, Berta guessed. There were bare spots up and down its flank, and its tail looked more opossum than coyote. The poor creature looked like it hadn't eaten in weeks.

When Cocoa finally caught sight of the animal, he tried to charge, barking like a banshee.

The coyote took two wobbly steps forward, curling its awful lips into a growl.

That's when Berta noticed the half-eaten rabbit, its entrails spread behind the coyote's two front paws.

The animal's fangs were covered by a thin layer of foam.

Berta backed up, which appeared to assuage the coyote.

Cocoa kept straining against the leash, the hair on his spine stiff as a razorback.

Then the coyote suddenly went slack.

The diseased animal with the foaming mouth, and the scene of carnage, was startling.

"Cocoa," Berta said, pulling the small dog back. "Do you want to be that animal's next meal?"

As Berta retreated, the coyote continued to waver. It twitched, she thought. There was no other word for it. Berta had gone to school with a girl who suffered from epilepsy. Occasionally, the girl had seizures. The coyote's sudden agitation reminded Berta of her old schoolmate.

After the tremor passed, the coyote turned in an agitated circle and fell down.

Rabies? Berta wondered.

In the movie version of *To Kill a Mockingbird,* Gregory Peck encountered a rabid dog, awkward and menacing, pacing down the center of the street. It was foaming at the mouth like this coyote. Rabid dogs were dangerous. The disease made them crazy aggressive, biting anything that moved, infecting whatever they managed to nip. Rabid dogs had to be put down.

Berta backed up to the rear entry of the motel, her eyes fixed on the twitching, prone coyote. She coaxed Cocoa onto the gravel perimeter, where he quickly relieved himself. Then she retreated to the confines of the motel.

Remembering the danger of rabid animals and knowing others might take their dogs to the rear of the motel, Berta dialed 9-1-1.

By the time Deputy Sandy Harju arrived, there was no need to discharge her weapon. She took two steps off the curb into the surrounding weeds and grass and could see the scruffy coyote laying quiet on the ground. It had the flaccid stillness of death. To be sure, she watched for breathing, staring at the coyote's flanks, but they were still.

The entrails of a rabbit, partially eaten, lay in front of the coyote's muzzle. The coyote had a bad case of mange. Its jaws appeared locked open. A thin layer of white foam coated its incisors. Clearly, it was an unhealthy animal. But Harju had seen animals with severe mange, and while this case was bad, half of its body was still covered in fur. Harju doubted it had succumbed to mange.

The woman who had called 9-1-1 thought it was rabies. Rabies was easily transmitted through bites by infected, maddened animals, and there was no telling how long this animal had been sick, or who or what it might have encountered. If this was a case of rabies, they would need to let people in Vermilion Falls know. The animal had to be tested.

She returned to her cruiser, took out her cell phone, found the Northland Animal Clinic, and dialed Phil Wirta, a local veterinarian.

Within 15 minutes, Dr. Wirta drove his truck around the north side of the motel, heading for the rear parking lot. There were three reasons it had only taken Phil Wirta 15 minutes to respond to Deputy Harju's call.

First, rabies in a coyote this near town was a potential public health hazard. If it was rabies, which Dr. Wirta doubted, they would need to issue a public notice, warning everyone in the area about the disease. He would also need to see if it cropped up elsewhere. If animals began acting crazy, he'd be a first responder.

Second, he was heading out to Art Calvin's place, south of Vermilion Falls. Art's feeder calves had a bad case of diarrhea and needed the vet's attention. The motel was on the way, more or less.

Finally, Sandy Harju had been one year behind Phil Wirta at Vermilion Falls High. They had always been friendly, in a casual sort of way. Any time that casual friendliness might have evolved into something more interesting, one or both of them were involved. Phil remembered one instance when he'd borrowed his parent's 24-foot Bennington pontoon boat. He'd been accepted to veterinarian school in the Cities and wanted to celebrate. Their group involved a dozen kids, including Sandy Harju, who had been invited by Kent, one of Phil's buddies. At one point, Phil and Sandy found themselves in conversation. He couldn't remember what they talked about, but he remembered the *feeling* of the conversation.

Kent was married now, with a kid. But Sandy Harju wasn't.

In a small community like Vermilion Falls, people—especially young people of a certain age (which Phil and Sandy were)—paid attention to who was available and who was not. Phil had heard two vet techs talking about Sandy Harju's social status, which was now, like him, single and unaffiliated. Phil Wirta was incredibly busy with his veterinarian practice. But is anyone ever too busy for romance? Especially when it involves a smart, beautiful woman in uniform?

As Phil drove up and parked, he confirmed what he remembered about Sandy in uniform. She was leaning against her cruiser, standing in sunlight, dressed in a policeman's jacket and squinting at him.

"Sandy," Phil said, getting out of his truck and nodding.

"Hi, Phil," Sandy said.

While he had always been interested in Sandy, for the moment he was more concerned about his professional duties. "Got a nasty looking dead coyote?" he said.

"Over here in the weeds. One of the motel guests was walking her dog this morning and interrupted it. Sounds like it was feeding on a rabbit and then just keeled over and died. It doesn't look healthy, that's for sure."

When Phil got near enough, Sandy extended her hand and they shook, professional enough, but both of them aware of the touch.

Sandy turned and started back toward the coyote with Phil beside her.

Phil approached the animal, stopping a few feet short. What he noticed first was the gutted rabbit. Clearly the coyote had been feeding. Phil also noticed unusual rigidity.

"How long ago was it called in?" Phil said.

"About 30 minutes," Sandy said.

"And the woman who called it in. The coyote was alive when she first saw it?"

"That's what she said."

The rigidity could have been rigor mortis, but rigor took longer than 30 minutes to settle in an animal's body. The coyote's stiffness was peculiar. Its jaw was stiff and partially open. He noticed the froth along the gums and teeth. Phil kneeled for a closer look, but he was careful not to touch anything.

"Hmm," he said, thinking.

"What?" Sandy said.

"I can definitely check it for rabies," he said. "Just to be sure. That foam around the mouth could be a sign of infection. But it looks to me more like poisoning. Possibly strychnine?"

"Strychnine?"

Phil nodded. "Maybe," he said. "Did you talk to the manager?"

"She's working up some signage to keep people away from the area."

Phil looked down the parking lot. "I can take care of these remains. I'd have her check along the back here and see if she finds anything else dead. Check into the edge of the trees too."

"Okay," Sandy said.

"Did she say anything about motel staff putting out strychnine baits for coyotes?"

Sometimes, Phil knew, farmers and ranchers used strychnine baits to rid themselves of chicken-stealing coyotes or foxes. But he couldn't imagine a motel would set out poison where a guest's dog might find it.

"No," Sandy said. "That'd be crazy."

She was using the same logic as Phil. Phil remembered that about her. They had an AP history class together, and she had always struck him as smart. And beautiful.

"It won't take me long to find out," Phil said.

"About rabies?"

"Rabies or strychnine, or some other kind of poison. This animal looks to me like it was poisoned. And if that rabbit is poisoned, which I'll also check, then these motel guests with dogs were damn lucky a coyote beat them to it."

"Who would put a poisoned rabbit back here?"

Phil shook his head. "No idea. Doesn't make sense."

He turned and walked back to his truck. He opened up a side panel and found a box of surgical gloves, pulling two from the pack. Then he turned to another panel and pulled down a plastic petri dish with a top and a long stick with a cotton swab on its end.

When Phil returned with the petri dish and swab, Sandy said, "Hey, I remember those. From Miss Tillapaugh's biology class."

Phil smiled. "I remember."

Sandy smiled back. Her reference to their shared high school days made both of them feel something more than casual acquaintance.

Phil spent the next 5 minutes getting a sample of the foam from the coyote's gums and teeth. Then he retrieved two large black plastic leaf bags. He used his gloved hands to carefully insert the coyote in one of the bags. In the other he stowed what was left of the rabbit. Then he used his boot to scrape over the earth where remnants of the dead animal's saliva had leached into the soil. He did the same thing to the soil where the rabbit's entrails had been pulled out and devoured.

Sandy was impressed by his thoroughness.

When Phil turned to Sandy, he thought he saw her look away. Interesting.

"Just tell the manager she needs to search through the rest of this back lot and make sure there aren't any more dead rabbits," Phil reminded her. "Or anything else dead, for that matter."

Sandy nodded. "How long before we get the results?"

"We use a lab in Eveleth. They'll fast-track it if I ask them. But I won't be able to run it over until I finish this house call. We should have it by noon."

Sandy had to get out to the White Pine Marina and talk to Jim Aho, Holden Riggins's boss. Then she needed to drive over to Arrowhead Marina to commandeer one of the department's speed boats. She was going to pick up Sam and Gray at the casino docks around 1. Fortunately, the marinas were near each other.

"I can run them over, if you help me load those bags into the cruiser's trunk and give me that dish."

"That'd speed it up," he said.

Phil loaded the specimens into the cruiser's trunk.

"Tell them Dr. Wirta needs the results ASAP, given the potential threat to public safety," he said.

He gave her the directions to the lab. Sandy recognized it as the same lab used by the medical examiner. Phil confirmed it, and then returned to his truck, where he lowered and locked the side panels.

All the while he was thinking about how he could approach the subject of a date. He'd had girlfriends, but he had always felt awkward about first dates. He made sure the rear of his truck was secure, and then he climbed into the cab and started the engine.

"Thanks, Phil," Sandy said.

"I'll ring you with the results as soon as I get them," Phil said, smiling out the open passenger side window.

Ask her, you idiot, he thought. But he felt his face flush, so he turned away.

Then he backed out of his parking place and turned the truck toward Art Calvin's place, where he needed to tend to feeder calves with diarrhea.

You are such a moron.

Deputy Harju and the motel manager scoured the rear grounds but found nothing else that appeared dangerous or deadly. Then the deputy got into her cruiser and punched in the address for the

Vermilion County lab in Eveleth. Twenty minutes, according to her app. Plenty of time.

She used her console radio to call it into the station, letting them know about the dead coyote and rabbit, and that she was running the samples over to the county lab for testing.

"The vet thought it looked like poison, more than rabies," Harju said. "But we'll know in a couple of hours. Over."

"Copy that," the dispatcher said. "Over and out."

Deputy Joe Haman sat on a stretch of highway between Tower and Ely, his radar gun pointed down the lonely road. The radar gun was off. He didn't want to be bothered with any pullovers, but he needed to appear occupied. He had just heard Deputy Harju's call on his cruiser's radio, and now he needed to think.

That goddamn mutt dodged a bullet, Joe thought. And when the lab finished its analysis, there were going to be questions about the strychnine. He reminded himself there were always going to be questions about the strychnine. He had expected it. There was no way anyone could tie him to the bait or the poison. He had been careful. Later, now that he thought about it, he might suggest the coyote could have carried the poisoned bait from some nearby ranch to the rear of the motel. Maybe carried it from a residence, for that matter, where someone had set it out because they were afraid a coyote could take their fuckin' Shih Tzu. Or a house cat.

For now, Sam Rivers's wolf dog had gotten lucky. But he couldn't stay lucky forever.

Earlier, at the station, Joe Haman had overheard Sam Rivers's request for another interview with the perp, Holden Riggins. That meant Rivers would be busy in interrogation room 2, and Sandy Harju was on her way to Eveleth. He didn't know where either of them would be later in the day. But he knew, at least for now, neither of them were anywhere close to the truth.

CHAPTER 31

The two men sat across from each other for the third time in as many days. Gray sat beside Sam, but he was looking at Holden. When Holden reached out his hand, Gray came out of his sit, approached, and sniffed with a tail wag.

Holden rubbed Gray's head and said, "Progress."

"Apparently, you've passed the smell test."

"Same to you," Holden said to Gray.

After reading the ME report, Sam wanted to ask Holden about watercourses on the east end of Lake Vermilion. The previous day, his interviews with the fish biologists confirmed Holden's suspicion that the walleye fish stocks in both Crane Lake and Vermilion were down. Sam could have confirmed Holden's hunches, but he was interested in watching Holden's reaction to some key details in the ME report.

"We received the ME report on Charlie Jiles," Sam said. "Turns out he drowned sometime Thursday afternoon. And not where they found him."

Holden appeared surprised.

"Where?" Holden said.

"Not sure," Sam said. "Your cabin's on Vermilion and you've been fishing the place most of your life. And netting too." Sam was referring to whitefish, but, of course, there was also the illegal netting from seven or eight years ago. "I'm guessing you know the lake pretty well."

Holden shrugged. "You get a feel for a place, living on it. I know it as good as anyone, I guess."

"Turns out CO Jiles had leaf particulate in his lungs. The medical examiner thinks he died at the mouth of a creek or river."

Holden again appeared surprised. If he had known about the location, he was doing a good job feigning ignorance. Or he was a good actor.

"Could be a lot of places, on Vermilion," Holden said, considering. "The lake is more than 40 miles long. More shoreline than any other lake in Minnesota. There are lots of streams and creeks."

"What about the east end?"

"Even if you cut it in half, there's lots of possibilities."

Sam nodded. "Maybe we can narrow it down."

"How?"

"Jiles was a conservation officer. The most likely scenario is he caught someone in the act of netting walleye and rather than get caught and serve time, they killed him."

Holden's face remained deadpan. "I guess," he said.

"So," Sam continued. "Is there a creek or river mouth on the east end that would be good for catching walleye?"

Holden looked away, thinking. Then, "Probably. Fish move. Especially walleye. They don't like light. This time of year, the water's getting clearer and colder. That means they usually go deep. Or at least deeper than they are in the summer. That place where they found me, where somebody set my net? Good walleye hole in the summer. This time of year, nothing but rocks."

Sam nodded. "I checked with the COs that pulled in your net. It was empty."

"Like I said, dumb place to set it, if you wanted to catch walleye."

"What if you were drunk?" Sam said. "Or high?"

Holden paused and glanced down. "People do stupid things when they're messed up. I know. I been there. If I wanted to net walleye," Holden said, "that spot where they found me would be the last place I'd do it. Even if I was dead drunk or sky high."

"You think a bottle and a half of whiskey would do it?"

"Wasn't mine," Holden said, quick, maybe a little edgy. "Didn't drink it."

They'd been over this, Sam knew. His prints were on the bottles and he appeared to be coming out of a deep drunk. They were still waiting for the results from his blood and urine tests, which should be definitive.

"If Jiles died near a creek or river," Holden said, "that means he was moved, 'cause there's no creek or river near that shoreline off Temple."

"Maybe," Sam said. "If not there, anywhere nearby . . . some kind of watercourse entering Vermilion where you could find walleye, if you wanted to net them?"

"If it was me . . . and it wasn't . . . the only two places I can think, this end of the lake, with deep enough water to find walleye, this time of year, would be the Trout River and Smug-glers Creek."

Sam had noticed the Trout River on a map. It was at the end of a huge bay on the north side of Vermilion's east end, flowing about 50 yards west of the Trout Lake portage. That portage was one of the few mechanized portages into the Boundary Waters. It would be easy enough to check.

"Where's Smugglers Creek?" Sam said.

"Near my place. Across the water there. It's kinda hidden back in a big bay on the north side. The water usually clears this time of year, but creeks like the Smugglers stir up stuff coming out of the woods and cloud the water. It makes things darker, down below. There's lots of rocks at the end of Smugglers Creek, about 25 feet down."

"Good for walleye?"

"Yup. Especially this time of year. There are a few things about that spot. The first is the cloudy water. The second is food. Bugs and stuff. Worms. That stuff attracts minnows. The walleye hunt the minnows. It's like a supper club. But it's also hidden. Even with GPS it's hard to find. It's a big bay with a long scrubby island in the middle of it. Unless you know the creek's behind that island, you'd never see it. There's a little spit of land that comes out in front of the creek, making it hard to spot even if you know it's there." He paused, looking at Sam. Then he said, "That spit hid my net, when I was poachin'."

"You netted a lot of walleye there?"

"When I was doin' it," Holden said. "One of the best things about that spot was a narrow sand beach to one side of the creek flow. If you knew where to go, you could run your boat up onto it, tie off, and pull your net in from shore, where you're completely out of sight."

"What about the Trout River?"

"That'd be a good spot. I never did it there, 'cause there's too much traffic. The portage is right there and it's pretty busy. Not so much this time of year. It's a truck portage. But the truck stops hauling people after Labor Day. People still use it, though. To haul their boats into Trout. The other places I can think of, at least at this end of the lake, are all pretty open and busy. Pike River empties into Pike Bay. The Vermilion River, over by the Vermilion Dam. But there are cabins and a lot of traffic around those places. And people fish them this time of year. No way you could set nets in those places. You'd probably catch fish. Lots of fish. But you'd get caught."

The two men went back and forth for a while. But after considering all the possibilities, and remembering that the last known ping of a cell tower by Charlie Jiles's phone was in Tower, near the casino, at the east end of the lake, the most likely place to check was Smugglers Creek.

"Okay," Sam said. "We're going to go check on your place. While we're over there, we'll check out that creek."

CHAPTER 32

When Deputy Sandy Harju dropped off the samples at the county lab, they assured her they should have the results within the hour, and that they would forward them to the veterinarian, Dr. Phil Wirta. Protocol, they told her, since the vet had made the request. She sent a text to Phil to remind him to let her know, and then started out for Lake Vermilion.

Her first stop was the White Pines Marina, where she spoke face-to-face with Jim Aho about his part-time employee Holden Riggins. She also checked Riggins's truck, still parked at the marina. Aho's comments and Riggins's truck had been interesting, but she wasn't sure what to make of them. She needed to think about it.

At the Arrowhead Marina she found her boat, a speedy runabout, gassed and tied to the dock. As she started to untether the stern rope from the dock, her cell phone pinged. Deputy Joe Haman.

She had worked with Haman off and on since she'd been hired by the sheriff. For the most part she considered him a competent, experienced, and professional law enforcement officer. But she thought he had a practiced veneer. Occasionally, she'd sensed a different person beneath the skin, one with a nasty temper. But only a flash, before some part of him managed to rein it in.

Harju's sense of Joe Haman made her curious enough to research his time overseas. She'd found a couple of public reports of Deputy Haman's use of excessive force. She decided it wasn't her place to say anything because she assumed the sheriff knew about the incidents. Besides, she wasn't the kind of colleague to gossip about a fellow officer—to the sheriff or anyone else in the department.

Still, it made her wonder about Deputy Haman, and convinced her she should keep their interactions professional.

Like now, when it would be unprofessional to ignore her colleague's call.

Besides, she wondered what he wanted.

"Deputy Harju," she said, picking up.

"It's Joe," he said. "A veterinarian just stopped by looking for you. Something about it not being rabies?"

"Oh, okay. I'll get back to him."

"Rabies sounded important, so I checked the rosters and told him you were patrolling that stretch of highway between Eveleth and Defiance, rest of the week, including tonight, if he needed to speak with you in person."

He's fishing, Harju thought.

Harju told Deputy Haman about the dead rabbit and coyote behind the motel, and how the vet thought it could be rabies.

"That doesn't sound good," Haman said. "If it wasn't rabies, what was it?"

"I'm guessing a lethal case of mange, given how bad the coyote looked. I'll text the vet and see what he thinks."

"Well, keep us posted," Haman said. "In case we need to alert the public."

"Will do," Harju said, and hung up.

Harju wondered if there was more to this call than reporting the vet's visit. Unlike some of her other male colleagues, she had never sensed a scintilla of physical interest from Deputy Joe Haman. If she had to guess, she would have said women weren't his thing. Again, like her sense of Haman's nasty temper, it was a suspicion she kept to herself.

After CO Jiles had been found along that empty stretch of Temple Island, Harju and Haman had been co-investigators of the scene. She had thought then he lacked the kind of intense interest he normally committed to crime scenes. When she remembered how he had been on Vermilion, and then later—awkward and aloof, she thought—and now, with the strange phone call . . . it made her wonder if something was up with Deputy Haman. Though she couldn't imagine what.

Sandy Harju was born and raised in northern Minnesota. She knew boats. It took her only moments to have the 150 HP Merc full throttle, skimming across Vermilion's waters, heading toward the casino docks. The trip normally took 15 minutes. But because the day was calm and Vermilion's surface glass, she made it in less than 12.

Sam and Gray were waiting on the dock. They watched Deputy Harju's approach. She decelerated at just the right moment, and then steered the boat into its mooring like a hand fitting into a glove.

Sam greeted her and held the runabout's gunwale.

"Okay, Gray," he nodded.

Sandy Harju stepped over and made space for the hybrid to jump into the boat.

"Good boy," she said.

Gray's tail wagged.

"He loves boats," Sam said. "But you've got to watch him. Otherwise, he'll jump in the lake."

As Sam pushed the boat away from the dock and jumped in, Harju's cell phone went off.

"Hello," Harju said.

"Sandy?"

"Yeah. Phil," Sandy said.

"The lab phoned with the results. Not rabies."

"I heard."

"Oh, yeah. Your office was on the way back to mine. I mentioned it to one of your colleagues. Dudley Do-Right."

Sandy smiled. "Deputy Joe Haman."

"Yeah. That guy."

"So, what was it?"

"That's the interesting part. Strychnine. That rabbit was filled with it."

"Strychnine!" Harju said.

Sam was sitting in the passenger side chair, near enough to overhear Harju's phone conversation and wonder.

"It was in a rabbit," she said to Sam. "Behind the motel."

"Yes. The rabbit," Phil said.

"Oh, I know," said Harju. "I was just telling my colleague about it."

Sam looked at Harju and said, "Ask him if that's common, to still use strychnine in baits?"

Harju asked, and Phil explained that strychnine today was commonly used as a pesticide. He never saw baits doused with it, the way they used to kill some predators.

"Interesting," Sam said, after Harju told him.

But it only took a moment for Sam to guess the poison was meant for Gray. The strychnine made him wonder about Monday's flat tire. Definitely suspicious.

Dr. Phil Wirta had spent the morning dosing Art Calvin's feeder calves. He had stopped by Deputy Sandy Harju's office because he told himself the next time he spoke with her he wasn't going to be stupid twice.

"What are you doing for dinner?" Phil said.

The offer suddenly shifted the conversation in a way Sandy Harju appreciated. Wanted. She was aware of Sam's presence. Even though he seemed to be respectfully not paying attention, he was close enough to hear everything.

She turned her head away and said, "Tonight?"

"Yeah," Phil said. "It's Wednesday night. Half-priced bottle of wine night at Daisy's out on the lake."

"I've gotta work tonight," she said.

Phil paused, and said, "Some other night, then?"

"Definitely," she said.

Thinking of the time, Deputy Harju knew there was much to do before she headed out on patrol later this evening. "I'll call you," she said.

Again, it was abrupt, and she didn't want it to sound that way. Frankly, she hadn't dated anyone in a while, and the image of his warm brown eyes popped into her head. After seeing him at the motel and watching him look at her through the passenger side window, she'd had a few moments to think about it. She'd been right about his interest. And she'd recalled a conversation on a pontoon boat ride about five or six years ago. She remembered something intense, something she liked. She'd been there with one of his friends. And Phil had been involved, as she recalled. At least back then.

The preceding all happened so quickly she didn't have a chance to think of something better to say.

"Okay," Phil said. "I would really like to hear about your job sometime. Call me." And then he hung up.

Now it was Sandy Harju's turn to feel stupid.

Sam glanced in her direction and said, "Maybe we could get going."

She was pretty sure he'd heard both sides of the conversation.

"Of course," Harju said. She waited for Sam to get in the pilot's chair.

But Sam remained seated in the passenger side chair and said, "You aren't driving?"

"I figured you'd want to," Harju said.

Sam loved to drive, especially boats on big lakes like Vermilion. But if Harju drove, he could keep an eye on Gray and make sure he didn't try anything foolish like jumping out of the boat.

"I'll keep an eye on Gray," Sam said.

Sandy Harju smiled. "Well, I do like to drive."

"Do you know where you're going?"

"I got the coordinates from the sheriff," she said, turning on their GPS. The screen came on and displayed the path she'd taken from the marina to the casino docks.

"It tracks you even when it's off?" Sam said.

"I guess," Harju said. "The GPS is new. Must be a feature." She plugged in her coordinates and the map refreshed.

CHAPTER 33

Holden Riggins's cabin was on the back side of Temple Island. It was a 20-minute boat ride from the casino docks.

Because of the cold, they hunkered down behind the boat's windshield.

Sam held tight to Gray's leash.

"Tell me about the coyote!" Sam said, over the engine noise.

"Some lady walking her dog found it."

"It was in the dog walk area?"

Harju nodded.

It made Sam wonder.

Harju quickly shifted to getting the subpoena for CO Jiles's cell phone records. The judge had agreed. Harju expected to have an electronic copy of his last two years' calls emailed to her by end of day.

She had also visited Holden's workplace, White Pines Marina, and this time spoken in person with Holden's boss, Jim Aho. He had basically reiterated what he'd told her over the phone. Holden was a model employee. Holden also owned a vintage Ford pickup truck he kept at the marina. Jim Aho found the keys in Holden's work area and Harju searched his truck. It was clean and well-kept. The only odd thing was a miniature plastic Buddha sitting on the dash. Harju had snapped a photo of the Buddha and showed it to Sam.

Sam shrugged. Holden didn't seem like someone who valued religious icons. But maybe it was like a plastic Jesus. Or maybe Ruth Walker had given it to him, so he was attached to it.

Sam was more interested in seeing who Jiles had phoned, the last day or two he was alive.

Sam was getting a feeling for the young deputy. She was smart, efficient, and could manage in a morning what it would have taken most deputies an entire day. He would have to put in a good word with the sheriff, though he knew the sheriff already had a high opinion of her.

After nearly 20 minutes, they turned into Holden's bay. They could see a narrow sand beach at the end of the bay, with a small cabin set just yards behind the beach, and a larger structure behind it. There was a dock to the right. Harju guided the boat toward the dock and, once they were near enough, Sam jumped out and tied the boat off, fore and aft.

Gray didn't wait for an invitation. He could see the lake's bottom rose gradually toward the sandy shore, an ideal place for a swim. In less than 10 seconds he was in the water, chest deep, oblivious of the cold, hunting for small fish.

Deputy Harju grinned.

The first thing Sam noticed about the property was the beach. Beaches were rare on Vermilion, especially beaches with clean, brown sand. Similarly, clean sandy bottoms that dropped gradually to deep water, more than 30 yards out, were also unusual.

The cabin was small and old, and from the outside appeared weathered but well-kept. Sam guessed it had a small room with a kitchen and two back bedrooms, probably divided by a thin plywood partition. Wide front windows opened onto the lake, facing the northwest. It had to be a cold view in winter. Cold, white, and icy.

As they approached the cabin, Sam imagined dented pots and pans hanging on the back wall, beside a propane gas range and small gas fridge. Working in wild places, he had visited many remote cabins. If Holden's was like others, there'd be a couple of wooden chairs in front of a simple wooden table, bordering a spare space, with cheap furnishings and two narrow rear bedrooms with barely enough room to step around threadbare mattresses.

The cabin's exterior was weathered log siding. Back behind the cabin they saw what Sam assumed was the work shed Holden had told him about earlier, where he had mended his whitefish net. The shed was sheathed in faded gray cedar siding and looked like a more recent construction. And it was bigger. Like a small barn.

Sam stepped up to the side door of the cabin and reached under the step to a ledge, where Holden had told him he would find the key. Then he stepped up to the door's plain beige-curtained windows, inserted the key, turned the lock, and opened it.

Sam stood for a moment.

Behind him Sandy Harju said, "Wow."

The place was nothing like Sam imagined. Its interior was carefully crafted, neat, clean, and, in an odd way, incredibly functional but also stylish. Not stylish, exactly. More like functional feng shui. The place had a feel.

There was a table in front of the windows. It was fashioned out of smooth pine. The table looked new and of simple construction, but the stain gave it the appearance of a beautiful, aged patina, the same color as the knotty pine interior walls. There were three chairs around the table—same wood, same color. There was a woven beige mat in the room's center, in front of the windows. The back wall, facing the work shed and woods beyond, had a stainless steel refrigerator, gas stove, sink, and granite countertop. The black granite had swirls and patterns with periodic flecks of gold, like some interstellar cloud with embedded planets and stars. There was a shelf below a pair of curtained windows. On it sat several different spices, including salt and pepper, but also red pepper flakes, paprika, onion powder, garlic powder, and an assortment of other spices. They were all carefully stacked, in three neat rows, arranged alphabetically.

The living space opened to a rear wall. The wall was paneled with those same golden knotty pine boards. Their surface was uneven, and its finish illuminated its knots and beautiful grains. The wall caught the sunlight spilling into the room through the front windows.

There were several shelves built into the wall, each of them filled with books.

"Not what I expected," Sam said. "I don't remember Holden being much of a reader. But then, neither was I, as a kid."

"Maybe he has a girlfriend. Maybe these are hers?"

Maybe, Sam thought. He'd have to ask Holden. Now he had more questions. Better, he thought; he'd ask Ruth Walker.

On the far-right side of the wall of books was a door, made out of the same wood as the wall. Sam stepped over and opened it into one spacious bedroom.

Basically, the cabin contained two rooms: the larger living space with a kitchen against the back wall and a large bedroom. There were wooden end tables on either side of the bed, with what appeared to be cast-iron lamps. The lamps, like the rest of the cabin, were stylish, clean, and dusted. The bed frame was constructed of cedar, but instead of having a smooth, varnished surface, the wood had been hewn with an axe. Blade marks gleamed over its surface. It had the texture of a lake's surface in a light breeze.

"Nice," Harju said behind him.

They returned to the main living area and Sam walked over to the table, staring out into the bay and then across into the wider part of the lake that stretched all the way to Trout Lake Portage. He peered out the window. It was a beautiful view. The weather was cold, but the air was still and the lake glass. Not yet frozen. It wouldn't be long, Sam knew, but for now, there was still time. He watched Gray knee-deep in beach water, staring beneath the surface with intensity. The small fish were entertaining him.

Out back they followed a flagstone walk to the work shed. Holden had told him the same key opened the cabin and the shed. He was going to use it, but as he approached, he could see the door jamb splintered.

"Uh-oh," Sam said.

Harju saw the same thing and said, "Break-in?"

"Looks like it."

The door was snug but opened with a slight push.

Sam and Harju walked into the room.

Atop two sawhorses in the center of the room rested a birch-bark canoe, almost finished. Its bark seemed to gleam under the overhead light.

"Look at that," Harju said.

"We need to try and figure out if anything's missing," Sam said.

"If I broke into the place, I'd steal that canoe."

"Good thing it wasn't you."

They both took a moment to admire the canoe. A lot of work had gone into it.

The rest of the barn also surprised them. The place had a larger footprint than the cabin. Its clapboard exterior had the same weathered appearance. Its outside made you think its inside would be rough-hewn, oil stained, and messy.

There were large windows without curtains in each of the walls. Overhead, two huge skylights were cut into the roof, the sunlight spilling into the room. There was a chest-high workbench that skirted the length of two walls. Numerous tools were positioned over the bench. In the opposite corner, there was a large built-in wooden trunk.

Sam remembered Holden's dad's garage. Mr. Riggins had been a plane mechanic at the airbase in Eveleth. One side of his garage contained a workbench brimming with scattered screwdrivers, wrenches, hammers, pliers, nuts, bolts, boxes of nails, elbow brackets, always two or three half-filled packs of cigarettes, and a minifridge filled with beer. And there was the locked cupboard on the back wall, above the bench, in which the boys had discovered the .45, liquor, and *Playboys*.

Holden's workspace also contained peg boards and wall shelves, but everything on them was organized by tool type and size. And the rough wooden counters beneath them were high enough to work while standing, and clean. There were no wayward nuts or bolts or nails or brackets out of place. The entire space looked like it had been apportioned by an engineer with OCD.

While the inside perimeter of the place was surprising, it all paled in comparison to the canoe, sitting in the room's center.

"I can't see anything missing," Sam said.

Deputy Harju walked over to the canoe again and bent down to have a closer look. She paused, almost like she was looking at a piece of art in a museum, and then ran her hand along its smooth surface. The canoe's internal skeleton had been molded out of thin wooden strips. The gunwales were straight and true, and the bow and stern curved up like stylish letters, or a symbol in an ancient script. The pieces of bark that made up the outside of the canoe were perfectly white and fit together as though they had been engineered to the micrometer. There were patterns in the bark and wood—natural patterns that accentuated the piece and, despite the perfection of its craftsmanship, gave the canoe an organic, almost living appearance and feel. It was a beautiful piece of work, and except for one small edge of the gunwale near the bow and stern, it was almost done.

Sam walked over to the built-in trunk in the corner. It was large and rough-hewn and had a top that could be easily lifted.

Inside, Sam found netting gear and the tools and parts used to repair them, but no nets.

"Someone came back for another net," Sam said. "Holden said he had three. One he set on Thursday, late. His whitefish net. Another was set for walleye, out near his legal net."

Harju walked over to the opened trunk. "And the third one's gone," she said. "You think he set a third one somewhere else?"

Sam thought about it. But the location, timing, and several other details about where two of Holden's nets were set didn't make sense. "I guess it's possible," Sam said. "Just doesn't add up."

"You mean the location and timing," Harju said.

She was smart. "Yeah," Sam said.

They had seen enough to share with the sheriff, who Sam remembered had worried about Holden's place. Sam would need to let him know his suspicions were justified.

They were surrounded by woods and water, and the only destination anchoring the narrow cove was Holden's dock, beach, and cabin. Holden's place would be easy to break into, just about any time, day or night.

Back in the boat, Sam got ready to untie from the dock and push off.

A wet Gray was getting into the boat.

"The place is like a monk's cottage," Sam said.

"That's it," Harju said. "I was trying to think. The first time I saw him, I thought he was a little rough. Like, scuzzy."

"I know what you mean. When you look at him, this isn't what you imagine for his cabin."

"Or shed," Harju said, a word that didn't describe what they'd walked into. She had re-seated herself in the captain's seat. Sam untied them and then pushed off and stepped into the boat.

Gray's tail wagged. Sam rubbed his head and said, "Now you might have a chance to lend a hand." He turned and said, "Holden gave me the GPS coordinates for Smugglers Creek. But even with GPS he said it wasn't an easy place to find."

Harju entered the GPS coordinates into the boat's navigation system, turned on the engine, and backed away from the dock.

In a moment they were full speed ahead, planed out level on the glassy water, racing toward Smugglers Creek.

CHAPTER 34

Deputy Joe Haman had made the call to Harju on his way to the casino. He was scheduled to do another drive-by circle of the lot, make an appearance, and sit for a time near the entrance in an obvious display of law enforcement vigilance. Then he needed to head over to the remote stretch of highway between Tower and Ely, where he would bag a couple of speeders, just to make his numbers look good and to assure Chief Deputy Barnes he was doing his job.

But *rabies* made him grin.

The veterinarian was young. Joe had noticed the vet's ring finger was ringless. There was no way to tell if he was already romantically involved. But a young guy like that, a fairly decent specimen, reasonably employed . . . Joe was pretty sure the vet's in-person visit to the office was because he'd been on the hunt. For Harju. Joe just hoped the vet kept his head up his ass and stayed too busy smelling Harju's tail to think twice about that coyote. If the vet was preoccupied with Harju, he might chalk up the mystery of the dead coyote to a severe case of mange.

Joe was well practiced in keeping his emotional cards close to his chest. When the veterinarian told him about what they'd found behind the motel, a wild coyote with possible rabies, Joe immediately understood Sam Rivers's mutt had dodged another bullet. But Joe kept cool and feigned concern.

For Joe, it was further evidence of Rivers's luck.

To be sure, he wasn't worried about the strychnine. If that vet determined it was poison, there was no way to tie it back to Joe. But poisoning behind the motel was much more suspicious than mange. And if Rivers thought about it, the idea the poison might have been meant for his mongrel didn't take a leap of insight. What Joe didn't like about uncovering strychnine was the way it might make Rivers cautious and careful, especially about his animal.

About the same time Joe was contemplating other ways to kill the dog, he spotted Rivers's Jeep. It was near the same spot as before, on the outskirts of the lot near the stand of red pines. The deputy drove by, slow, but didn't see any movement from inside the vehicle. Joe figured Rivers was in the casino, probably looking at video footage. Which meant his dog was asleep in the back seat.

Joe didn't stop. He was supposed to be cruising the lot, and that's what he did. He drove the lot twice, passing by the Jeep twice. But the dog never made an appearance.

This time Joe didn't have time to stop and sneak through the red pines. This time there was no point in hurling pinecones to harass the beast. For now, he would bide his time and carefully consider how to rid himself of the varmint, and the man who held its leash.

He pulled out of the lot and headed to his speed trap.

Deputy Joe Haman's cell phone buzzed. Or rather, the cell phone owned by his mother buzzed.

Joe counted five rings. Then it went dead.

He fished the phone out of his pack and examined the call history. "Unknown."

Phishing, marketing, or the poacher, he guessed. If it was the poacher . . .

But before he could finish his thought, his cell buzzed again. "Unknown." Somebody using *67 again. Had to be the poacher. He said he would call one last time.

Joe picked up.

Silence on the other end. Then, "Need to know," the voice said. Same voice. "Anyone around? Vermilion?"

To the best of Joe's knowledge, Sam Rivers was inside the casino, and Deputy Sandy Harju was monitoring a radar gun on the highway between Eveleth and Defiance. He had also overheard Chief Deputy Smith Barnes mention Rivers was visiting the sheriff tonight, to pay his respects to the new arrival.

"Clear," Haman said. "All day."

There was a pause, during which Joe wondered if the caller would hang up. The caller had gotten his information. If he wanted to keep the $2,000, all he needed to do was end the call. Joe didn't know the poacher. But if the man cheated him, Joe would track the man down and hurt him. Or kill him.

But the man finally said, "Two thousand. Big Bay reef." He gave Joe the GPS numbers. "Branch floating in the water, anchored to a line. It'll be there by 4."

Then the call ended.

Joe needed to head over to his lonely stretch of highway, where he could think. Technically, his shift was over at 4 p.m. If he got lucky with his radar, he could nab a couple of speeders by 3. Then he'd head over to the Arrowhead Marina, where he could commandeer one of the department's runabouts. If the chief deputy questioned him about the boat's use, he could tell him he wanted to take another look at the site near Temple Island where Charlie had been found. A hunch that didn't pan out.

Safely ensconced in his blind spot, Deputy Joe Haman aimed his radar gun toward the distant curve along the quiet highway. He waited less than 10 minutes before the radar picked up a Mustang coming round the bend—83 mph, 18 over the limit.

Joe smiled, started his cruiser's engine, waited until the Mustang sped by, and then turned on his lights and siren, pulling out after the scofflaw *like a muskie after baitfish.*

CHAPTER 35

Harju turned the boat north into a spacious bay. There was a narrow island in the rear middle of the bay, crested with scrub cedar, rimmed with brush-covered boulders, and surrounded by a trail of reeds stretching away from its shore on either side.

"Perfect smallmouth habitat," Harju said.

Sam agreed. "Holden mentioned that island. He said the creek's mouth was behind it, but you had to search for it."

Harju took another couple of minutes to turn around the west end of the island. Once they were behind it, there was a large stretch of water, maybe 100 yards to the mainland. They scanned the shore but saw nothing.

"The GPS says it's right here," Harju said.

From this vantage point, the shoreline appeared unbroken. "Move in closer," Sam said.

Harju slowed, turning the boat at an angle to the tree line. When they were 20 yards from shore, Sam noticed a floating branch, 40 yards down to the right. The lake's surface was still, but the branch was moving in a slow current. When Sam saw it, he looked farther down the shore and saw what looked like a fold in the trees and very small eddies across the lake's surface.

"Head over to that spot," Sam pointed.

Harju looked. "Where?"

He pointed to the floating tree branch.

As they neared the shore, a lip of land to the right seemed to separate from the shoreline behind it. It was an optical illusion. The land nearest the bay had the characteristic old cedars leaning out over the water. Behind the cedars rose a mature stand of red pines with one or two white pines towering overhead. It was one of Vermilion's iconic tree-lined shores.

But where the tall pines stopped, the trees to the left appeared smaller, scrubbier. The more they looked, the more it appeared there were two shorelines, noncontiguous. Sam pointed it out and Harju needed to blink, and peer again.

"It's like my depth perception is off," she said.

"Exactly. That's gotta be the mouth, back behind that mature stand of pines."

She angled the boat in that direction, but it wasn't until they were 30 yards off that they could clearly see the mouth of a slow-moving creek. Its entrance was maybe 10 yards across, but eddies in the current revealed water flow, coming out of the wilderness behind it. They saw a few leaves drift out of its mouth, turning slowly along the shoreline.

"There's that little beach," Sam said.

Harju looked but couldn't see it.

"To the left of the creek's mouth. It's tucked behind that spit of land. See the sand? It's like a 2- to 3-foot strip, between the overgrowth."

Harju, finally seeing it, said, "You want me to try and beach there?"

"Holden told me when he was netting, illegally, he would beach there, tether his boat to the bushes, and haul in his harvest in seclusion. Worth having a look, anyway."

"What exactly are we looking for?"

The truth was, Sam wasn't sure. "No idea," he finally said. "If this is where CO Jiles was struck and drowned, could be anything. Maybe nothing," Sam shrugged. "Pull in really slow. I want to have a look at that shoreline before you hit it."

Harju coaxed the boat to within 20 yards and put the motor in neutral. It was angled across the slow current, heading toward the inside spit of land with a speed and trajectory that should bring the boat's nose slowly onto a narrow strip of sand, providing the creek's current didn't catch it and turn the boat's prow.

Sam was standing in front, staring down into the water toward the closing shore. The water was cloudier, darker here, from the soil and particles carried down by the creek. When he glanced toward the narrow beach, he thought he saw a groove in the sand, the print from a boat's bow.

"Can you hold it?" Sam said. "Just hold it here?"

Harju slipped the throttle in reverse, and they could feel the engine's prop kick in, just enough to counteract its forward drift. But the reverse in the current brought them back faster than expected. She turned the wheel to compensate, but the combination of being pushed by the current and angling the boat's motor brought the side of the boat into the nearby overhanging brush.

Sam kneeled and grabbed a thick piece of brush. "Just cut it," he said. "Cut the engine."

Harju turned the ignition key and the motor died. Stillness.

Gray was peering over the side. He was excited, like he wanted to get into the water, but the brush angling out over the boulders and lake edge prevented it.

Sam was near the bow, still holding onto a clump of leaves and branches. But he wanted to have a closer look at that small spit of sand.

"Can you hold us here?" Sam said.

Harju moved to Sam's side and grabbed a handful of branches. Once he was certain the boat was secure, he stepped into the bow. From here he had a clear view of the sand, 10 feet ahead of them. "Somebody's been here," he said. "You can see a couple of places where somebody pushed up onto the sand with a boat keel."

"Jiles you think?"

"Who knows," Sam shrugged. "Could have been Holden, for all I know. Holden and Jiles. Or a complete stranger. But it's recent. Otherwise, the bow print would be washed away." Sam scanned the brush on either side of the sand. There were two or three places where the branches were bunched or broken. "And it looks like someone tied off a boat on that brush."

"Is there something behind that sand beach? Like a trail?"

Sam was already scanning. "Nothing I can see."

"So why tie up here?"

"Good question. Holden said it was a great place to bring in your net. You could anchor your boat here and if you set the net so its end came into the shore, you could haul it in unseen."

Harju looked around. "I can see that. You're really hidden back here."

Gray was leaning over the side, looking for a place to jump. Sam noticed and told him to stay. He didn't want the big hybrid going into the water, where it would be difficult to get him back in the boat. But the command wasn't easing Gray's interest. He whined and leaned out farther over the gunwale, his nose stretching toward an overhanging bush. Clearly, something had his attention.

Sam scanned the shoreline. Down near the water line, it looked like a piece of cloth was stuck in the branches, half of it floating in the lake.

Sam stepped over to Gray's side. "What'd you find, buddy?" Gray whined and stretched, but the cloth was out of reach. "Can you pull us in a little closer?"

Harju pulled until the boat's gunwale was overhung by branches. It was enough. Sam reached down, caught a piece of the material and pulled it free of the bush. When he held it up, its lower half soaked, he said, "it looks like torn underwear." The underwear had been white or off-white. Now it was stained dull gray by Vermilion's water, or the elements, or both. The elastic band was narrow.

"Women's underwear," he said.

There was thicker material in the crotch, and more stains, some darker. The waist band and both leg holes were torn, so the piece of clothing hung at an unnatural angle, one long strand of material hanging down.

"Gross," Harju said. "Where in the hell did those come from?"

Sam glanced upstream. "Could have floated down the creek, I guess."

Harju glanced upstream and said, "I can't see anything up there but dense trees and brush."

"Maybe it was dropped out of a boat?"

None of it made sense. If you pitched underwear out here, what would you replace it with? And why was it torn? Harju had no idea. Sam wondered if it might have involved hurried passion, but he kept the idea to himself.

"I don't know," Sam said. "But it was someone big." Sam pinched the thin elastic waist. He turned it and squinted at a tag. "Hanes. 9 2x."

"Definitely a bigger woman," Harju said.

Sam could see the clothing was for a bigger woman, though he had no idea how big.

"I'm a five," Harju said.

Sam glanced over, considering.

Harju shrugged and said, "Just sayin'. To give you an idea."

"Good to know," Sam said. So probably twice the size of Harju, he thought.

He'd double-check with Carmel tonight, guessing she was a six.

When he turned the underwear around, Harju said, "Is that a bloodstain on it?"

There was a double panel in the crotch, most of it stained a dark brown. Darker than Vermilion's stain. Sam recognized it as the color of blood set into cloth. "Maybe," he said. "At least it looks too light for excrement."

"Oh, gross." Harju's nose scrunched at the thought of it.

Sam was remembering the ME report. CO Jiles, before he died, had sex with someone. "Did you read the autopsy?"

"You mean the part about Jiles having sex with a menstruating woman?"

"Yeah. That part."

"You think these came from that woman?"

"Maybe," Sam shrugged. "The last cell tower Jiles pinged was in Tower. The whole east end of the lake would ping there. So, he could have been here."

They both thought about it.

"Those panties are pretty dirty, but they look new enough," Harju said.

"I don't know," Sam said. "Having sex out here? And then, why were they torn?"

Harju considered it. Then, "Maybe they couldn't wait?"

Sam had already wondered the same thing.

"I mean," she said, "don't get me wrong. That's not . . . my kind of thing." She blushed. "But I could see how someone might consider this place hidden enough for that kind of activity."

"And urgent passion could account for why the underwear was torn," Sam said.

Sandy Harju shrugged. "Could be."

Sam appreciated the young deputy's candor and perspective. "We have any evidence bags in here?" he said, still holding the underwear. "Something to put it in?"

"Should be something in the glove compartment."

Sam turned to the compartment and opened it. He pulled out a gallon plastic bag and managed to unseal its top. Then he dropped the soiled underwear inside it.

"Okay," Sam said. "You can let go."

Harju did and the boat slowly caught the creek's current, turned, and began to drift down the shoreline.

"I wonder if there's enough of a stain here to get a smear and test it?" Sam said. "At least to see if it's a match to what was found on Jiles."

Harju looked at the baggie and said, "I can run it over to the Eveleth lab as soon as we dock. All we can do is ask."

"Good idea," Sam said. He looked away, thinking. "Didn't you search the bottom of the area where Jiles was found with some kind of newfangled video camera?" Sam said.

"Yeah," Harju said. "An underwater video camera. With lights. Pretty sweet. But bulky."

"I was planning on heading over to the sheriff's house this afternoon. Bring him up-to-date and say hello to the new arrival. But now I'm thinking, given what we've found, our time might be better spent using that camera to check out the bottom here."

"We can do that," she said. "After I drop these at the lab, I could go into the office to get the equipment. But I'm supposed to be on patrol tonight."

Sam asked about the patrol, and Harju said it was routine—all the deputies needed to do occasional evening patrols, and this evening it was her turn to be out on the highway between Vermilion Falls and Defiance.

"Okay," Sam said, checking his watch. "I'll speak with the sheriff and let him know what we're doing. Let's keep this between you and me. If anyone asks, you're still going out on patrol. That's a lonely stretch of highway and I doubt you'll be missed."

Harju nodded.

"While you're running those errands, I'll have another quick look at those casino tapes. You think you can meet me at the docks by 4?"

"Sure," Harju said. "But that means we'll be using the camera after dark."

"Will that work?" Sam said.

"Sure. The lights that come with it are pretty intense. Better bring some lights for up top."

"We can do that."

Deputy Harju thought about it. "Might be better if we had a bigger boat. I was anchored when I was at that other site off Temple Island. And there was plenty of sunlight. Here, there's current and it looks pretty deep."

The boat was outfitted with a depth finder. Sam turned on the boat's power and pressed the ON button for the depth finder.

They had been drifting with the current and were now 10–15 yards farther down the shoreline from where they'd pushed up to the shore. When the depth finder's screen came up and refreshed, Sam could see the bottom at 25 feet, a scraggly, boulder-strewn line. And there were fish.

"Wow," Sam said. "It's deep and I see fish. Lots of them."

Harju came over to look. "And it's getting deeper."

The bottom was definitely deepening. As the boat drifted they watched the numbers blink from 25 to 26.

Sam turned on the boat and maneuvered it against the current, moving back toward the center of the creek's mouth. "I'm curious about how quickly it drops off," he said.

Back at the mouth, the depth finder read just 6 feet.

"That's a pretty significant drop," Harju said.

"That's what Holden said. That's why it was good for walleye."

"I'll have to remember that," Harju said.

"Yup. I don't see a lot of fish here. But there were plenty back there."

Sam cut the engine and it started to drift again, very slowly with the current.

"This could be a problem," Harju said.

"What?"

"Anchoring here could get dicey. Especially in the dark. If we can't find a hold or it's too deep, we'll need to keep the boat steady."

"We can do that," Sam said.

"But with lights?"

Sam could see the problem. If Harju was operating the camera equipment and he had his hand on the wheel, how could they use the lights?

"We need another set of hands," she said.

"And a bigger boat. With the equipment and another person moving around."

"In the dark," she said.

They both thought about it. Back at the Arrowhead Marina, the department only had access to three runabouts, this one the largest.

Sam thought about Holden's suspicions regarding law enforcement. For the time being, given what he'd discovered so far, he was inclined to keep the investigative work between him, the sheriff, and Deputy Harju.

"I'd rather not involve anyone else at the department, for the time being," Sam said, intentionally vague. "You're from around here. Do you know anyone with a pontoon who might be willing to let us borrow it? Might even be willing to help?"

Harju only took a moment to think about it. "I think so."

CHAPTER 36

Sam found an open wooded area off the casino parking lot where he could let Gray stretch his legs. Once in the woods, Sam phoned the sheriff, not really expecting him to pick up.

"Hey," Dean Goddard said. "How's it going?"

"It's going," Sam said. "How's fatherhood?"

"Ya know, I think I was born to be a father," Dean said. "I don't know if I've ever felt like this."

Sam thought he sounded a little shell-shocked. Maybe wistful. "That's a good thing," Sam said.

"It is. About all I can think about is how much I love this little guy, and how much I'm going to do for him. Him and his mom."

"How's mom?"

"Breastfeeding right now, which is why I answered. What's up?"

Sam wondered if he'd had a chance to look at the ME report. But the sheriff told him since John Michael was born, he hadn't looked at anything. Sam shared the medical examiner's suspicions about when and where Jiles died. He also told him about his interviews in Duluth, and his subsequent conversation with Holden, at least the part about where someone might set a net near a watercourse this time of year. There was the break-in at Holden's work shed, as well as the torn underwear near the mouth of Smugglers Creek. And they'd decided to return today, late afternoon, to use the video camera on the lake bottom, and see if they could surface anything.

On occasion the sheriff gave a voice nod . . . "Uh-huh." Once he said, "Interesting," without conveying a sense that it was interesting. Sam was sure he took it all in. But he could tell the sheriff's heart and mind had suddenly shifted, at least for the moment. Under the circumstances, Sam understood.

Sam also told him about the strychnine poisoning behind the motel. Given his flat tire and then the peculiar poisoning, Sam let the sheriff know he thought he was being targeted. He and Gray. The sheriff thought it was a distinct possibility and told Sam to watch his back. Sam reminded the sheriff it was all the more reason they definitely needed to keep the details of their investigation (especially what they were doing) to themselves: the sheriff, Sam, and Harju.

"And if anyone asks . . . even Smith Barnes . . . I'm visiting you tonight to bring you up to speed and welcome John Michael into the world."

The sheriff agreed.

Finally, Sam praised Deputy Sandy Harju.

"I told you," the sheriff said.

They exchanged a few more comments, enough for Sam to know the sheriff was up-to-date, for what it was worth, but that he was currently transfixed by John Michael's poops, and just about anything else the kid did—mostly sleep.

The sheriff hoped to be in the office sometime tomorrow morning.

Sam told him he'd meet him there and give him an update on this evening's search.

After Sam put Gray in the Jeep, he headed to the casino.

Amanda Goodacre was waiting for him in front of the hotel registration desk. They shook hands and said hello.

On the way to the Eyes-in-the-Sky she said, "I almost called you last night, but didn't want to bother you after hours."

"Call anytime," Sam said. "Everyone else does."

Amanda assured him she would. Then, "Remember that guy who called from the dock? Called Minnesota's TIP line and reported the boats?"

"Yeah."

"Remember how I said I thought I recognized the way he walked?"

"Yeah."

"Pretty sure I saw that guy walk into O'Donnel's Grocery last night. Must have been around 7. I was going in and he was walking in front of me and I thought, *that's the guy. In the video.* It was the same gait. I knew I'd seen him before."

"Who was it?"

"Guy by the name of Cray Halverson. I've never met him, but I've seen him around. I asked one of the checkout ladies and she told me. Said he has a place out Tamarack Lane. On the lake."

Sam took out his phone and made a note to himself. "What's he do?"

"Lady said he's a logger. We've got a few of those around here. Gotta say, he looked like a logger."

Sam asked about it, and she said he was short and thick, with broad shoulders. He wore a flannel jacket over a flannel shirt, Carhartt pants with heavy work boots, and a Mackinaw hat.

"Didn't appear to be married," she said. "At least didn't have a wedding ring."

"You got that close to him?"

"Passed him at the meat counter."

Up in the Eyes-in-the-Sky room, Sam said hello to Cal. Amanda had already told him Sam was going to visit. Cal had a desk and terminal set up for him and had already called up the day he'd been searching for.

"Before you get started, let's take another look at that dock pay phone. See if I'm right about that guy," Amanda said.

Cal spent a couple of minutes finding the right sequence. And then they all watched it.

The man's face was obscured beneath his bombardier hat. But Sam guessed he was about the right height and width. "What do you think?"

"Pretty sure that's him," Amanda said. "Cray Halverson."

"Cray Halverson?" Cal asked.

"You know him?"

"Not personally, but I've seen him around. He lives not too far from here. I think he lives with Rowena Melnyk."

Sam didn't remember the name.

"The waitress?" Amanda said.

Cal nodded.

"You mean in the casino restaurant?" Sam said.

"She works Thursday through Sunday. She's a part-timer."

Sam pulled out his phone and made another note. "So she's working tomorrow night?"

"Should be," Amanda said. "Should be in around 4, if I remember correctly."

Sam thanked them both. He wasn't sure it was important, but she hadn't been here last Monday, when he'd interviewed her colleagues, and he still needed to speak with her.

Sam spent the next hour reviewing every moment of video involving Holden Riggins. He watched Holden's movements in slow motion. After he was certain there was no contact with Holden, no one even close to him as he made his way from the dock through the main entrance up to the restaurant and the bar, he sped up that section of video. Then he watched again at regular speed.

After an hour, he broke to get a bite to eat, since it was probably going to be a late night. He went into the restaurant and sat where Holden had sat. He ordered a Greek Wrap with chicken and an Arnold Palmer. The sandwich came with fries, which Sam didn't turn down.

While he ordered and waited for his food, and then ate and drank, he watched the place. There was an opening behind the bar where you could see into the kitchen. It was a small opening, so you couldn't see much. There was a door to the left of the bar and one to the right, beside the bottles—the bitters, vermouth, and Canadian Club whiskey, Sam remembered. There was a sink to the left of the bottles. Sam wondered about it, the arrangement.

While he was eating his last French fry, his cell phone went off.

"Rivers," he said.

"It's Sandy Harju," she said.

"What's up?"

She told him she'd dropped off the evidence bag and told them they needed it ASAP.

"They said they'd try and get it to you before end of day tomorrow," Harju said. "Something about the specimen being tainted by lake water, but they'd try."

"Okay," Sam said.

"I'm getting the equipment now. I forgot how bulky it is. Especially with the underwater lights. It would definitely be easier to manage with a pontoon. And I think I know where I can put my hands on one. And someone to help us."

Sam thought about it. Citizens were often willing to assist law enforcement. He appreciated the sentiment. "That'd work," Sam said. "But we can't tell them what we're using it for."

"Oh, God no," she said.

"Okay. If you think you can borrow one and you think it'll work better, do it."

"It's the vet who analyzed the coyote and rabbit behind the motel," Harju said.

"He can meet us at the dock at 4?"

There was a pause. "I think so. I can ask, anyway."

Sam was pretty sure there was something else going on. But they needed another boat and an extra pair of hands. "Ask him," he said.

296 | CARY J. GRIFFITH

Sam continued using the video equipment, using the fast-forward whenever possible.

And then, watching the tape as the time marker sped toward noon on Friday, someone came out of the kitchen. A big woman wearing a large winter coat. Sam watched her step over to the sink. She took a glass from the nearby counter, glanced up casually, opened the ice bin, filled her glass with ice, and then poured herself something dark out of the soda gun.

Not unusual, Sam thought. An employee pouring herself a soda from the bar. Probably a violation, but during his tape viewing he'd seen several do the same thing, though never this woman.

As Sam watched, she turned and glanced down the length of the bar to where Amy, the bartender, was talking to another waitress, someone Sam didn't recognize. And then the woman in the coat had her back to the camera. She appeared to pause, however briefly, and then she picked her drink off the counter and disappeared through the kitchen door.

Sam rewound, pulled it up again, and watched.

She paused. But since her back was to the camera, Sam couldn't see if she was doing anything other than reading labels. According to the time stamp, the pause took about five seconds.

Sam rewound. He brought the blurry video to the point where she was holding the soda gun over her glass, and then he froze the frame.

"Cal," Sam said. "Do you recognize her?"

Cal swiveled over. "That's Rowena Melnyk."

The tape said 12:06. "The waitress who works part-time?"

Cal nodded.

"Does she come to work at noon?"

"I don't know their schedules," Cal said. "But that's Rowena. Hard to miss her." Cal smiled.

"Do the part-timers here, or the hourly workers, do they punch a clock?"

"Yeah. A virtual clock. They log onto a computer when they come in and enter their start time. They do the same thing when they leave."

"Can you look up an employee's record of when they worked?"

Cal nodded. "I can, because I'm security. But it's a violation of privacy."

"Can you look up Rowena's?"

Cal thought about it. "I suppose. I'll have to tell the boss."

Cal texted Amanda and in a couple of minutes received permission.

"Can you pull up her timecard for the last month?"

It took Cal a couple of minutes, but then Sam was looking at it. The entry for Thursday, October 12, had a code. "What's STS?" Sam said.

Cal peered at it. "Short Term Sick. She called in sick that day."

"Last Thursday?"

Cal peered again. "Looks like it."

"And here on Friday, she punched in 4 to close? She worked her full shift?"

"Yup," Cal said. "4 p.m. to 1 a.m."

"But we saw she was here around noon on Friday, October 13."

Cal shrugged. "Last Friday was payday. Maybe she was picking up her check? But she didn't punch in."

"Don't you guys do direct deposit?"

"They're trying to get everyone to do it, but we have employees who still like to get the check. And some of our employees don't have bank accounts."

Sam wondered about it. "Okay. Thanks."

He glanced back at Rowena Melnyk's timecard and noted she also worked full shifts Saturday and Sunday.

Sam went back to Friday night, to when Holden stepped, lurched away from the bar and into the darkened hallway. He noted the timestamp: 06:37.

Sam remembered, from lunch, he'd had a clear view into the kitchen through the opening behind the bar. At least into a narrow angle of the kitchen.

"Cal, can you show me the kitchen tapes for last Friday night?"

Cal swung his head out of his monitor and swiveled over. "Sure."

A few keystrokes later Sam had three angles to the kitchen. He had seen them before, but this time he wasn't looking for signs of anyone tampering with Holden's food. He played the sequence of all three, one at a time, covering the time from when Holden sat down at the bar to when he stood up and lurched into the hallway. In two of them he watched Rowena Melnyk peer from within the kitchen out into the restaurant area. She did it three times. Each time she ducked, glanced into the bar, and then resumed her waitress activities. The first time was 06:32, five minutes before Holden finished. Then she did it at 06:34. And finally, one last time, at 06:36. The last time she took a cell out of her pocket and appeared to text someone. 06:37.

Who was she texting and why? Maybe she was texting some-one at the end of the hallway, or outside, who was going to inter-cept Holden Riggins? Or maybe it was as innocent as getting a text from a friend and deciding she had a moment to answer it.

But Sam didn't think so.

CHAPTER 37

Traffic was slow on the highway between Tower and Ely, but Deputy Joe Haman got lucky. During the afternoon, he caught four speeders traveling more than 10 mph over the 55-mph speed limit. The last speeder was a young woman in a 2000 Mustang, rusted around the running boards, hurrying toward her barmaid job. When she handed Deputy Haman her driver's license, she tried a combination of distress ("I'm sorry officer, but if I'm late again my boss is gonna kill me") and charm ("you should come into Josie's for a beer sometime"). Joe ignored both comments and wrote her a ticket.

By 4 p.m., Joe was at the Arrowhead Marina. He spoke briefly with the dock hand and told her he'd forgotten to call ahead, that he needed to borrow a runabout, and that Chief Deputy Barnes knew all about it. He wondered if any of them were gassed up.

The dockhand had topped off the runabout Deputy Sandy Harju and Sam Rivers had used earlier, so she was sure it still had plenty of gas. It was still tied to the dock.

But to Joe all she said was, "Take that one that's tied up out there. I just filled it this morning."

"Thanks," Joe said, on a mission to retrieve $2,000.

It took 15 minutes to get from the marina into Big Bay. By the time Deputy Joe Haman entered the huge body of water, it was getting close to 4:30. An hour and a half before sunset, there was still plenty of skylight, even though it was low on the horizon.

A slight breeze was blowing in from the northwest, chilling the already chilly afternoon and adding a chop to the expansive stretch of bay. Joe had planned on first visiting the Temple Island site where they'd found CO Charlie Jiles, in case there were any other boaters out who might see him. But the day was brisk, and when he scanned the horizon he saw a single pontoon on the other side of the bay, probably a party boat heading out from the casino. It was 2 miles away, barely a speck on the horizon. So he said, "Fuck it," and plugged the coordinates he'd received earlier over the phone into the runabout's GPS device. A sharp arrow clarified itself on the screen, and he turned the runabout on a course that took the boat in a nearly straight line toward the hidden reef, and his money.

Minutes earlier, at the Lucky Loon Casino docks, Dr. Phil Wirta had tied off his 24-foot Bennington pontoon. The boat had a Yamaha 250-horsepower motor attached to its aft, plenty of power to quickly transport them to the mouth of Smugglers Creek. The pontoon was open and spacious and would be ideal for holding them steady in the creek's current as they used their equipment to scan the area's bottom and work their way down the shoreline. Phil had erected the boat's broad windshield screen across its front, which would add wind resistance to their journey across Big Bay. While the shield would slow them down, they should still reach the creek's mouth with plenty of sunlight left to work.

And they had the lights. More importantly, the shield would block the frosty breeze sweeping across the nearly frozen surface of the lake. They were thankful to be hunkered down behind it.

Harju had introduced Sam to Dr. Wirta.

"Call me Phil," Phil said.

"Sam."

"I told Phil about Gray," Harju said. "He's not joining us?"

"With all this equipment he'd just be in the way," Sam said. "He'll nap in the Jeep."

Sam explained that Phil would be helping in the course of an ongoing investigation and, because they were still trying to find out what happened, Phil would not be able to tell anyone what they were doing this afternoon.

Phil nodded and said, "Sandy already mentioned all that. I left word at the office I was helping out a friend but didn't really tell them what I was doing. A lot of our calls are confidential."

"Good," Sam said.

Phil nodded again and said, "I can keep a secret."

They all focused on getting their equipment aboard. As they were transporting the cameras and lights from the cruiser to the pontoon, Sam noticed the comfortable familiarity between Harju and Phil, tinged with palpable energy. Clearly, they knew each other. But it felt to Sam like they were both interested. In each other.

Sam, of course, was focused on the work ahead of them. But it still made him smile.

"This is a different boat than the one I remember," Harju said.

"Yup. They got rid of that old Bennington and traded it in for a 24-footer with a bigger engine."

"It's nice," Harju said. "Definitely a bigger engine."

They were talking about the pontoon, but Sam heard it as subtext.

"You can ski behind it," Phil said.

"I'd like to try," Harju said.

"Next summer. Pick a date."

The professional Harju made a rare, slight grin and said, "Definitely."

By a little after 4:30, they were pulling away from the casino docks, steering the bulky pontoon into the northeast end of Big Bay. Phil plotted a course that would take them around the end of Temple Island. Once they skirted the island, they'd head down the wide channel on its back side, separating the island from the mainland. The mouth of Smugglers Creek was a couple of miles down, behind a small channel island and concealed on the mainland's wilderness side.

The only other watercraft they saw was a runabout halfway across the bay, way out in the middle.

"That looks like our boat!" Harju yelled over the engine noise.

Sam peered across the water. The boat was quite a ways out. It was the only other boat on the water, far enough away so that its details were indistinct. But Sam thought it looked like the same boat. They watched someone behind the boat's wheel: a distant, indeterminant figure.

While they watched, the boat turned in a narrow circle, then turned again, as though it was looking for something that had fallen overboard.

Phil was piloting the pontoon toward Temple Islands' east end. His trajectory kept them at least a half mile from the runabout.

"Hey, Phil," Harju said. "Any binoculars on the boat?"

"You bet," Phil said. "In that compartment behind your seat. My parents are birders. Osprey, eagles, cormorants, loons . . . "

"Cool," Harju said. She opened the compartment and extracted a pair of 10x compact binoculars from a jumble of items in the large space.

The chop made it difficult to hold the binoculars steady. But after a few moments, Harju said, "Definitely a department boat. I think that's Joe Haman." She handed the binoculars to Sam.

When Sam peered through the eye pieces, he could make out the head and shoulders of the deputy, but not much else. He wore a patrolman's bombardier-style hat with its ear flaps pulled down. The head was turned away. But as Sam watched, the runabout made another arcing turn, one that brought the pilot's head around. Definitely Deputy Joe Haman.

"What the hell is he doing in the middle of the bay?" Sam said.

"Looks like he's turning in circles," Harju said.

Sam wondered if the deputy might be fishing. The deputy hadn't struck Sam as the kind of colleague who would commandeer department resources for his own purposes. But it was an odd place to be at this time of the late afternoon, in this kind of cold.

"Don't you have to sign those boats out?" Sam asked.

"Normally," Harju said. "I didn't today. I didn't want people to know what we were up to."

"Do you need to list what you're using it for? When you're signing out the boat?"

"Sure."

Sam knew they could check the roster and see what it said.

Phil was steady on the course toward the end of the island, increasing the distance between them and the other boat.

"We can go ask him," Phil said.

"Not now," Sam said. "We need to get over to the mouth of that creek while we still have some light."

In the middle of Big Bay, in the late afternoon sunlight, Vermilion's surface was slate gray. This far out into the water the breeze had time to create a chop, making it difficult for Deputy Joe Haman to see anything across the water's surface. At first, he spun around his coordinates a couple of times, beginning to wonder if he'd been cheated. He turned on the depth finder and could see there was a reef below him. At one point it was only 4 feet deep. But where in the hell was the float? And his money?

With the narrowing of each circle, he grew angrier. At one point, he heard a distant outboard. He glanced up to see a pontoon he had noticed earlier, chugging at an angle away from the casino docks. He saw figures in the boat and figured they were casino people, but the boat was too far away to see clearly. He also noticed it was headed at an angle that was gradually increasing the distance between them.

He returned to squinting across the slate-gray water.

Finally, he saw something that looked like floating seaweed or some kind of forest debris. It bobbed to the crest of a wave, and then disappeared. He looked for it again, and watched it surface again.

Joe's pulse quickened. It took him a few more minutes to steer the boat so that he was coming at the object straight into the wind, so the breeze wouldn't knock him off course. Whatever it was continued to appear and disappear. But it didn't move. He turned the wheel to the left, slightly, then right. By the time he was nearly on top of it, he thought he could see muddy twine wrapped around a very small pine bough. The needles on the bough made it look like seaweed.

He turned the wheel, flicked the throttle into neutral, and came near enough to bend over the side and retrieve it.

Had to be it, he thought, his pulse jiggering. When he pulled it out of the water, he could see the attached line. There was something weighty on the other end.

He rolled the twine—a thick monofilament—around the fake pine bough. He peered into the gray water, the line taut as he wound it. After a minute of hurried winding, maybe 20 feet of string, a wrapped plastic bag emerged from the depths.

Joe pulled it into the boat, set the package down on the boat's floor next to his seat, flicked the throttle forward, and scanned the horizon. The only other boat was the distant pontoon, now farther away from him, a small mark on the horizon.

Certain he was alone, he took a moment to pull the string netting from around the plastic bag. There were lead weights wrapped into the plastic. As he unraveled it, he could see markings, what looked like bills.

Joe glanced up again, but now he was definitely alone.

It took another five minutes to free the bills—20 $100 bills—from the wet plastic. The bills were dry. Deputy Joe Haman smiled.

He carefully pocketed the $2,000, tossed the line and faux pine bough branch and plastic wrapping over the side, and paid no attention to the trash floating away from the boat. Littering was, after all, a misdemeanor offense. But all Joe Haman thought about was his money. And how, even after Lake Vermilion had taken his old pal Charlie Jiles, its depths had coughed up more money. Looked like the gravy train Charlie started might continue.

CHAPTER 38

By the time Phil Wirta steered the Bennington into the mouth of Smugglers Creek, they had at least an hour of sunlight left. The pontoon was equipped with a depth finder. Phil had turned it on before they entered the waters around the creek. Now he used it to edge into the mouth, watching as it marked off 6 feet, 5 feet, then 4.

Phil cut the engine as the momentum of the pontoon took it directly into the creek's current.

"What're we at?" Sam said.

"Four feet. Getting shallower. The transducer is under the bow, so that's the depth right in front."

Finally, the boat's momentum began to slow, then stopped.

"Anchor in the mouth?" Phil said.

"Perfect," Harju said. "We can start right at the mouth and work our way down the shoreline and out into the lake." She turned to the equipment bag while Sam began readying the lights.

The bow of the pontoon had a 3-foot lip. A sizable anchor was tucked back near the fence against the front seats. There was a small gate in the front center of the partition.

Phil moved up to the gate, opened it, stepped onto the bow lip, and reached down for the mushroom-shaped anchor. He waited until the forward momentum of the pontoon stopped and began drifting backwards with the current toward the creek's mouth.

After the pontoon drifted about 4 feet, Harju looked up and said, "Here. This is good, Phil. Can you keep us here?"

Phil dropped the anchor while Sam and Harju watched the rope slip through his hands no more than 5 feet before it struck bottom.

"Hope it catches on something," Phil said. "It's pretty shallow."

He peered out over the boat's bow, but the water coming down the creek was too opaque to see farther than a couple of feet.

Phil gripped the rope and kept it from playing out. He could feel it drag 2 or 3 feet before it finally caught on something, something in the dark shallows below, and the rope went taut.

"Snagged on something," Phil said. He tested the rope and it felt secure. "Should hold here." He tied off the rope to the bow cleat.

The Bennington was 8.5 feet wide. Its bulk filled the creek opening. The creek widened where it went into the lake. The pontoon was halfway into the creek's mouth, and half in the lake. Its port side was a couple of feet from the bush-covered shoreline, and its rear starboard side opened out into the lake.

Sam took a moment to assemble the underwater lights and support pole. The underwater dive light panel was waterproof up to 164 feet deep and had four intensity settings. The panel had a mounting clip that connected to an extendable boom pole. The boom pole was designed for a microphone, but it also worked well for the light panel and could be extended up to 30 feet or shortened to 5 feet. They had a second boom pole with a grip attached to its tip in case they found anything they wanted to retrieve. For now, Sam extended the light panel pole to 6 feet, turned it on, set it to highest intensity, and stepped up to Harju's side, waiting for her to drop the camera lens over the pontoon's side.

While Sam worked, Harju unzipped the video camera carrying case and pulled out its 50-foot cable with a sinker weight to keep it submerged. She affixed the camera lens to the end of the cable, flipped up the viewing screen, and turned it on. While the screen was booting up, she dropped the cable over the side.

Harju had worked with the device earlier, scanning the bottom of the shoreline off Temple Island, where they'd found Charlie Jiles. She had already figured out how to maneuver the lens to look up or down or sideways. Now, as the image clarified on the screen, Harju kept the lens a foot from the bottom and angled its viewer to look down. The water quality was turbid, but the light panel helped. The bottom was muddy with sediment and leaves, but not much else.

"Let's move along the pontoon side toward the back," Harju said.

Sam worked in tandem with Harju, keeping the light panel angled toward the bottom, illuminating the lens and everything around and below it for a few feet.

As they neared the pontoon's aft, Harju said. "Nothing. Nothing but bottom."

"Keep working around the aft and up the starboard side," Sam said.

Harju did and they worked their way up the boat's starboard all the way to the bow. Once they'd made a complete circuit of the pontoon, Harju said, staring into the video screen, "I don't see anything."

"You see the bottom?" Sam said.

"Oh, I can see the bottom. And I can see for around 3 feet in any direction. Those lights are great. But it's just, bottom."

"What are you looking for?" Phil said.

Harju didn't answer and Sam finally said, "Can't say for sure. I mean, we cannot tell you why we've come to Smugglers Creek because it's an ongoing investigation and it's confidential. And we cannot tell you what we're looking for because we don't really know."

"Oh, okay," Phil said.

"Can you lift that anchor and let the pontoon drift down another boat length, Phil?" Sam said.

"Sure."

Phil worked to pull up the anchor. Once he'd freed it, the pontoon drifted in the creek's current. Phil watched the shoreline; when they'd drifted a boat length, he dropped the anchor. This time the rope fell at least 10 feet before hitting bottom. They dragged maybe a foot before the anchor caught on something— probably a boulder—and held.

They were now almost an entire boat length from the creek's mouth. In the same way they'd worked the lens and light panel earlier, they worked it again, moving along the 24-foot pontoon length down the port side near the shoreline, and then along the starboard side.

"More boulders this time," Harju said. "And it's getting deeper."

"Definitely deeper. Gets deep pretty fast," Phil said. "It's 10 feet beneath the bow."

"I bet it's at least 15 feet off the aft," Harju said.

It took a while to work the lens around so they could see beneath the boat. By the time they'd worked their way around the pontoon's aft, and were starting up its starboard side, Harju paused, peering more closely at the screen.

She moved the lens and said, "Got something."

Sam moved over to look and saw a flash of yellow on the screen.

"What is it?" Sam said.

"No idea."

"Phil, can you get that grab pole and see if you can use those grips to snag this thing?"

Phil came back from the bow, pulled up the snag pole, and said, "How deep?"

"Set it to 20 feet," Harju said. "I think it's 15 to the bottom."

He lengthened the pole to 20 feet and fished it over the pontoon's side. When the pole's end came into view on the camera, he tried to maneuver it toward the yellow object. All three of them were peering at the screen.

The pole's end had a hook with a maneuverable grip that could be used to make one end clamp down and tighten. Phil used it to move the yellow object—a kind of blocky square-edged item—to and fro.

"It looks like it's caught on something. Like a wire?" Sam said.

"Maybe fishing line?" Harju said.

"Can you tighten that grip on it?" Sam said.

"I'm trying," Phil said, peering into the monitor. "It's like doing surgery through a scope."

Finally, Phil angled the grip into position and clamped down. Something held and he began lifting the pole up out of the water. The yellow object lifted off the bottom and disappeared from Harju's screen.

Carefully, Phil kept the tension on the grip and lifted the pole, hand over hand, until the object lifted out of the dark water and came over the side.

"A Taser," Sam said.

"What the hell?" Harju said.

There were coiling wires coming out of the Taser gun. The wires were still hanging over the side. Phil started pulling up the wires, hand over hand. They were copper wires; after about 20 feet, he pulled its two ends, barbed electrodes, and fished them from over the side.

They all stared at the Taser on the pontoon deck as though it was some kind of incredibly rare fish. Definitely a rare catch.

"I don't know," Sam said.

"Did you expect anything like this?" Phil said.

"I did not," Sam said. "What about you, Harju?"

"A Taser? God no."

Sam handed the light panel pole to Phil and retrieved the Taser from the deck. The grip, the wires, the electrodes—all of it was clean. There were no official markings on it that would indicate it was the property of a law enforcement office.

"Looks new," Sam said. "And it looks like it was dumped here recently."

"And given that the electrodes and wires were uncoiled, it was apparently fired," Harju said.

"Before it fell into the lake," Sam said.

"But why?" Harju said. "And for what?"

"To subdue someone," Sam said. "But yeah, for what purpose?"

None of them could imagine how or why it was used, or for what.

"Let's keep looking," Sam said.

They'd been working steadily since arriving at the creek. The evening was cold and getting colder. There was still a snippet of sun visible on the western horizon, but it would soon be gone. Then they'd have another 30 minutes before the sky darkened enough for the stars to come out.

After taking another look at the bottom near where they'd found the Taser, Sam had Phil pull the anchor and let the pontoon drift back 4 or 5 feet. Then Phil dropped anchor a third time and waited for the weight to hold.

A few minutes into Harju's bottom search, she caught a flash on the video monitor. At first she thought it might be the flank of a big fish. But when she turned the camera directly on the object, she saw the flash again. When she moved over to it, they all had a look in the video monitor and Sam said, "Looks like an iPhone."

Sam and Harju looked at each other, and Sam was pretty sure they were both thinking the same thing. *Charlie Jiles's phone?*

They took another five minutes getting the phone up off the bottom.

Once in the boat, Sam turned it over and read: "Property of MN DNR" stamped on the back of it. Judging from how clean the phone looked, it had been in the water about as long as the Taser.

Had to be Jiles's phone, which was interesting. Sam recollected the ME report, and there was nothing in it to indicate Jiles had been hit by a Taser. The barbed Taser end would have left marks and other telltale signs.

Sam bagged the phone and they kept searching the bottom, working their way back in the current.

Now they were perhaps 20 feet from the mouth of the creek. There was still light in the western sky, but not for much longer.

Harju paused, looking at the monitor.

She had worked her way down the port side and was coming around the aft and said, "Look at this."

Sam, keeping up with the light panel, peered into the screen.

"Gill net," he said.

"But where are the buoys?" Harju said. "If this is a whitefish net, there should be buoys clearly marking it."

"Too deep for whitefish," Sam said. "That net was set for walleye."

In the distance, they heard the sound of a boat motor.

CHAPTER 39

Judging from the noise, it was a big engine, opened full throttle, and coming on fast. The boat was approaching from the other side of the channel island.

By now, the dusk light was beginning to fade. There was still some light in the western sky, but the world was becoming shadowy, and it would only be another 15 or 20 minutes until dark.

Sam lifted the light panel to the surface, hurriedly.

"Bring in your gear," he said to Harju.

Harju lifted the camera lens and cable to the surface.

As soon as Sam got the light monitor into the boat, he cut its power.

"Hit those running lights, Phil," Sam said. "Leave the anchor in but get ready to bring it up quick."

The running lights blinked out and Phil hurried into the front, untying the anchor rope from the bow cleat and taking hold of the rope.

"Fisherman?" Harju said.

"Too damn cold and too near dark," Sam said. "Poachers, more likely."

The boat was approaching quickly. They had been out here for nearly an hour and only seen one boat since they left the casino docks. Given they'd just found an illegal gill net anchored below them, whoever it was could be coming for their net. And their illegal catch.

As the boat neared the other side of the island its engine finally slowed. In another minute they watched as a shadowy runabout crested the island's eastern side and turned directly toward them. In another 10 seconds, they'd closed the distance to 50 yards.

Sam, Harju, and Phil were squinting at the runabout, looking for details. The outline of the craft was shadowy, but Sam thought he saw two figures in the boat: one behind the wheel, and another person sitting in the passenger seat.

Suddenly a massive high beam flashed on and all Sam, Harju, and Phil could see was blinding light. Everything else was obliterated by the intense illumination. The three of them shadowed their eyes and kept squinting, but the light remained intense.

There was a moment when Sam thought he heard, over the outboard motor, the word "sheriff," and then more words, maybe commands.

Then the runabout's engine roared back to full throttle and the boat took off rounding toward the other side of the island, the high beam still aimed straight at the pontoon, continuing to blind them and keeping the escaping boat in darkness.

"Anchor up!" Sam said, turning toward the captain's seat.

"They're using the light to hide!" Harju said.

Sam found the ignition switch, turned it on, and brought their engine to life.

"Anchor's up!" Phil said.

Sam put the boat in reverse long enough so his hard right would steer straight into the lake. Then he turned the boat as the runabout's waves washed against the pontoon's bow. Phil was coming through the front gate when the waves hit and he went down.

"Phil!" Harju said.

"Go. Go," Phil said, on all fours.

Harju was seated, gripping the pontoon's fence side.

Sam pushed the throttle all the way down and the bow of the pontoon lifted out of the water like a charging moose.

Now the only thing you could hear was the engine's roar. Sam was about to yell to Harju to turn the panel light on when the entire front of the pontoon was illuminated and then Harju picked up the panel and turned it to face in front of the quickening pontoon. The light illuminated at least 50 yards in front of them, but all they could see were the remnants of the runabout's wake.

"They turned around the other side of the island," Harju yelled.

After the runabout disappeared, Sam knew it had two options. Turn left, east, back down the channel toward the end of Temple Island and out into Big Bay, or right, west, which would put them in a long channel with Temple on the left, wilderness on the right, and not a lot of islands or cover for around 6 miles.

The pontoon's pursuit was taking them in the runabout's wake. Their boat had a 250 hp Yamaha engine and plenty of strength and speed. But it was pushing a 24-foot pontoon, no match for the smaller runabout. Sam had no idea what engine powered the runabout. Something big, judging from its earlier sound.

Whatever Sam did, continue straight following the runabout's wake, or turn left and hope to intercept the runabout as it turned east, he had five seconds to decide. By then, he'd be too committed to alter his course.

"Hold on!" Sam said, over the engine's roar.

He turned, sharp left. The pontoon hitched and groaned and then rose up on its port side, its starboard digging into the water. Harju fell to her knees, managing to hold the light panel upright, still shining in front of them. Phil, still on all fours, braced himself against the front seat. There was a moment during which Sam wondered if they'd sideswipe the island. And then they all watched the reeds brush by their starboard side as the pontoon found its footing and surged forward.

As they breached the left side of the island, the runabout suddenly shot out in front of them, not 40 yards away. The pilot was seated and focused on the water in front of them. His passenger was behind him, still holding the high beam up, aiming it directly behind their craft, assuming they would be followed. The pilot turned, looked to see the panel light coming on broadside, yelled something, though Sam couldn't hear anything over their own engine's roar. And then the high beam suddenly turned on the pontoon and blinded them again.

The runabout kept moving forward as the pontoon breached their wake and rose into the air like a water skier jumping a wave. As soon as they got to the other side, Sam managed to turn the pontoon left nearly 90 degrees and continue their pursuit. But they'd already lost 50 yards and now the runabout was increasing its distance. They swung in behind the boat's wake and Sam kept the pontoon at full throttle.

It took 2 miles of winding channel before the runabout reached the end of Temple Island. By then the speedier, lighter craft had increased its lead by a quarter mile. And then suddenly its high beam blinked out.

During the chase Harju continued to hold the light panel in front of them, lighting Sam's way. The jagged silhouettes of both shorelines breezed by. Sam knew they were in the middle of the channel and that for now, at least, pursuit was futile. But the light panel was highlighting the runabout's wake, which was still clear enough in the still water to easily follow.

For a second, Sam backed off on the throttle and put the boat in neutral. Then he cut the engine.

"Cut the lights," Sam said.

Harju fumbled with the panel and the lights turned off.

"Listen," Sam said. He thought he could hear the distant engine in front of them, but wasn't sure.

"It turned around Temple," Phil said. "It's still full throttle, but in another minute, on the other side of the big island, we won't be able to hear anything. But you should be able to follow that wake for a while."

"You hear it, Harju?"

"A little, like what Phil said. But it's getting dimmer."

Sam knew they needed to compare notes about what each of them saw, while it was still fresh in their minds. But for now, he turned the boat back on, and in a second they were continuing the chase at full throttle.

Harju turned on the light panel and shined it on the remnants of the runabout's wake.

By the time they rounded Temple's eastern end they couldn't see anything out on Big Bay. If the runabout had continued out into the big water it would have shown under the starlight, at least a shadowy figure. Temple Island stretched several miles to the south in a series of bays, inlets, and peninsulas that made the shoreline difficult to follow.

When they came around the island's end, Sam continued for another 100 yards, keeping the shoreline to the right, and then cut the engine.

In the distance they could hear the outboard. It must have been at least a half mile ahead, but it was still full throttle.

"He's sticking close to the shoreline," Phil said. "He's already around one of those points. No way we're going to be able to see him unless he turns on his running lights."

"No poacher's gonna turn on their lights," Harju said.

"I can still see what's left of their wake," Sam said. "And if they head out into Big Bay, we'll see them."

"I'd stick close to the shoreline and keep running till I got to the end," Phil said. "Once you get to the end of Temple Island you can turn in all sorts of directions. And there's lots of islands and places to lose yourself."

"And by then we probably won't be able to follow their wake," Sam said.

"Doubtful," Phil said.

"Let's follow it while we can," Sam said.

He turned on the engine and pushed it for another 30 minutes, but by then the remnants of the runabout's wake had dissipated and they could no longer see a trail across the lake's surface. Finally, Sam pulled up on the throttle and turned off the engine.

By now they were halfway down Temple Island. They all listened in the dark but couldn't hear anything.

"You think they stopped?" Sam said.

"Could have," Harju said.

"Could have gone anywhere along here. But my bet is if they kept following that shoreline, sticking close, they'd be far enough away now to be at the end of the island, and probably turned a corner. We wouldn't hear them if they went around the island's southwestern point."

"We need to compare notes," Sam said. "Now, while whatever each of us saw is still fresh in our minds."

"About the boat?" Harju said.

"Yeah. Any details at all you can remember seeing. About the boat, and anything you noticed about who was in it."

"Looked like a newer, 21-foot Crestliner," Phil said. "Pretty nice. With a Yamaha engine, probably about the size of ours. If I was to guess, I'd say it was a 200 or 250?"

"Catch any numbers? Anything on the side?" Sam said.

"There were numbers," Harju said. "But it was only a flash."

"Not me," Phil said.

Sam had seen them, but not long enough to read anything.

They continued comparing notes. After another five minutes, all they had was the type and size of the runabout, and that two people were in it wearing bulky camo. Harju was pretty sure the pilot was wearing a bombardier hat, one of those black ones with ear flaps and a forehead flap. She thought the ear flaps were pulled down over the pilot's ears, which made sense, given the cold.

Lots of people in the area used them this time of year, Sam knew. Especially outdoors people. But it made him wonder.

"What now?" Harju said.

"We gotta go back and take care of that net and those fish," Sam said.

"There were fish in that net," Harju said.

"We let go whatever we can, and harvest the dead ones," Sam said. "But it's gonna be late. I suppose we could wait until morning, Phil. If you need to get back."

"Can't wait until morning," Phil said. "I took an oath as a vet. We've got to go free as many of those fish as possible. Some of them won't survive the night."

"Good answer," Sam said.

"Besides," Phil said. "This is about the most exciting night I've had in quite some time."

Phil Wirta returned to the mouth of Smugglers Creek, relocated the underwater net, managed to hook one of its floats, and began hauling it in.

The veterinarian worked tirelessly beside them, releasing the live fish from the net, and tossing the others into a large plastic leaf bag. By the end they were forced to harvest seven large walleye.

When they finally hauled in the entire net, they found an owner's tag near its bottom. Holden Riggins. His second stolen net.

Of course, Holden Riggins was in the county jail. Sam knew Holden could be working with someone on the outside. But it didn't make sense. Why use a net that could be clearly tied back to him? And why tell Sam that the place he'd set it, if he was looking to poach fish this time of year, was in the mouth of Smugglers Creek?

What made more sense was Holden Riggins's innocence, a likely possibility Chief Deputy Smith Barnes would be reluctant to admit.

CHAPTER 40

Thursday, October 19

O ver Sam's first cup of coffee he fired up his laptop.
There was already an email from Carmel. Sam had slept longer than usual, but it was only 7 a.m., too early to place his call to Amanda Goodacre.

"Check it out," her subject line read. Then:

> I wanted to get this done before work. Here's the link to the place I was talking about, off Birch Point Road. It looks so nice, particularly with the party boat. So I went ahead and booked it. I guess you'll be stuck with visitors this weekend. Prepare yourself.

Sam knew Carmel meant those last couple of words as a joke. But her comment reminded him of the conversation he wanted to have with her. He had been so busy and preoccupied he hadn't thought about it.

Why rock the boat? Sam thought. *Why quibble with the status quo?*
Because you love her.

"So buy her flowers," Sam said.

Sam's voice made Gray's tail thump.

"Whose side are you on?" Sam said.

His tail thumped again.

Sam told himself to snap out of it; there was too much going on. He needed to focus.

Still, he followed Carmel's link. The place had three bedrooms, the master with a hot tub overlooking the lake. There were two baths, an outdoor sauna, and a large deck. From the deck the view overlooked a long, bisected dock with a tri-hulled pontoon boat on a hoist. Beyond it, there was a narrow slice of Vermilion waterway, presumably the connection to the rest of the lake.

When Sam checked the cabin's address on Google Maps he could see it was on a long, narrow bay that opened out into Vermilion's Big Bay. The cabin was probably a 30-minute boat ride to the back side of Temple and Holden's cabin.

The thought of the back side of Temple and Smugglers Creek returned him to reality.

Sam replied, "Perfect. Thanks for reserving it. Looking forward to seeing you, Jennifer, and the rest of the pack. And for the record, you would be wise to get prepared yourself."

That might make her think, he guessed.

He clicked send.

Sam felt certain the end of this day would bring the closure he needed so he could spend the weekend with his pack unpreoccupied. He knew it was going to be a busy day, even though he was still fuzzy about how, exactly, it was going to unfold.

When he returned to his emails, he saw farther down the list another late-night send from Deputy Smith Barnes.

"Suspect's Toxicology Report," its subject line read.

Attached is the lab report on the suspect's blood and urine. They found something. I don't have time to get into it right now.

Sheriff's in tomorrow morning—wants to make sure you're here to bring him up to date on case. 10:30.

Sam downloaded the toxicology report. A few columns and several rows populated the bulk of four pages. Each row appeared to be a tested substance. They fell into recognized categories: alcohol, amphetamines, barbiturates, opiates, etc. Almost all of the rows tested negative. But there were two, alcohol and benzodiazepines, that tested positive. Under the alcohol category, Holden Riggins's urine and blood contained .06 *ethanol*. By Holden's own testament and from the video Sam had already reviewed, Holden had two drinks Friday night, which would be consistent with the .06 finding of his blood-alcohol level.

Under the category Benzodiazepines, there were several drugs listed, all of them except one—Rohypnol—with no trace amounts. The street name for Rohypnol was roofie, also known as a date-rape drug. The drugs were often surreptitiously deposited in people's drinks, mostly women. The victims became amnesic, docile, and, in higher doses, unconscious. The amount shown was consistent with how they found him, unconscious and just about dead.

In Holden's case, hypothermia was a complicating factor. But regardless, it appeared he'd been drugged.

The report's comments section provided further details about Rohypnol. In addition to a list of street names and likely symptoms, depending on the dose, the comments concluded: "The amounts detected in the subject were very high and, depending on the subject's size and weight, would likely result in unconsciousness and memory loss."

Holden had suggested he'd been drugged. The toxicology report confirmed it. He'd been seriously drugged, which accounted for why he was found nearly comatose in the bottom of his boat and couldn't remember anything from the previous evening.

It appeared Holden was guilty of being a felon in possession of an unregistered weapon, his father's .45. But Sam couldn't imagine how anyone could consider Holden guilty of anything else, including consuming any of the alcohol from the open bottles in his boat, despite the damning evidence of his prints.

Everything Sam had learned to date supported Holden's version of events. CO Jiles died on Thursday, drowning in a flowage more than a mile distant from where he was found (if Smugglers Creek was the correct flowage). Even if the waterway was elsewhere on Vermilion, the autopsy confirmed CO Jiles could not have drowned where he was ultimately found. He was clearly placed into Holden's net. And presumably someone had moved CO Jiles's DNR runabout from wherever Jiles had drowned to where his body was found.

Deputy Smith Barnes was suggesting Holden killed CO Jiles Thursday afternoon, hid the body, and on Friday, after his casino dinner, he boated to wherever Jiles and his boat were stashed, hauled the CO's body and his boat to the location beside Temple Island and Holden's whitefish net, and then placed Jiles into his own net, while also setting an illegal walleye net. Holden also left an empty bottle of Old Crow and a half-filled bottle of Jack Daniels on the floor of his boat, for good measure, before drugging himself with a roofie. For an alibi?

It made no sense. The evidence told him something had happened, but that Holden Riggins had nothing to do with it. Other than being framed.

Sam was pretty sure he knew who was involved. But he needed to follow up on his hunches to figure out the details of what had been done. He hoped he could do that before his 10:30 meeting with the sheriff.

Sam hit reply to Barnes's email and typed, "See you and the sheriff at 10:30. I'll let Deputy Harju know."

Gray was growing impatient, but he was too much of a team player to complain. "Okay, buddy." Sam showered, shaved, and then turned to Gray, got him breakfast, and within 20 minutes he had Gray leashed and outside, walking in the woods behind the Vermilion Falls Motel. Sam made sure there were no poisoned baits, and that otherwise the trees behind the motel were safe. Then he unleashed Gray.

The day was bright and sunny but still cold. According to Sam's weather app, it was cold, but by the afternoon the winds would come out of the south, bringing warm air. Carmel had been right: Friday was good, Saturday was going to be beautiful.

By 8 a.m., Sam took a moment to text Amanda Goodacre. "Need to review video from last Friday again. Can I stop by?"

Within five minutes, Amanda texted, "Of course. When will you be here?"

"8:30."

She'd meet him in front of the hotel registration desk.

Back in his room, he checked his emails. There was one from his boss, Kay Magdalen.

"Rivers," the email began. Sam knew Kay well enough to hear her voice over his screen. He also knew what she wanted.

"Do you think you could let me know what's going on? I was under the impression you were investigating the murder of a conservation officer and violation of the Lacey Act. Update, please. Or you could always be bounced back to Colorado, where you could tell me in person."

Sam smiled. He could count on his boss for two things: she had his back, and she loved to threaten him. He hit reply and gave her a thumbnail of his most recent activities and told her, vaguely, that while he hadn't solved the murder, he was getting very close. He was prevaricating, but Sam knew Kay would appreciate hearing that some progress was being made. He promised to return to his reports as soon as he was finished here—where he was pretty sure he'd be working through the weekend.

On a party boat.

He didn't mention the party boat, cabin, Carmel, or any of the rest. He wasn't stupid.

After answering Kay his phone rang. Sandy Harju.

"Yeah," Sam said.

"Morning, Sam," she said, pausing long enough to give him a chance to use her first name.

"Morning, Harju."

"I just sent you two emails," she said. "One with the ME tech's analysis of the torn underwear. And the other with CO Jiles's phone records for the last year."

"Find anything interesting?"

"I haven't had a chance to look at the phone records. But the ME's analysis was why I called. Turns out the torn underwear was too tainted to test the blood sample, but the underwear's elastic band contained skin cells, so they have DNA, but owner unknown. They had more luck with the semen. The semen is Jiles."

Good God, Sam thought. "Source unknown, for now. But we know her size."

"Hanes. Size 9 2x," Harju said.

"So we know Charlie Jiles had sex, presumably before he died. And he probably had sex in the mouth of Smugglers Creek."

"Probably."

Now, Sam knew, they needed to find her.

"Can you do me another favor?" Sam said.

"Of course."

"Can you check the DNR's boat registration database and see if there are any boats registered to Rowena Melnyk or Cray Halverson?"

Sam waited while Harju took down the names, making sure about the spelling. Then Sam told Harju about the meeting at the sheriff's office at 10:30.

"I'll be there," she said.

"But text me about the boats. Make and model," Sam said.

As soon as he was off the phone, Sam dialed Amanda Goodacre.

"Do you test your employees for drugs?"

Amanda, surprised, said, "Sure. We do pre-employment and random drug tests. We're a casino. Can't have drug users working at a casino."

"You do random drug tests?"

"Sure."

"What do you use? A saliva kit?"

Amanda nodded. "Yeah. I forget the brand. But it's a saliva drug test kit. We don't do it very often."

"Is it a swab, or . . . ?"

"They spit into a sterilized cup and we send it off to a lab for testing."

"That'll work."

"What's going on?"

"Any chance you can call Rowena Melnyk and have her come in," Sam said. "This morning."

"Uh, sure," Amanda said. "What's this about?"

"Just," Sam said. "I can't explain it just yet. I have some hunches. I still don't know everything, but if we could get Rowena Melnyk's DNA, it might clear up some things."

Or make them muddier. But Sam didn't think so.

Amanda was surprised. She explained that Rowena was one of those steady employees. You could always count on her showing up and doing her shift. She was efficient, courteous, and friendly to the casino's customers. She wasn't like some of the other women waitstaff, table workers, dealers, hotel maids, and the like, who were sexually harassed on a regular basis. Rowena was friendly but cool.

And from the video, Sam had noticed she was a larger woman.

"By 'steady' do you mean she always shows up for work?" Sam said. "Never calls in sick?"

"That's right," Amanda said. "I don't think she's ever called in sick. At least as long as I've known her."

"She was sick last Thursday," Sam said.

"She was?" Amanda said. "I didn't know that."

Sam spent the next few minutes examining the last month of Charlie Jiles's phone calls. He went back to September 15 and worked forward. Most of the calls were work related. He saw several calls made to Ben Connors, Jiles's boss. He saw several other calls to people he assumed worked for the DNR. Sam found his first interesting, non-work-related call in late September. A 60-second call to Cray Halverson. Too long for a mistaken call, Sam knew. But short enough so they were just exchanging a brief message.

Interesting.

He continued working forward and found another call to Cray Halverson in early October. About the same time, he made a call to Deputy Joe Haman. Then the next day there was a call to Rowena Melnyk.

Sam was beginning to get the picture. Or at least, what he thought the picture might be. And then he saw four text messages made on the Thursday CO Jiles died. The first was outgoing to Rowena Melnyk. She answered it a few minutes later. Then another text from Jiles to Rowena and, finally, one from Rowena to Jiles. The last call was at 12:48 p.m.

CHAPTER 41

By the time Sam Rivers arrived at the casino it was 8:30. Amanda Goodacre met him in front of the registration desk.

"Did you get ahold of Rowena Melnyk?" Sam said.

"I did. I asked her if she'd come in and she wanted to know what it was about."

"What did you tell her?"

"Routine HR issue, just trying to clear up some records. She sounded," Amanda hesitated, "suspicious."

"You didn't say anything about the drug test?"

"No," Amanda said. "Testing is sensitive. We try to keep it quiet and confidential until we do it, for obvious reasons."

So no one could get out of it, or try and game the test, Sam knew.

There was a conference room down the hall from the main floor doorway to the Eyes-in-the-Sky room. Amanda told Sam to wait for her there, she'd get the testing kit and bring Rowena, when she arrived.

On his way to the conference room, Sam thought about Rowena Melnyk. He didn't know much about her, but everything he knew was, well, fishy. On the day CO Jiles was murdered, she called in sick. The next night, when Holden Riggins was apparently drugged in the casino restaurant, she worked a full shift in the restaurant. If Sam was judging the angle of her glance out of the kitchen correctly, she was watching Holden, around the time he got up from his bar stool and stumbled into the hallway. And then she texted someone. And if Sam had to guess, she looked like the kind of woman who would fit into Hanes underwear, size 9 2x.

What else?

She was living with that logger. What was his name? Cray Halverson. According to Amanda, he was the same guy who phoned the TIP line around 4 a.m. last Saturday, to report seeing Holden's and CO Jiles's boats. If Amanda's powers of observation were accurate, what was a logger doing on the lake at 4 in the morning? Especially when it sounded like he lived on the mainland. If he lived on an island, Sam could understand the early morning sighting and subsequent call. The man said he was boating to his car. But if he lived on the mainland, that excuse didn't make sense.

And he was wearing the same kind of bombardier hat as the pilot in the fleeing runabout.

Sam had several questions to ask Rowena, but he reminded himself that her eyes, face, and body language could tell him as much as her words.

Around 9 a.m., Amanda Goodacre and Rowena Melnyk entered the conference room. Rowena was startled when she saw Sam, sitting across the conference room table.

"Have a seat," Amanda said. She pulled out the chair directly across from Sam Rivers and Rowena sat down. Amanda sat to Rowena's right, at the head of the table.

The fluorescents flooded the windowless conference room with intense white light.

Rowena wore black jeans and a plaid work shirt. She was hard to ignore, stepping into a room. She had long dark hair with some salt-and-pepper strands starting to show. It was pulled back behind her shoulders and fastened with an amber clasp. Her face was round and cute, in a Northwoods barmaid kind of way. He'd be surprised if, as Amanda alluded, she didn't occasionally attract the attention of some of the male patrons.

"This is Sam Rivers, a special agent with the U.S. Fish & Wildlife Service."

Rowena nodded to Sam and said, "Oh?" She was tentative. "What's Fish & Wildlife have to do with the casino?"

"I'm helping out with the investigation into the death of Conservation Officer Charlie Jiles," Sam said. "Did any of your colleagues tell you I spoke with them last Monday?"

At Sam's mention of Charlie Jiles, something changed. Sam saw it on her face. It wasn't fear, exactly.

"I guess I heard about it," Rowena said.

"Since you weren't here on Monday, I just wanted to ask you a few questions," Sam said. "About last Friday night."

"Okay. That was almost a week ago. But I'll try."

"Do you remember seeing anything strange or out of place? Particularly anything involving Holden Riggins?"

"Holden Riggins?"

"Yeah. Do you know him?"

Rowena nodded. "Know who he is. He comes in on Fridays."

"So do you remember him coming in last Friday night?" Sam said.

Rowena thought about it. "I guess. I mean, he's pretty quiet. Keeps to himself. But since he comes in every Friday, he must have been there. But I don't remember it, exactly. I don't wait on him. He always sits at the bar and Amy takes his order. You should ask her about him."

Sam nodded. "Yeah. I spoke with her earlier in the week. But I was just curious about what everyone saw that night. So, did you work the whole shift last Friday? Until, what, 1 a.m.?"

Rowena nodded.

"But you were sick last Thursday?" Sam said.

Rowena's eyes took on a deer-in-the-headlights look, and she didn't answer.

"Did you have the flu on Thursday?" Amanda said.

"No. I just . . . didn't feel great."

"It wasn't the bottle flu, was it?" Amanda said.

It was an attempt at levity, but it was lost on Rowena. She shook her head and said, "Bad cramps."

That made them pause. Then, just to clarify, Amanda said, "Bad period?"

Rowena nodded, once. She wasn't embarrassed. Her countenance betrayed something else.

"I've been reviewing some of the security footage from last Friday," Sam said. "I noticed you came in around noon on Friday."

Another pause. "I guess."

"To pick up your check?" Amanda said.

Rowena thought about it, and then shook her head. "I was in the neighborhood, and just wanted to say hello to those guys. The day staff. I don't see them a lot."

"At one point you got yourself a glass of ice and some soda," Sam said. "Do you remember that? It was around noon."

Rowena stared, for a moment almost catatonic. "Did I? I don't remember."

"You did," Sam said. "You were wearing a big jacket, and on your way back into the kitchen you paused for a moment, in front of some bottles. Looked like you did something."

Rowena looked startled but tried not to show it. Then her head was shaking no. "Probably just thinking, I guess. Do you think I stole something?"

"It looked like you might have switched bottles," Sam said.

Another startled look she tried to brush off. "What?"

"Apparently Holden Riggins was drugged Friday night. We're trying to figure out how that happened. Just wondered if you might have been involved."

"No. Why would I want to drug Holden Riggins?"

"We can't figure out why anyone would want to drug Holden Riggins," Sam said.

"Did you see anything odd about Holden that night?" Amanda said.

"No. But then, I don't have much to do with him. My tables are usually on the other side of the room."

"How well did you know Charlie Jiles?" Sam said.

There was a flash of what looked like alarm during which Sam thought Rowena was going to say something. Maybe confess to having sex with him out at Smugglers Creek?

But then her face softened, and she said, "Charlie Jiles?"

"Yes," Sam said. "The conservation officer who was murdered. How well did you know him?"

She paused, thinking again. "I knew who he was."

She was lying, Sam knew. The day Charlie Jiles died he'd texted Rowena, and she had responded. Sam didn't know what those texts said, but clearly, she knew him.

"How did you know him?" Sam said.

Rowena tried to think. "Everybody knows Charlie. He was one of those guys who knew a lot of people," she said.

There was another pause, after which Amanda said, "Are you familiar with the casino's random drug testing policy?"

Rowena thought about it and nodded, slowly.

"The casino's required to do at least five per month." Amanda explained how the casino was governed by the Minnesota Gaming Control Board, as well as tribal laws, and they needed, for obvious reasons, to make sure their operation was squeaky clean. That's one of the reasons they were required to perform random drug tests. "Guess it's your lucky day," Amanda said. "If it's okay, we'd like you to take one now."

Rowena thought about it, then nodded. "Okay."

Amanda handed her the Saliva Drug Test Kit and explained how to use it.

As Rowena began working with the screw top, Sam said, "Do you live nearby?"

Rowena looked up. "Tamarack Lane."

She finally managed to break the seal, and looked back down, starting to unscrew it.

"Is that close?" Sam said.

Rowena nodded again, looking up. She explained how to get there from the casino. It was about 5 miles down the road to Tamarack Lane, then a right for less than a mile. Their cabin was on Vermilion.

The cap was off the container and she peered down into it.

"You just need to spit a few times into the cup," Amanda said.

"Somebody told me you lived with a logger," Sam said.

She looked up. "Yes," she said. "Cray."

"Cray?" Sam said.

"Cray Halverson. It's his place at the end of Tamarack Lane."

"How's the logging business?" Sam said.

She looked at Sam. "Slow," she said. "This time of year." Then, back to Amanda. "Just spit?"

"In the cup," Amanda said. "Two or three times should do it."

They watched as her mouth worked, gathering saliva.

"I figured it was a slow time of year for a logger," Sam said. He wasn't making small talk. Sam knew she was paying attention.

She spit into the cup. Then she said, "Yes. Logging's slow in the fall. It'll pick up in a month or two, when it gets colder."

She looked back into the cup.

"Does he ever net whitefish?" Sam said.

This time she glanced at Sam and then Amanda. Her expression shifted, along with the color of her face, which paled . . . ever so slightly.

"Whitefish?" Rowena said.

"This time of year," Sam said. "The season just opened. Been open for a little over a week. Do you know whitefish?"

"Sure," Rowena said. "But no. Cray's never netted."

"The only fish you can legally net are whitefish," Sam said. "I hope he's never netted walleye."

"No."

"Just a couple more times," Amanda said, about the cup. "So, do you know any employees who might be using?"

"Drugs?"

Amanda nodded.

"No. None of us in the bar. I don't really know other areas. The people who work there."

"What about roofies?" Sam said. "Rohypnol? Have you ever seen it used?"

There it was again. She tried to remain calm, neutral. But what he noticed was the effort.

"Roofies?"

"We've had incidents before," Amanda said, referencing the cases they'd prosecuted. "You remember?"

"Oh." Then she nodded. "That's the date-rape drug?"

"That's it."

"I've never seen it done," Rowena said. "I heard about those times, but I wasn't here those nights. Are you testing for roofies?"

"No," Amanda said. "People don't take roofies recreationally. Predators use it. This test is for the usual stuff. Marijuana, opioids, meth, barbiturates, that kind of thing."

"Oh." She nodded. And then she spit again.

"The part-time gig works pretty well for you?" Sam said.

She nodded. "Yes."

"That should be good, Rowena," Amanda said.

Rowena handed over the cap and the cup. Then she glanced at her wristwatch and said, "Is that it? I've got some errands to run."

Amanda and Sam both stood and thanked her. Rowena stood quickly, nodded, and left.

After the door closed, Amanda looked at Sam and said, "Most people ask about when they can expect the results."

Rowena had been anxious to leave.

"She's scared," Sam said.

CHAPTER 42

S am returned to his Jeep and had enough time to run Gray and then head over to the sheriff's office. While he was running Gray in the nearby woods, Sandy Harju texted him.

"Cray Halverson owns a Crestliner, Commander Elite," she wrote. "Twenty-one feet, seven inches. White. With a 200 hp Yamaha. Nice boat."

Deputy Harju was too smart not to recognize the importance of Cray's boat. "Thanks," Sam texted back. "See you at the sheriff's office."

By 10:30 in the morning, Sam, Deputy Harju, Deputy Smith Barnes, and the sheriff were all crowded into the sheriff's office. Sam had brought in two extra chairs and he, Harju, and Barnes sat in front of Sheriff Goddard's desk. The sheriff appeared tired but content.

"How's John Michael?" Sam said.

"The kid keeps his own hours," the sheriff said, shaking his head. Then he grinned. "But God, he's cute."

"It'll get better," Smith Barnes said. Barnes had two sons, both now in their 40s.

"So I've heard." Then, with a yawn, the sheriff said, "So, where we at?"

Harju and Barnes both looked at Sam. Sam said, "Well, everything's taken a few unexpected turns."

Then Sam took the next 15 minutes running through some of what they'd learned, chronologically. Smith Barnes had told the sheriff a few of the details, about the autopsy report and Holden's toxicology report.

When Sam covered the pertinent details of those reports, Smith Barnes finally recognized that the only logical conclusion was Holden's innocence. Barnes still believed once a criminal, always a criminal, and from Barnes's perspective, Holden had been heading toward committing murder since high school. But he was smart enough to keep the thought to himself.

"The evidence supports Holden Riggins's innocence," the sheriff said.

"What about a felon having an unregistered weapon?" Barnes said.

The sheriff paused. "You're right. Good point. Keep the gun in evidence. I'll consider that charge later. But those other charges— illegal netting, open container law, and murder," the sheriff said, pointedly. "I think we can release Holden Riggins. Now."

Barnes looked at the sheriff and was thinking about reminding him of the open bottle law. But he knew the sheriff. He saw his familiar resolve. So, he finally said, quietly, "Okay."

Then there was a knock on the door, and Lois, the sheriff's gray-haired admin, poked her head in. "Sheriff, there's a man here who wants to see you."

"Gotta wait," the sheriff said. "We're in the middle of something."

"He says it's about Charlie Jiles. He says he knows what happened."

"Who is it?" Sam said.

"Cray Halverson."

Sam turned to the sheriff and said, "I haven't had a chance to tell you about Cray Halverson. You should hear him out, Dean. Probably best if you record it, after you read him his rights. How about if we talk to him in the interrogation room?"

Sheriff Dean Goddard appeared surprised. But he paused for a moment, considering, and then sighed again. "Lois, can you please escort Mr. Halverson to the interrogation room? Tell him I'll be there in a sec."

After the door closed, they all looked at one another, and the sheriff said to Sam, "You think he knows something?"

"Yes. I also think he's a poacher and has been poaching walleye for a while. And I think Charlie Jiles was involved."

This time Smith Barnes was startled. He was about to protest the idea that a Minnesota DNR conservation officer could be involved in poaching. But before he could, the sheriff held up a finger.

The sheriff looked at Sam and said, "Apparently you've been busy."

"I have. Me and Deputy Harju," Sam said, nodding toward Harju.

"And you have evidence?"

Harju looked to Sam. Sam said, "I was starting to lay it all out. But yes, there's plenty of evidence, and it took us in an unexpected direction. There are one or two gaps. The poaching is an educated guess. We have evidence of a connection between Cray Halverson and Charlie Jiles. And we have evidence of some other kind of connection between Cray's live-in girlfriend, Rowena Melnyk, and Charlie Jiles."

The sheriff's eyebrows raised. It was a lot to take in. But the sheriff knew Sam Rivers and was willing to roll with the unexpected developments.

"I'm guessing, but I suspect Cray Halverson is going to fill in some gaps," Sam said.

The sheriff paused, thinking. Then, "Barnes, maybe you should go and take care of Holden Riggins. That interrogation room is too big for all of us. Sam, Deputy Harju, and I can hear what Cray Halverson has to say." Sam remembered the room was small, but the sheriff's directive was also a subtle way of excluding Smith Barnes.

"Okay," Barnes said, subdued.

After Barnes's departure, the sheriff wanted to know what he was walking into, with regard to Cray Halverson.

"Cray was the guy who made the call to the TIP line," Sam said. "The caller indicated he was out by Temple Island at 4 a.m. But Cray, who lives with Rowena, has a cabin on the mainland."

"Interesting, but maybe he was heading to a favorite fishing hole," the sheriff said.

"We're pretty sure we intercepted Cray and Rowena last night heading to an illegal walleye net," Harju said. She explained about what they were doing, what they found, and how they chased after Cray's Crestliner.

"The day Charlie Jiles died," Sam said, "he sent two texts to Rowena Melnyk, one to Cray, and Rowena texted back, twice."

Finally, the sheriff raised his hands and said, "Okay. Let's see what Cray Halverson has to say."

Lois was back at the door. "Uh, sheriff," she said.

"What is it now?"

"Mr. Halverson is in the interrogation room. But now there's a Rowena Melnyk here to see you. She asked if Mr. Halverson was here."

The sheriff looked at Sam and then Harju. Then back to Lois. "What did you tell her?"

"That I was not allowed to discuss departmental business."

"Good. Where is she now?" the sheriff said.

"Front room."

"Let's talk to Cray first," Sam said. "Put Rowena in your other interrogation room. I suspect Cray is here because he knows we know something. But he doesn't know what we know."

"Or what we don't," the sheriff said.

CHAPTER 43

When they entered the small interrogation room, the first thing Sam noticed was the smell. The odor was fetid musk, like a wild animal. Aged sweat with something else mixed in; some kind of strong emotion—anxiety or fear or anger—with, Sam thought, a hint of fish. Cray was unshaven and, judging from the rims under his eyes, hadn't slept much. He wore a disheveled flannel shirt under taupe Carhartt coveralls.

"Before we talk, Mr. Halverson, I need to explain the ground rules," the sheriff said.

First, he introduced Sam and Deputy Harju. Cray seemed to know about Sam. Then he nodded to Harju.

The sheriff read him Miranda, setting a recorder on the desk in front of him so he'd see it and know he was being recorded. He waited for Cray's acknowledgment, that he understood his rights. He nodded, but the sheriff asked Cray to give him a verbal.

"I understand," Cray said.

After everyone was seated, Cray waited less than 10 seconds before he said, "Charlie Jiles raped my Rowena."

For a moment, everyone remained silent.

"Your girlfriend?" Sam said.

"Partner," Cray said. "Like a wife. But we don't have no rings or paper that says so."

"When?" the sheriff asked.

"First time was late September. Jiles told me to go to Crane Lake." Cray looked away. "I been takin' walleye for two years. With nets. That sonofabitch Jiles'd tell me where to set, and when."

"So he told you to set on Crane Lake?" the sheriff said.

Cray nodded. "Said the coast was clear. Set 'em night before, he said. Then bring 'em in at dawn. He knew I'd stay over. Not the first time I done it. But that bastard trapped my Rowena. Said he needed help on some cleanup at the creek. Bullshit," Cray said. Then, "Rowena trusted Jiles 'cause we'd been partners for two years. So, she went."

When Cray didn't continue, Sam said, "And he raped her there?"

He nodded. "Boat ride over, he got her to drink some of that drug he uses on women. He told me about it once. Gave me some, case I was interested. But I wasn't."

Cray glanced at a nearby wall, thinking.

"What kind of man drugs women and rapes 'em?" Cray said. "That's what the sonofabitch did. Drugged my Rowena and raped her," he spit. "He goddamn took a video of it. On his phone!" Cray said, incredulous.

"He filmed it?" Harju said.

Red faced, Cray Halverson nodded.

"When did you find out about it?" Sam said.

Cray glanced at the wall again. Without looking at any of them, he said, "Week ago. Drove down to Two Harbors for supplies.

That's when the sonofabitch did it again. Thursday. Used that video to trap her again. Said he'd get rid of it but needed to tell Row he was sorry. Got her to Smugglers Creek."

There was a long pause during which Cray continued staring at the wall.

"Row went, 'cause she was going to beat the shit out of him."

The law enforcement people in the room had no doubt Rowena Melnyk could have done it.

"But he had a Taser?" Sam said.

Cray nodded. "Rowena didn't stand a chance. He knocked her out with it. Raped her again." There was no spit in it this time. Only disgust.

After a moment of silence, during which Cray let the news of Rowena's second rape sink in, he continued.

"If Row had told me about the first time, I would have killed Charlie Jiles sooner than I did."

There it was, Sam thought. *Cray's confession.* Sam, Harju, and the sheriff didn't blink. But they all recognized there were still details to be filled in.

"He hurt her, that second time," Cray said. "Taser left marks. So did his hands."

"Did you kill Charlie Jiles last Thursday?" Sam said. "At Smugglers Creek?"

Cray looked at Sam and nodded.

"Need a verbal, Cray," the sheriff said.

"Yeah. I killed Charlie Jiles. He raped Rowena. Twice."

"How did you find out about it?" Harju said.

"Rowena was hurt. Needed help. She called me."

Another long pause. Harju said, "She called you from Smugglers Creek?"

Cray nodded.

"Jiles was still there?" Harju said.

Cray nodded again. "In his boat."

Harju wondered about it. Would Charlie Jiles let Rowena call for help? Maybe she did it surreptitiously, but it couldn't have been easy, with her rapist nearby. She glanced at the sheriff, to see what he thought. He was focused on Cray. But Sam looked at Harju in a way that told Harju he wondered about it too.

"So you boated out there to help her?" Sam said.

"Uh-huh," Cray said.

No one said anything, thinking about it.

"Can you tell us what happened?" the sheriff said.

"I got out there and seen what happened and jumped into Jiles's boat and hit him with his fire extinguisher. Knocked him into the water and left him there."

Sam was having a hard time imagining Charlie Jiles sticking around to be confronted by Cray Halverson, after Jiles raped Rowena a second time. But the details were correct. Jiles had been killed with the fire extinguisher. A blow to the head.

"I called Row in sick. Then I fished Jiles out of the water and ran him and his boat up the creek. Then I got Rowena home and tried to figure out what to do."

He didn't sleep that night.

Friday morning, Cray had a plan. Everyone knew about Holden Riggins's past. Jiles had told Cray that Holden could be a problem, though they'd never done anything about him. The previous afternoon, when Cray raced to Smugglers Creek to help Rowena, he boated by Holden Riggins setting his whitefish net off Temple Island. That evening, trying to figure out how to cover their tracks, he thought about Holden Riggins. If law enforcement found Holden drunk, out with his nets, Jiles tangled in Holden's whitefish net, beside an illegal net for walleye, Cray knew they'd finger Holden for illegal poaching and murder.

"Then on Friday," Sam said, remembering the video, "Rowena swapped out the bottles used to mix Holden's drink? That's how you drugged Holden?"

Cray reminded them the snake Charlie Jiles had given Cray some roofies. Cray still had them.

"Jiles had a bug up his ass about Holden. But me and Rowena never would have done nothin' about him. 'Cept he was the perfect guy to throw the law off our trail. And to give us time for one last walleye haul. We knew Holden'd get clear, once the dust settled."

Sam was less sanguine about the law eventually clearing Holden. Especially given his history with Deputy Smith Barnes and others in local law enforcement. But Cray Halverson's confession cleared up several issues, including Holden's innocence. Sam and Harju both wondered about the time gap between Cray Halverson's arrival at Smugglers Creek and his confrontation with Charlie Jiles.

"Sheriff," Sam said. "I need a private word with you and Deputy Harju."

The sheriff looked up, thought about it, and nodded.

"I'll have someone type up your statement, Cray. Then you'll need to sign it."

Cray nodded.

The sheriff turned off the recording, picked up his phone, and he, Sam, and Harju stepped out of the room, closing the door behind them.

"We need to speak with Rowena Melnyk," Sam said.

"Sure," the sheriff said. "But Cray's confession clears up a lot."

"But there's something that doesn't add up," Harju said. "Charlie Jiles was in his boat at the mouth of Smugglers Creek. He convinced Rowena to meet him in her boat. When she arrives, he tases her. Then he rapes her. Why did he stick around?"

"To make sure she was okay?" the sheriff said.

"First he tases her," Harju said. "Then he rapes her, brutally. Then he worries about her well-being?"

The sheriff shrugged. "Dumber things have happened."

"I'm with Harju," Sam said. "Even if you assume Rowena Melnyk managed to make a call to Cray Halverson and tell him what happened, Cray was away from their house. Down in Two Harbors, he said. It would have taken him quite a while to get to Smugglers Creek."

"There's no way Charlie Jiles is waiting there the whole time," Harju said.

The sheriff, recognizing the anomaly, said, "Let's see what Ms. Melnyk has to say."

They entered the second interrogation room. Rowena Melnyk sat across from them. After Sam, Harju, and the sheriff sat down, the sheriff repeated his Miranda warning, and explained about recording their conversation.

Rowena nodded and said, "Is Cray here?"

The sheriff paused. "Yes. Cray is here and we've spoken to him."

Rowena looked away, and for nearly a minute she didn't speak. She was thinking. Then, "I got an idea what Cray told you." Her voice faltered and her eyes teared up. She held a handkerchief in her hand. She reached up and blew her nose.

After she calmed herself, she said, "When we met this morning, at the casino, I was pretty sure you guys had figured it out. When I went home and told Cray about it, he said he'd go talk to you. That he'd set it right. He'd tell you he killed Charlie Jiles. But I told him no. And then I was so upset I had to lay down. When I got up, Cray was gone."

"And you assumed he had come to speak with us?" the sheriff asked.

Rowena nodded. "No one. No man ever done anything like that for me. We're quiet people. We don't talk much. Specially about us. But we love each other," she said, a whine in her voice, then more tears.

They waited while she calmed herself a second time. Then, "But Cray never hit Charlie Jiles. I killed him."

To the best of her memory, she tried to convey what happened, though some of the details were understandably hazy.

When Charlie Jiles finished raping Rowena a second time, she was in such a deep state of shock she struggled to reach full-throated consciousness. It wasn't the first time she'd been used for sex. But she'd never been tased or tied. She lay there, stunned, and barely noticed when Charlie Jiles cut the ties that bound her.

"Get yourself dressed, Rowena," Jiles said.

She remembered his first words, when he was finished.

When she didn't move, and still weeping, he repeated, "Get dressed."

"I tried to pull myself together," Rowena said. "I was still on my knees. I . . . I remember getting my jeans on. There was blood. When I saw my panties on the boat's bottom, torn and soaked, I got sick. Threw up over the side. Then I remember sitting on the side seat and crying. I tried to stop. I tried to but couldn't."

"What was Charlie Jiles doing?" the sheriff said.

"I don't . . . remember. I think he was picking up the cut ties. He was sorting things out," she said.

She paused for a moment, looking off with a long, unfocused gaze.

"I know at one point he turned away from me. He was close, but his back was to me.

"I didn't know what he was going to do," Rowena said. "He shot me and tied me up and raped me . . . he had to know I couldn't keep the marks from Cray. Cray was going to see them. He had to know Cray would kill him."

She raised the handkerchief to her eyes again, wiping tears.

"And . . . I . . . just . . . something in me . . . something in me . . . Charlie Jiles was going to kill me. I knew he was going to kill me."

She paused again, in a hard place of telling.

"The fire extinguisher was stuck to the wall," Rowena said. "Close."

Fourteen inches long, four inches in diameter, and weighing two and a half pounds, they were designed to be wielded against sudden conflagrations.

"I couldn't breathe," Rowena said. "I jus' . . . something came up inside me and . . . I took that red cylinder out of its bracket. I was good with a bat . . . in high school. Good with a bat. Before Charlie Jiles turned, I swung at him. Hard as I could."

Sam knew it had been a few years since Rowena was in high school. But swinging a bat was like riding a bicycle, the grip and the way you pivot on your left foot and step into it, your entire upper body leading the bat's arc. All of it naturally recalled. Muscle memory.

Sam guessed there was more to her swing than the memories of her high school softball prowess. He guessed Rowena Melnyk swung at all those times men—bad men—used her, forced themselves on her. Sam knew those men. He knew they were the ugliest kind, who thought their dicks were lodestars, every fiber subservient to its need. Sam could imagine there were these kind of men in Rowena's past. The kind of men who did not think about a woman. They focused on climax. The woman, Rowena, might as well have been a blowup doll, forced into whatever posture satisfied their monomaniacal urge. The woman was an orifice, a means to an end.

Until Cray Halverson.

Forensics determined the extinguisher struck Jiles against the back right side of Jiles's head, just under the ear. Struck him hard enough to crack his skull. Probably resulting in instant unconsciousness.

"I knocked off his green cap and he started to go down," Rowena recalled. "After I hit him I must have dropped the extinguisher. Or it slipped out of my hands. I would have hit him again. I still wanted to tear him apart. I charged behind that swing and hit him with my shoulder. With everything. He fell in the lake."

She watched a mass of green make an oversize splash. Then disappear beneath the surface, briefly. The air trapped in his clothes brought him bobbing to the surface, face down.

Rowena, caught up in the adrenalin, was ready to follow him into the water. She fell forward and would have plunged on top of him, ready to tear the man apart, if the gunwale hadn't prevented her.

"I sat," she said. "I don't know how long. Long enough to watch the body float away. Toward shore."

After several more minutes her heart finally eased its hammering. "I knew he was dead," Rowena said. "Pretty sure I killed him when I hit him. But nobody can survive that long face down in water."

Thinking about the scene, Harju recognized the signs of shock. Being tased, raped, and then striking out, Harju guessed Rowena Melnyk would have been practically catatonic.

"I sat there for a long time, I guess. Long enough for Charlie Jiles to float into some weeds and get stuck there. Long enough for Cray to get back from Two Harbors. And then I just . . . cleaned up."

She felt the blood in her jeans. Her bloody underwear lay in the back of the boat, beside Jiles's phone and his spent Taser.

"I wrapped my panties around the phone and threw them into the lake. I never wanted anyone to find his phone or see that video.

Then I threw in the Taser, so no one would ever know anything about it." She looked away and paused. "Except Cray."

Rowena explained there was no other way. She had her phone and used it to call Cray. As soon as she heard his voice, she sobbed.

"Cray knew to come. I told him where I was and that I killed Charlie Jiles."

Cray told Rowena to stay there. He'd get there as soon as possible. And he did.

"Then I told him everything."

Rowena explained how Cray held her for as long as it took, until the sun went down and the woods turned dark and a bone chill entered the air. Cray fetched coats from the boat's storage compartment and made sure Rowena was wrapped up warm. Then he took a flashlight and stepped into Jiles's runabout, untethering it and steering it toward the shoreline, where the green-clad officer lay face down, stuck in the weeds.

Then everything else happened the way Cray told them earlier. He took Rowena home, towing her boat.

And she slept.

And Cray Halverson got busy.

Finally, Rowena was finished. She looked pale and tired. If she hadn't been solid as stone, Sam might have worried she was close to a heart attack. But Rowena was strong. The last week, Sam guessed, was incredibly hard on her. But they were left with few alternatives. When they all filed out of the room, the sheriff asked Deputy Smith Barnes to escort both Ms. Melnyk and Mr. Halverson to holding cells, at least for the time being.

CHAPTER 44

Friday, October 20

S am was finished at the sheriff's office by Thursday afternoon. Deputy Harju and the sheriff took over the details of processing Rowena Melnyk and Cray Halverson. They were guilty of poaching, as well as poisoning and framing Holden Riggins. And attempted murder, given Holden almost froze to death. But did Rowena murder Charlie Jiles? Clearly, it had been murder. But didn't it involve an element of self-defense?

Cray Halverson argued they had never intended to kill Holden Riggins. If he'd wanted to kill him, why would he have placed the predawn call at the casino docks, reporting the suspicious boats and providing their exact location? He would have left Holden to freeze to death. They'd only used Holden as a decoy, knowing he would eventually be cleared. They needed time to make one last haul of walleye, to fulfill his order for Char Peigan. They used Holden to cover their tracks and buy them time.

Sam and the sheriff let them know they could argue whatever they wanted to a prosecutor, or a jury. But for now, the charge was attempted murder.

But the murder of Charlie Jiles? Given the rape charge, if what Rowena described to them was true (and she had the bruises and Taser marks to prove it), the sheriff would need to consider those charges. Especially since Rowena feared for her life. He'd made a call to the prosecutor's office and set an early Monday-morning meeting to discuss them with her.

Surprisingly, when Holden Riggins was finally informed of all the details, he said he did not want to bring charges against Cray and Rowena for drugging and framing him. He wanted them to pay for poaching, and for whatever else the sheriff thought fitting, but he reminded the sheriff that he had known desperate times. Holden believed the best way to atone for his past and theirs was to show mercy.

While they'd been inside, interviewing Rowena and Cray, the winds continued out of the southeast. By the time Sam left the county offices, the mercury had climbed to 57 degrees.

On Friday, Sam checked out of the Vermilion Falls Motel. By 4 p.m., he and Gray were on their way to Birch Point Road, when Carmel called.

Carmel's pack had taken off early and had just got into their Vermilion hideaway, and it was terrific. Jennifer was crooning over every room. Frank and Liberty had already leaped off the end of the dock, in vain pursuit of a pair of mallards. Where were he and Gray?

Sam pulled in behind Carmel's Expedition and could hear barks from the cabin's lakeside. He and Gray found everyone on the dock, enjoying the late afternoon sun and warmth.

Carmel was sitting on a bench beside a cooler. Jennifer was throwing sticks for Frank and Liberty, one of Gray's favorite games. He thundered down the dock and was airborne by the time the stick left Jennifer's hand. Frank and Liberty, surprised, followed Gray in trailing pursuit.

Sam wasn't sure he had ever seen anything so nice: the lake in sunlight, Jennifer playing catch with the dogs, the dogs soaked, Carmel with her face golden in the light, and a bottle of Sam Adams in her hand. And then in Sam's.

He wasn't on the deck 10 minutes before his cell rang. It was Holden's friend, Ruth Walker.

She had already spoken with Holden and heard the good news. She wanted to surprise Holden and was hoping Sam would join them for dinner out at Holden's cabin tomorrow night.

Sam told her about Carmel, Jennifer, and the dogs, and Ruth said, "They're invited. Holden will love it. Just don't tell him. Do you know how to get there?"

Sam did.

While they sat in the unusual heat of the waning October day, Carmel told Sam about her day. Perhaps most importantly, she and Jennifer had talked on their drive north. A short while after crossing Hellwig Creek, it was Jennifer who brought up sleeping arrangements.

"Seriously, Mom. Every night I'm home I hear you sneaking to the study! You don't need to sneak around."

The 12-year-old sounded indignant, on the verge of becoming a teenager. And a woman.

Sam started laughing.

When it was Sam's turn to talk about his day, he didn't know where to begin. The week had been so crazy, and the last two days filled with so much emotion, he decided just to sip his beer and enjoy the evening with Carmel. And the night, now that Jennifer was onboard with the facts of life.

Saturday was glorious, boating much of the east end of Lake Vermilion, a huge body of water with beautiful wilderness and stunning cabins. By dinnertime they cruised to Holden's hermitage and, to their surprise, saw the sheriff department's boat and a second boat tethered to Holden's dock. They had to beach the pontoon, which was fine with the dogs, who loved the way Holden's sand tapered into the water.

Ruth Walker had also invited Sandy Harju and Phil Wirta, plus the sheriff, his wife Dr. Susan Wallace, and newborn John Michael. Ruth, who didn't seem old enough, had nonetheless schooled Harju and Wirta when they were seniors. It had been her first year, and it had been difficult, but one of the reasons she'd managed to get through it was because of stellar students like these two.

Holden, of course, was shocked, surprised, and, eventually, pleased.

In fact, he was so pleased, he agreed to share his favorite whitefish recipe. But only if they swore to keep it to themselves.

Sam transcribed.

Per two pounds of whitefish fillets, mix the following in a large zip-top plastic bag:

1½ tsp. paprika

1 tsp. garlic powder

1 tsp. onion powder

½ tsp. salt

½ tsp. pepper

¼ cup grated Parmesan cheese

¼ cup shredded Parmesan cheese

¼ cup panko breadcrumbs

Cut the fillets into large slices, about the size of a potato wedge.

Break two eggs into a cup of milk and hand whip into a light froth.

Drop the whitefish slices into the milk-egg mixture.

Drop the coated whitefish into a large zip-top plastic bag containing the spice-cheese-breadcrumb mixture.

Shake to coat well.

Cover the bottom of a cast-iron pan with oil. Heat. Then fry the breaded fillets until golden-brown. If you wanted them with less oil (which Holden didn't), you could also place them on a greased cookie sheet and bake at 425 degrees for 10–12 minutes.

DIPPING SAUCES

Aoli:

4 cloves of garlic, minced

2 tsp. fresh lemon juice

¼ tsp. salt

¼ tsp. pepper

½ cup good mayo

¼ tsp. Dijon mustard

1 tbsp. Heinz ketchup

Sweet, salty, and spicy:

2 tbsp. maple syrup

2 tbsp. balsamic vinegar

2 tbsp. Dijon mustard

½ tsp. garlic powder

1 tbsp. Chohula Hot Sauce

The recipe produced the finest fried whitefish any of them had ever tasted. When dipped into Holden's sauces, the culinary experience was transcendent, maybe even spiritual.

They all promised to never share the recipe with anyone.

EPILOGUE

Rowena's murder of Conservation Officer Charlie Jiles was determined to be self-defense.

After the dust settled, Cray and Rowena were convicted of poaching. And since they sold their poached walleye commercially, it was a violation of the Lacey Act. Given the ambiguous circumstances, the judge was lenient in sentencing. Combined, Rowena and Cray each received 4-year sentences and would be eligible for parole after 2.

The sheriff's suspicion about a county law enforcement insider assisting Charlie Jiles's poaching operations was warranted. Cray confessed to having paid off an anonymous informant with money dropped on a reef in the middle of Vermilion's Big Bay. While Cray confirmed the man's existence, he could not confirm his identity.

Sam recalled seeing Deputy Joe Haman on that reef. To double-check, he called up the GPS memory of the runabout Joe Haman had used to get to the reef. Joe's alibi was that he was acting on a hunch and wanted to re-examine the location where they found Jiles's body. The GPS showed he boated straight to the reef and back.

When Joe was questioned, he said he thought he saw something on that reef, so he'd gone out to investigate. By the time he was done looking over the reef, it was getting dark, forcing him to return to the marina. The explanation wasn't plausible.

But they needed more evidence. For the time being, Deputy Joe Haman was suspended until further notice.

The sheriff asked Sam Rivers for assistance. The most logical place to begin was Charlie Jiles's Eveleth home. The sheriff remembered Joe Haman's cursory reports. The man had visited the place three times, initially to search for Charlie's cell phone and anything else that might look suspicious, and to make sure Charlie's house was locked and secure.

The sheriff gave Sam the cursory reports and a key to Jiles's home. Given the sensitive nature and purpose of Sam's visit to Jiles's home, the sheriff told no one about Sam's search.

Now that Jiles's house was somewhat cleaned, the place appeared spare.

Sam searched throughout the house, making a careful inventory of its contents and cubbies. He looked in the freezer. He peered into all the kitchen cupboards. Similar to Deputy Joe Haman's initial search, he looked through Jiles's closets, through each of his numerous pairs of shoes, through his dresser drawers, through the end tables on either side of his bed. He looked in the basement. He even took a flashlight and shined it into some side registers and cold air ducts.

But he found nothing.

Something about Jiles's bedroom made Sam return to it. As soon as he walked in, he realized the obvious. One of the bedside bookshelves held four novels, two nonfiction books, and a dictionary. Everything but the dictionary appeared relatively new. Sam thought two of the novels were especially odd for a guy like Charlie Jiles: *The Streel* by Mary Logue and *Where the Crawdads Sing* by Delia Owens. Sam was familiar with both books; they were quite good. But both books looked like they'd never been opened.

Incongruously, the American Collegiate Dictionary appeared ratty and moth-eaten.

Sam pulled out the American Collegiate and opened it. Most of the book's center was hollowed out. Inside, Sam found three stacks of bills and a flash drive.

Sam flipped through one of the stacks of bills and saw they were all $100s. The other two stacks were the same. They were nearly an inch thick. Sam had confiscated contraband before. These looked like stacks of $100 bills, or $10,000.

Clearly, Charlie Jiles had not been a reader. But he was a recorder. Since none of the files were password protected, they were easily called up on the sheriff's computer, back in his office, when Sam shared what he found, behind a closed door.

The flash drive contained several audio recordings, some videos, and still shots, all apparently taken with his iPhone. Presumably, it was some kind of insurance. Or something he might be able to use someday to bribe or extort?

The sheriff was pleased about the nearly $30,000 in cash, which would help fund the department, prosecutors, and the state crime lab. But he was more pleased with what they found on the flash drive.

Along with pictures and videos and some audio of Cray Halverson and Rowena Melnyk, there were several in which Deputy Joe Haman was featured. Most of the Haman files were nearly two years old. The audio files were short, and chronicled detailed discussions of how their operation would work, and what Charlie Jiles needed in terms of county law enforcement information.

Deputy Haman was heard making several pertinent suggestions, all involving illegal activities. There were negotiations regarding payment. For Haman's small role in the operation, he was paid $1,000 per month.

Through late morning, calls to Deputy Joe Haman went unanswered. Either someone alerted him to his imminent arrest, or he sensed something awry. Truthfully, Joe Haman assumed Cray Halverson was the person who phoned him wanting information about law enforcement whereabouts, after Jiles was dead. He also assumed Cray Halverson had told the sheriff and Sam about it.

Regardless, when the calls from the sheriff's office became persistent, he suspected they had connected the dots.

Joe Haman spent the morning at home, thinking hard about next steps. Finally, he opened his cold air duct, took out the $20,000 in cash he had accumulated over the last two years, gathered some other supplies, and headed out to his boyhood farm. He turned into the long drive and parked behind the barn.

The more he thought about it, the more he figured his best next step was Canada. But if he drove they could easily catch him on the highway or at the border.

The barn was full of traps, packs, camping equipment, everything he'd need to disappear into the woods and survive, even with the cold and winter coming on. He could cross the border through the wilderness and vanish on the other side.

Earlier, the new owner of Joe's boyhood farm had driven by and noticed there were fresh tire tracks in the drive. He'd seen them before. Days earlier, when he checked on his property he'd also seen where someone had broken into the barn through the grain chute door, though he couldn't find anything missing.

Now he wondered if the thief had returned. He called the sheriff's office and reported the suspicious activity.

The sheriff knew Joe Haman was from the area and had been raised on a farm. When the sheriff heard about the patrol request, he verified the property had been the Haman family farm. The sheriff and Sam thought they'd check it out.

They found Haman's car behind the barn, but Deputy Joe Haman had disappeared.

"We'll find him," Sam said. "Or Gray will."

The deputy was a neatnik. In the car's front seat they found a towel Joe Haman used to wipe down his car's interior. It was covered with Joe's scent.

Sam brought it out, placed it in front of Gray's nose, and said, "Find!"

It had always seemed like a game to Gray. One he loved to play because he was so good at it.

His tail wagged, his nose went to the ground, and within five minutes he was heading into the shorn cornfield behind the farmhouse. Sam and the sheriff followed. They occasionally saw what they assumed were Joe Haman's boot prints. The two law enforcement officers needed to hustle to keep up with Gray.

At the tree line they hesitated. The forest was dark and thick, and they knew if they entered the woods it might be a while before they came out. But the trail was fresh.

By the time Gray had gone about a mile into the trees, he was 100 yards in front of Sam, who was more than 50 yards in front of the sheriff. Gray saw movement through the woods. As he closed toward it, he glimpsed the backpack on the backside of Deputy Joe Haman.

Gray was far enough ahead of Sam and the sheriff to have at least a full minute of Joe Haman to himself.

Gray didn't really think like a human. He didn't think about things like retribution or revenge. For Gray, it was all about pursuit and capture. If Gray had thought like a person, he might have remembered the time when Haman harassed him with pine cones and piss at the casino, or maybe recognized Joe's scent and associated it with Sam's flat tire and the strychnine-laced rabbit.

Regardless, Gray's sprint to overtake the errant lawman was as quiet as a wolf in pursuit of an unsuspecting whitetail. At least until he was upon him.

A minute later, Sam Rivers arrived. The sheriff was still struggling through the pines.

Gray had Deputy Joe Haman on the ground, on his back, hands and arms raised like an overturned turtle, screaming for Gray to back off. For his part, Gray had knocked the deputy down and then taken a few gnarly bites at his forearm to make sure he stayed down.

For Deputy Joe Haman, crime did not pay; instead, it accrued some decidedly painful debts.

Cray Halverson's full, ardent confession included a list of his customers. Cray had lied to all of them. After interviewing them, everyone except Chef Char Peigan confessed they were suspicious about the provenance of Cray's walleye. Then everyone except Char pled guilty to a gross misdemeanor and paid a $3,000 fine.

Char, down in the Cities, maintained her innocence. She hired a large downtown law firm to take her case. Through a series of filings and counter filings, during which she declined to take the advice of counsel and settle, Char held her ground. She did so because she feared anyone convicted of this kind of crime would never become a James Beard Award winner, and it had long been her ambition, vision, and mission to become one.

Over two years of accepting poached product, Char had saved nearly $24,000. Eventually, she settled for a gross misdemeanor and a $3,000 fine. She spent nearly $40,000 on attorneys' fees.

Because Char's story was such an interesting one, a young Minnesota-based reporter for *Restaurateur*, a national trade magazine, covered it. The monthly's May story featured an elegant, smiling Char Peigan on its cover, standing in front of her restaurant, Field & Stream. The cover tag line read: *How the mighty have fallen.* The story explained that the photo was taken three years earlier at the restaurant's opening. At that time Char had been featured as an up-and-coming star in the Twin Cities restaurant market, perennially in the running for a James Beard Award.

The article quoted two former James Beard judges, each explaining that, based on their understanding of the case and Ms. Peigan's egregious, illegal activities, if it was up to them she would be disqualified from ever applying for the prestigious award. "When all her competitors are playing by the rules, and this restaurateur is obtaining an advantage through the purchase of illegal product, that's not fair. There have to be rules in competitions," the judge concluded. "You break the rules, you pay."

And so, Char Peigan did.

When the prosecutor understood Holden's .45 was a family heirloom, and that Holden had been clean for the last seven years, they registered the weapon, returned it to him, and said no more about it.

Holden took some time off work. He finished his birchbark canoe. In early November, the weather yielded the season's final warmup, keeping the waterways open. Holden called Sam and told him there was something he needed to do, and that he could use Sam's help.

Sam agreed to come up, and on a sunny midday, Holden explained what needed to be done.

Sam was against it. He considered the canoe a work of art. He knew Holden had taken a lifetime to sojourn in wilderness and harvest all of the materials that went into its construction. And another lifetime exercising the craftsmanship required to build it. But Holden felt it must be done.

They gathered the necessary supplies, tied an aluminum canoe to the back of Holden's birchbark, and then both he and

Sam paddled it across Vermilion, up into Trout, and eventually into Pine.

During the entire journey north, they said little. Recognizing the importance of what they were about, they focused on their breathing, their paddling, and their journey into wilderness.

By early afternoon they came into the old familiar lake. They paddled out from the waterway that had taken them into Pine, the aluminum canoe trailing behind them, their wake breaking the still water in a shallow riffle, like a water bird in search of refuge. They paddled to the island.

There was almost no wind. The sky was clear and a beautiful, late-autumn blue, the angle of light making the lake's mirrored surface resplendent.

Once on the island they beached both canoes. Then they found three heavy stones and placed them in the wooden canoe's bow, middle, and stern. They covered the bottom of the canoe with dry tinder, filling it to the gunwales. Finally, they both stepped into the aluminum canoe and, towing the loaded birchbark, paddled to the lake's center.

Holden did not need any words to be spoken, because with every narrow strip of wood that went into the making of the beautiful canoe, he had already uttered them. Apologies to his father. Confessions aplenty. Atonements to everyone he'd struck in anger, and to the wilderness and its animals he'd desecrated over the years, through his mindless, inattentive, soulless activities. The birchbark was his offering.

Sam could not let the moment pass without saying something.

"A very long time ago I lost a friend. You and I and your dad paddled into a storm on this lake. Your dad died. A lot changed after that. That storm has followed both of us. I know your offering, and the way you've lived for the last seven years, should provide us, your dad, the wilderness, some atonement," Sam said. "I am glad to have my old friend back."

Sam paused. There wasn't much more to be said. He managed to reach his paddle forward and touch Holden's shoulder with it. Holden reached behind him and gripped the paddle's end.

Then Holden struck the match and touched it to the canoe's tinder and watched it lick and burn. It did not take long to catch fire and grow. Then he and Sam backed off and watched the pyre flare. The smoke reached into the windless sky like a column into the house of the gods. Its sides withered first, caving in on themselves. Gradually, everything above water burned. Finally, near the canoe's low-hung center, the gunwale fell and opened a space large enough for the sluice of water to rush in. When the water touched the red-hot coals they hissed, steamed, and eventually the water won out. And when the lake finally silenced the fire, what was left of his personal project, weighted down by three heavy stones, disappeared into Pine's depths the way Holden's father had so many years ago.

Before Holden returned to work, he invited Ruth out to his cabin for dinner. After a dessert of ice cream and chocolate sauce, he asked Ruth if she'd spend the night. She did.

Two days later Holden called Sam. He told Sam about Ruth. But the real reason he'd called was to find out if Sam had anything to do with local DNR fish biologists Cindy Hill and Andy

Nivens asking Holden for his assistance. Their winter fish counts were coming up, and they needed someone who knew Vermilion and knew how to net and where to place them. Also, they needed someone who was familiar with the numerous species that could be found in Vermilion. It was a subcontractor role, part-time job, but the pay was excellent and if things worked out, they could use him after ice out too.

Sam smiled, congratulated Holden on his news about Ruth, and said he didn't know anything about the fish biologists.

"Right," Holden said.

The flurries came in mid-November, sudden and ticking like a snow bomb. Four inches in the Cities, but it didn't stay around. Still, it was a sign. Something shifted in Sam Rivers.

Maybe it was also hearing about the good fortunes of his old friend Holden. Maybe it was admiring Holden's boldness, his sudden willingness to throw himself into life's breach, his acceptance of his past in a way that paved the right path for his future.

Maybe it was John Michael Goddard, the sheriff's son, barely a month old and growing like a weed.

On Friday morning, Carmel's first surgery wasn't scheduled until 10:30 at the vet clinic. She made sure Jennifer had breakfast and got onto the school bus. It was Carmel's turn to fix breakfast for her and Sam. She fried a couple of eggs and made some turkey bacon with buttered whole wheat toast.

Sam was reading the news on his iPad. Carmel set the plate down in front of him, with a full glass of fresh-squeezed juice. And then they both started eating in silence.

Sam's fork was midway between his plate and his mouth when he paused.

For such a long time he'd felt the tension of a huge boulder balanced atop a plateau, held in place by the thinnest purchase of stone. Now, it seemed, worn by time, wind, and weather, and everything else that happened over the last several months, it felt like it was ready to topple. The boulder, Sam knew, was doubt. Reluctance. Fear. A refusal to move on. Now he felt a geologic shift.

"What?" Carmel said, looking at him. She'd sensed something in Sam.

Sam lay his fork on his plate, looked at Carmel, and said, "Do you think you'd be willing to do this permanently? This breakfast thing? This living together?"

When you know someone as well as Carmel knew Sam (and vice versa) you could easily differentiate a flippant comment or a joke from something serious. It was a tone and the way it was said, accompanied by a certain demeanor. A point-blank stare that pierced her like an arrow.

But she was having none of it. "Is that really how you want to ask?"

Sam, confused, said, "What?"

But it only took him a second to recover. His eyes widened. He held her gaze. She didn't look away. Sam's hands closed the space between them and she returned his grasp with her own. And then his doubt toppled like a stone.

He told Carmel how the first time he'd met her, he had felt something. Ineffable, startling, tangible as a heart skip. He had admired the way her attention focused on Gray, and how her capable hands demonstrated so much care and sensitivity. There wasn't a day that had gone by that he had not wondered at how it had all unfolded, his love of her, his admiration, the fate that brought them together when they were both at points in their lives to appreciate and respect it for what it was. Genuine, deep-seated, mature, and profound love. Love that rises unbidden in the heart. In fact, regardless of their infrequent squabbles—Sam was sensible enough to give a nod to his shadow . . . their shadows—Sam wanted her to know that he was ready to take the next step, whatever that step might entail. Marriage or no marriage. A commitment to stay together. From Sam's perspective, it was a commitment he knew he was ready to make.

Sam was going to say more. But Carmel's tears triggered a mist in his own eyes, and for a moment neither of them spoke.

"Yes," Carmel finally said. "To whatever you're asking. Yes."

ACKNOWLEDGMENTS

Missing Peter Geye, I enrolled in one of his Master Mondays classes at the Loft, where for eight weeks a dozen of us, led by Peter, sat around and critiqued each others' work. During that class I wrote most of the book's first chapter, which my classmates read and reviewed. My heartfelt thanks to all of them for their invaluable input and support, including Amy Bethke, Derek Dirckx, Eleanor Frisch, Peter Geye, Glenn Miller, Jodi Yatckoske, Judy Borger, Lara Palmqvist, LaWayne Leno, Madeline Graham, Rebecca Wurtz, and Star Wuerdemann.

I met several excellent fellow writers in Peter Geye's year-long novel writing course. After the course ended, four of us met for a time as an impromptu writing group: Amit Bhati, Brian Duren, and Drew Miller. When I shared some of *Dead Catch* with them, they had several excellent ideas for improving it, and convinced me to keep writing. While our group no longer meets, some of their helpful input survives in this book.

Novels cannot see the light of day without numerous friends willing to read flawed, early drafts. Many thanks to Steve Sauerbry, Laurie Sauerbry, Eli Nemer, Anne Torrey-Nemer, Bill Torrey, Anna McCourt, Noah Griffith, Doug Johnson, and Heidi Hammond. I appreciate all of them taking the time out of their busy schedules to both read the early work, and to provide invaluable feedback. In particular, Doug Johnson is not only a voracious reader, great writer, and a world traveler, but he is also an engaging conversationalist whose wide-ranging conversations have entertained and edified, especially when hiking in the woods. I first met him years ago while fishing a pond on Arlo Vanscoy's western Iowa farm. Ever since, I have been fortunate to have his critical perspective and friendship.

The Sam Rivers Mystery series has been significantly improved by Mary Logue's careful, judicious, rapier-red-pen. Mary is a well-known writer and writing teacher, as well as an award-winning poet, children's book author, mystery writer, and more. I highly recommend her recent historical mysteries: *The Streel* and *The Big Sugar*. Pick them up; you won't be disappointed. She has made every Sam Rivers novel better, and *Dead Catch* is no exception. If you enjoy this novel (and the others), Mary deserves mounds of credit.

My publisher, AdventureKEEN, produces some of best outdoors books in the world. Before I ever had a chance to work with them, I acquired and used several of their outdoors guides, which accompanied me on my trips into the woods to learn more about the trees, birds, cacti, mammals, wildflowers, and just about anything else you can expect to encounter in wild places. While their usual genre is nonfiction, they decided to take a chance on the Sam Rivers Mysteries, and I am so glad they did. I cannot imagine working with a better partner. At every turn AdventureKEEN has gone out of its way to offer important guidance and support. In particular, thanks to Publisher Molly Merkle for believing in and continuing to support the Sam Rivers Mysteries; Chief Product

Officer Travis Bryant for his help on book covers and much more; Developmental and Managing Editor Holly Cross, as well as additional editorial assistance from Emily Beaumont and Jenna Barron; and Annie Long, for her design and typesetting expertise. I would be remiss if I failed to give a special callout to Marketing and Media Relations maven Liliane Opsomer, who has assisted with this series in general, and *Dead Catch* in particular, in more ways than I can enumerate here. Her support in promoting and marketing these mysteries to numerous media outlets, bookstores, presenting venues, and more has been indispensable. I am profoundly grateful for her assistance.

When I was a boy, my buddy Steve Sauerbry invited me up to his family's recently acquired rustic cabin on Northeastern Minnesota's Lake Vermilion. For a kid who loved to roam the forests and fields of Eastern Iowa, experiencing Minnesota's pine woods and clear waters struck me like a hammer blow (but in a good way). Ever since, I have considered this region a spiritual landscape, albeit also one of recreation.

My friend's Pine Island cabin sits in a stand of beautiful red pines in Canfield Bay. You can only get there by boat. Over the years, Steve, myself, Jim Gray, Eli Nemer, Mike Reeve, and Drew Skogman began visiting the place for an annual fishing trip, a journey that has happened for more than five decades. Many have joined us off and on over the years. But these five guys have provided me with invaluable friendship, comradery, and laughter. We often remark, "What happens up north, stays up north." That said, I don't think it's a violation of that edict to recognize that what we have experienced and shared on Vermilion has had a profound impact on my life, and taught me what it means to be a friend over time, sentiments which I hope made it into this book. I am thankful for their continued friendship.

Finally, no one hears more about a book, from its inception to the conclusion of a final draft, than my life partner, Anna. She is a sounding board for plot twists, character developments, and more, and patiently listens and gives advice when it is painfully needed and when it is not. Her advice is informed by more than three decades of service in the mental health industry, and I am so lucky to be the beneficiary of her wisdom, perspective, and aplomb.

ABOUT THE AUTHOR

Award-winning author Cary J. Griffith grew up among the woods, fields, and emerald waters of eastern Iowa. His childhood fostered a lifelong love of wild places.

He earned a BA in English from the University of Iowa and an MA in library science from the University of Minnesota.

Cary's books explore the natural world. In nonfiction, he covers the borderlands between civilization and wild places. In fiction, he focuses on the ways some people use flora and fauna to commit crimes, while others with more reverence and understanding of the natural world leverage their knowledge to bring criminals to justice.

About Dead Catch *and Discussion Guide*

On the first full day of whitefish netting season, Holden Riggins is passed out in the bottom of his boat, less than 30 yards from a murdered Minnesota conservation officer. The officer's body is tangled in Holden's net. Holden has apparently secreted a second net nearby, in the hopes of poaching walleye.

From the looks of it, Holden has consumed more than a bottle of whiskey, which is why he's passed out and nearly dead from hypothermia. When he returns to consciousness, he claims he knows nothing about the CO nor the illegal walleye net, though both nets are clearly his.

To complicate matters, the population of walleye, Minnesota's most prized game fish, has been unaccountably dropping throughout a handful of the state's most picturesque northeastern lakes. Has Holden resurrected his illegal netting ring, cashing in on the state's $25 million walleye industry? Or is he as innocent as he claims?

When county and state law officers begin to question Holden, he stops talking. Rather than prove his innocence with the help of local law enforcement, the only person he is willing to speak with is his boyhood buddy, Sam Rivers.

Holden and Sam have not seen each other since a tragic event separated them when they were 12 years old. Holden is a known scofflaw, poacher, and ex-con. Sam Rivers is a special agent for the U.S. Fish & Wildlife Service. In the past, Holden has used wilderness and everything in it for his own nefarious purposes. Sam puts people like Holden in prison.

Now both men must work together to solve the CO's murder and figure out why walleye stocks in some of Minnesota's most picturesque and best fishing lakes are falling.

1. How large is the walleye fishing industry in Minnesota, and why could it be a possible inducement to crime?

2. Why would netting walleye be illegal, while netting whitefish is not? Why is it important to the story?

3. What are some of the points of evidence that lead law enforcement to believe Holden Riggins is the obvious murderer?

4. Holden Riggins has asked for Sam Rivers to investigate his case and the death of CO Charlie Jiles. Are there any other reasons Sheriff Dean Goddard agrees to go along with Holden's request? Are the sheriff's reasons for recruiting Sam reasonable? Ethical?

5. Discuss some of the reasons Sam Rivers decides to take on the informal investigation of Charlie Jiles's death.

6. Why is Lake Vermilion a good setting for the story?

7. Why did Cray Halverson believe Holden Riggins would be a good fall guy for their crimes? Why did he believe Holden would be exonerated?

8. When Rowena Melnyk confronted Charlie Jiles the second time, at the mouth of Smugglers Creek, do you think her actions were justified? Do you think she should have been charged with murder?

9. Was the ultimate punishment of Cray Halverson and Rowena Melnyk justified? Should it have been harsher?

10. Why did Holden burn and sink his birchbark canoe on Pine Lake? Why did he invite Sam Rivers to accompany him?

The Story of AdventureKEEN

We are an independent nature and outdoor activity publisher. Our founding dates back more than 40 years, guided then and now by our love of being in the woods and on the water, by our passion for reading and books, and by the sense of wonder and discovery made possible by spending time recreating outdoors in beautiful places.

It is our mission to share that wonder and fun with our readers, especially with those who haven't yet experienced all the physical and mental health benefits that nature and outdoor activity can bring.

In addition, we strive to teach about responsible recreation so that the natural resources and habitats we cherish and rely upon will be available for future generations.

We are a small team deeply rooted in the places where we live and work. We have been shaped by our communities of origin—primarily Birmingham, Alabama; Cincinnati, Ohio; and the northern suburbs of Minneapolis, Minnesota. Drawing on the decades of experience of our staff and our awareness of the industry, the marketplace, and the world at large, we have shaped a unique vision and mission for a company that serves our readers and authors.

We hope to meet you out on the trail someday.

#bewellbeoutdoors

READ ON FOR AN EXCERPT FROM CARY J. GRIFFITH'S NEXT NOVEL

RATTLESNAKE BLUFF

AVAILABLE SUMMER 2025
WHEREVER BOOKS ARE SOLD

CHAPTER 1

J ulio Vargas Ortega loved Minnesota's Driftless.

Ever since he was a young boy Julio—Jules to his friends, colleagues, and especially Izzie—rose before dawn. Even with the windows shut to birdsong and the blinds pulled, Jules could feel first light. It didn't matter if the previous evening he and Izzie had been out past midnight at a tequila fest, doing the Marimba two-step, and then home to bed, beating out a rhythm all their own. When the eastern horizon grew pale, Jules shuffled into their galley kitchen to brew coffee, his tighty-whities tented by his tumescence and the memory of Izzie's charms.

At 27, Jules liked his coffee black. Not that he needed the caffeine buzz, being someone who took care of himself. He was five foot eight, built stout and thick-muscled, with jet black hair and a tan patina he claimed was from his mother, Esmerelda, who was one quarter Mayan. Apart from a taste for occasional tequila, Jules and Izzie lived clean. And even though Jules missed Esmerelda, who he had not seen in nearly three years, there wasn't a morning that passed without Jules feeling lucky he lived in Minnesota's bluff country.

He stared at the kitchen calendar, admiring the photograph. It was a morning shot in July, looking out across the only place in Minnesota that escaped the Ice Age glaciers. It featured green land undulating in sweeping ridges all the way to the horizon. The verdure hung in mists like the treetops of an Amazonian rain forest.

Today was Tuesday, July 11, 2023. He had always believed Tuesdays were the most productive day of his week. Similar to his instinctual sense of first light, he felt certain today was going to be something special.

He was usually on a construction site an hour before anyone else, especially on a Tuesday. He enjoyed sitting in the company's F-150, sipping double-strength. By 7 a.m. the sun was off the horizon, turning the fields of bluestem golden. And on this morning, his first on Alta Vista, a new construction site, he loved watching the goldfinches flash their yellow regalia, trolling for mates, getting ready to nest when, later in the month, the mullein and thistle seeds would start to come in. Whether they were calling for the chiquitas, or just because the morning was blue, clear, and warm, it didn't matter to Jules. Things were going great for him and Izzie. The beautiful midsummer morning in the heart of resplendent country filled with birdsong and sunlight seemed like the perfect accompaniment to his mood, which on this day was ebullient.

Yesterday, Leslie Warner, owner of Warner Construction, made him foreman on this site.

"You're the best man for the job," Leslie said.

At 40, she had been in the business long enough to recognize an excellent worker when she saw one. With an equally excellent demeanor. Jules always did exactly what she asked. And despite Leslie being what men considered attractive—in face and bearing—Jules had always been respectful. Unlike most men, whose eyes wandered over Leslie's body like magnets caught in a forcefield, Jules always looked her in the eye.

The previous afternoon she and Jules had walked to the tree edge of the proposed Alta Vista development, where scrub brush was perched atop a limestone bluff. They'd bushwhacked through 10 feet of undergrowth until they were right at the cliff edge.

The limestone-topped escarpment dropped more than 100 feet to the valley below. When they stood on its edge, the panorama unobstructed, they were blessed with a view as fine as the one on Jules's kitchen calendar. The hills, undulating in front of them, took their combined breath away.

"I'll be bringing out some potential partners this week," Leslie said. "The first one tomorrow, over the lunch hour. Can you make sure and clear out some of this brush. Doesn't have to be a lot. Just enough so he can see this."

"Of course," Jules said. "I'll get the Bobcat this afternoon and start on it first thing in the morning. I'll make sure there's a view by 11 a.m."

"Perfect," Leslie smiled, already thinking about the words she'd use to sell the site to her new investors. *From here you can see across the Driftless to the Mississippi River. And you're only 45 minutes from Rochester.*

The setting was bucolic, the vista magnificent, and its proximity to the medical complex practical. Her potential partners were doctors who wanted all three. Leslie had a feeling about this, her most ambitious project. It was going to sell out fast. And it was going to be lucrative, providing they didn't run into any snafus.

Unfortunately, Leslie had been working in construction long enough to know unexpected issues always arose. Her first issue had been getting the county to agree the site could be developed. She hired a surveyor to mark off the site. Then she worked with an architect to address the potential issue of building on an area bluff. If everything went as smoothly as the site's start, she could expect clear sailing.

But she knew bumps in the road were inevitable. She just hoped they didn't slow her down.

On Monday afternoon, Jules drove 45 minutes to the Warner Construction Equipment lot outside Winona. The yard was near the Mississippi, and like everything in bluff country, Jules liked to pause and admire the flow of big water. He was back at the bluff site by 5 p.m. It took another 15 minutes to position the flatbed on the gravel shoulder and unhitch it, making sure the cat was still chained to the bed and secured for the night. The trailer had a rear black metal gate that doubled as a ramp. Jules unhitched the rear gate and dropped it to the ground, making it ramp-ready for his early morning work. Then he returned to his truck, anxious to tell Izzie the good news, and to celebrate at the tequila fest.

Before Jules pulled away, a pickup came up beside him. A man rolled down his passenger side window, nodded to Jules, and said, "What's goin' on?" indicating the trailered equipment.

He looked like a local farmer, Jules thought. Maybe in his 70s, with what sounded like the hint of an English accent. He seemed friendly enough, but you could never tell.

"Doing work for Warner Construction," Jules said.

"What kind a work?"

Jules knew enough to play dumb. Leslie Warner never wanted others knowing her business, until it was well enough along for them to figure it out on their own.

"Clearing land."

The man seemed to think about it. Then, "I always thought, remote as this is, but still being close to Rochester, it'd be a bonny site for a row of townhouses, or maybe a big house," the man said. "Providing you're a multimillionaire." He smiled.

Jules smiled back. "I guess," he said. "Definitely a nice view."

"Once you get beyond those trees," the man said.

Jules agreed. "You live around here?"

Jules knew he'd tell Leslie about the man, and his questions. He knew she'd be curious.

"Down the road about a mile. Name's Joe Smiley. Got a dairy farm in the valley."

"Jules," Jules said, shaking Joe Smiley's hand.

In the winter, when Warner Construction work slowed, Jules sometimes worked dairy.

The two talked cows for a while. The man was interested to know Jules knew dairy. It was hard work, and he was always looking for help, which he didn't mention, wondering if the man with tan skin and an accent was legal. Must be, he guessed, working for a construction company. He didn't know Warner Construction, but he made a note of the name, and would look it up when he got a chance.

They finally said their goodbyes, and Jules headed back to Rochester, excited for the evening's entertainment.

Tequila and dancing always made Izzie frisky.

By 7:30 a.m. the next day, Jules stepped out of his cab, fully caffeinated and ready to take on the day. It felt like he could lasso the sun and ride it into the heavens, if need be, so much was going so well for Jules these days. His work as a foreman meant more money. And Izzie was in her last year at the university. She was working as a teacher's aide. But if all went well, by next year she'd have a classroom of her own, and a big raise in pay. There'd been talk of marriage, but Jules was waiting until he put away enough money for a proper ring.

Thinking about marrying Izzie reminded him of his mom. He had not seen her for three years, and it was hard. Super hard for Jules, who loved his madre. If he was worth anything, it was because of her. And his father. But his father had passed when he was a boy. And his madre had never remarried. Though thankfully, there was plenty of family around Llanos, a dirt-poor community less than two hours southwest of Ciudad Juarez. The area was destitute, with little work and no future.

So, Jules came north.

He sent his mother money and Facetimed her the Sundays she could borrow a phone. But it was a poor substitute for being at her table and enjoying hot tortillas off the stove with huevos, queso, frijoles, and pimientos out of her garden.

It was hard not giving his madre a hug or being hugged by her. But it was one of the sacrifices you made when you crossed the border in search of better fortunes north.

Jules walked down through the bumpy pasture, thinking about how his raise would give him enough money to send his mom a bus ticket, to get her up here for their wedding—providing he bought the ring, asked the question, and Izzie said "yes."

Before offloading the Bobcat he scanned the tree line ahead of him. He walked down to the bluff and stepped into the brush, surveying the work he was about to begin. He paced off what he figured was about 10 feet. When he fired up the Bobcat and began pushing forward with the front loader, he'd have free reign with the first 5 feet of brush. Then he'd need to be careful. The last edge he'd need to cut by hand. And he needed to hustle.

The boss wanted an open view by noon.

The trailer's ramp was already down. When he circled in back to step onto it, he noticed a boot print in the gravel dust; a distinctive, familiar waffle pattern. A Redwing work boot. He'd priced them, but they weren't cheap. Maybe now that he was earning a foreman's salary . . .

The print looked fresh, though the weather had been sunny and calm the last few days, so it could have been made anytime.

He glanced over his equipment, but everything appeared fine. And there was only the one print,

Jules thought no more about it. He stepped up onto the bed and unlocked the chains, pulling them from the Bobcat's four wheels.

The day was beginning to warm. The cat had been sitting all night, so its front handle was cool. Jules unlocked its front door, grabbed its handle, and swung it open. He pulled it wide, stepping onto the front loader's lip, getting ready to twist into the cab seat. Maneuvering into the lone front seat was tricky, like shoehorning a foot into a tight boot. But he'd been doing it all summer, so the movement was second nature.

Before twisting and sitting he glanced onto the seat and noticed something different, something unexpected, what looked like a thick coil of colorfully patterned rope. He hadn't put it there, so he paused, admiring the way it was coiled.

Then it rattled.

It was a sound he hadn't heard since the day he'd left home. It was a rattlesnake. Dangerous. The sound and its appearance made him scream and spring back, catlike, onto the trailer bed.

Once he was certain he was at a safe distance, he breathed. The unexpected shock of seeing a rattlesnake rocketed his pulse.

"Mierda," he said, an expletive.

In northern Mexico and Texas, rattlesnakes were commonplace. There were several kinds, all of them easily recognized. When he was young, he and a friend had killed a 4-foot timber rattler, skinned it, and roasted some of its meat over a fire. It smelled good over the flames. They'd taken a few bites, the flavor a cross between frog legs and turtle. A little gamey but tasty. And filling for a couple of kids who seldom had enough to eat.

Then they tossed the entire carcass—less its head, where the venom was stored—to the hogs.

When Jules's mother found out, her eyes turned fearful, then angry. Esmerelda's Mayan heritage always made her think a little differently. Especially about things in nature. When that side of her bloodline came across snakes—any snakes, but especially rattlesnakes—it was an omen.

"No good comes from killing a snake," Esmerelda said.

She instructed them about giving the rattler a wide berth or using a long stick to shoo it out of their path. They should never kill it.

But this snake was on the front seat of his cat. And Jules needed to get on with his day. He needed to get that tree line cleared by 11 a.m., so Leslie could show her client the view.

The rattlesnake wasn't moving. The inside of the cat was cool, Jules knew, so even though the snake had rattled, it wasn't ready to slither away any time soon. Jules couldn't imagine how it had gotten into the cat. Or why, for that matter. Probably following a rat, he guessed. Though none of that made any difference.

He fetched a long-handled shovel from the cargo hold of his truck and returned to the flatbed.

When the snake saw the shovel blade, it made a quick rattle. Jules brought the metal down flat and hard, whacking the reptile. It writhed and rattled, and he struck it again, twice. Then it stopped.

Jules had known lots of rattlesnakes. But he had never seen a rattler like this one. It was covered with beautiful dark-brown splotches. There was a pattern to the splotches, along the top of the back and around the sides. The top splotches were the largest, separated by tan skin. Its head was in the shape of an arrow point. He watched it for a full minute, making sure it was dead. He admired the snake's pattern and intricate design. He was surprised that even for a millisecond, when he first saw it, he had mistaken it for a coiled rope. Clearly it had been alive and beautiful, and for a moment Jules felt bad about the snake, that it had somehow gotten into the cat and slithered onto his seat. He regretted killing such a beautiful creature.

He recalled the scolding he'd gotten from his mom. She was always using herbs, to spice their food but also for native rituals she remembered from childhood. After the boys had killed the rattlesnake, eaten part of it, and thrown the rest to the hogs, she'd pulled down a bundle of dried sage. Then she made the boys go out to the livestock tank and wash their hands and faces. When they were finished, she lit the dried sage and waved the smoke around their heads, hands, and upper bodies, saying something in Mayan, some kind of incantation Jules had never heard. To cleanse them.

Jules wished his mother was here to help him. But this morning he didn't have time for ritual. Jules was a foreman and he needed to get into his Bobcat and use its front loader to plow up the bush edge, cutting the last part by hand. The boss needed her view.

Once he was certain the snake was dead, he used the shovel blade to scoop it up. He dropped the snake on the road's shoulder, well away from his truck and trailer. Then he returned to the cat, checked it for more snakes, didn't find any, and within five minutes he'd backed it off the trailer and was motoring to the bluff edge.

He knew he'd clear a view for his boss well before noon. It was his job.

But it was hard not to recall his mother's voice.

"Snakes are omens. No good comes from killing a snake."

PRAISE FOR *WOLF KILL*

"Griffith's prose makes you feel the winter chill . . . and the twisty plot delivers a chill down your spine. This is a Minnesota mystery with razor-sharp teeth."
—Brian Freeman, *New York Times* best-selling author of *The Deep, Deep Snow*

"*Wolf Kill* is a terrific read! The writing is so good that you can feel the frigid winds blowing through this dark and masterfully crafted novel even as the suspense heats up. And the wolves are as magnificent and frightening as you could hope.
—David Housewright, Edgar Award–winning author of *What Doesn't Kill Us*

"In northern Minnesota, winter is full of dangers that can kill: hard cold, hard men, and hungry wolves. Cary Griffith brings the menace of all three into play in his riveting new thriller. Returning to the childhood home he fled 20 years earlier, Sam Rivers finds himself battling a group of scheming reprobates and struggling against an avalanche of painful memories. Griffith's intimacy with the territory he writes about comes through in every line. I loved this novel and highly recommend it. But I suggest you enjoy it under a warm blanket. Honestly, I've never read a book that evokes the fierce winter landscape of the North Country better than *Wolf Kill*."
—William Kent Krueger, Edgar Award–winning author of *This Tender Land*

"Up here in the North Country, we have a bounty of fine mystery writers. Krueger, Housewright, Eskens, Freeman, Mejia,

Sanford . . . Add to that list Cary Griffith, whose *Wolf Kill* thrills for its plotting, superb writing, and unforgettable characters, not least the brutal Minnesota winter. Sam Rivers is not only a fine sleuth, but a complicated man with a complicated history and a fair family grudge. Taken together, he's a force, both on the page and long after you finish reading his story. Good thing there's more of him to go around, and I'll be first in line for the next Sam Rivers novel."

—Peter Geye, author of *Northernmost*

"Cary J. Griffith defines the savage, howling beauty of a Northern Minnesota winter in this taut, compulsively readable mystery. I want more Sam Rivers!

—Wendy Webb, author of *The Haunting of Brynn Wilder*

"Fans of Paul Doiron's *The Poacher's Son* or the Joe Pickett books will appreciate this descriptive novel with an intriguing plot and well-written characters."

—Lesa Holstine, *Library Journal*

"Involving, fast-paced . . . [Cary J. Griffith's] writing is so vivid the reader wants to bundle up and enjoy the beauty of the landscape, even at 20 below zero."

—Mary Ann Grossmann, *Pioneer Press*

"The latest from accomplished Minnesota author Cary J. Griffith brings us a new North Woods hero to join the ranks of William Kent Krueger's Cork O'Connor and Allen Eskens' Max Rupert. He even gives Brian Freeman's Minnesota-to-the-core Jonathan Stride a run for the money."

—Ginny Greene, *Star Tribune*

PRAISE FOR *COUGAR CLAW*

"In this highly anticipated second novel in the Sam Rivers series, Cary J. Griffith delivers another finely researched and compellingly written thriller. Both the beauty and the savagery of our natural world form the heart of a Griffith story. In this case, it's the predatory habits of cougars. When the killing of a Twin Cities man in an apparent cougar attack brings Sam to the Minnesota River Valley to investigate, what follows is a gradual and fascinating revelation of not just the predatory nature of cougars, but that of humans as well."

—William Kent Krueger, Edgar Award–winning author of *This Tender Land*

"*Cougar Claw,* the second installment in the Sam Rivers series, sends the U.S. Fish & Wildlife special agent to the scene of a grisly cougar killing on the outskirts of the Twin Cities. As usual in Sam Rivers's world, all is not as it seems. Griffith doubles down on his strengths in this series, giving us another vibrant cast of allies, suspects, and a misunderstood predator, while navigating a path between animal rights and human fears of the natural world. I can't wait for Sam Rivers's next assignment.

—Mindy Mejia, author of *Everything You Want Me To Be* and *Strike Me Down*

"A deadly threat from the wild comes far too close for comfort when an urban bicyclist is found mauled to death by a cougar. In this second book in the Sam Rivers mystery series, Cary Griffith takes this U.S. Fish & Wildlife special agent on a hair-raising hunt to find the cougar—and the truth. Mixing deep knowledge of the natural world with the twists and turns of the best suspense novels, *Cougar Claw* is a thoughtful and thrilling story."

—Mary Logue, author of the Claire Watkins mysteries and
The Streel

"From the first page to the last, *Cougar Claw* blends high suspense with the quiet observations of the predator's predator, Sam Rivers. Between Griffith's descriptions of Minnesota's natural beauty and the human nature of his characters, this is a book you won't want to end."

—Debra H. Goldstein, award-winning author of the Sarah Blair
mystery series

"Griffith—and his very engaging hero, Sam Rivers—both know the Minnesota wilderness inside and out. But be careful. After staying up all night to devour *Cougar Claw*, you may find yourself listening for a low growl the next time you're alone in the forest."

—Brian Freeman, *New York Times* best-selling author of
The Deep, Deep Snow

PRAISE FOR *KILLING MONARCHS*

"In *Killing Monarchs,* Cary J. Griffith combines monarch butterflies, a Mexican cartel, and compelling characters—both human and canine—to deliver a chilling thriller you won't want to put down. Sam Rivers and his wolf-dog partner, Gray, make a terrific, crime-fighting duo!"

—Margaret Mizushima, author of the award-winning
Timber Creek K-9 Mysteries, including *Striking Range*

"What do murders disguised as overdoses, endangered monarch butterflies, and international heroin smugglers have in common? U.S. Fish & Wildlife Special Agent Sam Rivers and Gray, Sam's rescued wolf-dog hybrid with a nose for narcotics. As the bodies pile up in the Land of 10,000 Lakes, Sam and Gray are on a mission to stop the killer before he claims his next victim. A gripping thriller highlighting the ironclad bond between man and his best friend, *Killing Monarchs* had me turning pages all night long. Sam Rivers and his faithful wolf dog are my new best friends."

—Brian Malloy, author of *The Year of Ice* and *After Francesco*

"Both thriller and mystery, *Killing Monarchs* mixes an elementary-school science project with scorpions and drugs. Totally surprising is how butterflies flit into this fast-paced and tantalizing story. Cary Griffith has laid out another fabulous tale, based on solid knowledge of the natural world, with a provocative sense of the deviousness of humankind."

—Mary Logue, author of *The Streel* and *The Big Sugar*

"*Killing Monarchs* is an exciting, thrilling, and suspenseful page-turner! Griffith weaves together an intriguing mystery with fascinating environmental concerns, young adults facing the reality of their past, and the dangerous world of drug cartels. Sam Rivers, a U.S. Fish & Wildlife agent, is a captivating character, and, as a K-9 handler, I especially enjoyed Rivers's sidekick, the extraordinary wolf dog, Gray. Together, Rivers and Gray make an outstanding team. Readers will be rooting for them and stay up late to find out what happens next. *Killing Monarchs* hooked me from the first page, and I couldn't put it down. I highly recommend this series!"

—Kathleen Donnelly, author of the award-winning National Forest K-9 series and K-9 handler for Sherlock Hounds Detection Canines

"With one sharp eye on the world of nature and another carefully watching the evil antics of two-legged species who roam the earth, Sam Rivers is one part teacher and two parts crime solver. *Killing Monarchs* floats like a butterfly and stings like a scorpion. Prepare to be schooled."

—Mark Stevens, author of *The Fireballer* and The Allison Coil Mystery Series